SECRETS OF MOTH

SECRETS OF MOTH

THE MOTH SAGA, BOOK THREE

DANIEL ARENSON

ISBN: 9781927601204

MOTH

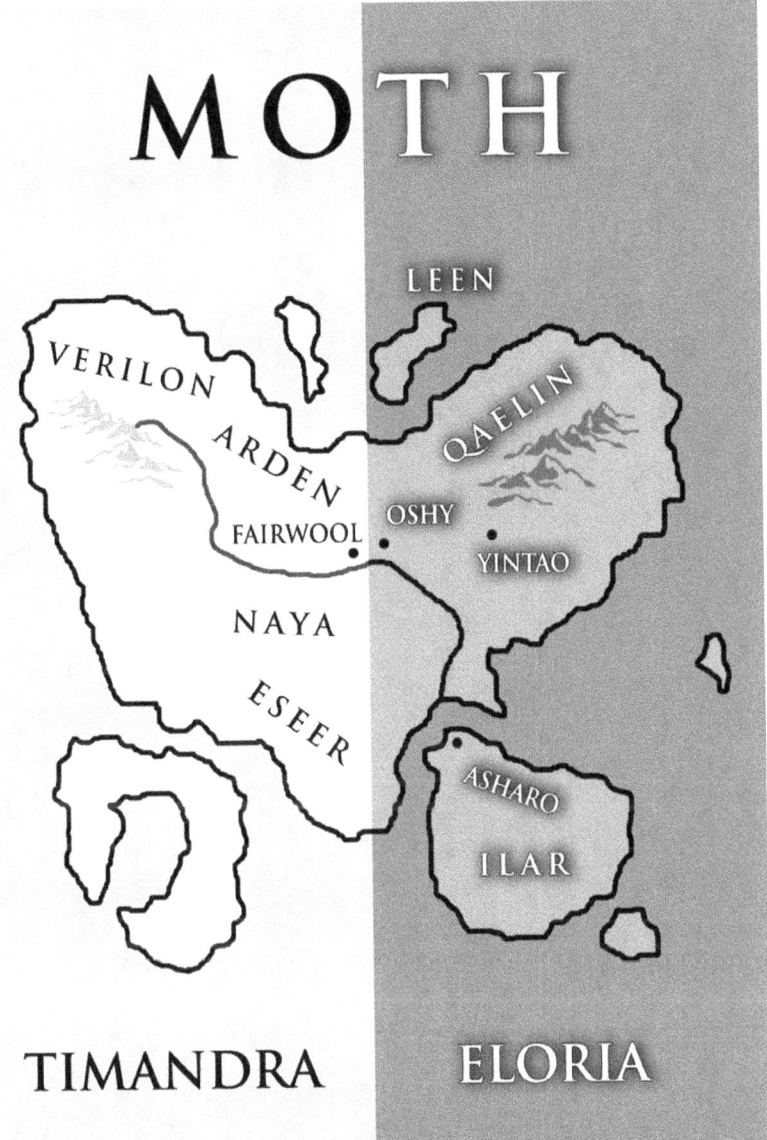

LEEN

VERILON

ARDEN

QAELIN

FAIRWOOL • • OSHY

• YINTAO

NAYA

ESEER

ASHARO

ILAR

TIMANDRA   ELORIA

View the full map at DanielArenson.com/Moth

CHAPTER ONE
THE CLOCKWORK CLERICS

First of Four stood upon the mountain, watching the sunrise.

The first indigo glimmers flowed into pink curtains, gilding mist over fields of swaying grass. Sunbeams followed, piercing orange and red clouds, and finally the sun herself emerged, painting the world. Hills and mountainsides gleamed like beaten gold. Anemones and dandelions bloomed in the valleys, reaching out to the light. The cold, long night had ended. Warmth and light once more bathed the world.

"A last dance," First of Four whispered, the wind ruffling his fur. "A last painting in fire."

He gazed upon the land. The foothills rolled to distant valleys, and a river coiled between barrows. He sniffed, his long snout twitching. The scents of life—flowers, grass, trees—filled his nostrils. *Soon the aroma will fade in the east. Soon darkness falls.*

He turned around to face the clock upon the mountainside.

The Cabera Clock loomed upon the limestone facade like the eye of a god. The sunrise caught its dial; it shone like a second sun. Inside the mountain, beyond the stone doors his brotherhood had been guarding for millennia, echoed the sound of gears and springs, a song ten thousand years old.

The song of harps rose behind him.

He turned to look down the mountainside, and he saw them there. His brothers walked in the valleys below. The wind ruffled their thick, golden fur. Each brother's six hind legs moved through the grass; their front two limbs rose like the arms of men, playing harps of bone. They raised their heads, amber eyes gleaming, snouts inhaling. They climbed the mountainside, moving toward the clock as they did every thousand years.

"The four Clockwock Clerics," First of Four whispered. "United at another millennium . . . perhaps our last."

His back six legs stood upon stone. He raised his foremost limbs, holding a flute in each paw. He placed both into his mouth and he played his ancient song, calling his brothers home, summoning them to hear the clock ring, to see the orrery turn.

As the sun rose higher, his three brothers climbed the mountainside until they stood before him. Their eyes watched him, gleaming marbles of molten gold. Their fur undulated like the grassy valleys below. Their harp strings fell still.

First of Four gazed upon them, one by one, and spoke in a deep voice.

"The sun rises upon a thousand years gone by. For ten millennia, we have guarded the Cabera Clock. For ten millennia, we—the Clockwork Clerics, the Guardians of Time—have watched the children of men kill, steal, sin, and burn. Today the doors will open for the tenth time." He lowered his head. "Today the dance ends."

His three brothers lowered their heads, and tears streamed down their long faces. They spoke together. "The dance ends."

They approached the doors, the four Clockwork Clerics, the four pillars of time. They played their music, ancient notes of guardianship, chords from before the children of men had walked the earth, from the very first turns of the world and flutters of wings.

The music flowed upon the mountainside.

The sun blazed against the dial above.

The clock hand turned . . . leaving the number nine, the last number marking the centuries. The ancient hand, forged of never-rusting brass, caught the sunlight. It turned like the world. It pointed at the new millennium, at the number of beginning and end and nothingness, at a golden zero upon the white face.

Another thousand years of stewardship ended with the chime of bells.

Beneath the dial, the stone doors upon the mountainside opened.

"We enter the chamber," said First of Four as the bells chimed. "The orrery calls."

He led them through the doorway.

First of Four no longer knew his age. He could not recall the passage of time before the clock had existed, only vague dreams of color and blackness, of water and smoke, of fire and stone. Nine times he had entered this chamber. Nine times he had seen the worlds turn. Now, for the tenth time, he stepped into the mountain and beheld the orrery.

The machine filled the chamber, taller than the greatest oak. A great, mechanical sun blazed in its center, its embers burning within a round iron grill. Eight worlds spun around the sun, spheres of metal moving on circular tracks, large as boulders. Around each world, moons moved along metal rings. Gears turned and clanked upon the floor, intricately fitted between stone tiles. Silver stars shone upon the ceiling. Bells chimed. The clock kept turning. The worlds danced on.

"Behold the orrery," said First of Four. "Behold time itself. Behold the secret of the Cabera Clock . . . and of the dancing worlds."

The Clockwork Clerics gazed upon the contraption of gears, rods, rings, and spheres, their song silenced. The dance, as always, continued.

First of Four moved forward. His six feet pattered onto the astrolabe forming the chamber floor—a circle of runes, grooves, and moving pieces, a star-field of marble and bronze. He approached one of the dancing spheres—a humble ball of metal, smaller than the others, far from the mechanical sun. A single moon moved around it. Upon this world's surface, etched in platinum, appeared continents shaped like a moth—two wings spread into the oceans. The sphere spun around the sun, and it spun around it axis, as it had for time beyond measure.

"The world of Mythimna," First of Four said. "Our domain. A world where man rises." He lowered his head. "A world of war. Of hatred. Of jealousy and sin."

His brothers came to stand around him.

"A world of bloodshed," said Second of Four.

"A world of cruelty," said Third of Four.

"A world which man has ruined," said Fourth of Four.

First of Four turned toward his brothers. He saw himself reflected in their eyes. He saw the sadness in them. He saw the pain that man had brought.

"We have watched over mankind for ten thousand years," he said. "We built this clock to guide them, to show them that life is quick and time is slow. Yet they have abandoned our teachings. They have turned to shortsightedness, to jealousy, to blind faith, to cruel leaders, to wars and the destruction of life. They slay their brothers and sisters, they cut down forests, and they poison rivers. The three kingdoms of men fight upon the wings of the moth, and blood spills upon the world." First of Four looked back toward the mechanical world that spun behind him. "We have only one more lesson . . . one last hope. Brothers, fetch me three pieces." Pain stung his eyes and tore at his throat. "The dance must end."

His brothers wailed, heads tossed back. Their cries echoed in the chamber, and the mechanical worlds swayed upon their tracks. Yet they obeyed him.

For ten thousand years, they had guarded this sacred clock. Today they broke it.

The bells fell silent.

They returned to him with the broken pieces.

"A gear from the heart of our clock," said Second of Four. Upon the astrolabe floor, he placed down a gear the size of a wagon wheel.

"The number nine," said Third of Four. "The last number of a turn." He placed down a heavy metal rune.

"The hand of the clock," said Fourth of Four. He placed down the brass hand that, only moments earlier, had moved to a new millennium.

First of Four nodded. "The clock is broken. The world has fallen still."

He looked back at the orrery. The mechanical sun still crackled, embers bright within the round grill. The worlds still traveled around it, moving along their circular tracks. But one world—Mythimna—no longer turned around its axis. Forever its one side would now face the sun, lit by the fire of embers. Forever its other side would face the chamber walls, shadowed and cold.

First of Four turned away. He left the orrery. He stepped outside onto the mountainside.

He looked to the west. The sun hung there, golden and warm and good. The grass swayed, robins and chickadees sang, and the wildflowers sent forth their sweet scents. He looked to the east. The day was gone. The light had left that land; shadows cloaked the hills and valleys. Above him, the great dial—missing its hand, missing its nine—stood still. So was the sun now still.

"The light will remain in the west," he said. "Shadows will remain in the east. Brothers of mine! Gather around me. Second of Four—take the gear far into the darkness, and hide it among the islands of the seafaring men. Third of Four—take the rune of nine, and hide the number in the rainforests where the sylvan kingdom reigns. Fourth of Four—take the brass hand, and hide it under the dunes where the desert kingdom sprawls." He stared at the horizons, imagining those distant lands. "The world is broken. To fix Mythimna, to let the dance continue, the children of men will have to unite, to bring three pieces back to our home, to fix the clock as one people. Only peace between them can save their frozen world."

"The children of men are petty and will not know what to do," said Second of Four.

"Then we will teach them." First of Four nodded. "As you hide these broken pieces, spread the tale. Write it in books. Sing it to bards. Tell the children of men who suffer how to heal Mythimna. I will await them."

His three brothers nodded. Holding the broken pieces of the Cabera Clock, they walked down the mountainside . . . and over the horizons.

First of Four remained standing upon the mountain for a long time, the wind in his fur.

The light hung in the west. Darkness blanketed the east. The clock remained still. Summer faded into autumn, and the snows of winter fell, and spring sent green across the west, and still the sun did not move, and still his brothers did not return.

First of Four waited on.

The years turned and still he stood, and the winds chilled him, and snow filled his fur, and summer's sun baked him, and rain ran down his face. He lost count of the years he waited, and for the first time in his long life, he felt his age. White filled his fur, and his joints hurt, and he could no longer play the same old tunes on his flute.

When winter came again, he turned away from the valleys and hills, opened the doors in the mountainside, and stepped into the chamber.

He stood at the doorway for a long time, shielded from the rain and snow, and watched the horizon and waited . . . waited for his brothers to return. Waited for the children of men to bring him the three broken pieces, to fix the clock, to let the world turn again.

The years went by, and the winds ached in his aging joints, and when the snows were coldest, First of Four took a step back and let the doors close.

Shadows and light filled the chamber, and the mechanical sun crackled. The orrery spun as always, eight worlds orbiting, one side of Mythimna always facing the heat, one side always dark.

For a long time—centuries, perhaps millennia—First of Four stood facing the doors, waiting for them to open, waiting for mankind to forge peace, to work as one, to fix the clock.

And still he aged.

Old and frail, he finally stepped away from the doors, bent his many knees, and hobbled into a smaller chamber. Gears, springs, and rods rose around him, a dead machine. The back of the clock's dial, a disk like the sun, rose above him, frozen; he stood behind the mountain's blinded eye. He curled up among the gears. He waited.

CHAPTER TWO
SAILING ALONE

Koyee limped along the riverbank, fleeing a city of fire and death.

"One step at a time, Eelani," she whispered.

She took a step and her wounds blazed. She gasped in pain. She inhaled deeply, waiting for the agony to subside. She took another step and nearly fainted. She balled her fists and took a third step. She moved along the river.

"One step . . . at . . . a time." She struggled to form words, her lips shaking. "We have to keep moving."

She had pulled out two arrows from her body only moments earlier. They lay upon the riverbank, red with her blood. More of that blood seeped from her shoulder and thigh. Adding to her pain, countless scratches and bruises covered her.

"But we still live. We still breathe. We can keep moving."

When she looked behind her, she saw the inferno. The city of Yintao, capital of Qaelin, had fallen to the horde of sunlight. Ferius and his army had stormed the walls, crushed towers and homes, and killed so many. Even from here, miles away from the city, she could see the sunburst banners rising from what walls remained. She could see the smoke of burning homes, smell the scent of charred corpses, and hear the chants of sunlit victory.

Her eyes stung. "Did you escape, Okado? Did you sail south, Torin?"

They were the two men of her life—the two souls she loved most. Her brother, brave and wise, a leader of men. Her lover, a child of sunlight, less a warrior but just as wise, just as strong, a beacon of morality for the people of the sun.

"Do you sail south to Ilar?"

She turned to look south again. The Yin River flowed through the dark plains, a strand of silver. The last ships had sailed past the horizon, bearing the survivors of the slaughter. If Koyee ever found them, would she find those she loved or only strangers . . . only mourning?

She took another step, blood trickling.

"Step by step," she whispered. "We must keep walking, Eelani."

She could barely feel her invisible friend, only a hint of warmth upon her shoulder. Perhaps Eelani too was hurt, maybe even dying. Koyee ground her teeth and moved on. She would save her spirit friend. She would save herself . . . even if she could no longer save the night.

She walked for what felt like hours. She fell into mud. She pushed herself up and walked again. No stars or moon lit her way; smoke covered the sky and ash rained. She tossed off her armor; it was too heavy, weighing her down. She kept only her sword—the old blade Sheytusung—slung across her back. Step by step. Limping. Falling. Bleeding. *Just keep moving.*

"Perhaps we walk to our death, Eelani." She shivered with cold now, yet also felt so hot—burning up. "Perhaps we walk to death in darkness. But we'll keep walking nonetheless. If we must die, we'll die far from the hosts of the enemy . . . in a quiet, peaceful place."

Another mile and her foot twisted on a rock, and she fell onto the muddy riverbank.

She lay on her stomach, too weak to rise. She reached out and felt the water. She let it flow around her fingers, soothing like silk. The mud was cold but warm ash fell from the sky like snow.

"This is a good place to die," she whispered. "It's dark and quiet and I'm at peace."

She raised her head, wanting to look south one last time, to imagine Torin and Okado sailing downriver to safety. Lights gleamed in the distance and Koyee smiled. Were those the lights of afterlife—the souls of the fallen awaiting her? Her father. Her mother. All those who had died in this war. They gleamed in the shadows, reaching out, welcoming her home.

I come to you now . . .

Mud filled her mouth.

Her wounds blazed.

She blinked and coughed. She was still alive, still trapped in her body. She raised her head and reached out to those lights.

"Mother . . . Father . . ."

The lights swayed. When Koyee squinted she could bring them into focus.

Two lanterns. Two lanterns swinging upon poles, their light casting beads upon the river.

She pushed herself onto her elbows, blinking and struggling to see. A gasp fled her lips.

"It's a village, Eelani. A small village outside the city walls. We have to go there."

Trembling, she pushed herself to her feet. She nearly fell again. She sucked in breath and she walked on, reaching toward the lights. As she approached, she saw several huts, a pier, and a swaying boat. Dizzy and gasping for breath, she stumbled into the village and found it abandoned. Aside from a single dinghy, the docks were bare. The people had fled.

"Is anyone here?" she called out, voice raspy. No one answered.

Koyee raised her chin and tightened her lips. She inhaled through her nose and hugged herself.

"We will not die yet. Not yet, Eelani!" She clenched her fists. "We will sail on."

She unhooked a lantern from its pole and stumbled toward the dinghy. Wounds throbbing, she untied the rope and grabbed the oar. The current caught the boat at once, tugging her south along the Yin . . . south to those fleeing ships. To hope. To those she loved.

She sailed in the dark. She sailed alone. As she flowed south, the smoke cleared from the sky, and the Leaping Fish stars shone above, and Koyee could smile for despite her wounds, despite the loss of her homeland, despite the ache in her heart, there was still beauty in the world. There was still goodness and hope in the dark.

"Do you remember how we sailed from Oshy almost two years ago?" she whispered. "Do you remember, Eelani? It was in a boat like this. We sailed to seek help for our home." Tears now streamed down her cheeks. "We still sail. Just you and me. We still haven't lost our hope in the shadows."

She reached into the pocket of her tattered, bloody tunic, and her fingers closed around her flutes. She pulled out two musical instruments: an old bone with some holes drilled in, a trifle she had played in the dregs of Pahmey; and a beautiful silver flute, a costly instrument she had played in The Green Geode as a yezyana.

I played these flutes in my darkest hours, living as an urchin in rags, and then as an enchantress in silk, she thought. *Today I am alone again in darkness. Today I play the old bone.* She placed the silver flute away.

An old tune called to her, the music Little Maniko had taught her. Eyes stinging, she raised the flute to her lips and played again.

We call this song Sailing Alone, she thought, *for it is the tune of a boat on the water, of a lone soul in darkness, of hope when all hope seems lost.*

The boat sailed downriver and her music flowed.

The stars turned, the hills rolled at her sides, and the fires behind her faded into darkness. All the world was this: stars and shadow, water and stone, song and silence. She stood at the prow, playing her flute until she saw the light ahead.

The distant lantern bobbed, growing closer, and Koyee smiled.

"Look, Eelani. Another boat."

She sailed downriver. The light moved upriver toward her. Boat approached boat, two glowing wisps in the darkness. A man was rowing toward her, the lamplight falling upon him.

"Koyee?" he asked, hesitant, and then shouted and waved. "Koyee!"

She looked at him—his dark hair, his mismatched eyes, his laughing mouth—and she laughed too.

"Torin!" She reached toward him, tasting her tears. "Torin."

Their prows met and she stumbled into his boat. He wrapped her in his arms, and he held her close, and they stood embracing and weeping and laughing.

"I had to come back for you," he whispered. "I rowed from ship to ship, and I couldn't find you, and I knew you were back here. I knew you were alive. I had to save you."

She laughed and touched his cheek. "You didn't save me. I found a boat. I saved myself."

He pulled her closer against him and kissed her forehead.

Their lamps joined—starlight and sunlight—together again. They sailed south into the endless darkness.

* * * * *

Ishel walked through the ruins of Yintao, spear in hand, stabbing the wounded.

"Filthy demons," she said and spat.

The debris spread around her: fallen walls, smashed
pagodas, and cracked columns. Shattered blades, shields, and
helmets lay upon piles of bricks and roof tiles. Everywhere Ishel
looked she saw the ruin of flesh too: blood on cobblestones,
severed limbs, and corpses. But she cared not for ruin or death.
Ishel, Princess of Naya, sought the living.

Her pet tiger growled at her side. Ishel stroked the beast's
head.

"Yes, Durga," Ishel cooed. "Soon, my sweet, we will find
you a meal."

Durga bristled and tugged at his chain, but Ishel held him
fast. She was a princess of the rainforest, and he was a king of
beasts. Though far from home, traveling under a dark sky, they
did not forget their nobility. Blood now stained Ishel's tiger-skin
cloak, dents marred her iron breastplate, and dust dulled the
gleam of her golden armlets, but she was still a great leader, a
shining light even here in the dark.

Moaning rose ahead. Ishel stepped around a toppled
column and fallen street lamp, oil still burning behind its glass
panes. There he lay, his legs trapped under the column's capital, a
young soldier of Eloria. His large eyes—freakish things the size of
limes—stared at her in pain. Blood stained his long white hair,
and he reached out to her, begging in his tongue, pleading for aid.

Ishel came to stand above the soldier, placed a boot upon
his chest, and laughed.

"I can't speak your wicked tongue," she said, pressing her
toes down into a wound upon his chest.

The man was too weak to even scream; he could only
whimper. Tears budded in his eyes. He seemed young to Ishel,
not yet twenty.

"My brother was young too," she said softly, staring down
upon this soldier. She removed her boot from his wound, knelt,
and caressed the boy's cheek. "He was only a youth but already

old enough to fight. He marched into the night, vowing to light the darkness . . . and they slew him. The Chanku Pack, cruel wolves of the night, murdered him upon the moonlit plains."

The young Elorian soldier whispered to her, still speaking his tongue, and some softness filled his eyes, some relief.

"Help . . ." he said, his accent heavy, finally speaking her language. "Help . . ."

Ishel laughed and mussed his hair. "Such a clever boy! How did you learn to speak?" She patted his cheek. "But I don't want to hear you speak . . . I want to hear you scream."

His eyes widened with fear as she straightened and raised her spear.

She drove the blade down.

And he screamed. He screamed as she twisted the spearhead in his gut, and it was beautiful, and she smiled.

"Good boy . . ." she cooed as he died upon her blade.

Her tiger growled at her side, and Ishel nodded and loosened the chain.

"Very well, my pet. You may feed."

The tiger pounced upon the dead man . . . and feasted.

Ishel kept walking through the ruins, listening to moans and screams, driving her spear down to silence them. Soldiers, mothers, children—all died upon her blade. All were filthy Elorians, creatures to exterminate, lower than maggots.

"Yet my greatest kill was the traitor." She speared a moaning woman found trapped under a dead wolf. "The fat boy. The Ardish scum." She spat.

All in the Nayan army—perhaps across the entire host of eight Timandrian kingdoms—knew of the traitors, those four children of sunlight who had defected into the darkness.

Torin Greenmoat.

Camlin Shepherd.

Linee Solira.

Ishel licked her lips. "And the one I killed—Hemstad Baker."

She smiled to remember firing her arrows into his portly form. He had died silently—a disappointing death. Ishel craved screaming almost as much as blood. She vowed that when she found the other three, she would make them scream and squeal. Elorians were insects to crush, but those Timandrians . . . they were something even worse.

"Treachery will be punished." She stroked her tiger. "We will find them, my sweet Durga. They fled this city, but we will find them. You will feed upon them too."

She reached a section of wall that still stood, rising from rubble, its crenellations chipped. She walked up the inner stairway, stepped onto the battlements, and beheld her army below. The hosts of Naya roared in a shadowy courtyard, banging spears against shields. Tiger pelts draped across their shoulders, fang necklaces hung around their necks, and blood stained their breastplates. Tigers growled among them, chained to their wrists. Bone beads filled the warriors' long, red hair and beards. Ishel's own hair—the color of fire—fluttered in the wind. Standing upon the wall, she raised her bloody spear.

"Warriors of Naya!" she shouted.

"Ishel! Ishel!" they chanted.

She swung her spear above her, spraying droplets of blood. "I have sworn to lead you to glory. The empire of Qaelin has fallen, and the spoils are ours!"

They roared in triumph.

Seven other kingdoms of Timandra had marched into darkness with her host, and they would squabble like hens for seeds. But Ishel swore to herself: *The choice cut of Eloria will be ours. And revenge will be mine.*

"Linee Solira," she whispered as her army roared below. "Camlin Shepherd. Bailey Berin. Torin Greenmoat."

The names of the traitors. The names of those she would kill. As her warriors brandished their trophies below—katanas, helmets, and jewels seized in the war—Ishel imagined spearing her enemies and smiled.

CHAPTER THREE
THE LIBRARY

Cam stood on the palace balcony, gazed upon a city of black bricks and red banners, and felt loss and fear claw inside him.

The port city of Asharo, capital of Ilar, spread across the hills and coast. Every building here—from home to shop to silo—looked like a fortress. Battlements crowned every roof, and soldiers stood upon them, clad in lacquered plates of black steel, bows and spears in their hands. Braziers burned atop dark towers. Troops marched in courtyards. Crenelled walls lined the coast, and beyond them a hundred warships patrolled the sea, lanterns bright. Everywhere he looked, Cam saw the banners of this southern island empire—a red flame upon a black field.

Unlike Qaelin—an empire of philosophers, buskers, priests, and beggars—Ilar was a land of steel, fire, and war.

"And war is coming here," Cam whispered and shivered in the cold wind. "Ferius conquered Qaelin, the largest empire of the night. Now he will sail to Ilar."

Beside him, Linee whimpered. Cam turned to look at her. When he had first met her, Linee had been a queen of sunlight, a young woman clad in a gown and gems, a fairy tale creature. Her gowns had torn in the long wars of the night. Her jewels had been sold or lost. Here in the darkness she wore the accoutrements of an Elorian noblewoman—a red silk dress embroidered with black dragons, a golden sash around her waist, and a single ruby upon her throat. Her blond hair, once a masterwork of curls and braids, now hung straight to the sides, and her eyes, once bright and joyous, held the shadows of haunting memories.

"Maybe we should go home." She lowered her head. "Look at this place, Camlin. A dark sky. Elorians in black armor. A war between monks and the children of night. This isn't our war." She looked at him, eyes pleading and damp. "We can rent a boat; I still have some jewels to sell. We can sail back home, Camlin. Home!" Her eyes lit up. "Do you remember home? The blue skies, white clouds, and yellow sun. Trees and grass and shrubs and flowers. The song of birds. The taste of bread and fruit." She sighed. "We belong back there. This isn't our war."

Cam closed his eyes. He could barely remember that home. He could barely remember the warmth of the sun, the light of day, the blue of the sky and the green of forests.

"I want to go home more than anything." He hugged himself in the cold. "I don't like the darkness or the cold of this place. I don't like eating mushrooms, glowing fish, and whatever meat can be found in the dark. And worst of all, I don't like this war—the constant fear of Ferius arriving in this city. But Linee . . . Ferius now rules in Arden, our old kingdom, and his monks are spreading to many lands in Timandra. If we did return to sunlight, he would hunt us. He knows our names; half the world must know our names by now. I never thought I'd be famous." He laughed mirthlessly. "We're among the Five Traitors, the Timandrians who fight for the demons of darkness. Well . . ." That old chill gripped him, and he lowered his head. "Four Traitors now."

The memory of Hem, lying dead and peaceful in the ruins of Yintao, returned to him like icy wind. Cam closed his eyes, and he knew why the memories of home evaded him. In all those buried memories, Hem was with him—singing in The Shadowed Firkin tavern, imitating Bailey behind her back, offering their gang freshly baked bread . . . and following them to war in the night.

"And now he's gone," he said. "Now that big, fat, stupid loaf of a boy is gone. And . . . I don't know who I am anymore."

He opened his eyes and looked at Linee. "For so long, we were Cam and Hem. Bailey would call us the two-headed beast. I don't know how to just be Cam."

Linee moved closer to him and slipped her hand into his. Cam was used to being the shortest one among his friends— barely reaching the shoulders of giants like Bailey and Hem, and even Torin towered over him—but Linee stood just as short, and her eyes gazed straight into his. He saw softness and kindness in those green eyes.

"Maybe . . . maybe I can be your new best friend." She bit her lip and lowered her head. "I mean . . . not to replace Hem or anything. I know I can't do that. Just . . . " She looked up at him, eyes damp. "Just to be a new friend. We can be Cam and Linee maybe." She looked away, cheeks flushing. "I guess it's a stupid idea."

He pulled his hand from her grip, and she looked ready to cry, but then he placed his arm around her, pulled her close, and held her tightly.

"I think it's a fantastic idea," he said. "It's the best damn idea I've heard since entering the night."

Her face lit up. "Really?" She laughed, mussed his hair, and pinched his cheek. "Good! Because I'm a very very good friend, even if I annoy you sometimes. I know most people wouldn't believe me. They think I'm dumb and childlike and pampered, and maybe they're right. Maybe I am those things. But I'm also loyal and kind."

The cold wind gusted, billowing a thousand red banners across the black city. Clouds trailed over the moon, ships patrolled the coast, and the warriors of Ilar marched upon battlements and courtyards below. Cam and Linee stood together on the balcony, holding each other, watching the night.

* * * * *

Koyee walked through the refugee camp, too hollowed for tears, too weary for grief. The thousands crowded around her, exiles of her empire, but she sought only one soul.

"Look again!" she told the old man with the scrolls. "He must be on the lists. Okado son of Salai. My brother."

The elder shook his head, white beard swaying. He held a bundle of scrolls that rolled down to his feet. "I am most sorry, my child. But no Okado son of Salai has joined our camp." He patted her hand. "So many lost loved ones in the battle. His soul was strong. He shines now among the stars."

She pulled her hand back and glared at him. "Do not be so quick to bury him." She left the old man and marched through the camp, mud squelching under her feet. "I will find him. Okado!" She coned her hand around her mouth and cried out. "Okado! Has anyone seen him?"

She wouldn't listen to the old man with his lists of survivors. She wouldn't listen to those soldiers who claimed they had seen Okado fall in Yintao's port, burned by Ferius himself, giving his life to protect the people of that captured city. If there was no body, there was still hope.

"Okado!"

The refugee camp, home to the survivors of Qaelin, spread across the valley. A mile away rose the walls of Asharo, the capital of the Ilari empire, a city of bricks and tiles and steel. But here in the wilderness rolled a place of mud, of crude tents, of frightened survivors.

Koyee was not the only one searching. Others walked between the tents, their feet muddy, calling out the names of loved ones. Wives called for husbands. Mothers called for children. Everywhere she saw them—skinny, wounded refugees, their clothes in tatters, crying for the missing. And Koyee knew:

Most of those loved ones were dead. Thrice their elders had moved from tent to tent, collecting the names of all the survivors.

"And you're not among them, my brother." Koyee looked up at the stars. "Do you truly now shine above me, watching from a place I cannot reach?"

She kept walking through the camp, silent. She had fought to save thousands. She had left behind a brother. She lowered her head and could not breathe for the ache in her heart.

I lost my mother in childhood. I lost my father two years ago. Now my brother is gone, and I am truly alone.

"Koyee?"

She turned to see Torin, and her eyes stung because though she had lost her family, and she herself was lost in a strange land, she was not alone—not with him here, the man who had followed her from sunlight into shadow, from war to exile, from water to fire and finally to mud. He wore his armor of the night—a shirt of steel scales and vambraces carved with moonstar runes. Instead of his old longsword, a katana hung at his side. When she had first met him, he had seemed a soft boy to her, his cheeks smooth, his eyes afraid. She saw a man stand before her now. A beard darkened his cheeks, his face was gaunter, and two years of bloodshed had hardened his eyes like hammers on hot steel.

"I can't find him, Torin," she whispered. "I must have searched every tent. He's . . ." She lowered her head, voice choking.

He took her hands. "I'm sorry, Koyee. I'm so sorry."

She nodded and wiped her eyes. "I have to tell you something. A secret." The pain constricted her throat; she could barely speak. "I was with Shenlai when he died. The last dragon of Qaelin. He spoke his last, dying secret to me." She touched Torin's cheek. "Come with me back to Asharo. We must find the city library. And we must find a clock."

* * * * *

The Library of Asharo loomed above the streets. Black columns stood in a ring, supporting a dome so large it could have enclosed all of Oshy. A banner of the red flame thudded from the roof, and iron statues of panthers guarded the stone doors. Koyee had visited Minlao Palace, home of Pahmey's elders. She had met Empress Hikari in her hall of stone and steel. She had fought in the courts of the Eternal Palace of Yintao. She had sailed upon ships like floating forts. This, however, was a place of learning, and it was the greatest building she had ever seen.

"If there is hope for the night, it will be revealed to us here," she said.

Torin sighed. "I don't know, Koyee. 'Fix the clock and the world will turn again?' What does that mean?

"I don't know. Maybe the books do. That's why we're here." She smiled. "I hope you remember the reading lessons I gave you."

They climbed the stairs, moving between the panther statues. Soldiers stood outside the doors as if guarding a palace, for knowledge too was power, mightier than swords and cannons. Koyee stepped between them, entered the library, and gasped.

Despite her grief, her fear, and her aching wounds, she smiled shakily and tears of awe stung her eyes.

"It's beautiful," she whispered. "Oh, Torin . . . it's beautiful."

He twisted his lips. "It looks dusty. Dust makes me sneeze."

"The only thing dusty here is your empty skull." She held his hand, dragged him deeper into the library, and grinned. "Look . . . oh stars above, look at all those books."

Shelves spread along the walls, rising toward the domed ceiling, and more bookshelves rose along the floor like a labyrinth. Countless books filled them, wrapped in leather or metal, books more plentiful than soldiers in any army. Paintings of flying dragons covered the ceiling, statues of queens and kings stood between columns, and mosaics of birds and panthers spread across the floor, but Koyee spared these wonders but a glance or two. Instead she gaped at the books, things of wonder and mystery. Some were large, elaborate codices, their titles golden upon their spines. Others were smaller, humbler things, simply sheaves of parchment wrapped in a bundle, dusty and curling. Some books looked too heavy to lift, and others she could have hidden in her pockets. A few had covers forged from precious metals inlaid with jewels. She saw books of poetry, of history, of medicine, of astronomy, and some—how she wished she had time to read them!—stories of epic tales from long ago.

At that moment, more than boats, swords, or flutes, Koyee knew that she'd discovered her true love: books.

She walked between the shelves, smiling. It felt like all the horrors of the world—the loss of her family, the flame of war, the light of day—could never reach her. Here between these books was a different plane of existing. Here were knowledge and wisdom themselves, a realm of thought and memory. She walked among the stars. Every book here was a world unto itself, a world she could lift off a shelf, open up, and delve into like a spirit.

"I don't know where to start!" she said, still smiling.

"I don't know either." Torin looked miserable. "There must be a million books here. We'd grow old, shrivel up, and die before we could read a tiny fraction of these. Blimey, just reading the titles would take a lifetime." He sighed. "I'm a humble gardener from a humble village; I don't know how to be a scholar."

"What we need is a librarian." Koyee walked between two shelves and pointed.

Down an aisle, maybe a hundred yards away, rose a stone desk. A figure sat there, white of hair, too distant to see clearly.

Koyee inhaled deeply, savoring the scent of the books, and walked toward the librarian.

When she reached the desk, a wizened, whitened creature raised his head from a book. He was an old man but so ancient and small he seemed to Koyee like some spirit from a tale, someone to be found behind a mushroom rather than a desk. His nose thrust out, long and thin as a finger, supporting golden-rimmed spectacles. Curtains of white hair like cobwebs hung around his face, and his beard flowed across the desk like a tablecloth. His ears thrust out like antennae, and his eyes—very large and very blue—blinked at her.

"Well, hello young . . ." He adjusted his lenses. ". . . young woman. Welcome. I am Fen, Guardian of Books, Lord of Lore, Keeper of Knowledge, Augur of Wisdo—" He began to cough, patted his chest, and cleared his throat. "I'm the librarian. What knowledge do you seek?"

The old man seemed barely larger than Little Maniko. Koyee smiled. "A book about clocks, Master Fen."

"Ah!" The little man rubbed his hands together. "Clocks! Purveyors of time. Keepers of moments and eras. Masters of horology. Very important devices, yes, for us here in endless night. Did you know, child, that the world would once turn? Did you know that all hourglasses are made to track the dance of old days and nights?" His voice was a high, quivering sound like a harp string. "Not many believe it, but I have books of old . . . books that speak of those times, yes. What clocks does your eager mind seek to study? Hourglasses? Water clocks? Mechanical clocks of gears and springs? Perhaps the buried sundials of the ancients? Or maybe—"

"I don't know," Koyee said, feeling it best to interrupt before he started coughing again. "It's a riddle. Something about a clock that's broken, that has to be fixed."

". . . or perhaps astronomical clocks or—" He blinked and gasped. "A clock that is broken?" His voice dropped to a whisper and he leaned across the desk. "Surely you don't mean . . . oh Flame of Ilar."

Torin reached the desk, holding a small bestiary with a bird on the cover. "What's so wrong with broken clocks? I mean besides maybe being late for dinner."

"Many things, young master!" said the librarian, frowning at him. "Hosts have been late to battle because of broken clocks, letting their kingdoms fall. Lovers have missed their trysts, then jumped into the sea to drown their pain. Broken clocks can topple empires and shatter souls. But . . . ah . . . there was *one* clock . . . one clock that did far more than crush an empire."

Koyee shivered. "What can be worse than crushing an empire?"

Old Fen smiled, revealing small golden teeth. "Breaking the world itself." He hopped off his seat, rushed around the desk, and clapped his hands. "Come now! Old Fen will lead you to knowledge."

He rushed down the aisle, his robes fluttering and his slippers thumping. Koyee and Torin followed. They moved through the labyrinth of books, and Koyee longed to stop, to reach to the shelves, to explore all the words around her. Every book seemed to call out to her, begging to be read. But Fen was moving too quickly, and Koyee only caught glimpses of the titles she passed—books about beasts, magical artifacts, star maps, and histories of heroes.

Fen led them under an archway, past obsidian statues of dragons, and into a dusty chamber. Lanterns shaped as laughing spirits hung upon the walls, fur rugs covered the floor, and armchairs stood against walls. A fireplace crackled in the back, its burning blocks of tallow casting orange light. Books filled more shelves here, seeming more ancient than any Koyee had seen.

Their leather spines peeled back, the runes upon them so faded she could barely read them.

You'd have loved this place, Okado, Koyee thought, a sudden sting of pain shooting through her. *You were a warrior but wise too. I wish you were here with me.*

Fen grabbed a wheeled ladder, pulled it toward a wall of shelves, and climbed. He reached for a heavy codex almost as large as he was. As he pulled out the book, dust showered. Standing below, Torin sneezed.

"Ah!" said Fen. "Here we go. The Cabera Clock Chronicles by Master Zenafren." He pulled the book to his chest, hobbled toward Koyee, and handed her the codex. "This should teach you a few things. This book is about the greatest clock that ever existed—a clock that tracked the dance of the stars themselves and the spinning of the worlds . . . a clock of legend, the clock that broke Moth."

Koyee took the heavy book, leaning back and nearly crumpling under the weight. "Thank you . . . Master Fen!"

Torin hurried forward to help her. Together, they carried the oversized book toward an armchair. Koyee climbed into the seat and wriggled into the soft cushion. The chair was large enough for two, and Torin sat beside her. They placed the book upon their laps.

Koyee opened the tome with a new shower of dust. She swallowed a sneeze and stared at the first page. An illustration covered the parchment, depicting a mountain rising from the dusk, the light of Timandra to its west, the shadows of Eloria to its east. A dial appeared upon the mountaintop, inlaid with numbers from zero to nine. Ilari runes appeared beneath the illustration, and Koyee read aloud.

"The Cabera Clock." She gasped. "It says it's over twenty thousand years old, Torin! I didn't even know people existed to build a clock twenty thousand years ago."

Torin flipped the page, revealing a new illustration. Here appeared an animal Koyee didn't recognize. It reminded her a little of a bear, large and shaggy and covered in golden fur. It had eight limbs—six of its paws stood upon the ground, and the foremost pair rose to hold a harp. Its face seemed sad to her, long of snout and large of eyes.

"A 'Clockwork Cleric,'" she read. "Maybe humans didn't build this clock after all."

Torin leaned down and squinted. He struggled to read the language of Ilar and stumbled over the words. Koyee smiled and patted his shoulder.

"Don't hurt yourself. Let me read for you." She flipped the page, began to read the story of the clock . . . and slowly her smile vanished.

CHAPTER FOUR
DAUGHTERS OF SUNLIGHT

Bailey stood alone in shadow.

A single candle burned upon her table, and she stared into her tall mirror. She did not know who she saw. A woman. An orphan. The daughter of a lord from a minor house, an exile, a warrior of the night. A lost soul.

"I am alone."

Her reflection stared back at her. Her brown eyes seemed weary. Her skin, which had always been tanned and freckled, now looked pale. Her old pride—her two golden braids—did not shine here in the darkness. Where was the girl she had known, an adventurer who swam through rivers, chased butterflies in fields, climbed trees, and wrestled Torin—he was always the monster in their games—on grassy hills? That girl had died long ago. That light had left her.

"And you left me too, Torin."

She had joined this quest—her greatest, most tragic adventure—to look after him. And now he spent all his time with Koyee. Even Cam, whom Bailey used to deride and tug by the ear, would have been welcome company here in this city, but he only spent time with the exiled queen.

"And here I am—Bailey Berin, alone in a room in a city of shadow."

The empress of this land had given Bailey a chamber in some fortress. It was fine enough a place—the chair upholstered, the bed soft—but to Bailey it felt like a prison. She was raised in sunlight and grass and water, and in this city of shadows and stone she felt herself wilt.

She turned away from the mirror.

Maybe I should go home. Her eyes stung. *Hem is gone, and maybe Torin and Cam no longer need me. I came here to protect them, but they found new women.*

She knuckled her eyes, ground her teeth, and cursed.

"Don't be stupid, Bailey!" she scolded herself. She punched the wall. "Don't be some stupid . . . cry baby! You're a warrior. You're strong. The others are weak. Torin?" She snickered. "A babyface. Cam?" She barked a laugh. "A runt of a shepherd. I don't need them. I don't need anyone."

Lips tight, she grabbed her sword. Torin perhaps had switched to a katana, but Bailey had not forgotten her roots, and she kept her longsword of sunlight, the pommel shaped as the half-sun of Idar. Buckling the weapon to her belt, she stormed out of her chamber.

She burst outside onto the streets of Asharo. A cobbled boulevard stretched before her, lined with houses of black bricks. Chimneys pumped out smoke. The red flame banners thudded from crenelled roofs. Everywhere she looked, she saw soldiers waiting for war. Back in Qaelin, the fallen empire of the mainland, soldiers had seemed to her like mystical spirits, slender men clad in silvery scales, their spears tall and pale like orchids. But here in Ilar, the southern island of Eloria, soldiers seemed to her more like demons of darkness. They wore heavy plate armor, the steel lacquered and black, and their helmets were shaped like scorning demons complete with bristly mustaches. Many marched back and forth, clanking like oversized beetles, tasseled swords and bows hanging across their backs. Others rode upon great panthers, the beasts growling beneath them.

Yet when Ferius arrived here with his hosts of sunlight—knights on horses, hammer-wielding barbarians riding bears, and archers upon elephants—could this army of the night, for all its might, withstand them? Bailey had thought Yintao safe too, and yet those walls had fallen. Perhaps there was no safety in the night.

"Bailey!" A voice rose across the street, and a small shadow came racing toward her. "Bailey, by the light, I've been looking for you."

She frowned. "Camlin Shepherd! What do you want?"

He reached her and wiped sweat off his brow. He panted and it was a moment before he could speak again. "They found something! Torin and Koyee. Some way to defeat Ferius with a giant clock and a spider-bear and a missing hand . . . or something like that."

Bailey sighed. "It's finally happened. You've contracted stupidity from Linee." She shook him. "Cam! By Idar. What are you talking about?"

"I don't even know!" He grabbed her arm and began pulling her down the street. "Just follow me to the library. Torin can explain it better."

She rolled her eyes but she followed him. "Yes, I'm sure that when Torin explains about missing hands and spider-bears, it'll make perfect sense."

When Cam finally dragged her into the library—Bailey cursing at him to slow down all the while—she found everyone else inside. Torin and Koyee stood at a table, a book the size of a heater shield open before them. Linee stood at their side, hugging herself, and Cam went to stand beside her.

"What's all this about?" Bailey said, hands on her hips. "Why did you call me here?"

She couldn't curb her rage. So the babyface had his girl of the night. The runty shepherd had his queen. What did they want her here for—to gloat? To scorn her for her loneliness? She snorted. She was better than them. She was taller, stronger, faster, and wiser. What did she care what any of them thought?

"Well, speak!" she said. "Tell me or I'm leaving."

It was Koyee—that damn little urchin—who stepped forward and spoke first. Bailey was tempted to throttle the pale waif. Koyee Mai—with her slender frame, large purple eyes, and perfectly smooth white hair—made Bailey feel clumsy, awkward, too tall and gangly, some lumbering giant beside a fairy. She hated the girl for that, and she hated her for stealing Torin.

"We found a way to undo the lies of Ferius." Koyee spoke in Ardish for her benefit, her accent thick. "We can make the world turn again. Day and light can return to the world of Moth."

Bailey covered her eyes and laughed. "Oh dear Idar, the lot of you are mad."

When she turned to leave, Torin raced around her and blocked her passage.

"Bailey, wait." Pain filled his eyes. "Just listen to what we found out."

She glared at him. The damn boy perhaps sported some stubble now, and maybe he'd grown a few muscles during the war, but he was still a damn babyface. She didn't care what anyone else said. Bailey knew who he really was. She had taken an orphan into her home, had wrestled him into submission in the fields, and had seen him jump at rabbits in the dusk. Maybe now, with his armor and battle scars and a couple more years of weariness, he could fool Koyee, pretending to be some warrior. But he wasn't fooling Bailey.

You're still my Winky, she thought. *You're still the little boy I took into my home . . . the boy I love. Even if you now love another.*

"Oh, fine!" Bailey said. "Merciful Idar, anything to stop those puppy eyes of yours. It's not very manly when you make them."

She stomped toward the others and glared down at the open book. Torin spoke, sometimes letting Koyee interject, and Bailey listened.

She listened for a long time.

When they were done, Bailey stood silently for a moment, mouth agape. Finally she laughed and raised her hands incredulously.

"So you're telling me . . . that a fabled, ancient dragon held a secret for thousands of years, then finally spoke of an even older clock, which was built by a race of creatures called Clockwork Clerics, and which controls the movement of our world. Oh, and wait!" She laughed again. "Our world is apparently round and used to spin around its axis like a marble. And . . . wait . . . this is the best part: We can only get the world to spin again if we find three pieces of the clock—in a rainforest, a desert, and an island—and repair it, because the spider-bears want mankind to work together as a team. Did I miss anything?" Bailey slapped the book. "Seriously, did I? Maybe about pink elephants with swan wings, guarding a windmill inside a volcano that belches out the winds of the world? And tell me, what causes the seasons—a giant faulty furnace protected by magical beavers?"

Torin sighed. "I know it sounds like a bit of a stretch . . ."

"Do you think, Torin?" She twisted his arm. "Really, do you think?"

"But look, Bailey!" He tugged himself free from her grasp. "What if it's real?"

"It's not real."

"Just think about it." Torin looked back at the book. "The Sailith Order is all about the day fighting the night, about light banishing the darkness, about the forces of the sun vanquishing the demons of the moon. Well, what if everyone had a day and night again? What if the sun could rise in Eloria and darkness could fall in Timandra? What if the ancient dance returned?"

"There never was an ancient dance!" Bailey grabbed her head in frustration. "Merciful Idar! Those are just stories. The world never turned, and no fabled Clock of Magical Belly Button Fluff can fix it. Those are just fairy tales."

"Well, I thought dragons were only fairy tales until I saw them," Torin said. "And one dragon told Koyee about this clock. So I believe it's true. And I believe it can undo all the rhetoric Ferius has fed the people."

Bailey groaned. Torin actually believed this story! She looked at the others, seeking some support, but they only stared at her solemnly. They too believed.

With an enraged grunt, Bailey tugged her braids. "I can't believe I'm hearing this. You lot are a bunch of naive children." She blew out her breath. "Look, even if it *is* true, and even if we *could* find these three missing pieces—the gear, the hand, and the number—and even if we fixed the clock and the world *did* turn again . . . so what? Ferius would just preach something about how Elorians carry the ancient curse and still need to die. You think day and night rotating again can change his mind?"

Torin shook his head. "No. Ferius is bloodthirsty and mad. Nothing can sway him. But his soldiers, Bailey. Do you know why they follow him? Because for decades now, Sailith has been teaching them that daylight is good and that night is evil. When day and night are everywhere, Sailith falls apart. It loses all legitimacy. Its dogma becomes some bad old joke. How could Eloria be cruel if the sun rose upon it? How could Timandra be righteous when cloaked in night half the time? You want to fight Ferius? His greatest power isn't his armies—it's his *narrative*." Torin nodded. "Let's tear that narrative apart."

Koyee nodded. "We'll have to find the three pieces. We can tell nobody else of this. We cannot risk Ferius learning of our task." She looked from one to another. "We'll split into three groups and retrieve the three pieces of the Cabera Clock."

Bailey narrowed her eyes, tilted her head, and stared at the young Elorian woman.

So . . . you would go with Torin on yet another quest, she thought. *Like you traveled with him last year, leaving me out of the picture.* Bailey felt that old rage flare anew. *I see your little plan, Koyee Mai of Eloria.*

Bailey looked back at Torin. The babyface believed in this little picture book story, and if Koyee had her way, Bailey would be cast aside again.

This is my chance, Bailey realized. *This is my chance to break them apart . . . and to keep the babyface near me where he belongs.*

"Very well," Bailey said, hands on hips. "We'll go on three quests again. Cam and Linee! You two will travel to the desert of Eseer to find the missing clock hand. Torin! You and I will travel to fetch the missing number from the jungles of Naya. Koyee! The gear is the only piece hidden in the night. You are Elorian and accustomed to darkness, so that will be your quest."

She smiled thinly, staring at the young Elorian. *That's right, Koyee. You can travel alone this time.*

Torin cleared his throat. "Bailey . . . shouldn't we all discuss this together?"

"No." Bailey shook her head vigorously. "Those are our quests. We Timandrians have spent too long in the darkness. For over a year, we haven't seen daylight, and we're growing pale. We're growing weak. Within Timandra's armies, they speak of a shadow curse, an illness that strikes Timandrians who haven't seen the sun in too long. Ferius is now sending soldiers back every six months, replacing them with fresh recruits. We've lingered in the dark for too long. Koyee, the only Elorian in our fellowship, will remain alone in the night. We Timandrians must return to the sunlight."

They all turned to look at Koyee . . . all but Bailey. She stared at Torin and saw the pain in his eyes.

Yes, it hurts you to part from her, doesn't it? She smiled thinly.
*Good. Now you know how I feel. But you belong with me, Winky. We've
been together all our lives, and we will be together again.*

Koyee nodded and pain filled her eyes too. She lowered her
head and spoke in a small voice. "Bailey speaks truth. You're all
weary and pale, suffering from lack of sunlight. We Elorians
thrive in the night, but you need the light of day. I'll travel to the
distant island in the dark, and I'll find the gear. Cam and Linee will
seek the hand in the desert. Torin, you and Bailey can seek the
number in the rainforest. Let us meet at the spring equinox at
Cabera Mountain in the dusk. The Cabera Clock lies broken on its
peak."

Bailey closed her eyes, and her fingertips tingled, and her
knees shook.

Home. I'm going home.

Not home to Fairwool-by-Night, perhaps. Not even to
Arden, her old kingdom. But she was going back to sunlight—just
Torin and her. They would run through grass again like in their
youth. They would lie in the sunlight and talk of their dreams.
They would climb trees, and she would tease him for being too
slow. That to her was home more than any particular village or
kingdom.

She walked toward Torin and slung her arm around him.
She pulled him close and smiled at the others.

"Again we part three ways," Bailey said. "Again the hope of
Moth lies upon our shoulders. I don't know if the Cabera Clock is
real. I don't know if we can find its missing pieces. But if they
exist . . . if this is the way to defeat Ferius . . . we'll find them. I
would travel to the very ends of the earth for a sliver of hope."

And for you, Torin. And for you.

Cam and Linee looked at each other, held hands, and
nodded. Koyee stared at them all with strangely blank eyes, and

she caressed her arm, perhaps still feeling the wound Ferius had given her in Pahmey.

The book lay open upon the table, and when Bailey glanced toward it, it seemed as if the Cabera Clock—just an old illustration on parchment—was looking at her too, its dial a single, all-seeing eye.

* * * * *

He sat alone upon Qaelin's captured throne, gripping the armrests so tightly the gilt cracked.

"She escaped," Ferius hissed, fingernails digging into the seat. "Koyee has fled . . . and she knows."

He looked across the throne room of the Eternal Palace, the great hall he had conquered. Columns rose in rows, holding a vaulted ceiling. Braziers shaped as wolves, birds, and fish held burning embers in their mouths, casting red light. A mosaic spread across the floor, depicting blue dragons coiling around silver stars. The true blue dragon of Qaelin—the creature Shenlai—hung from the ceiling on chains, gutted and stuffed, his eyes replaced with glass balls.

"You lie dead in my hall," Ferius said through a clenched jaw, staring at the beast. "Yet still you haunt me, creature of darkness."

He had ordered his men to slay the beast. He knew that Shenlai had known of the clock, that the dragon would reveal his secret with his last breath. His men had reported seeing the reptile fly out of Yintao, bristly with a hundred arrows, Koyee upon his back. When Ferius had finally found the dragon, the creature had lain dead in the wilderness . . . Koyee gone.

Ferius rose from his throne. He walked down the hall, boots thudding upon the mosaic. His fists trembled, and he bit his cheek and tasted blood.

"You *know*," he said, voice trembling with rage. "You know of the clock, my half-sister."

He walked toward the dead dragon. With a snarl, he grabbed one of the beast's horns and tugged. The horn came loose into his hands with a sound like ripping leather. Ferius shouted and drove it forward, stabbing the corpse.

"I will find you, my wretched beast of a sister. I vow to you. I will find you, Koyee, and I will hang you here in the hall of your fallen empire, but I will keep you alive. You will live to scream and weep as I hurt you."

The doors to the hall opened.

A woman's silhouette stood there, hands on her hips, lamplight behind her.

"Leave this place!" Ferius shouted and tossed down the horn. "I ordered my guards to let none enter. Who are you?"

The woman at the doorway—with the light behind her, he could only see her shadowed form—laughed.

"Having a little tantrum in the shadows, are you? No guards can hold me back." She took a step into the hall, revealing a beast that growled behind her, eyes gleaming. "So this is the mighty Ferius, Lord of Light, Commander of the Sunlit Hosts . . . throwing a fit like a toddler."

The woman stepped closer, and the light of braziers fell upon her. She smiled crookedly. She was a Nayan woman, a daughter of the rainforest; she wore tiger pelts and a breastplate painted with claws. Wild, fiery curls cascaded from her head, war paint covered her cheeks, and her eyes shone bright green. Tattoos of jungle beasts coiled up her arms. She held a spear bedecked with a string of fangs, and a bow and quiver hung across her back. A live tiger growled at her side, a chain running from its collar to the woman's wrist.

"To enter my hall is death," Ferius said.

The woman snorted. "Not to me. I am Ishel Who Cuts Bones with Iron, Daughter of Kewana Who Shatters Stone, Granddaughter of Tihotek Who Feasted on Man Flesh, Princess of Naya . . . and your betrothed."

Ferius narrowed his eyes, scrutinizing her. "You are early. Your father, Kewana Who Shatters Something or Other, promised to deliver you only in the spring."

She laughed. "When I heard tales of your might, I traveled early into darkness. Yet now I see a short, hunched over, bitter man pretending to be a dragon slayer. I slew soldiers in this battle. Did you hide indoors, stabbing stuffed animals? Perhaps I should return home to sunlight."

Rage flared in Ferius, emerging in a growl. He stepped toward her. He was a short man, it was true, and Ishel—like most people—stood taller than him, but Ferius had always overcome his short stature with ferocity. He grabbed Ishel's wrist, digging his fingers into her, and stared into her eyes. He knew that his stare—hard, cold, and pale blue like forge fire—unnerved people. His eyes were eerily far set, beady and gleaming with the hint of danger, eyes small like a Timandrian's but bright and piercing like an Elorian's.

"You will return to the rainforest," he said. "You've traveled far into the night, but I will send you back to sunlight."

She raised an eyebrow, and in the instant it took her to speak again, Ferius knew that he had unnerved her, and he smiled thinly.

"Our people had a pact, *Lord of Light*." She spoke his title with scorn. "I am to be your Lady of Light, to rule Nightside by your side, first among the eight kingdoms of sunlight. In return, my family—and our people of the rainforest—will convert to your faith. The banners of Sailith will rise in Naya, and the banners of Naya will rise in the night. Do you renege on our deal?" She snorted. "Do you prefer to play at dragonslaying in your hall, a boy with his toys, or will you honor our deal and marry a princess of tigers?"

Ferius turned away from her. "You still stink of the jungle."

Leaving her, he walked across the mosaic, stepped between two columns, and approached a map that hung upon the wall. The parchment stretched as wide as a boat, ridged and grooved into the shape of mountains, valleys, and rivers. It showed all of Mythimna, this world the commoners called Moth. One landform thrust into the daylight like a white wing, another into the darkness like a black wing, a world shaped like the duskmoth that flew in the twilit forests.

Ferius traced his fingers across the dusk, that strip of shadows between the wings of the world. In that land—only a few miles wide—rose Cabera Mountain and upon it the clock. For many years, the Sailith Order had kept this sacred secret—the source of its power . . . and the potential for its undoing.

"If Koyee fixes the clock, it is over," he whispered, and for the first time in many years, the chill of fear washed his belly. "If the world turns again, and if day follows night in all lands, all my work is undone."

Ishel came to stand beside him, her tiger at her side. The smell of Elorian blood clung to her. She narrowed her eyes, staring at the map. She held her spear with her right hand, and her left hand stroked her tiger.

"What clock are you talking about?" She snorted. "I care not for clocks or dusty old maps. I care for *conquest*. Will you respect our pact?"

He ignored her. He walked along the wall, caressing the map, whispering.

"The gear in a dark island." He touched an isle east of Ilar, hidden in the shadows. "A hand in the desert." He walked toward the sunlit wing and stroked the sandy lands in the south. "And the number nine in the jungle of the barbarians." He tapped the rainforests of Naya.

Ishel snorted. "Barbarians? We are the strongest kingdom of sunlight. We will rise highest among them." She grabbed Ferius's arm, her eyes blazed, and she sneered. A necklace of tiger fangs hung around her neck, and her own teeth gleamed with as much ferocity, her canines almost as long as fangs themselves. "Tell me, Ferius, do you renege on the deal you forged with my father? Speak! Or I will spear you, gut you, and hang you beside your dragon."

He smiled thinly. "You are fierce. That is good. You will do well for this task. Do you know of the Five Traitors, the Timandrians who joined the forces of the night?"

She tilted her head. "Of course. All know their names. It was my bow that slew the fat one, the baker named Hemstad." She growled. "I will kill the remaining four when I find them."

Ferius's smile stretched into a grin. "I do not renege on our deal, but I am changing it. We will be wed, Princess Ishel of Naya, and your kingdom will rule the greatest ruins of the night. But first you will travel back to your homeland . . . to a temple among the trees. You will meet the traitors there. And you will bring me their heads."

CHAPTER FIVE
THE GIRL AND HER GIANT

Koyee was loading supplies into the *Water Spider*, her trusty old rowboat, when the girl and her giant came walking along the pier toward her.

Koyee had told only two other souls about her journey: Jin, exiled Emperor of Qaelin, her fallen homeland; and Empress Hikari, ruler of Ilar, this island of their exile. If word spread of the Cabera Clock, enemies would race to stop Koyee, and they had sworn to keep the secret.

"Shenlai the Wise believed," Koyee had told them. "I must go on this quest . . . for him and for all the night."

Jin had kissed her cheek, tears in his eyes, and prayed for her safety. Empress Hikari, however, had railed that this was a fool's quest, only a legend. She had demanded that Koyee remain to fight, yet Koyee would not.

"We cannot fight the army Ferius musters," Koyee had said. "Not with a million swords. So I must sail away . . . to chase a dream, to find a hope."

And so she had come alone to this pier, and so she now loaded all her belongings onto the *Water Spider*: a new suit of armor, not a Qaelish shirt of scales but the black, lacquered plates of Ilari warriors; jars of mushrooms, packs of meat and fish, and skins of wine; fur blankets and spare tunics; and rolled-up maps of parchment. These supplies would take her to the distant Montai Isle in the east . . . where she would find hope or desolation.

When she saw the girl and giant approach, Koyee kept packing, not sparing them a second glance.

"If Empress Hikari sent you to stop me," she said, "you're wasting your time. I sail today and you'd have to shackle me to stop me."

The girl laughed. "Stop you? By the stars above, no no no, we don't want to stop you. Why would we want to do that? Stopping is so boring. A stop is an end, a stop is a wall, a stop is like falling asleep just as the party gets interesting. My dear young lady, we're here to join you! Yes yes, that's far more interesting and fun, I find, joining . . . going on journeys . . . seeking adventures and—" The girl bit down on her words. "Oh dear, I've done it again, haven't I? I've gone off talking too much, just like I always do, just like I've done as a child. My mother always told me: Nitomi, do not let your mouth run off a mile a minute, or your tongue will fall out. Well, my tongue hasn't fallen out yet, but sometimes it does hurt, and—" She slapped a palm over her mouth and spoke in a muffled voice. "Sorry. I did it again!"

Koyee placed a rolled-up rug into the boat, turned around, and stared at the girl. In truth, she was more of a woman, probably a few years older than Koyee's own eighteen years. But she stood even shorter than Koyee, as close to four feet as to five. Her face was impish, her eyes huge and blue, her nose small, her ears large. She wore tight, black silks that covered her like a second skin. Many daggers hung around her belt and across her chest.

Behind her towered the tallest man Koyee had ever seen. He must have stood over seven feet tall. Even in the cold, his chest and arms were bare, revealing muscles the size of Koyee's rolled-up rugs. His face was wide and stony, his eyes narrowed to blue crescent moons. His snowy hair cascaded down his shoulders. He held an axe that could, Koyee thought, chop down a tower with a single blow; it must have weighed as much as her.

"Qato protect," the giant said, voice a deep rumble. "Qato serve."

Nitomi, the short woman in black, loosened her fingers and spoke between them. "That's about all he says, that one. Qato this and Qato that. I tried to get him to say three words once, but he hurt himself so badly he almost passed out, so I just let him be. He's my cousin, supposedly, but I don't see any relation. I think my aunt must have found him hatching from an egg on a cliff. But he's strong, he is. I saw him hammering a nail once, only he hammered his thumb instead, and the hammer head broke right off. Didn't even feel a thing, the big brute. We both serve in the Dojai Order. You know what that is?" Nitomi let her hands drop from her mouth, and the speed of her words increased. "It's this very special school, very competitive, and all the way up in the mountains. They train real assassins there, real killers, not like the dumb soldiers who just roam around everywhere in the city, slashing their swords and obeying orders. No no no . . . we dojai are something special, much deadlier, and we move in silence, and—"

"You don't seem very silent to me," Koyee said, feeling it best to interrupt; she had a feeling the only way to have a conversation with Nitomi was to interrupt a lot.

"Oh dear, I've done it again." Nitomi slapped her head. "Stupid, stupid Nitomi! Probably why I got kicked out of the school. Oh well, my point is: Empress Hikari sent us to help you. Qato and me, that's right. We're going to sail with you to wherever you're going, and we'll watch your back. We're good warriors, we are. I'm sneaky and quick, and Qato's stronger than a dragon. You'll be safe with us, so long as Qato doesn't sink the boat." Nitomi stared at the *Water Spider* and bit her lip. "By the stars, it's a bit small, isn't it?"

Koyee stared at the two, moving her eyes from one to another, and shook her head.

"No," she said. "Just no. I travel alone."

But Nitomi leaped forward—indeed sneaky and quick—and scuttled into the boat. She sat down and grabbed an oar. "Too late! I'm already here. Qato! Into boat!"

The pale giant nodded, walked around Koyee, and climbed into the boat too. The vessel dipped several inches into the water. "Qato sail."

Nitomi patted his shoulder. "Good Qato."

He nodded. "Qato good."

Still standing on the pier, Koyee gasped. "Get out! Both of you. I can't endanger you. I'm sailing somewhere dangerous."

A grin split Nitomi's face. "That's why we're here, my dear! We love danger. Danger is exciting! Danger is our specialty. We're here to protect you! Well . . . and because Empress Hikari says we're the two worst dojai in the empire, and she wants us off the island. But also to protect you!" Nitomi patted the bench beside her. "Well, climb on board. While we're young. Don't make us wait or we'll row east without you. Ooh!" She turned toward the back of the boat. "Are those matsutaki mushrooms? Those are my favorites!" She grabbed a jar, unscrewed the lid, and began to feast. "Mmm . . . these are good. Mmm . . . can't talk now, eating."

"Hey, put those down!" Koyee stamped her feet, then turned toward Qato; the giant was busy feasting on a slab of salted meat. "You too, Qato, don't eat that. Those are mine! I—Oh dear."

Koyee sighed. She was about to leap into the boat, grab the two, and try to drag them out, but a voice rose behind her, and she froze.

"Koyee?"

She closed her eyes. She took a deep breath. It was him.

She turned around, opened her eyes, and saw him there.

"Torin," she whispered.

He stood farther back on the pier, staring at her as if hesitant to approach. He stood alone. He wore his armor, a katana hung at his side, and a heavy pack hung upon his back. He too was prepared to leave on his quest—a road that would take him a world away from her. When Koyee looked over his shoulder, she saw Bailey far in the distance. The tall, golden-haired woman was rearranging her pack and not looking Koyee's way.

"I came to say goodbye," Torin said.

Koyee looked back at him. "I know, you silly thing. I wasn't going to leave without saying goodbye to you."

She stood stiffly, not sure what else to say. Sometimes she thought she hated goodbyes less because they were heartbreaking, more because they were awkward. She never knew what to say when parting from others, let alone Torin, the man she loved . . . the man she might never see again if their quests failed.

Torin seemed just as uncomfortable. He took an awkward step toward her, seemingly unsure whether to hold her hand, embrace her, or pat her on the back.

"Oh you are a silly thing!" she said, grabbed him, and embraced him tightly. "You can speak so eloquently about fighting for peace and justice, but when you have to say goodbye, you're as tongue-tied as a toddler sucking on candy."

He laughed softly, holding her close. "Goodbye, Koyee."

She touched his cheek, and he kissed her—a small, tight kiss at first, then smoothing into a deep, desperate kiss. Koyee closed her eyes in his arms, and she remembered her first time seeing him, a boy wheeling the bones of her father, and she remembered fighting him in Pahmey, then fighting at his side. She thought of the first time they had made love—back in the hospice—and her eyes stung, and she could barely breathe, and she did not know how she would be away from him for so long.

"I love you," she whispered when their kiss ended. "Be safe. Stay near Bailey always, and she'll watch over you. She's good with the blade."

He nodded. "I'm not too bad with one myself, you know." He squeezed her against him. "I love you too, Koyee. I'll think about you until we meet again at Cabera Mountain. We will meet there. We will do this."

As he walked away, Koyee looked back at Bailey, and she saw the woman staring at her from the distance. Koyee waved but Bailey would not return the gesture; she only stared, and even from this distance, Koyee could see the hatred in her eyes.

She loves Torin too, Koyee knew. *But he is mine, and he loves me, and I'm sorry, Bailey. I'm so sorry because I know how much it hurts.*

A sniffle sounded behind her, followed by a trumpeting sound. Koyee turned to see Nitomi blowing her nose into a handkerchief, tears in her eyes.

"That was beautiful!" said the little assassin. "Just . . . so sad and . . . so beautiful . . . and . . . " Her tears rolled and she blew her nose again; the handkerchief fluttered. "True love. There's nothing better. Well, maybe only a nice plate of fried matsutake mushrooms with a side of chanterelles. Say, Koyee, you got any chantrelles on this boat? I could go for some now, if you have them, and oh—let me look. Ooh, wait, you've got salted bat wings! I love those too and . . ."

Koyee stopped listening, letting Nitomi prattle on. She climbed into the *Water Spider* and sat between the girl and her giant. As they left the docks and oared into the sea, Koyee looked back and saw Torin still on the boardwalk. He stood still, watching her leave, and raised his hand. She waved to him until he faded into the distance.

CHAPTER SIX
TORN

After endless turns in endless darkness, they flew toward the sunlight on the back of a dragon.

"Home," Torin whispered, the wind stinging his eyes. "Dayside."

Tianlong, the black dragon of Ilar, flew upon the wind, wingless but flowing forward like a snake upon water. His black scales chinked and his red beard fluttered like a banner. Torin and Bailey sat in the saddle, pressed together, as the dragon flew across the last miles of darkness toward the sun.

The stars and moon still shone above, indigo spread across the sky, and shadows cloaked the land below. But ahead Torin saw it: the dusk, the glow of his homeland. The memories pounded into him, as stinging and mighty as the wind. He could smell the fresh breads dear old Hem would bake, feel the softness of woolen cloaks, hear the song of birds, taste the cold ale in The Shadowed Firkin tavern . . . and most of all, feel safe. Feel warm. Feel at home. Until now, fighting for the night, he hadn't realized how much he missed the sunlight. Now his eyes watered.

"There it is, Bailey," he whispered as the dragon flew. "The light of our home. Don't you— Bailey? Bailey! Get down!"

Sitting before him in the saddle, Bailey was unbuckling herself and struggling to rise. Torin grabbed her waist, trying to pull her back into the seat.

"Let go of me, Winky." She wriggled herself free, placed her ankles under her backside, and stretched out her arms. Slowly she began to rise.

"Bailey, you'll fall!" Torin winced. "We're flying a mile above the world."

She grinned over her shoulder at him. "And it's wonderful." With a single, fluid movement, she rose to her feet in the saddle, stretched out her arms, and stood upon the flying dragon. Her two golden braids flew behind her like comet tails. She tossed back her head and laughed. "It's wonderful, Torin! Stand up with me. Fly with me! I— Whoa!" She wobbled, windmilled her arms for balance, and steadied herself. "Almost fell there."

Torin grimaced. Sitting in the saddle behind her, he held her ankles. "I'm holding you until you sit down! You're going to get yourself killed."

Bailey shook her head, arms stretched wide, head tossed back. She inhaled deeply, the wind flowing around her. "It would take a silver arrow to kill me. Stand with me, Torin! Stand up and feel the wind and see the sun."

He shook his head, wincing. The dragon coiled as he flew, the wind gusted, and Torin clung to Bailey's legs. "Sit down. Please."

She kicked her legs about, tearing his grip off, and slowly raised her right foot, bringing it to rest against her left knee. "Look at me, Torin! It's like flying. Stand with me or I'll hop around and then surely fall."

"Don't you dare hop, you'll—"

"Then stand with me!" She looked down over her shoulder and grinned. "Hold onto me if you're scared. I dare you, babyface. I dare you! If you don't stand, I'll trumpet the news around Moth that Torin Babyface is the most cowardly coward in both day and night. I'll— Whoa!" The wind gusted, Bailey tilted, and her arms windmilled until she steadied herself. She kept one foot raised, teetering on the other.

Torin grumbled. "If I stand, you have to put both feet down."

"Deal."

Cursing with every vile word he knew, Torin unbuckled himself. His heart thrashed madly. As he slowly began to rise, he winced and held his breath. Damn Bailey could always do this to him! Back home, she would dare him to swim across the river, then laugh as he floundered and nearly drowned. She would goad him until he climbed the maple tree in the village square, then taunt him when he fell. And now this, the worst challenge of all— standing on a damn flying dragon.

Barely daring to open his eyes, Torin rose to his feet in the saddle and wrapped his arms around Bailey's waist. They stood together, him rigid and clinging to her, her with her arms outstretched and her head tossed back. Her flying braids slapped his face, and she laughed.

"Look at the sun, Torin. Look at the day. Isn't it beautiful?"

The dragon undulated beneath them, scales rattling. The wind shrieked. Torin felt sick and his head spun. He clung to Bailey, staring at her neck, not daring to look anywhere else. "Can we sit down now?"

"Not until you look, Winky. You're not looking. Don't make me hop." She leaned sideways, revealing a view of the landscape and the dusk ahead.

Torin stared through wincing eyes . . . and lost his breath. Through his head still spun, the beauty pierced him. Sitting in the saddle, Bailey and the dragon's horned head before him, had been one thing. Standing in open sky, Torin felt like he himself were flying. The horizon spread before him, curving and lit with orange and gold. Sunbeams pierced the clouds. Distant forests rustled, and sheets of rain fell in the north upon green hills. They stood in silence, watching.

Tianlong the dragon turned his head and looked back at them. He grinned, revealing fangs. His red beard billowed. "We land here, friends!" The dragon's voice was deep and rumbling like boulders falling underground. "I am a creature of darkness, and I cannot take you into the light. Hold on tight!"

With a deep laugh, Tianlong began to dive.

Torin winced and even Bailey squeaked. Wobbling, they sat back down in the saddle as the dragon descended. They were flying somewhere over the vast, lifeless plains of the Qaelish empire, and beyond the dusk lay the rainforest of Naya. No city, town, or village could be found for miles, according to Torin's maps. Their journey would take them deep into the jungle—to the ancient temple of Til Natay, to the number nine, and to hope.

The wind whipped their hair as Tianlong spiraled down. The dragon landed upon a hill, the dusk to their west, the darkness of Eloria spreading to their east. When Torin dismounted, knees wobbly, he found actual moss upon the hill— the first greenery he'd seen in over a year.

Bailey dismounted too, wrapped an arm around his neck, and rubbed her knuckles against his head. "Torin old boy, you survived the flight. Now we travel on foot, and I bet I'm a hundred times faster. And I'm not waiting for you to catch up, snail."

He grumbled and shoved her off. "I'm glad to see you're in a good mood. The night is burning, Ferius is mustering new forces, and only our quest can save the world. And you're having a laugh."

She shrugged and her grin widened. She stretched out her arms as if she still stood upon a flying dragon. "When the world is burning, that is the best time to laugh."

Torin wondered. During their stay in Asharo, capital of the Ilari empire, Bailey had seemed sullen. Whenever he had invited her to join him and Koyee for a walk or meal, Bailey would only grunt and claim to be busy practicing with her sword. She had spent all her time locked in her chambers or swinging her blade in a training yard, her eyes flashing and her lips always frowning. As soon as they had left the city, her mood had improved. She was the old Bailey again, the one he had grown up with.

The open air and sunlight are good for her, Torin thought, looking at his friend. She was now busy pulling their supplies off the dragon's back. Asharo had been a city of bricks, steel, and flame, enough to crush any spirit.

And yet the thought still niggled at the back of his mind. Had it truly been the city that had darkened Bailey's mood? What if it had been Koyee? Looking back, it seemed that whenever Koyee was with them—especially when the young Elorian took center stage, speaking of her plans—Bailey's mood had run foulest.

"By Idar's blistered feet!" Bailey said, glaring at him. "Winky, are you going to help, or are you going to keep standing there like a lump of dirt?"

Torin shook his head clear of thoughts. He stepped forward, reached across the dragon's back, and helped untie the straps holding down their belongings. He slung his pack over his back. It bulged full of supplies for the journey: jars of mushrooms, smoked sausages, skins of wine, a tinderbox, knives and sharpening stones, and a bundle of maps. Next he buckled his new sword to his hip, a katana the Elorians had gifted him, its hilt wrapped in black silk. Finally he grabbed his walking stick and stood ready for the journey. Bailey stood at his side, carrying a similar pack and her own weapons: her old longsword, her bow, and a quiver of arrows.

"My pack is larger than yours, Winky," she said. "You didn't pack enough supplies."

He rolled his eyes. "Merciful Idar. Everything is a competition with you, isn't it?"

Hovering three feet aboveground, the dragon turned his head toward them. His red eyes gleamed. His scaly body undulated behind him like a standard in the wind, and his beard flowed down to the ground.

"Here we part, children of sunlight," said Tianlong. "I am a warrior of darkness; in sunlight, you must fight alone. I do not know your quest, but I will think of you in the shadows of the night. I pray we meet again."

Torin placed his hand on the dragon's scaly brow. He bowed his head. "Goodbye, Tianlong, noble friend. Goodbye, last dragon of Ilar, and may your wisdom forever guide the night. May—"

"Move it, poet!" Bailey said, shoving Torin aside. She wrapped her arms around the dragon's head, squeezing him in an embrace, and kissed his snout. "Goodbye, Tianlong old boy. Don't worry about the babyface. I'll watch over him." She pulled back and patted the dragon's cheek. "Now go on, fly! Get out of here before he gets poetic again."

With a grunt and a chuckle, Tianlong soared into the sky, spun toward the east, and flew into the darkness. Torin watched him leave for a moment, feeling strangely sad. For two long years, he had dreamed of returning home to sunlight. Now he felt that Nightside was a place of wonder and magic—of shining crystal towers, fish that glowed with inner lights, wise mystics with gleaming eyes, and dragons like those from the pages of storybooks. He left that wonder here in the shadows. He left Koyee and all her noble people of the shadow. And there Tianlong flew away, a last whisper of magic gone into—

"Winky!" Baily grabbed his arm and tugged. "By the light, what's gotten into you? Come *on*! We have no time to gape at the stars; you've been doing that for ages. We've got a piece of clock to find."

Torin sighed as he stumbled downhill after her. He had fought in battles and slain men. He had made love to Koyee in a hospice of the plague. He had dueled Ferius, the Demon of

Daylight, and flown upon a dragon. Yet in the sight of the sun, to Bailey he was just a humble boy again.

"Fine!" He wrenched his arm free. "Slow down, all right?"

"Never. Keep up or be left behind." She tramped downhill toward the dusk.

He followed, pack bouncing across his back and his sword banging against his thigh. They headed across a valley. Moss gave way to grass and grass to shrubs. The sun appeared over the horizon, and they stepped into its light.

* * * * *

They trudged through the brush, lashing their swords at vegetation, slapping at mosquitoes, and sweating in the heat of sunlight.

"I thought I missed Dayside." Torin spat out an insect that flew into his mouth. "Idar damn it! I forgot about the bugs and the heat." He sighed. "I miss the night already."

Bailey swiped her sword, cutting through hanging vines, and climbed over a fallen log. "Not me. Too cold back there. Too cold and lifeless." Sweat dampened her shirt, burrs covered her cloak, and mud rose to her knees. "Give me light, heat, and life all around me."

A second insect flew into Torin's eye. He cursed, blinked it free, and slapped another critter that landed on his cheek. "Life all *over* us, more like. I swear, I— Bailey!" She was rushing ahead, disappearing into the brush. He called after her. "Bailey, I told you, slow down. If we separate here, we'd never find each other."

Somewhere ahead, she snorted. "Well then keep up! According to Koyee's book, the number nine is all the way in Til Natay, a temple miles and miles from here. We have to hurry."

He jumped over bulging tree roots, raced around a boulder, and reached her. He leaped back as her sword swung; she nearly sliced through him as well as the vines. They kept moving through the rainforest.

Torin had grown up in the northern, temperate valleys and hills of Arden, then spent over a year in the night. Naya seemed to him just as strange as the endless darkness. The canopy hid the sky, rustling and raining leaves. Vines and bushes grew everywhere, tangling around him. Water dripped and flowed and mist hung in the air. The insects were not the only animals; frogs trilled in streams, birds of every color flew overhead, and furry critters Torin had only read about in bestiaries—monkeys, he thought they were called—hooted and swung from branches above.

"Are you sure you know where you're going?" Torin could barely see a dozen feet ahead; the greenery obscured everything.

Bailey nodded. "Of course. Koyee's book said that Til Natay rises at the end of the Great Nayan Escarpment. We're walking atop that escarpment right now." She smiled and took a deep, dreamy breath. "When I was a girl, Grandpapa would say that the escarpment was the spine of an ancient giant who had collapsed atop Naya. His blood seeped out, feeding the rainforest which grew upon him." She pointed northward where the land sloped down. "See how we're walking atop a cliff, moving westward? Down there the forest is much lower. It rolls all the way to the Sern River and to our own homeland of Arden." She turned back west. "We just keep walking atop the hilly spine, and we'll get there."

Torin groaned. "I don't see an escarpment. I don't see west, north, or south. I just see, well . . . trees everywhere."

She glowered at him. "That's because you're an empty-headed, winky-eyed boy. If I shove you down the escarpment, I bet you'll see it."

Torin groaned and made his way over a slippery boulder. "That's assuming Tianlong dropped us off at the right place. We could be walking atop an unrelated mountain."

"An *escarpment*, you woolhead, not a mountain. And the dragon did. Dragons always know these things." She swung her sword, forcing him to leap back. "I know a lot more about dragons than you do, Winky, so be quiet."

She was about to swing her sword again when Torin caught her wrist. He stared at her, holding her fast, planting both feet firmly on the ground. "You don't know everything, Bailey."

Slowly, she turned her face toward him. Her eyes narrowed and a dangerous light filled them. "Let go of me."

He tightened his fingers around her wrist. "You've spent the past few hours tugging me, twisting my arm, and nearly lobbing off my head every time you cut a vine. I've had enough. You don't know everything about dragons, and you don't know everything about escarpments, and you don't—"

She shoved him. She shoved him so hard he slipped in the mud, let go of her wrist, and reached down to catch his fall. Before he could even hit the ground, Bailey pounced onto him, growling like a rabid animal. She shoved a knee into his belly and he grunted. He tried to knock her off, but she pinned his arms to the ground, knelt above him, and sneered.

"Don't ever talk to me like that again." She glared down at him, her face a mask of rage. "Don't ever grab my wrist like that. You're . . . you're just a ba—"

"A babyface, yes." Torin stared up at her. He could barely breathe with her knee in his belly, but he wouldn't tear his gaze away. "I've heard it a million times. Only I'm not. I've got scruff on my cheeks now. And I've fought in battles and I've killed men. And you will stop treating me like a child. Do you understand?"

He expected her to scream, to slap him, to storm off into the wilderness without him. Instead she lowered her head, and her cheek pressed against his, and her eyes closed.

"I don't want you to be that person," she whispered. She removed her knee from his belly, and suddenly instead of pinning him down, she was lying atop him, holding him in an embrace. "I don't want you to be anything but a boy."

He sighed and wrapped his arms around her. She nuzzled his cheek.

"Why?" he asked.

She shrugged and buried her face against his neck. He felt her warm tears. "Because I don't want things to change. I don't want you to be some warrior, some . . . some soldier who loves Koyee, who fights in wars, who doesn't need me anymore." She raised her head, her eyes red, and cupped his cheek in her palm. "Because I miss the old times. Do you remember them? I miss Fairwool-by-Night. I miss you being a scared little orphan, younger and shorter and slower than me. You were a precious child and you needed me. And I protected you. You were mine. Not Koyee's. Not the night's. Not even your own man. You were my little babyface and nobody else's, and I miss that. That was home to me."

Torin spoke in a soft voice. "I've grown."

"I don't want you to grow up. I don't want anyone to."

He held her in his arms. "I miss home too. I miss those times. And more than anything, I want us to return home. I want us to live together again in your grandpapa's cottage. I want us to climb Old Maple, run through the fields, and fish in the Sern River. But to do that, we have to fight this war. And we have to change. We have to grow."

She nodded, eyes damp, still lying atop him. "I know. I'm sorry, Torin. I'm sorry that I . . . that I goad you on like this, that I mock you sometimes, that I tug you and twist your arm. You're the best person I know and I love you." Tears filled her eyes, and her voice became only a choked whisper. "I love you so much."

He held her, and she kissed his cheek, and they lay together in the grass and leaves.

"I love you too," he whispered, and he meant it, though he didn't know how he loved her. As a friend? As a foster brother? As a man loves a woman?

As they lay together, he thought of Koyee: her large lavender eyes, her smile, her hand in his, and the battles they had fought together. Like this world of Moth, he was torn . . . torn between a woman of daylight and a daughter of the night.

Bailey caressed his cheek and kissed his lips, then sprang off him and rose to her feet. She adjusted the pack, bow, and quiver that hung across her back, then reached down her hand.

"See? I'm not tugging now." She wiped her eyes. "Hold my hand and I'll help you stand, and we'll keep walking together."

He took her hand. They kept walking through the rainforest, and she did not release her grip.

CHAPTER SEVEN
SUNLIGHT

"Aaand . . . the flowers and the bees and the singers and the trees, and they all went hopping awayyy . . . Aaand—"

"Linee!" Cam scowled at her. "Please! For Idar's sake, *please* stop singing."

She opened her mouth wide, prepared to sing another verse, then closed it. She tilted her head and stared at him quizzically. "You don't like my singing?"

Walking along the beach under the moon, Cam glowered. "I told you a million times, Linee. I hate your singing. The fish hate your singing. The crabs hate your singing. The damn stars above hate your singing by now. Please can you be quiet?"

She thought for a moment, tapping her cheek. "Let me think. Uhh . . . no." She cleared her throat, tossed back her head, and sang with new vigor. "And the puppies and the cats and the birds and the bats, and they all went hopping awayyy . . . And—"

"Linee!" Cam stopped walking, turned toward her, and grabbed her arms. "Please. I'm begging you. We've been traveling for almost a month, and you're still singing the same song. I can't take it. Can you at least sing another song?"

"But I don't know any other songs!" Tears welled up in her eyes. "And I'm so bored here. It's so quiet and lonely on this beach, and it's so dark, and singing makes me happy, and . . . " She sniffled, covered her eyes, and sat down in the sand. She wept into her palms, mumbling between sobs. "I miss home, and you're so mean to me, and it's not fair, and if I were still a queen—"

Cam groaned and began stomping away. "Fine! Stay here. I'm walking back to sunlight, and if you want to be alone in the dark, singing your song, that's fine with me."

She wailed behind him. Her feet padded in the sand, and she leaped onto his back, nearly knocking him down. "All right, all right! I'm here and I'll be quiet."

He struggled to pry her off. "Get down."

She clung to him. "I want a piggyback ride."

He cried out in frustration, tugged her arms off, and sent her falling into the sand. "No piggyback rides! Just walk quietly like an adult. Merciful Idar, you're three years older than me, but you act like a baby."

She stuck her tongue out at him. "Well, if I'm a baby, you're a grumpy old man, Grumpy." She danced and pirouetted at his side. "If I can't sing, I'm going to dance as I walk."

"Fine! So long as you dance silently."

Last month, they had left Ilar upon an oared ship bearing the Red Flame banners. That ship had taken them north to the coast of Qaelin, the dark empire Ferius had crushed, and then west until they saw the glow of dusk. Beyond that orange horizon lay Timandra, the land of sunlight. The Ilari sailors, though brave and strong, had dared sail no farther.

"Our journey takes us to Eseer," Cam had told them. "A desert kingdom in the sunlight."

The sailors, however, had refused to sail into the light, and Cam could not blame them; if the Timandrians saw an Elorian vessel in their waters, they would likely sink it. And so, a few hours ago, Cam and Linee had climbed onto the shore, the dusk gleaming on the horizon. They had been walking toward the light since.

"It's so beautiful," Linee said, pointing at the dusk. "Oh Camlin, I missed the sunlight."

With every step, they came closer to the light, and Cam found himself agreeing. He had spent over a year in the darkness. The sight of sunlight brought back memories so powerful he nearly stopped breathing. He could hear songs in the tavern, taste beer, smell flowers, and remember his carefree days with his friends and family.

"I wish you were here to see this too, Hem," he said softly.

Patches of pink, blue, and bronze rose ahead like a watercolor painting. Beads of light glimmered upon the waves to his left, and gold seemed to coat the sand beneath his feet. To his right, hills rolled into the horizon, and for the first time in many turns, Cam saw grass—real green rustling grass that filled his nostrils with its scent. After walking for another mile or two, he saw the sun itself rise from the horizon, a burnished disk casting rays between thin clouds.

"Home," Linee whispered and held his hand. "I missed it so much, but . . . " She stopped walking. "But I'm scared now."

Cam raised his eyebrows. "Scared? What are you talking about? You've spent the past year blabbering on about butterflies, flowers, hummingbirds, and strawberries, complaining how cold and bleak and dark the night is. And now you're scared of the sunlight?"

She nodded. Her voice was soft. "I am. Because I'm not the same person anymore. A queen lived in sunlight long ago, enjoying those flowers and butterflies. But I don't know who I am now. I'm not a queen anymore, not since Ferius killed my husband and took over my kingdom. I'm just . . . maybe I'm just a girl of the night now. Maybe there is no more home for me here. I know, Camlin, I know I've spent all this time talking about Dayside, but . . . strangely, I don't want to go there anymore."

Cam sighed and turned toward her in the sand. "None of us are the same. I left the daylight a boy, just a shepherd following

Bailey on one of her adventures. I come back now as . . . I don't know who. But we have to go on. You know that, right?"

She nodded, head lowered, then took his hands and looked into his eyes. "Can we rest for a bit first? Maybe sleep for a while, then go into the sunlight next turn?"

He nodded. "We've been awake for a long time. We can do that."

They lay a blanket upon the sand, sat down, and ate a meal of cold mushrooms, sausages, and salted fish. The waves whispered before them, blue and gold, casting foam onto the sand. Countless seashells gleamed. When Cam lay on his back to sleep, Linee cuddled at his side and tossed an arm and leg over him. He wanted to shift away—how could he sleep with her holding him?—but when he looked at her, he sighed.

Her eyes were closed, her cheek soft and pale in the light. Her hair cascaded, golden like the sand. Her breathing deepened. When awake, Linee was the most annoying creature Cam had ever met—singing discordantly, tugging his arm when bored, and, worst of all, crying far too often. When she slept, however, she seemed a different sort of woman—a vulnerable, hurt woman, a widow grieving, a lost soul. And so he placed a hand on her thigh, letting her nestle closer to him. He closed his eyes. They slept in each other's arms.

* * * * *

When they woke and stepped into the sunlight, they beheld a desert of golden dunes, rustling palm trees, and a river thick with white sails.

"Timandra," Linee whispered, gazing in wonder. "The land of daylight."

Cam nodded. "Specifically, the kingdom of Eseer, a southern realm in Timandra—and probably the most inhospitable one. It's mostly sand and rock." He smiled wryly. "You won't see many butterflies and strawberries here."

"Oh yes I will." She pointed. "See that green stain in the northwest? That's an oasis. They have butterflies and strawberries in oases. I read it in a book."

Cam hitched up his belt. "It's also quite a long walk." He took out his map, unrolled the parchment, and showed it to Linee. "That green patch must be Kahtef, an oasis city in south Eseer on the Kae river. According to Koyee's book, somewhere around here, we need to find the 'Ziggurat of Ferisi.' The missing clock hand will be there."

"A ziga-what-now?" Linee blinked.

"A ziggurat."

She frowned. "What's that then? Some kind of rodent?"

"Not a rodent! Why would the clock hand be in a rodent? You know . . . a ziggurat!" Cam gestured with his hand. "That sort of . . . zigs."

"You don't know either, do you?"

He sighed. "No, but the people of Eseer will know, and we'll ask them. Now come, enough stalling. Let's keep walking."

They hefted the packs across their shoulders and walked on through the sand.

The night had been cold, the dusk cool. Here in full sunlight, heat bathed them and sweat soaked them. It had been hard to keep track of seasons in the night, but as far as Cam knew, it was winter. And yet here on the southern coast, the sun beat down, as hot as any summer back in Arden. As they walked and his sweat trickled, Cam almost missed the night already, and he removed his heavy clock and stuffed it into his pack.

After an hour or two of walking along the coast, they reached a delta. The Kae River—the artery of the Eseerian desert—split here into a dozen rivulets that flowed into the sea. Rushes, palm trees, and mangroves grew between the streams, lush and green and fluttering with birds. Dozens of vessels sailed here: humble reed dinghies, long boats with many oars, and great ships with wide canvas sails. Scorpions were painted onto hulls and banners—the sigil of Eseer.

When they reached the first rivulet, they found a pebbly path that ran along the water. They left the sea behind, walking north through the delta. Storks, seagulls, and cranes flew above, and grasshoppers hopped among the rushes. As ships sailed by, Cam watched their sailors. The Eseerians were a tall, slender people, their skin bronzed by the sun. Some of them—perhaps wealthy merchants—wore rich white robes with golden hems, and canopies rose upon their ships' decks. Others seemed to be humble fishermen, rowing reed boats, clad in nothing but loincloths, their faces browned and wrinkled.

When one fisherman saw them and came rowing their way, Linee squealed with fright and ducked among the rushes. Cam pulled her back up.

"He seems friendly." He waved to the man. "I think he wants to give us a lift."

Moments later, they sat in the fisherman's reed boat between baskets of tilapia. The man wore a white cloak and hood, protecting him from the blazing sun, and a scorpion bracelet circled his wrist. He chattered as he rowed them north toward the city, but Cam could not understand the language.

"Daenor?" the man asked. "Sania? Naya?"

Cam pointed at himself and Linee. "We're from the kingdom of Arden."

The fisherman raised his eyebrows. "Arden?" He began to talk again in his tongue, sounding amazed; the kingdom of Arden lay many miles in the north. As far as Cam knew, he was the first Ardishman to have ever visited this desert.

As they sailed upriver, the rivulets began to gather into a single stream—the mighty Kae. Fish leaped in the water, a family of crocodiles stared from the rushes, and when Linee gasped and pointed, Cam saw two hippopotamuses battling in the distance. Storks and cranes cawed and flew overhead, dipping to catch fish.

Many vessels sailed around them. Some were humble fishing boats carrying baskets of flapping tilapia and perch. Others were galleys of many oars, bearing treasures from distant lands: parti-colored parrots in cages, exotic plants in pots, and jugs of wine. Cam cringed to see one ship ferrying men and women clad in rags, metal collars around their necks—slaves.

Soon the city of Kahtef appeared upon the horizon, and Cam watched it approach. Sandstone walls grew from an oasis of palm, fig, and sycamore trees. Scorpion banners beat atop turrets, and upon the city battlements stood guards in breastplates, round helms hiding their heads, spears and bows in their hands. Behind the walls, Cam could make out the tips of tall, narrow buildings capped with platinum. A gatehouse rose around the river ahead; the water flowed between two towers and under a stone arch, entering the city like a road through gates. It seemed to Cam a city as exotic as anything he'd seen in the night.

The fisherman pointed at himself. "Izmat. Izmat." He pointed at Cam and Linee and raised his eyebrows.

Cam tore his eyes away from the city. He pointed at himself. "I am Cam." He pointed at Linee next. "This is Linee, my companion."

Izmat grinned, showing crooked teeth. "Ah! Cam and Linee! From Arden!"

Cam cleared his throat. "Yes. You speak a little Ardish?"

The fisherman's grin widened. "Little."

With that, still a mile away from the city, Izmat began to direct his boat toward the riverbank. Rushes bent and slapped against the reed hull.

"What are you doing?" Cam crossed his arms. "I thought you're taking us to the city." He pointed to the distant walls and towers. "Kahtef! To Kahtef."

The fisherman smiled, bobbed his head, and held up a finger as if to say: *Just one moment.*

The boat drove closer to the marshy bank. Rushes now rose several feet high, hiding the world. Cam could no longer see other boats or the distant city.

"Maybe he has to go to the bathroom," Linee said.

Cam felt a chill, and his hand strayed toward the hilt of his sword. "Maybe he wants to rob us."

When the boat drove into the sandy riverbank, Izmat sprang out and landed between the rushes, leaving Cam and Linee on the boat.

"Cam and Linee from the kingdom of Arden." Suddenly his accent was less pronounced. His smile vanished, he reached between his robes, and he pulled out something that looked like a long flute or hollow reed. "My master, Ferius the Lord of Light, told me you would be arriving up the delta."

An amulet came free from Izmat's robes. It was shaped as a round sunburst, sigil of Sailith. As he raised the pipe to his lips, Cam understood what it was: not a flute but a blowgun. Cam leaped sideways. Izmat blew into the tube. A dart shot out.

Cam glimpsed steel and red feathers. As he jumped off the boat, the dart slashed through his cloak. Linee screamed and ducked. Cam landed in the shallow water, cursed, and drew his sword. As he ran toward his enemy, the fisherman loaded a new dart and brought the blowgun to his lips again.

"Cam, duck!" Linee screamed behind him.

He obeyed and kept running, hunched over.

Another shard of metal flashed.

Cam winced, for an instant sure that Izmat had blown his dart. *I will die here in the rushes, far from home, and our quest will fail.*

He grimaced, expecting to feel poison seep through his neck. Instead, the fisherman gasped and froze. Cam gasped too. It was not a blowgun dart that had flashed. An Elorian throwing star pierced Izmat's neck. The fisherman gave a last gasp, blood spurted, and his blowgun fell into the mud. An instant later, Izmat followed.

Cam froze and spun around, sword raised.

Linee stood in the boat, holding a second throwing star. She stared at the fallen man, then back at Cam.

"Suntai gave me a few throwing stars once, and . . . I've been practicing in secret. I didn't think . . . that I'd ever . . . Oh Idar. Camlin, are you all right?"

His mouth hung open. He blinked a few times, then ran back to the boat, jumped inside, and hugged her. "Soggy sheep bottoms, you're full of surprises, aren't you?"

"I killed someone." Her voice was barely a whisper.

He nodded. "And probably saved our lives. This land is more dangerous than we thought, and Ferius knows we're here. I'll fetch the man's cloak. At least one of us can hide under the hood."

He returned to the body. Grimacing, he removed the man's cloak, rinsed it in the water, then brought the garment back to the boat. As the white cotton dried, Cam rummaged in his pack for his small mirror and razor, then spent a few moments shaving his head.

"You look silly," Linee said, hugging herself. "I don't like it."

"Get used to it, because I'm going to grow a beard too. Ferius knows what we look like." He nipped his scalp and winced. "Damn!"

"Well, he'd know you anywhere, Camlin," Linee said. "You're too short. Maybe you should grow to normal height to blend in."

He grumbled. "Maybe you should grow a brain."

When his work was done, he stripped off his old clothes from Arden—a woolen cloak and a tunic. He removed the half-sun amulet from around his neck—the symbol of Idarism, the faith of North Timandra—and hid it in his pocket. He remained in only his breeches. Shirtless and hairless, he looked at Linee.

"Do I look Eseerian?"

She gaped. "Oh, Camlin! You're skinnier than I am." She placed a hand on his chest. "You need more muscles. I can feel your ribs. Forget searching for a clock hand; try searching for a solid meal."

He muttered and turned away. "Be quiet. Now grab that hood and cloak. They're dry now. Hide yourself. I haven't seen anyone else here with blond hair and green eyes."

Cam grabbed the oar and pushed the boat away from the bank, leaving the dead man among the rushes. They sailed on—a bald young man, clad only in breeches, and a young woman hidden in cloak and hood. They rowed on toward the city, looking—Cam hoped—like nothing more than two Eseerians returning home.

Kahtef grew closer ahead, its walls looming, its archers gazing down from the battlements. A hundred boats sailed back and forth around them, and the sun beat down, glimmering in the water and nearly blinding Cam. They rowed toward the stone archway that crested the river, welcoming them into the city.

"We've been in Eseer for only a few hours," Cam said as he rowed, "and already one of Ferius's minions tried to kill us. We'll have to be more careful."

Sitting at the prow, Linee gazed at him from inside her hood. "Let's find that zigzagging rodent as fast as possible and get back to the others."

"A ziggurat, Linee. Not a rodent."

With one more thrust of his oar, their reed boat sailed between the guard towers . . . and into a city of light, stone, and steel.

CHAPTER EIGHT
THE HENGE

Through mist and shadow, Koyee watched the island grow near.

"And one time, I ate *twenty-nine-and-a-half* entire bat wings!" Nitomi was prattling behind her. "And then I was sick, and then I ate another *fifteen* wings, only they said that doesn't count because I threw up the first ones, but I still think I won the contest, and— Oh! Land!"

The little dojai assassin, barely larger than a child, scuttled forward on the boat. She stood by Koyee at the prow and gasped.

"The island of Montai," Koyee said softly, holding her lantern. "The land of silver and silk, of dreams and darkness . . . of an ancient gear and a hope for the night."

From here in the dark waters, the island seemed like a humble, black bulge rising from mist, barren and smooth and rolling across the horizon. Koyee saw no lights, no other boats, no walls or towers. It seemed a lifeless land.

"A land of monsters," Nitomi whispered and clutched one of her many daggers. For once, she did not prattle on but stared, silent, her lips tightened.

Koyee frowned and looked down at the shorter woman. "What do you mean?"

Nitomi gulped so loudly her head, neck, and shoulders bobbed. "You haven't heard the tales of the monsters of Montai? Did you grow up under a rock where nobody tells any tales because the rock is squishing them? All children in Ilar know of this place—the cursed island of, well, curses. None of our ships ever sail to Montai. I think we're the first ones to ever come here in thousands of years. Sometimes *their* ships arrive in Ilar, though, carrying silver and silk and stories . . . terrible stories, Koyee. Stories of a demon that deforms their children, and of giant worms the size of whales who wrap you in cocoons and eat you, and . . . and . . . " She covered her eyes. "I was trained in the Dojai School in the mountains, and they taught us to never be afraid, but . . . they didn't know I'd go *here*, and now I'm scared, Koyee. Monsters are real and I'm so scared."

Koyee placed a hand on the young assassin's shoulder. "I've been all over the lands of night, Nitomi. I climbed the crystal towers of Pahmey and shivered in its alleys. I rode upon a dragon in Yintao. I fought hosts of sunlight and creatures from across Timandra. I faced the curse of mages whose scars still cover my arm. But I've never seen a monster that cannot be defeated." She smiled. "You are quick and silent and carry many daggers. I carry a sword, and dear Qato here is larger than a nightwolf. Whatever evil awaits here, we will defeat it."

At the sound of his name, the towering Qato lumbered across the boat. He stood by them, his shoulders soaring over their heads, and stared at the distant island too. The wind whipped his white hair, but he remained shirtless as if immune to the cold.

"Qato brave." He pursed his lips and nodded. "Qato strong."

Nitomi tilted her head back and looked up at him. "Qato *row!* Get back to the oars, you big pillock. The boat's tilting."

The giant assassin grunted but obeyed. The *Water Spider* moved through the mist, and the island grew ahead, looming above them and hiding the eastern stars. The wind grew colder, and Koyee wrapped her cloak around her and shivered. Beneath the silk, she wore her new Ilari armor. The dark steel plates were heavier than her old Qaelish scales but fit snugly, allowing her to move just as freely. Her companions wore no armor, for they had trained in Ilar's Dojai School for speed, silence, and slinking through shadows. Their silks were black, and even their blades were painted a dull charcoal.

When Koyee looked back eastward, she glimpsed a light soon gone. She narrowed her eyes and pointed. "There! I saw something."

As they oared closer, she scanned the island but still saw only darkness. Boulders rose from the mist like sentinels of stone, the water crashing against them. Koyee stepped back to the stern, grabbed the rudder, and they navigated between the jutting obstacles. The waves rose and fell and the sea grumbled, and though she kept scanning the shores ahead, the light did not return.

"I didn't see anything," Nitomi said. "What did you see, Koyee? Did you see a monster? Oh by the stars . . . was it big? Did it have lots of teeth, or—"

"I saw a light." Koyee leaned forward, squinting. "I must have seen a light. Maybe . . . maybe it was just a leaping lanternfish. It certainly wasn't a monster, though. It—"

A moan rolled across the land.

Koyee froze and a chill ran through her bones. The moan rose louder than thunder, a keen like a drowning god, like a dying nation, the sound her heart had made when Shenlai had fallen upon the plains of Qaelin. It went on for long moments, rippling the water and filling the air, a sound that seemed to come from everywhere and nowhere. When it finally died, the sea seemed silent, and even the waves against the boulders hushed.

"The monsters," Nitomi whispered and hugged herself.

Koyee shook her head. She remembered a time almost two years ago—by the stars, it felt like another lifetime!—when she had chased a thief into the graveyard in Pahmey. Ghosts had moaned and flowed around her, and it wasn't until Koyee had faced them that she found wind chimes and hanging strands of silk.

"In strange shadows, the only monster is fear." Koyee nodded. "We heard trumpets, that's all. Trumpets to scare us away. Look! The light shines again. We sail toward it."

As they sailed closer, the glow rose in the mist like a veiled moon. They navigated around another boulder—Koyee had to lean off the hull and push them away from it—and made a beeline to the light. A mile from the coast, Koyee could make out lanterns, huts, and a small port.

"A town." Hope rose within her. "This is no wasteland. This is no wilderness of monsters. People live here."

Nitomi chewed her lip. "If you can call the Montai 'people.' I've seen drawings of them, and they're horrible, all tall and silent. Well, everyone is tall compared to me, and I'm not sure why I think they're silent, because drawings are always silent, but . . . they just sort of stared at me from the paintings, and I could *hear* their silence through the parchment, if that's possible. Do you think it's possible to hear silence, Koyee?" She tapped her cheek. "I don't know, because normally it's never silent around me, not even when I'm sleeping, since people say I talk in my sleep, and—" She slapped her hands across her mouth and mumbled between her fingers. "I've gone and done it again, talking too much. Hush, Nitomi, hush!"

When they sailed into the port, Koyee sucked in her breath. At her side, Nitomi hissed and drew a dagger, and even Qato—almost always silent himself—grunted.

"Sheathe your blade, Nitomi," Koyee said and raised her hand high, a gesture of peace. She called out across the water. "We come peacefully, friends!"

A dozen figures stood on the docks, robed in pale silk, aiming bows at the approaching *Water Spider*. They were lanky and barefoot, and their robes hung across their chests, revealing their left shoulders. Their skin was black as the night, their hair long and silvery like moonbeams, and their eyes were gleaming blue pools, brighter than lanterns. Each man and woman carried a thin, curved blade upon the hip.

When Koyee saw the two youngest figures, she gasped and narrowed her eyes. One was a child of six or seven, the other a babe held to her mother's chest. Both sprouted six arms from their torsos, and their heads were blank, black bulbs with no features save for huge blue eyes—no hair, no mouths or noses or ears, only those dead, insect-like orbs.

"This place is cursed." Nitomi shivered. "Koyee, the children are . . . are deformed, and the adults have bows and arrows, and I'm not wearing armor. I'm a dojai, we don't wear armor, we need to be sneaky, and . . . and if they shoot us, we'll—"

"Hush, Nitomi," Koyee said. "We keep going." She held up both hands now. "Friends! I am Koyee of Qaelin. I've come seeking a—"

An arrow sailed through the air and slammed into the hull of the *Water Spider*.

Nitomi squeaked. Koyee froze and clutched her sword.

"Sail away, foreigners!" called one man from the port; his accent was so heavy Koyee could barely understand. "No strangers may visit our isle. Return to your lands!"

Nitomi squeaked and scuttled toward the stern. "They're hostile."

Koyee stared ahead, eyes narrowed, and shook her head. "No. They're afraid. Qato, row on." She raised her voice. "Do not fear, friends! Whatever plagues you, we can help you."

The *Water Spider* moved closer to the port, and the Montai folk upon the boardwalk tugged back their bowstrings. Their eyes narrowed, glowing crescents in their dark faces, and Koyee winced, for a moment sure they would fire again. Yet she would not turn back.

I fought Ferius in the dregs of Pahmey. I faced a horde of sunlight upon the walls of Yintao. I know cruelty. I know evil. She looked at the archers' tightened lips, their taut muscles, their quick breaths. She saw several children who hid behind barrels, peering with large eyes; most appeared healthy, but one had the same six arms and bald, dark head, its only features large blue eyes. She saw a village with no color, almost no light, no more joy than could be found in that old graveyard of ghosts. *I see no cruelty . . . only fear.*

"We are friends!" she called out again. "We bring help to Montai." She did not know what plagued this island—whether it was poverty, disease, or the monsters Nitomi feared—but whatever it was, it would be foremost on these people's minds. Her words would conjure that blight . . . and hopefully a welcoming.

She held her breath as they sailed, then shakily released it when the Montai lowered their bows. One among them, an old man with a wrinkled face, raised his hand in welcome.

"You may dock your boat, Koyee of Qaelin, though it has been many years since your people have set foot upon our shores." His voice was deep like underwater currents, his accent flowing like waves on stones. "I am Siyun, sage of this town. Tales have reaches us of your courage, daughter of Eloria, the fabled Girl in the Black Dress who fought the sunlit demons. Our island is distant but our ships sail far, and our people crave tales. Moor and we will speak of the evil in your land . . . and the evil in ours."

They docked and stepped out onto the boardwalk. Koyee's legs wobbled after so long at sea, and her companions swayed at her sides, seeming just as unstable, their sea legs like boneless fish. Elderly Siyun turned to head into the town, gesturing for them to follow. The world still swaying around her, Koyee walked after him, her two dojais flanking her. The other townsfolk remained behind.

Koyee beheld a town of black and silver. Black were the bricks of the houses and shops, black were the cobblestones, and black were the banners that rose, showing no sigil or rune, upon the roofs. Silverwork gleamed around her: doorknobs and hinges, belt buckles and sword hilts, and goblets and figurines in shop windows. Through other windows, Koyee saw silversmiths hammering, twisting, and coiling their masterworks, forming cutlery, hourglasses, jewelry, and buttons. Even the silken robes the Montai wore were colored silver, as if they too were made of the metal; they gleamed against their charcoal skin like moonlight upon water.

As they passed by a school, Koyee looked inside to see twenty children sitting upon rugs, reading from scrolls. One child sat in the back, her six arms hanging loosely at her sides. Her blank head rose to stare at Koyee, and her sapphire eyes gleamed. Slowly, the child raised her six hands toward the window, spiderlike, and Koyee gasped. Mouths full of sharp teeth opened and closed upon the six palms.

They walked on. In the village square, between braziers, rose a silver statue of a woman. It stood twice Koyee's height. Like the strange children, the statue sported six arms, and its face lacked a nose or mouth but stared with cold eyes. Montai folk knelt around the statue, whispering prayers and kissing the flagstones. It almost seemed to Koyee that the idol's eyes watched her, moving in the bald, silver head as she walked by.

Siyun led them past the houses and onto a pebbly, hillside path. They climbed to the hilltop where they found a henge of boulders, each inlaid with a metal disk. Some disks were large and bright, others small and dim, some ringed, others surrounded by smaller circles. When the company stepped into the henge and stood among the stones, the stars seemed to brighten above;

Koyee had never seen them so bright. She stared, head tilted back, and gasped, for it seemed to her that the runes upon the stones—disks and rings—filled the sky like floating lanterns torn from their strings. Great, blue spheres gleamed above her, and she saw maps upon them—the shapes of strange lands and seas—and around the spheres shone smaller circles, each bearing its own terrain. The spheres seemed so close to Koyee—she could reach out and touch them, she thought—yet so far, countless miles away.

"They're worlds," she whispered. "They're round worlds in the sky."

Siyun nodded. "And upon those worlds the same henges stand, and eyes there gaze upon us in Mythimna, for we too are but a single world, a sphere in an endless sky." He lowered his head. "And now our world is fading, for an evil rises."

"The Demon of Daylight," Koyee said. "Ferius. He leads the hosts of the sun, and his light will blind us."

Siyun regarded her. "I speak of an older evil, child. Tidings have reached us of the demon Ferius, yet for many years, we in Montai have been suffering under a greater demon's heel."

He looked between the henge stones, and when Koyee followed his gaze, she saw the silver statue below in the town. The woman with six arms seemed to stare back at her, face blank. People were still kneeling before the idol, singing prayers.

"The silver woman with six arms?" Koyee asked. "But you pray to her. Some of your children look like her."

Siyun nodded. "We worship her from fear, and only here in the henge dare I speak these words, for only among the glow of the worlds is our speech veiled to her. We pray to a statue, but the true creature lives far in the mountains, and her name is Shalesh, and she is as ancient as this island. Every year her shadow sweeps into our town as the worlds align, when the power of the henge fails to protect us. Every year she takes a single child—a child lost to us, a child who grows four new arms, who loses a mouth to scream with . . . and ears to hear others scream. Some of these children Shalesh returned to us, and they do not age; some among them are centuries old. Most remain with their mistress, serving Shalesh, praising her name in caves and tunnels."

Koyee could not tear her eyes away from the distant statue of Shalesh. Its eyes locked on hers, tugging, calling to her, whispering into her ears, speaking of all those secrets in her heart. In those eyes, Koyee saw her shame—an urchin upon the streets of Pahmey, a daughter who let her father die in flame, a coward who fled the desolation of Yintao as the enemy killed and burned, as her brother died. In those eyes, it seemed to Koyee that she herself was the monster Nitomi had spoken of, an evil worse than any in sunlit or shadowed lands. She winced and hugged herself, and her head spun, and—

"Koyee?" Nitomi was tugging her arm. "Koyee, what's wrong? You look like you've seen a ghost . . . or a monster. Oh dear, have you seen a monster? I knew it. I knew they existed here. I wanted to turn back but—"

Koyee shook her head wildly, clearing it of thoughts, and turned toward old Siyun.

"We seek a gear. I don't know its size or its material. But stars and moons are engraved upon its teeth, and it's ancient, a gear from before the empires of Eloria had risen, from before there was an Eloria." Koyee unfolded a page she'd removed from the library codex, displaying a drawing of the gear. She showed it to the old man. "Have you seen this artifact?"

Siyun examined the page and shook his head. "This is a craft beyond Montai knowledge. We work with silver and stone, but we forge no gears; it is a lost art. Of these things only the weaveworms upon the mountain possess knowledge, for they collect many gears, sprockets, and axles for their looms. They are great weavers of silk, and though they forge no metal of their own, they gather the crafts of men and build machinery to spin, dye, and weave their fabric. If you seek knowledge of gears, you will find it among them, but beware, for they hold no love for the children of men. They are an ancient breed, more ancient than us, and they have lived upon this island since the days when the world still turned."

Nitomi squeaked and hid behind Koyee. "The weaveworms?" Nitomi's voice dropped to a whisper. "Monsters?"

"To some." The old man nodded. "They trade with children of men, but they do not suffer our feet to tread upon their mountain, for it is holy ground to wormkind. In years of old, they would allow our sages to climb and speak with their masters, but those times have passed, and now they slay all who approach. Often we have found the bodies of our children who had strayed onto their land, cocooned and lifeless, wrapped in shrouds of their silk."

Siyun pointed between two of the henge's stones. Koyee turned to see a distant mountain rising in the east. Its crest glowed as with white fire or a crown of fallen stars.

"We will climb the mountain." Koyee folded the page and placed it into her pocket. "Perhaps they'll try to slay us, but if they possess the knowledge we seek, we must face them. We will visit the weaveworms."

CHAPTER NINE
MEMORY IN DARKNESS

Jin stared into the dark sea, remembering his fallen home and his fallen friend.

"I miss you, Shenlai," he whispered into the cold wind.

The black waves whispered below, their foamy crests silver in the moonlight. Beyond that sea lay his fallen home, the lost empire of Qaelin. Beyond that black horizon, his best friend—the blue dragon Shenlai—lay forever sleeping.

Jin closed his eyes, and he could see it again. His city crumbling. The sunlit demons spreading across the night, bearing torches and blades. The thousands dying and the arrows and swords driving into Shenlai, cutting through scales, slaying this ancient dragon who had protected the empire for millennia . . . who had protected Jin for the humble ten years of his life.

A hand stroked his hair. "He flies now among the stars, child. He still looks after you."

Jin nodded. Born without limbs, he used to ride upon Shenlai, but now he hung in a new harness, snug like a baby against Empress Hikari's chest. When he tilted his head back, he saw her looking down at him, her face framed with long white hair. She smiled softly, and her hand kept stroking his head, again and again. Jin's mother had died giving birth to him; some whispered that she'd died of shock upon seeing the limbless babe emerge from her womb. Jin had never known the touch of a mother. Perhaps it felt like this.

The empress stood upon the northern walls of her empire, this distant land named Ilar, a place of safety in the darkness. His own empire had fallen, but he had a new home now, and he had a new friend.

"He gave his life to save the world," he said, returning his eyes to the sea. "He died so he could reveal his secret to the right person . . . to Koyee." He sniffed. "For so many years, assassins and armies tried to kill him. Only with his dying breath could Shenlai reveal his old truth. But he always lived. He always waited. It was Koyee he had to speak to. She is very brave and very strong." He stared into the darkness, trying to imagine her there in the distance, traveling across distant lands. "And now she's out there, walking the road he sent her on. Shenlai told her to save the night. And she will . . . she will."

Hikari sighed. Jin rose and fell with her chest, feeling as if he floated upon those waves below.

"When Koyee first came into my hall, I thought her weak," said the empress. "I thought all Qaelish folk weak; they were an enemy to me. Yet now I see all Elorians as one people, and Koyee is strong. But Jin . . . we cannot place all our trust in an old story, in a clock that might only be a legend. If there is safety for the night, it stands upon these walls."

Hikari turned from side to side, affording Jin a view of the wall they stood on. It stretched along the coast, topped with battlements and guard towers. Countless soldiers stood here, clad in plates of black, lacquered steel, their helmets shaped as snarling faces with fur mustaches. They held bows and torches, and tasseled katanas hung from their belts. The banners of Ilar thudded among them, showing and hiding red flames—symbols of this southern island—upon black fields. Out in the sea, more lights blazed; the navy of Ilar patrolled the coast, its ships like towering fortresses, their decks lined with cannons and topped with pagodas. When the empress turned her back to the water,

Jin—slung across her chest—saw the city of Asharo, the capital of Ilar. More walls rose here, bristling with more men, and behind them rose the dark towers, barracks, and minarets of the city, a bristly heap that covered the hills. Crowning the city, dwarfing all other buildings, rose a black pagoda of six tiers—the palace of the empire. Upon its roof blazed an eternal red flame taller than a man, the sigil of Ilar brought to horrible life.

"Here is safety," said the empress. "In wall, tower, and blade. In might. Not in a secret quest in the shadows, but in the flame of many warriors who will die to defend the night."

Jin closed his eyes. "Who will die to defend the night . . ." The images of the dead back in his own empire, in his beloved fallen land of Qaelin, still danced behind his eyelids. "We stood upon walls in the city of Yintao. Many soldiers fought there too. And they died, Hikari." He opened his eyes, tilted back his head, and stared up at her pale face. "They died and I still hear their screams. He will come here too . . . Ferius, Lord of Light, and he will lead a great host, a host to dwarf our own. And we will die here."

Hikari snarled and drew her katana. She held the blade high; it gleamed red in the torchlight as if already bloodied. "Not so long as I draw breath, as I hold steel, as I stand in the night."

Jin thought back to the great warriors of his empire. His palace guards. His soldiers. The brave Okado and Suntai, leaders of wolves. They had raised swords, they had vowed to always fight . . . and they had died.

And yet I survived—weak, limbless, afraid. He let his chin fall to his chest. *And Koyee survived . . . and the four children of night who had joined us. The young. The frightened.*

"Shenlai told her a secret. He was the wisest soul I know. You say he's still looking after me, Hikari, and I believe he is—through Koyee and through her friends."

Hikari stiffened and seemed ready to say more when a roar pierced the night.

They spun back toward the sea and Jin gasped. Around them, the soldiers muttered, clanked, and tightened their grips on their bows.

A fleet sailed ahead, rising from the horizon—two hundred ships or more, their lanterns bright, their sails and banners white. At first Jin was certain that the war had come, that Ferius sailed here with his army. But when he squinted, he saw the sigils upon the banners and sails—great diamonds painted onto the silk.

"Leen," he whispered. "The empire of Leen sails to us."

The roar sounded again, distant across the sea, and Jin finally saw its source. A dragon flew above the distant fleet, silvery like a strand of moonlight. Here flew Pirilin, the guardian of the north, sister to Shenlai, one of only two dragons who still lived in the night.

Hikari placed an arm across Jin and clutched him tightly. He heard the smile in her voice. "Leen brings aid! Leen sends an army to fight alongside ours."

Across the walls, the soldiers cheered and waved their swords, but no hope filled Jin. His heart sank and ice seemed to fill his belly.

"That is no army," he whispered. "They do not bring us aid . . . but seek it."

He could smell the blood on the wind. He could hear the prayers and whimpers. Jin led a camp of refugees, thousands of wounded, frightened souls exiled to this island. Here ahead in the sea, he sensed the same desperation.

When the fleet sailed nearer, his fears were confirmed. The people of Leen stood upon the ships, not soldiers but women, children, elders. Their eyes were haunted, their bodies bandaged. Burns stretched across the hulls of ships, and holes filled the sails.

Several men lay in carts, missing limbs—wounded soldiers whose pain Jin knew too well.

"The island of Ilar!" the people cried upon the decks, pointing and weeping and praising the stars. "Safety!"

Tears stung Jin's eyes.

Pirilin the dragon flew toward him, gliding wingless upon the wind like a snake upon water. Her white scales gleamed in the moonlight, and her violet eyes shone like two lanterns. Leaving the ships behind, the dragon coiled down toward the walls, dived over Hikari and Jin, and landed behind them upon a cobbled expanse. Her tongue lolled as she panted, cracks filled her scales, and one of her horns ended in a chipped nub.

"Pirilin!" Jin cried.

She blinked, her eyelashes—each as long as a human arm—fanning him, and the pain of a dying empire filled her eyes.

"We are fallen," whispered the northern dragon. "They came on a thousand ships. They swarmed into our city." Tears rolled down her cheeks, freezing and clinking onto the cobblestones. "The white towers of Taenori, Jewel of North, fell like shattered icicles. The fires of the enemy melted the snow until a sea rolled through our halls. Our homes are vanished, gone underwater like the fabled islands of old. All our soldiers, brave souls of the north, burned in fire and drowned in water. All our darkness is lit." Pirilin tossed back her head and cried out, a great keen, louder than armies, a mourning wail that rolled across the sea. "Leen is fallen!"

Empress Hikari breathed in with a hiss, stepped closer to the dragon, and placed a hand on Pirilin's cheek. As the empress leaned forward, Jin—hanging from his harness upon her chest—found himself staring into one of the dragon's great, purple eyes.

"Pirilin!" said the empress. "Where is he? Where is Ferius?"

The dragon did not remove her eye from Jin. She spoke in a low voice, answering the empress . . . but speaking to Jin.

"With a thousand ships. With more soldiers than hearts beat in the night." In her eye, Jin could see it—the battle of the north, the thousands falling to the fire and water. Pirilin's voice dropped to but a whisper, but her words filled him with the power of beating war drums. "He is coming here."

CHAPTER TEN
VALLEY OF THE TITANS

They walked upon moss, ferns swaying around them, when they crested the hill and beheld the valley of titans.

Bailey had spent the past few hours cursing, spitting, and grumbling about Ferius, about the fools who followed him, and—just as vigorously—about how slow Torin walked. Standing here, the wind in her hair, she gasped and her eyes dampened. She reached out and held Torin's hand.

"Look," she whispered. "Oh, Torin. Look."

He stood at her side, caked in mud, his clothes tattered and his sword green with the juice of leaves. His eyes dampened and a soft smile spread across his face.

"It's beautiful." He squeezed her hand. "It's . . . the most beautiful thing I've seen."

She grinned and pinched his cheek. "You gardener boys." She hopped and began racing downhill, tugging him with her. "Now come on, tree lover! Let's go explore."

The valley sprawled below the Nayan Escarpment like a courtyard below a wall, full of mist, ferns, and grass. A grove of giants rose here, the trees hundreds of feet tall. Bailey had seen the castles of Kingswall, the towers of Pahmey, and the palaces of both Yintao and Asharo, capitals of night. She thought these trees rose taller than them all.

The temple she sought—the ruins of Til Natay—lay farther west along the escarpment, but Bailey could not miss a chance to explore this place. She ran downhill between ferns, laughing. She felt like she had as a child, tugging Torin with her to hill and

meadow, chasing grasshoppers and butterflies and new flowers
for their parents. Before these towering trees, she felt as small as
that scrawny girl with bee stings and scraped knees, and still she
tugged Torin with her.

When they reached the valley and the first titans, she froze,
gasped, and tilted back her head. Her grin stretched so wide it
hurt her cheeks. The roots of these trees rose taller than her, and
their boles were wider than her home back in Fairwool-by-Night.
When she craned her neck back, she saw the trunks soaring,
higher and higher, rising through mist and into cloud, their
boughs swaying and rustling their leaves in the cold heights.

She tugged Torin's hand, laughing. "Come on, let's find the
biggest one."

She expected him to laugh too, to run with her, to race
around the grove, but he only stood with his feet planted firmly in
the moss. He shook his head, and his voice was soft.

"Let's walk slowly. This place seems . . . holy. We shouldn't
run here." He began to walk, holding her hand, his grip soft and
warm. "These trees are ancient and wise. They are guardians of
the forest, old priests of the world."

Bailey bit her lip. "Wanna climb one?"

"No. They're not for climbing, I don't think. They feel
almost like the columns of temples. I was never a religious man. I
never prayed much to Idar or any other god. But now I feel in the
presence of wisdom that's very old, that's very real." He smiled,
head tilted back, and inhaled deeply. "Let's just walk and sense
them."

Bailey mussed his hair. "You really mean it, don't you? Oh,
you're still such a babyface. All right. I'll walk with you nice and
proper-like for a bit."

Sighing, Bailey let him set the pace. They walked between
the trunks, each one wider and taller than the towers of men's
cities. Birds, marmosets, and insects made their homes in the

trees, peering down from branches and holes. The aroma of leaves, wood, and grass filled Bailey's nostrils, and mist floated around her. At every tree they passed, Torin placed his hand against the trunk, smiled softly, and whispered under his breath, perhaps prayers to the titans.

At the fifth tree, Bailey let out a groan.

"Oh, Winky, this is boring." She placed down her pack and weapons, then grabbed a tree trunk. "I'm climbing this bad boy, and you're climbing with me." She pulled herself a foot up, driving her fingers between coils in the trunk. "We need a good look to scout the land; I bet we can see the temple from up there. I'll race you."

"Bailey!" He stared up at her. "That tree must be hundreds of feet tall. This isn't like Old Maple back home."

She gave him a crooked smile and a wink. "Scared?" She stuck her tongue out at him and kept climbing. "Chase me!"

He crossed his arms. "I'm not climbing."

She shook her leg, spraying mud off her boot onto him. "Then I'm going to keep pinching your cheek for the rest of the journey, and when we sleep, I'm going to snore right into your ear and drool right onto your neck."

"You do those things anyway!"

"We'll, I'll do more of them. Now come on, scaredy cat. Climb with me." She smiled down at him. "Like we used to. Like we climbed as children. We need to be children for a while."

As he stared up at her, his eyes softened, and he sighed—a sigh of resignation and of memory. He reached into his pack, rummaged around, and produced a rope that ended with a fist-sized grapple.   "It's a good thing I brought this with me." He began to unwind the rope.

Clinging to the tree, Bailey gave a swift kick, knocking the grapple from his hand. "That's cheating. No grapple! Climb like me—hands and feet only."

He groaned but he grabbed the trunk and began to climb.

Full of grooves, holes, and branches, the tree was massively wide and tall but easy for climbing. Bailey inhaled deeply, a smile on her lips, savoring the earthy scents. Parakeets sang around her, and marmosets fled into holes in the bole. Torin climbed several feet below, and with a grin Bailey climbed faster, determined to leave him far below.

Yet as she climbed, Bailey found that tears stung her eyes, and she wiped them with the back of her hand. It was just pollen in her eyes, she told herself, or maybe the mist that floated everywhere in Naya. She kept climbing, lips tight. She had ascended thirty feet, maybe more, when she paused for breath and looked around her. The rainforest spread into the horizons, the titan grove rising like towers over the lesser trees. In the north, she could make out a stream carving its way through the foliage, and she pretended that it was the Sern, the river that flowed along Fairwool-by-Night. When she looked down at Torin, she imagined that they were climbing Old Maple, the tree that grew from the village square.

After we climb, we'll go home and sit by the fireplace, she told herself. *He'll sit in his armchair, reading a book, and I'll wriggle in beside him and pinch his cheek if he complains. And we'll play a board game and drink mulled wine and laugh, then fall asleep in each other's arms.* Often they had slept together like that, curled up in the oversized armchair, a quilt pulled over them, their limbs all tangled together and their breath warm against each other's cheeks.

And there they were again—her tears, stinging her eyes and flowing down to her lips. Because she missed those days. And she missed that girl. She hadn't yet killed men then. She hadn't seen thousands die. No nightmares of burning children had filled her. She could laugh freely in those years, tease Torin, and be a girl, be happier than she was now, so far from home.

"Bailey, are you all right?" he called up to her, several feet below and grunting as he climbed.

"Don't you worry about me. Race you to that big branch up there!"

She sniffed and blinked the tears away. She kept climbing, clinging to that memory of home.

She slung her arm across a branch as wide as a normal tree's trunk, pulled herself up, and stood upon the beam. She wiped her brow and paused for a moment, catching her breath. This branch was as high up as the Watchtower's battlements back home, and she had climbed only a small part of the tree. The wind rustled the branches and leaves around her, and she dug her fingers into a crevice on the trunk. She looked around her, gasping at the view.

"Oh, Winky, it's beautiful."

He was struggling a few feet below, trying to reach the branch, but his fingers only skimmed the purchase. "A little help?"

"Not now! I'm admiring the view." A smile spread across her face, and her braids fluttered in the wind. She had flown upon a dragon, but that had been in the night, and she had seen only stars and shadows. She had never been so high up in daylight. She could see for a dozen miles in every direction from up here. A hundred other titans grew around her, and between them spread the canopy of the lesser trees. The rainforest covered the land, rolling over hills and valleys, undulating like a green sea in the wind. The escarpment rose to her left, a great green shelf. Upon its distant western facade, she thought she could see a waterfall. Birds flew below her, mist floated, and—

"Bailey!" Torin grunted below her, pawing at the branch. "Can you just . . . a hand?"

She groaned and rolled her eyes. "Oh, you baby! Fine." She leaned down, grabbed his wrist, and hoisted him up onto the branch beside her. He wobbled for a bit and clung to a higher, thinner branch for support. They stood together upon the limb, most of the titan tree still above them, the rest of the forest rustling below.

"Now this is how you admire a forest," Bailey said and nudged Torin with her elbow, winking as he wobbled and clutched the branch. She pointed westward. "See those bulges rising from the trees on the horizon? I reckon that's the temple we're seeking."

She had to squint to see them; they still lay a dozen miles away, rising upon the edge of the escarpment, overlooking the valleys below. From here, she could see only gray shards like boulders protruding from the greenery. With many roots, vines, and fallen logs to impede their progress, she thought it would take another two or three turns to reach the place.

"They might just be rocks," Torin said, squinting at the distance.

"Rocks that size? No. Whatever is rising there is massive, the size of palaces. That there is our temple. That's where we'll find the clock's missing number." She turned to face him, grinning, and mussed his head. "We're almost there."

He nodded. "Good. Now that you've had your little look-around, can we climb down?" The wind gusted, and he winced and clung for purchase, his feet wobbling upon the branch. "I'm dizzy."

Her grin only widened further, and she tickled him. "You know that's only encouraging me. Come on—higher! We've only climbed about a third of this tree, and I want to reach the damn top. I want to stand on top of the world, Winky. Follow me! I dare you."

She hopped, for an instant touching nothing but air, and grabbed a branch above. She slung herself up and kept climbing.

She had climbed several more feet, scurrying over branches like one of the marmosets, when she saw the rope ladder.

She paused, tilted her head, and narrowed her eyes. She had seen no civilization since entering the rainforest; most of the Nayan folk lived miles north from here along the Sern River, their fabled cities of stone thriving on fishing and trade. Gingerly, wondering if this was only a mirage, she reached up and touched the rope ladder with her fingertips. It swung and felt real enough.

"There's a ladder!" she called down to Torin. "I'm climbing up."

"Wait. A ladder? Bailey, this could be somebody's home. Should you just barge in?"

But she was already climbing, the wooden rungs smooth against her palms. The ladder took her through tiers of leafs and mist. Branches crisscrossed above, forming a lattice, seeming almost unnatural to Bailey, as if folk had guided and shaped the branches over centuries. The rope ladder took her between a wreath of branches and past a carpet of foliage.

She brushed aside leaves and gasped.

"Oh merciful Idar . . . it's a village."

She laughed softly, climbed higher, and stepped onto a flattened branch. She gaped, the smile not leaving her face. A staircase coiled around the titan's bole, and many shelves sprung out around it like mushrooms, holding tents and huts. Branches spread out from that central pillar like spokes, flattened to form roads. Rope bridges and ladders swung between them, forming a web more complex than the most masterful spider could weave. Between these branches swung hammocks, and even little huts—made of twigs and leaves—rose like great, woody acorns. Water flowed through wooden pipes, pots of herbs hung upon ropes, and vegetable gardens flourished upon ledges. The village spread up and down in a hodgepodge.

"A village in the sky . . ." she whispered.

The villagers bustled across the tree, climbing ladders and stairs, crossing bridges, tending to gardens, and lounging in their hammocks. Bailey had seen the soldiers of Naya's northern tribes before, burly men and women clad in tiger pelts; they knew the craft of metalwork, and they wore armor of iron and bore cruel spears. This southern, treetop tribe seemed a simpler, gentler folk. They wore clothes of leaves, and beads hung around their necks and arms. Their skin was pale, their hair red and wild, braided and chinking with bone clips and beads. Their eyes were bright green. Bailey saw no metal here, no weapons, no fire; it was a tribe lost to time, a tribe living like the most ancient men when the world had still turned.

Two villagers—young boys clad in leaves—saw her and pointed and chattered to their elders. More eyes turned toward Bailey, and soon a hundred villagers came swinging down ladders, leaping between branches, and racing down wooden stairs toward her.

"Bailey, what . . . " Torin began, climbing to stand beside her. His voice trailed off when he saw the village.

The children reached them first, their green eyes so large they looked almost Elorian. With twig-like fingers, they tugged at Bailey and Torin's silken, embroidered cloaks, garments woven in the night. They tapped their bits of metal—belt buckles, Bailey's simple bronze bracelet, and Torin's dagger—then gasped and whispered amongst themselves. An elder stepped forth, brushing the children aside. His white hair and beard flowed down to his knobbly knees, and he wore only a loincloth. He touched Bailey's cheeks with fingers like gnarly roots, then turned to Torin and spoke rapidly in his tongue, a tinkly language like rain on leaves and water on pebbles.

"We're friends!" Bailey said. "We're from Arden. Friends." She pulled off her bracelet, a humble circle, and held it out. "Here—a gift for you."

The elder squinted at the bracelet, lifted it, and tapped the metal. A grin split his face, showing only three teeth, and he nodded.

Bailey looked at Torin and whispered, "Give them a gift too."

"I don't have any jewelry."

"Just give them something!"

He reached into his pocket, produced a few Elorian coins, and held them out. The elder took these too, sniffed, tapped the copper, and grinned again.

"Great, we've just introduced them to both metalworking and currency," Torin whispered. "We've probably just corrupted an ancient, pure culture untouched by civilization. You see what your climbing can do, Bailey?"

"Oh, hush. A bracelet and a few coins won't corrupt anything."

The villagers grabbed their hands and clothes and tugged them. Bailey and Torin followed, walking along the branch, across a bridge, and up another ladder to a plateau formed of wood, vines, and rope. There the villagers sat them down upon rugs of lichen, softer and springier than any fabric, and brought forth a feast. In wooden bowls they served mushrooms and berries, water scented with flower petals, and—Bailey gasped to see it—all manner of insects from skewered grasshoppers to wriggling grubs. The villagers pushed the bowls forth, mimicking eating.

Torin paled as a villager held out a bowl of grubs. "I'm not hungry," he said, holding out his palms.

"You're being rude." Bailey reached into the bowl, picked up a wriggling grub, and waved it at Torin. "Eat up. We're guests."

He winced. "I'll just have some berries."

She rolled her eyes and snorted. "You're worse than Linee." She tossed the grub into her mouth, forced herself to swallow, then grinned. "See? Delicious. Tastes like chicken."

Torin looked queasy.

Around them, the villagers laughed and joined the meal. Bailey stuffed ten grubs into her mouth, chewed vigorously, then leaned toward Torin and opened her mouth wide, sticking out her grubby tongue. He turned green, and she mussed his hair and kissed his cheek, smearing a bit of grub onto him.

Hours went by, it seemed, hours of eating and drinking, listening to the villagers sing, and watching dancers perform in wooden masks. Sitting on the lichen mats, Bailey leaned against Torin, placed a hand on his knee, and rested her head against his shoulder. She tugged his arm, slinging it around her, and he did not resist.

"I wish we could stay forever," she whispered, smiling softly as she watched the dancers. "When this war is over, we should live here."

"I'd starve to death," Torin said.

"Good." She nodded. "More grubs for me."

After the dance ended, villagers brought forth skirts of wide, flat leaves and necklaces of wooden beads. At first Torin only grumbled some more, but with a few taunts and pokes from Bailey's elbow, he relented. Soon the pair stood clad in nothing but leaves, their limbs bare, beads around their necks.

When Bailey saw Torin—clad in a leafy skirt, his chest bare, his expression miserable—she burst out laughing. "Look at you!"

He grumbled. "You don't look much better."

Bailey glanced down at her body. Her leafy skirt hung halfway down her thighs, and thick necklaces of beads hid her chest. She looked back up at Torin and grinned. "I'm a beautiful princess of the jungle. And you look more awkward than a fish riding a horse."

He grumbled and walked along the branch to the hammock the villagers had given them. "I'm going to sleep. When I wake up, we're dressing back in our clothes, climbing off this tree, and moving on."

He entered the hammock, turned his back toward her, and lay still. Bailey hopped into the hammock too, landing atop him. The supporting branches creaked and Torin grunted. She climbed over him and lay facing him, grinning.

"Get your own hammock," he said.

She wriggled around and slung an arm around his waist. She gave his nose a playful bite. "I'm comfortable here."

"I'm not!"

She shrugged. "So?" A yawn stretched across her from fingertips to toes. "I'm tired and going to sleep." She nuzzled against him, swung her leg across him, and closed her eyes.

Torin sighed. "I can't sleep like this. Your leg weighs about as much as an elephant, and your elbow is poking my stomach."

She smiled softly, eyes still closed, and nestled closer. "Torin . . . do you remember our armchair back at home? The one by the fireplace?"

After a moment's pause, he spoke in a soft voice. "I do."

Her smile turned sad upon her lips. "I've often thought about that armchair. When we slept in the darkness of night, war and blood around us, I'd try to imagine that I still sat in that big, oversized chair, and that you were there with me. I remember how, as children, we'd sit there together, a book open on our laps. We'd sometimes fall asleep like that . . . and just spend a whole turn cuddled together, holding each other, safe and warm by the fireplace." She opened her eyes and touched his cheek. "Do you ever pretend that we're back there?"

All the harshness and anger flowed away from his face, and she saw the memories in his eyes. "I do. A lot. I miss that home."

"I do too. That's why I'm happy here. Because I'm with you now—climbing like we used to, teasing you like in the old days, and going to sleep together in a safe place. Because when we're like this, it feels like home, and I can feel like a girl again, not like a soldier . . . not like Bailey the warrior who killed, who bled, who saw so much death. Here I can be just a girl. And that's the best feeling in the world." She closed her eyes again, wriggling against him. "Hold me and let's pretend that we're back there, cuddling together in the armchair, sleeping in safety."

She felt his hand on her waist, and she laid her head against the warmth of his chest, and he stroked her hair.

"You're safe, Bailey Berin," he whispered. "You're home."

She smiled and she slept.

CHAPTER ELEVEN
THE STREETS OF KAHTEF

They walked through the market of Kahtef, the great oasis city, imagining enemies everywhere.

"Remember, Linee," Cam whispered, "don't speak loudly in Ardish, and don't remove your hood. We don't know who might be another Sailith spy."

She walked at his side, shivering, clad in the oversized cloak and hood of the assassin she had slain. In a southern land of searing sunlight, not much shadow filled her hood, and her northern features—green eyes and freckled cheeks framed with golden hair—seemed as foreign here as a camel wandering the arctic. Cam had often thought his dark eyes plain, but here he was thankful for them. With those eyes, his shaved head, and simple canvas breeches, at least he fit into the crowd.

And that crowd was everywhere—countless Eseerians bustling across the market. Many of the poorer folk were dressed like Cam in nothing but trousers, their thin chests bronzed. Even the wealthier folk, better fed and brighter of eyes, did not wear much, only humble skirts or tunics of white wool, revealing their legs, arms, and often their chests. What they lacked in fabric they made up for in jewels, sporting many rings, earrings, and necklaces of burnished gold and gemstones. Soldiers marched here too, the butts of their spears clanking against the cobblestones. Sandals held their feet, their breastplates displayed scorpion sigils, and their khopeshes—swords shaped like sickles—hung at their sides.

"Cam, do you see a zigzagging rat?" Linee whispered, walking at his side.

He glared at her. "I told you a million times, it's a *ziggurat*, and I don't even know what that means. But if the clock hand is anywhere in this city, maybe we'll find it in this market. So keep an eye open!"

As they walked along the streets, they passed many stalls. Hundreds of merchants lined the roadsides, calling out their wares. Cam scanned every stall. One merchant, a toothless old man, hawked a hundred spices from a hundred tin bowls; Cam recognized cardamom, cinnamon, coriander, and cumin. Another merchant, a woman clad in shawls, called out over barrels of olives, raisins, dried figs, almonds, and dozens of other comestibles. Some merchants sold jewelry, anything from rings to plates of gemstones worn across the chest, while another sold animals—snakes, parakeets, and even monkeys—in cages. Cam and Linee walked by stalls selling blades with antler hilts, figurines carved from olive wood, drums and flutes, and even—Cam cringed to see it—a roadside market selling slaves in iron shackles. The smells of spices, sweets, wine, frying fish, and sweat filled his nostrils.

Above the colorful stalls rose the tan, brick walls of shops and homes. Awnings stretched out between them, revealing only a strip of sky. Weeds grew between the streets' cobblestones, and palm trees and pines grew at every corner, full of dates and nuts, conures, and chattering monkeys. Down the street, Camlin caught glimpses of a distant palace—or perhaps a temple—its stairs lined with statues of men and women with insect heads.

"Camlin, look!"

Linee grabbed his hand and pointed to a palm tree. Cam's heart leaped into a gallop. For an instant he was sure Ferius's spies had found them, but when he looked at the tree, he saw a rat scurrying around its trunk and into a sewage hole.

"A ziggurat!" Linee whispered in awe. "Do you think the clock hand's in the sewer?"

"Why don't you go look?" Cam said. "For pity's sake, it's not a rodent. Why can't you understand that?"

She pouted and crossed her arms. "Well, at first I thought the rat was zigzagging. But . . . I guess you're right, Camlin, he did move in more of a beeline. I'll keep looking."

Cam sighed. "Why couldn't I have gone looking for the number with Bailey? I'd take all the arm-bending and ear-tugging in the world over this." He stared at a few monkeys in the palm tree; they were busy picking the fruit. "Linee, let's keep going. I— Linee?"

He turned and couldn't see her, and his heart raced anew. Again he could imagine Sailith monks tugging her into an alley. He scanned the marketplace, then breathed in relief when he saw her. The exiled queen had approached a stall of embroidered shawls and was busy browsing.

"Oh, Camlin, can you buy me this one?" she asked when he approached. She held up a pink shawl, its wool embroidered with flowers and its hems tasseled. "I promise if you buy me this, I'll find you a zigzagging rat."

"No, we have to save our money. We—"

"But I want it!" she said, voice rising louder, and stamped her feet.

Cam winced. If any heard them speaking Ardish, the language of the north, their disguises would be useless. More to keep Linee quiet than happy, he dug through his pocket and produced a few Eseerian coins. Empress Hikari had given them to him, having taken them from the corpses of Eseerians who had invaded Ilar. Grumbling under his breath, he paid the shawl vendor—a child barely older than ten. Linee grinned, tossed the shawl around her shoulders, and kissed Cam's cheek.

As they kept walking through the city, they emerged from the marketplace and found themselves on a boulevard of wide, white flagstones, each engraved with a different insect. Cam saw scorpions, scarabs, dragonflies, and many others. Columns lined the roadsides, their capitals supporting statues of deities, their humanoid bodies supporting insect heads, the bulging eyes inlaid with gemstones. An obelisk rose in a square ahead, hundreds of feet tall and tipped with platinum, and priests in white robes swayed around it, blowing ram's horns. City folk moved toward the pillar, everyone from beggars in loincloths to wealthy, bearded men in jeweled chariots. Hundreds of doves and starlings flew above, darkening the sky, flitting from palm to fig to pine tree.

"Camlin, I'm hungry." Linee tugged his arm. "And I'm sleepy. Can we find food and a bed?" She pointed to a stone building on the roadside, palm trees framing its door. "That looks like a tavern."

Cam was about to glare at her, to roll his eyes, to insist they kept searching, but before he could open his mouth to speak, his stomach gave a growl. He too was famished and weary; he couldn't remember the last time he'd eaten or slept.

"Just a quick bite and nap," he said. "Then we keep looking for the hand."

Linee managed to simultaneously rub her belly and yawn. They walked along the street, skirting a woman carrying a basket of grapes, a child juggling for coins, and an old man riding a donkey laden with jars of preserves. When they reached the tavern, Cam saw a sign shaped like a dragonfly, and through the windows, he glimpsed men drinking and eating. The sound of flutes and the smell of frying fish wafted into the street.

"Remember, don't speak loudly in Ardish, and—" he began, but Linee ignored him and raced through the doorway. With a sigh, Cam followed.

They found themselves in a hot, dusty chamber. Jugs of wine stood along the walls, painted with scenes of soldiers fighting dragons. Several dozen men and women reclined upon tasseled pillows, eating pears, figs, and chickpeas from low wooden tables. Upon a stage, a woman clad in palm leaves and silver played a timbrel, swaying to the beat.

Cam found a small, low table in a shadowy corner, only a foot tall. He and Linee sat side by side upon an embroidered cushion, their backs to the wall. Cam knew only a few words in Eseerian—mostly studied from old books on the journey here—but managed to order them a meal, wine, and a bed for the night.

The food arrived: a roasted duck upon a bed of leeks and apricots, wild rice mixed with pine nuts and shallots, pears stewed in honey and wine, and grainy bread dipped in olive oil. After so long in the night, eating little more than mushrooms and fish, the meal was heavenly. The meat melted in his mouth, gravy dripped down his chin, and the wine tingled through him. He let out a contented sigh, and Linee's eyes rolled back with every bite.

After their meal, a serving girl led them upstairs into a bedchamber. It was a humble room, and a large straw bed occupied most of it. When the server had left them, Cam closed the door, and Linee doffed her cloak and hood. They found a basin of water, washed off the grime and sweat of their journey, then sat upon the bed. A sandy breeze blew from the window, and the palm trees rustled outside.

Sitting beside him, her hands folded in her lap, Linee laid her head against his shoulder.

"I missed this," she said softly. "Real food. A bed in sunlight. The song of birds. I wish . . . I wish we could just stay here. Well, maybe not here in this tavern. And maybe not even in this kingdom. But in sunlight. I wish we could forget about that war back in the night." She placed a hand on his knee and looked at him, her eyes earnest. "Camlin, maybe we can do that. We have some money. Maybe we can just find a home here—you and me. Let's forget about clock hands, Sailith spies, and all those scary things. Let's buy a little house with a garden, and we can eat duck every turn, and . . ." She looked down and sniffed, and when she looked up again, her eyes were damp. "I don't even need a palace anymore. I don't need to be a queen. I can be a wife to you. Or just a friend if you prefer! We can live together, the two of us, here in the daylight. I know you think I'm silly and a little stupid, and I know I sing too much, but if you agree, I promise I'll learn. I promise I'll be good to you."

Her hand was warm against his knee, her lips parted, and her eyes shone. She leaned forward, waiting for an answer.

Cam had spent the past year scolding her, rolling his eyes at her, sometimes even yelling at her. Sitting so close to Linee now, her body warm and her eyes damp, his anger melted away, his throat felt too tight, and his own eyes stung.

"I would like that," he whispered and placed his hand upon hers. "I would like nothing more. Even if you sing too much, and even if you're silly. But I think of our friends in Eloria. I think of Suntai who died for us. And I think of Koyee who's sailing into danger. And I think of Hem who gave his life in this war." His voice was hoarse. "We can't forget about them. We have to keep going. We have to do our part and not let down our friends."

Linee lowered her head and nodded, and her tears splashed against her lap. "I know. I know, Camlin. I'm just so afraid all the time, and . . . and I love you. I really love you so much."

He squeezed her hand. "Linee . . ."

She trembled. "I'm sorry. I mean . . . you're the only person who listens to me." She touched his cheek. "Everyone thinks I'm just a baby, but you go on quests with me. And you listen to me, even if you think my words are stupid. Nobody ever treated me that well—not my father, not my late husband . . . only you, Camlin Shepherd." She leaned forward and kissed his cheek.

He drew back a strand of her hair, tucked it behind her ear, and found himself caressing that hair, running his fingers over and over through the silken gold.

"You're not stupid." He stared into her eyes. "Don't let people tell you that. Don't let *me* tell you that. You solved the last riddle in Pirilin's court, a riddle Suntai and I couldn't answer. You learned to speak Qaelish and Ilari faster than I did. And I bet you find this clock hand before I do, at least if you stop looking for rats." He couldn't help but smile when she giggled. "All your life, Linee, people told you you were a silly, childish princess, and you wanted to please them. You wanted to be what people expected you to be. So you played along with it. But there's more to you. Somewhere deep down, there's more. I've seen it. That's all."

Her tears spilled and her body shook. "That's a lot."

She embraced him with a crushing urgency, her arms wrapped tightly around his back, and he held her closely, and he found himself kissing her, and her kiss tasted of wine, honeyed pears, and tears.

They lay upon the bed, wrapped together, and they could not stop kissing, not even as Linee's silks slipped off her body, as they pressed together, naked and warm under the blankets, their fingers entwined. Cam had never loved a woman before, and it was strange to him, a dance of heat and shadows, of confusion and laughter as their teeth banged together, then of silent gasps as they found their rhythm. It seems hours before he lay on his back, drenched in sweat, breathing deeply as Linee slept against him, her head on his chest, her leg tossed across him.

"Camlin," she mumbled in her sleep, nestling closer to him. "My Camlin."

He stroked her hair, and he felt more confused and lost and happy than ever before. He was about to close his eyes and sleep too when he saw the painting on the wall.

He had not noticed it when entering the room, but lying on the bed, it hung before him in a beam of sunlight. The canvas featured a triangular building, stairs running up its facades, its crest flattened. The foremost stairs, lined with statues, rose toward a shadowy archway leading into the structure. A figure stood there, painted no larger than Cam's finger. At first he thought the figure a warrior in armor, but when he squinted, he saw a creature constructed of springs, sprockets, and scraps of metal like the toys artisans would make in Pahmey, little soldiers that marched when you wound them up. Standing in the archway, the automaton stared at Cam from the painting, its eyes red, its metallic arm raised in condemnation—a limb made from the hand of a clock.

CHAPTER TWELVE
MEMORY IN FIRE

They stood on the palace balcony, gazing upon a city of steel, stone, and silk.

Asharo, the last standing city of the night, rolled down the hills toward the black sea. Its sisters had fallen. Hives of color and crystal, ports of glowing towers, cities of mighty walls—all had burned in the sunlit fire. Empires had crumbled; nations were gone. The night blazed and yet here they stood, a last corner of darkness, a last bastion of shadow in a sea of sunlight.

"Asharo must stand," Jin said, hanging in his harness from Hikari's chest like a babe in a sling.

The empress nodded, hands upon the balcony railing, gazing at the city and the sea beyond. "It will stand . . . or all the night will fall."

The entire city seemed like a single great fortress. Pagodas of black bricks and red roof tiles rose upon every hill, full of soldiers. Archers stood in minarets along the city streets. Homes and shops alike sported crowns of battlements, and men stood upon them, clad in black steel. From every roof flew the banners of Ilar, Qaelin, and Leen, silken standards showing flames, moonstars, and diamonds. The people of each empire huddled within these walls; the refugee camps outside the city had been dismantled, and the last survivors of Eloria now hid in homes, in workshops, in cellars, or simply along the streets. The old empires were gone; they were one people now. They were all Elorians. They were all the night.

"Death will come from the sea," Jin said, the wind in his hair. "They are near."

He stared at the city walls. Many soldiers guarded them, armed with arrows, cannons, and catapults. Beyond those walls, the ships of Eloria patrolled the water, their cannons ready, their lanterns bright.

But it will not be enough, Jin thought and shivered. *Not when the thousand ships of sunlight arrive.*

Empress Hikari wrapped her arms around him, pressing him close to her chest. She leaned down and kissed his head. "The night will be victorious, sweet child."

But Jin only saw the bloodshed back in his home—his guards, his people, and his dearest friend Shenlai slain in the onslaught.

"I'm afraid," he whispered. "Shenlai taught me that it's all right to be afraid, that you can be afraid and still be brave. But I don't feel brave. I feel helpless." Tears stung his eyes. "I wish I had legs to run to battle with. I wish I had arms for wielding a sword and shield. How can I help our people? I feel so weak without Shenlai."

Hikari turned away from the city, leaving the balcony and returning into the palace.

They entered the empress's bedchamber. Polished black tiles covered the floor, and the walls were painted crimson and gold. Swords hung over a crackling fireplace, and candles burned in iron sconces, illuminating a granite table, gilded chairs, and a bed topped with silk blankets. Statues of dragons held crackling embers behind their iron teeth, and jewels shone upon their scales.

Hikari pulled shut a sliding door, hiding the city outside, and sat in an armchair by the hearth. She pulled Jin free from his harness and cradled him in her lap. He lay, wrapped in silk, gazing up at her face. She stared into the flames, seeming to be lost in thought.

I wonder if my mother looked like her, Jin thought. When he had first seen Hikari, he had feared her. She had stormed into his city, clad in black armor, her body bristly with blades and throwing stars. She had ridden into his hall upon a shadow panther, her eyes blazing, her lips snarling, blood dripping from her katanas. He had thought Hikari a demon at first—the infamous empress who ruled Ilar, the southern island that had so often tormented his own empire.

Yet now . . . now he saw a softer woman, a hurt woman lost in memory and pain. The first wrinkles of age or worry spread out from her eyes and framed her mouth. Her hair cascaded and tickled Jin's face. Her eyes gleamed orange in the firelight—large Elorian eyes, full of sadness. She rocked Jin gently. He was already ten years old, too old to be cradled like a babe, but this felt good. This felt right. He had never known the comforting touch of a mother.

"I had a son once," Hikari whispered.

"What happened to him?"

She smiled softly. "He was born fighting. He was born two moons early, a tiny little thing, his spine crooked, red and wrinkled and so small . . . small enough that he fit into my palm. The masters said he was weak. They told me to toss him into the sea. They do so with other weak babes." She returned her eyes to the fire, her smile sad. "Yet how could he be weak? How could something so small that clung to life, that fought for every breath, not be a warrior? He fought against his own body. That is the greatest fight one can face. And so I kept the babe . . . and nursed him and loved him and watched him grow. He never learned how to walk; his back was twisted like a snake. Everyone thought him weak. They told me he would never be a warrior. But he was strong . . . he was strong in his own way." She stroked Jin's hair.

"He died younger than you are now, and I burned him in a great flame, and his spirit now shines in the stars."

Jin lowered his eyes. "I'm sorry, Hikari."

She held him close. "We are in Ilar, the land of the Red Flame, where we worship strength and courage, where warriors are more esteemed than sages. Yet I loved that small, struggling little boy, and I refused to believe him weak." She looked into Jin's eyes and touched his cheek. "Never call yourself weak. You have no limbs but you have strength. When the enemy lands upon our shores, we'll need more than swords and arrows. We'll need leaders. We will lead our people."

Jin nodded. "I lost Shenlai, my dear dragon. My soldiers are fallen and my friends are gone into shadow. But we will lead our people. When the enemy arrives, I cannot fight with sword or bow, but if you carry me, I will still go to war, and I will try to give courage to our people." He swallowed. "But . . . as we wait, can I stay here with you? Can I sleep in your bed and feel safe for one turn?"

Hikari laughed softly and kissed his forehead. "Of course."

He slept in her arms that night, feeling safe and warm. The fire crackled in the hearth, and Jin dreamed of flames blazing over walls, homes, and the children of night.

CHAPTER THIRTEEN
BLOOD AND WATER

Bailey snickered. "Please, Winky, I'm a much better warrior than you. I *fought* through all seven layers of Yintao, and you just sailed past four or five of them." She swung her sword, lashing vines. "I'm faster than you, stronger than you, much deadlier, and much more experienced. You can pretend to be some fighter now, but you're just a gardener."

They had been walking through the jungle for what seemed like eras. Every turn, whenever Torin swung his sword to lash through the brush, Bailey would laugh and mock him for pretending to be some fighter—it didn't matter that he was only fighting vegetation now, not Sailith monks.

"Yes, Bailey, I've heard it all before." He rolled his eyes.

"Good. Because you need to learn this, or you'll just get yourself killed." She looked at him, brown eyes narrowed. "Do you hear me? If Ferius and his gang show up in this jungle, you step back and let me fight. Do you understand?"

A frog hopped between his legs, and a macaw fluttered above, its parti-colored tail nearly brushing his head. "Sort of how you fought Ferius in the gardens of Kingswall, ended up in his dungeon, and I had to come save you?"

She gave an enraged roar. "You know nothing! I only ended up in prison because I didn't want to kill them outside the palace. But I could have. I could have *easily* killed Ferius and his men."

Torin blew out his breath and slapped a bug that landed on his leg. "So far, Bailey old beast, two people have drawn Ferius's blood. I scarred his cheek and back, and Koyee wounded his leg.

You, meanwhile . . ." He tapped his cheek, feigning deep thought. "Well, I suppose you annoyed him a few times, but then again, you annoy most people you meet. And please keep your voice down. We don't know that Sailith isn't tracking us through this jungle, and when you shout, you—"

She shouted again. She shouted so loudly a hundred birds fled from the trees. Tossing down her sword, she leaped, slammed into him, and knocked him down. She began to wrestle him, struggling to pin his arms down.

"You apologize!" She snapped her teeth at him, narrowly missing his nose. "Apologize now or I'll make you wish you only had a wounded cheek, back, and leg."

"Bailey, get off!" He tried to shove her off, but she wouldn't budge. "You can't keep doing this when—"

Something whistled above.

A shaft flew over them—an instant blur.

An arrow slammed into a tree trunk a foot away.

Bailey and Torin froze. They both looked up, seeing nothing but the brush.

As slow as dripping honey, Bailey—still lying atop Torin—reached toward her discarded sword.

Another arrow whooshed and slammed into the ground between her fingers.

Laughter rose between the trees, and a voice called out, "Silly children! You make more noise than boars in heat. And you are the heroes who are to save the world?"

The brush parted. A woman emerged and came to stand before them. She wore tiger pelts and a breastplate. A mane of red curls cascaded across her shoulders, and tattoos of jungle beasts coiled up her arms like sleeves. Her eyes were green, her lips mocking, and she held a bow, its nocked arrow pointing at them. A spear hung across her back, and a sword hung from her side.

Behind her growled a tiger, its leash running from its collar to the woman's belt.

"Who are you?" Torin asked. Still lying under Bailey, he reached for his sword.

"She's a dead woman, that's who!" Bailey said, glaring up at the woman. "Are you going to shoot us? Because you have time to shoot one of us. Before you can nock another arrow, the other will run you through."

The woman laughed again. "Arrows are for battle, but this . . . this here is not a battle. This is entertainment. I heard you two boasting of your prowess for miles."

"Who are you?" Torin repeated, his voice lower, his eyes narrowed. He probably would have felt more dangerous with Bailey off him and a sword in his hand, but he made do with what he had.

The woman shot her arrow into a tree, slung her bow across her back, and drew her sword—a wide scimitar engraved with Nayan runes. With her other hand, she attached her tiger's chain to a branch.

She stroked the animal. "Here is Durga, King of Tigers, the greatest of the Nayan beasts. And I am Ishel Who Cuts Bones with Iron, Princess of Naya, and we share a mutual friend. Ferius sent me to find you. He thinks highly of you, but I see only weaklings. Stand up, children, and dance with me."

Bailey leaped up, grabbed her sword, and lunged at the jungle warrior before Torin could take another breath.

Longsword crashed against scimitar, and the leashed tiger growled.

Torin jumped to his feet, reached for his sword, and found that his belt had moved around during his wrestle with Bailey. Cursing, he reached behind his back, found the hilt, and drew his blade.

The two women were dueling—Bailey screaming, Ishel only smirking. When Torin jumped into the fray, hoping to skewer Ishel while she fought, the jungle warrior raised her spear with her free hand. Still dueling Bailey and not even sparing him a glance, she drove the spear Torin's way.

With a grunt, Torin tried to parry. He knocked the spear aside, but its head still lashed his arm, tearing through his tunic and nicking his flesh. He tried to swing his sword again, but again the spear thrust, forcing him back, its range longer than his blade. As Ishel drove the weapon toward him with one hand, she kept her eyes on Bailey, dueling the young woman. Their two swords clanged and sparked.

"Torin, get out of the way!" Bailey shouted as she fought, swinging her sword with both hands, trying to find an opening. "I'm better at fighting than you."

"Not everything is a competition!" he shouted back, then lunged sideways as the spear thrust. It sliced a line across his shoulder.

He pulled back out of the spear's range, abandoning hope of reaching past it. Instead he ran around a cottonwood, hoping to attack Ishel's other side. Yet when he skirted the tree, he found Durga growling at him; the tiger stood leashed to the bole, protecting his mistress.

"Torin, stop playing with that cat!" Bailey shouted.

He groaned and ran back to Ishel's left side, only to find the spear thrusting at him again. When Bailey yelped, he looked up to see blood on her thigh; Ishel's scimitar had sliced off some skin, but Bailey still fought, screaming with rage.

"Scream for me, children!" Ishel said and laughed. "This is more fun that I thought. Ferius was so worried about you, but you're only little pups."

Torin stepped back, reached down, and grabbed Ishel's arrow from the ground—the arrow she had shot between Bailey's fingers.

"I might not be a great warrior like Bailey," he said. "But unlike you, Ishel, I'm willing to fight dirty."

He tossed the arrow toward her.

Ishel's eyes flicked his way.

She raised her spear, diverting the arrow away from her neck. The projectile changed course and flew upward, grazing Ishel's cheek and spurting blood.

With a howl, Bailey slammed the scimitar aside and thrust her longsword. Ishel leaped back, avoiding a wound to her chest, but the blade still sliced her arm.

Blood sprayed and Ishel gasped, eyes widening.

Torin slammed her spear aside and thrust his sword.

Ishel jumped away.

With a single, fluid moment, the jungle princess jumped onto her tiger's back and tugged its chain free. The beast burst into a run.

Bailey and Torin began to run in pursuit.

"Come back here!" Bailey shouted. "Coward! Come face us!"

Vines tangled around them. Branches slapped them. Grass rose around their feet. They ran, following specks of blood. They hurdled over fallen logs, mossy boulders, and brambles. Parrots fled before them, squawking madly.

Torin's side was aching when they reached a wall of trees, shoulder-high grass, and vines that grew along boulders. He paused, panting and holding his side. His wounds dripped. Mist floated and he heard crashing water somewhere nearby.

"She's gone, Bailey." Sweat dripped into his eyes. "We can't expect to catch a tiger in its natural habitat."

She ignored him, attempting to scale the wall of stone and brush, only to fall back down. "Push me up! I'm going to catch her and finish the job."

Torin winced. One wound on his arm and another on his shoulder blazed and dripped. Bailey too had suffered a cut along her hip; her leggings were torn, revealing blood. And yet she ignored the wound, grabbed a vine, and tried to keep climbing.

"We have to find her, Torin. We have to. She'll return with reinforcements. Now push me up!"

"Wait, wait!" He reached across his back for his rope and grapple. "I knew this would come in handy. Let me—"

"No grapple!" Bailey shouted. "Put that down and push me."

Grimacing, Torin shoved Bailey up the wall of boulders and brush. Once on top, she reached down, grabbed his wrist, and helped him climb. They emerged onto a shelf of stone, the highest point of the escarpment. Cliffs dropped down beneath their feet, and more cliffs rose in the west, framing a verdant valley. The canopy rustled below them, too thick to see through, breaking only for a rocky stream. Nearby, a waterfall crashed down the escarpment into the valley, spraying mist.

Far in the west, past mist and green haze, treed hills rose into blue clouds. Here the escarpment finally seemed to end, leading to highlands that rolled into the horizon. Through sheets of distant rain, Torin could make out faded structures of gray and green—ancient towers melted by years of water and wind. When sunbeams broke through the clouds, falling upon the ruins, they blazed against a piece of metal on a tower's crest like a jewel in a crown of stone.

"The temple of Til Natay." He pointed. "We're almost there. It can't be more than ten miles away."

She looked around, chest rising and falling, sweat dripping down her brow. "Where's Ishel? I can't see her." Her hand trembled around her hilt. "It's her we must find."

Torin looked around. The rainforest stretched for many miles in each direction. "She's gone. We won't find her in this forest. We might meet her again before the end, but for now we must bandage our wounds. I don't want to bleed to death before we complete our quest."

Bailey began to object, insisting that they pursued Ishel at full speed, but when Torin showed her the wound on his shoulder, she winced and nodded. It was a red, ugly thing, already full of mud and leaves.

They trudged down into the valley, reached the rocky stream, and approached the waterfall. The crashing torrent roared and mist enveloped them, dampening their clothes and hair.

"Take off your shirt," Bailey commanded. "I have a needle and thread and I'm going to wash you, then stitch you up good."

"I don't need stitches."

She glowered. "You need stitches on your wound *and* your mouth. Shirt—off!"

He winced as he doffed his cloak and peeled off his shirt. The mist stung him like tiny arrows. "Now you, Bailey. You're wounded too. Leggings—off."

She raised her eyebrow. "Me? It's just a flesh wound."

He glowered. "Don't be funny. We're taking care of you too."

After placing down her pack and weapons, she kicked off her boots, wriggled out of her torn leggings, and pulled her tunic over her head. She stood before him in her underclothes. A wound ran along her hip, dripping blood down her thigh. They stepped into the pool, stood in the waterfall's mist, and splashed water into their wounds.

"Ow!" Torin flinched when Bailey began to stitch the cut on his shoulder. "Merciful Idar, be gentle."

"Be tough! I thought you're a warrior." She broke a branch off an overhanging mangrove and handed it to him. "Bite down on this if you must." She thrust the needle in again.

He stitched her wound next. She bit down on a branch too, and she growled and turned red, but she did not scream. When he was done, he splashed water onto the stitching, clearing off the last blood.

"There, only a scratch." He patted her hip. "All better. You're lucky I was there to save you."

Her eyes flashed, and she grabbed his arms painfully. "You saved me? It was my sword that cut Ishel! I'm the one who dueled her! You just danced around and tossed a stick at her."

He tried to pry her hands loose, but she held him tightly. "It was an arrow, and without it you'd probably be dead. I think we proved in battle that I'm the greater warrior."

Her face reddened and she looked ready to scream, but then her eyes became sly. "You're just goading me now."

He smiled. "It's so easy."

Bailey lowered her head, and a small smile curled her lips. "I know it is. I must be a right nightmare to travel with." She touched his damp hair, leaned forward, and kissed his cheek. "You played a small part in the battle, I'll admit it, and I'm glad you were there. Thank you."

She kept caressing his hair, and her body—clad in only her wet underclothes—pressed against him. She kissed his cheek again, then his ear, and then the corner of his mouth.

"Bailey, what—?" he began.

"Hush," she whispered, lips against his ear. She placed both hands on his cheeks. "Do you remember how we kissed back in the crater in the night? I've been thinking about that kiss since then. And I want to do it again."

He closed his eyes as they kissed, and her lips were warm, her tongue seeking his, her body pressing against him. He wrapped his arms around her, surrendering to her warmth, but then pulled back.

"Bailey, we can't do this." He looked away, still holding her. The pool swirled and the waterfall crashed down behind them. "I can't."

She pulled his face back toward her. "Because of Koyee?"

He nodded.

Bailey cupped his cheek in her hand and gazed at him earnestly. "Are you married to her?"

"No."

"Betrothed?"

"No."

"Did you sleep with her?"

Her comment surprised him. "I . . ."

"Tell me." Anger filled her eyes. "Tell me the truth."

He nodded. "Yes."

Tears dampened her eyes but she blinked them away. "Forget about her, Torin. She's wise and strong, and she's exotic and tempting to you. But I'm from your village. I've been your best friend since we were babies. I'm the one for you." She kissed his lips again. "Forget about Koyee and love me instead."

For a long moment, he stood with her under the waterfall, kissing her, holding her, and he thought about all their years together: playing in the fields as children, traveling into the night, fighting together upon ships, atop city walls, and here in the rainforest. All his life, she had been there by his side, his Bailey, his closest friend—Bailey of angry but loving eyes, of mocking lips, of courage and kindness, of strength and frailty.

"I love you, Bailey," he said, holding her close to him. "But I'm confused. This still feels wrong."

She reached into the water and began to unlace his breeches. "Let me make you feel right."

For a moment, he let her fingers work, but when he closed his eyes this time, he saw another woman. He saw Koyee. He saw a gentle woman of starlight and shadow, a woman of strong eyes, of a kind heart, a woman he had fought for, then fought with, a woman with whom he'd traveled through darkness into hope. In his mind, he saw Koyee's lavender eyes gazing at him with love . . . then the pain of betrayal.

He turned away.

"I can't, Bailey. I'm sorry. You are the closest person to me in the world. I love nobody more than you. You are my oldest, dearest friend, but I can't."

He saw the hurt in her eyes, a pain deeper and greater than her wound. "Because of Koyee."

He nodded. "I'm sorry. I'm—"

Her eyes flashed and he winced, expecting her to slap him, to knock him down, to scream and hurt him. But instead, tears filled Bailey's eyes, and she only pulled herself free from his embrace. She waded away, stepped out of the water, and began to dress.

"Bailey," he said softly, climbing out of the pool beside her. "Can we—"

"We keep moving." She wriggled into her leggings, pulled her tunic over her head, and clasped her sword to her belt. "We have to save the world for Koyee. So let's keep going."

They walked through the forest in awkward, painful silence.

CHAPTER FOURTEEN
INTO SHADOW

The dunes rolled golden into the distance. The azure sky spread above, embracing the simmering sun. The horizons undulated with heat and distant mountains rose, yellow and white, sentinels of stone. The land was a painting of ancient secrets, of a glory greater than found in poem or song, temple or palace, or all other crafts of men. The camels traveled across the sand, their saddlebags tasseled, their riders cloaked in white—tiny figures in an endless landscape of majesty, magic, and—

"Eww, it's licking me!" Linee said, whining as the camel twisted its head around to sniff her foot. "Face forward, you stinky animal. Forward! I hate this stupid desert."

Sitting on his own camel, Cam groaned. "Linee, please! I was trying to enjoy the beautiful landscape, and you had to ruin my mood."

She grimaced as the camel licked her toes. It took several shakes of her foot before the animal turned its head forward again and kept walking across the dunes. Cam sighed as he rode beside her, bouncing atop his own camel's hump. Ahead of them, upon his own dromedary, rode their guide—a scrawny boy lazily flicking a crop.

"How far are we from the ziggurat?" Linee called out to the child.

Cam scowled. "I told you, don't speak Ardish to anyone. We're still undercover."

The boy looked over his shoulder at them. His grin spread across his sun-bronzed face. "Ferisi Ziggurat!" He pointed ahead and spoke in his tongue; Cam only understood the word *serana*—close.

"He says it's nearby," Cam explained.

Linee pouted and crossed her arms. "He said that hours ago." The wind gusted, full of sand, and raised her tasseled shawl from her shoulders to slap against her face. She tugged it down and whimpered.

Cam held his canteen over his mouth. Only a few drops spilled out, blessed relief against his dry tongue. His lips were just as dry and cracked, and he licked them. He wore a white cloak he'd bought back in Kahtef, and it offered some protection from the sand and sun, but after a turn in the open desert, he missed the oasis city like a drowning man misses land.

Far north in Arden, his homeland, it would be winter now. Snow would be glittering upon the fields and roofs. If not for this war, he would be sitting in The Shadowed Firkin by a roaring fireplace, nursing a mug of ale, listening to Hem sing, speaking to Torin of old tales, and teasing Bailey just to see her get angry. Another gust of wind blew sand into his eyes, and Cam sighed and lowered his head, blinking the grains away.

But Hem is dead now, he thought. *And Ferius rules in Arden. And maybe Torin and Bailey are gone too. That home is forever gone.*

"Camlin, there's drool on my shoe!" Linee said, wrinkling her nose and kicking, spraying camel cud into the sand.

Cam blinked and looked at her, the memories of home fading in the sunlight. She looked at him, face twisted in misery, but then she grinned, her teeth very white in her golden face, and laughed. The sun gleamed upon her bracelet and necklace of bronze and topaz; she had bought the jewels back in the city, which now lay miles behind. And now a new memory filled Cam—a memory of last turn, making love to Linee under the blankets in a stifling tavern room, their naked bodies slick with sweat, moving together, their lips locked in a kiss. As she smiled at him now from her camel, she was beautiful—her golden hair streaming, her smile bright, her green eyes full of love for him.

Maybe she is my new strength, Cam thought. *If my old home is gone, maybe she is the new light in my life.*

He was about to speak these thoughts when their guide stood upon his saddle, pointed ahead, and called out, "Ziggurat! Ziggurat. *Look.*"

Cam turned his head northward. Their three camels crested a dune, the wind died, and he saw it there in a sandy valley.

"The Ziggurat of Ferisi," Cam whispered.

Based on the painting back in the tavern, he had imagined a building the size of a manor, maybe even a small palace. But here loomed a structure to rival the greatest pagodas he'd seen in Eloria—it was a monument that could house a nation. It still lay several miles away, a triangular edifice with staircases rising along its facades. The top ended with a plateau, and upon it rose a square structure like a barracks, and a dark gateway loomed upon its southern wall.

"That was where the clockwork man stood," Cam said. "In the painting. He stood in that doorway at the top of the stairs."

From this distance, he could see no mechanical figure, no glint of metal—only the tan bricks, crumbling and ancient. They rode their camels down the dune and into the valley, leaving a trail of footprints, heading toward the monument.

As they rode, Cam pulled out a dusty leather book from his pouch. After seeing the painting back in the tavern, he had scoured the city's shops for information, finally finding this book in a dusty hovel that sold scrolls, codices, crystals, amulets, and other items of power. Books, the old shopkeeper had claimed, held the most power of all, more than potions and hexes, for they held knowledge.

Cam dusted off the book and squinted down at the small letters. Half the pages were full of Eseerian hieroglyphs, which

Cam couldn't read; the runes were written from right to left, shaped as animals and plants. The book's other half, however, was written in High Riyonan, an ancient language that was the root of Ardish, Verilish, Magerian, and the other tongues north of the Sern River—the ancient realm of Riyona, a northern empire that had fallen a thousand years ago. Cam could read a little Riyonan— rare for a shepherd's boy, but he'd always loved the books of adventure found in Bailey's house. Riyonan was older than Ardish, and many of the words were different, but the alphabet was the same, and Cam could understand at least half of these words.

"It says here . . . " He brought the book closer to his eyes and blew off dust. "The ziggurat was built over four thousand years ago by Kah— by Khar— Kaer . . ."

Linee rolled her eyes. "Kaeorin the Conqueror, Son of Asharpel, Blessed King of Ancient Eseer."

He gave her a sidelong glance. "When did you sneak a peek at this book?"

She groaned. "I do not sneak peeks, Camlin Shepherd. I'm an educated woman. I went to school. Granted, I spent most of my time there drawing birds and butterflies in my books, but I picked up some things. Don't bother giving yourself a headache reading that tattered old thing. All educated, highborn ladies like myself know of Kaeorin the Conqueror, Son of Asharpel, Blessed King of Ancient Eseer. He's a legend."

He slammed the book shut. "Well I've never heard of him."

"You'd never heard of a peacock until we saw one in the city. I might be silly, but unlike you, I did receive a proper education. My teachers told me the tale. Kaeorin built the ziggurat for his wife, the beautiful Queen Ferisi, to entomb her when she died. He died too just after completing the monument. They buried them together." She clasped her hands together. "It's such a beautiful, romantic story."

"Two lovers who died and were buried? That's romantic?"

She nodded. "Yes! You and I will be buried together someday in a magnificent mausoleum too."

Cam rolled his eyes. "You're making this up. If you'd heard the story before, you'd have known what a ziggurat is. You wouldn't have spent your time in the city chasing zigzagging rodents."

"Well . . ." She looked down at her lap. "Maybe I forgot that part of the story until you reminded me. But I'm almost certain my teachers never called it a ziggurat. They probably called it a beautiful palace."

"And they probably called camels 'horses,' sand 'gardens,' and scorpions 'butterflies,' knowing that's the only way you'd understand."

She nodded. "They probably did. Oh, Camlin, do you think we'll meet the beautiful Queen Ferisi and her noble, brave husband Kaeorin the Conqueror, Son of Asharpel, Blessed King of Ancient Eseer? Do you think they're still here?"

"If they are, they're nothing but dust."

As they kept riding through the desert, they passed by ruins protruding from the sand. A woman's face carved in sandstone rose to their left, larger than a carrack and staring skyward. A stone hand, large enough to hold a whale, rose not far beyond it, the sand rising halfway up its palm. As they kept riding, they passed the tip of an obelisk, the capitals of buried columns, and the sandstone head of a cat, large as a hill. This place had once been a great city, Cam realized, full of temples and palaces and soaring statues. He wondered why the ziggurat still stood while the other artifacts were buried, then realized: most of the ziggurat *was* buried, and the massive structure ahead—larger than any palace he'd seen—was simply its peak.

Finally they crossed the valley and reached the ziggurat's steps. Sand fluttered around them. Upon his camel, Cam tilted back his head and gazed up the staircase. It rose a thousand steps or more, crawling up the windowless facade like a spine, leading to the archway at the ziggurat's crest.

"Amaran," whispered their guide and clutched his amulet. It was shaped as a man with the head of a dragonfly—the god Amaran the Guardian, a deity of the desert. The guide spoke some more in his tongue, and Cam didn't need to understand Eseerian to know the child was scared, that he spoke of old curses.

"We climb from here," Cam said. "*Kei! Kei!*"

At the command, his camel knelt and Cam dismounted. Linee climbed off her own camel, slipping and falling onto her backside in the sand. Cam helped her up, then loosened his sword in its scabbard. The child was still muttering, sweat on his brow. Cam didn't believe in curses or monsters, but the guide's behavior unnerved him.

He pointed up the stairs. "We climb. Come with us." He took a step onto the stairway and gestured for the guide to follow, but the boy only shook his head, speaking feverishly in his tongue.

"The poor boy is terrified," Linee said. "Do you think there are monsters here? Or ghosts? What's he saying?"

Cam shrugged. "You saw the city of Kahtef. Every road has five stalls selling charms and potions. Superstition fills the desert. But you and I are Ardish folk. We believe in the evil of men, not spirits or magic."

He tried not to think of the dark magic of Mageria shattering the walls of Yintao, the fiery magic that had engulfed Ferius in flame, or the dragons he'd seen. Linee didn't need to think about that now either, or soon she'd be trembling and fleeing.

He reached into his pocket, fished out three coins, and handed them to their guide. "Come with us." He pointed up the stairs. "We could use help."

Hand shaking, the boy reached out to take the coins. Before he could grab them, a metallic shriek cascaded down the ziggurat.

Cam winced. It sounded like rusted sheets of metal scraping together, rising higher and higher until the sound shattered and vanished. He spun back toward the stairway, stared upward, and saw a shimmer in the doorway like dulled armor. Whoever or whatever stood there quickly vanished.

"Clockwork men . . ." Line whispered. "Like in the painting."

"*Het, het!*" rose their guide's voice. When Cam spun around, he saw the child back on his camel. The animal burst into a gallop. Its two friends, the camels Linee and Cam had ridden here, ran with it.

"Come back!" Linee shouted, waving, and turned toward Cam. "He's escaping with our rides!"

Cam bit his lip, placed a palm over his eyes, and stared into the desert. The camels were racing in a cloud of dust; Linee and he would never catch up. The city of Kahtef lay beyond the horizon.

"Looks like we walk back." He sighed. "The same damn thing happened in Leen. Why do our guides always abandon us?"

"They abandon *you*, Camlin." Linee glared at him. "I'm fun and beautiful. You're always scowling, and you're always leading us to these scary places, so of course they run. *I* wanted to find a cute little rodent, but you had to choose this ziggurat. Well, fine! Let's find your stupid clock hand and go home."

Cam reached into his pack and pulled out his tunic of scales, the armor the Chanku Pack had given him. It unrolled, chinking like a bag of coins, and Cam pulled it over his head.

"Linee, armor on!"

She shook her head. "Armor is ugly."

"So are the wounds clockwork men can give you. Armor!"

She groaned but she reached into her pack, pulled out her own shirt of scales, and donned the clanking garment. Cam drew his sword and Linee drew her dagger. They began to climb the stairway, moving up the ziggurat's outer plain.

The stairway was wide enough for a dozen men to walk abreast, and the steps were carved for taller folk than them. After a hundred steps, Cam was sweating and wheezing, and he had barely climbed a tenth of the way up.

At his side, Linee looked just as weary. "Camlin, can I have a piggyback ride?"

He glowered. "No!"

She pouted. "But I'm tired."

"Good, maybe you'll be too tired for sulking soon. Keep climbing."

After what seemed like hours, soaked in sweat and dizzy with weariness, they finally reached the top. Panting, Linee had to crawl the last few steps. The desert rolled around them into the horizons. Before them loomed the doorway into the ziggurat, a square of stone and shadow tall enough for a ship to sail through. A scorpion engraving glared down from the keystone. Cold wind blew from within, scented of mold and death. When Cam peered into the shadows, sword raised, he no longer saw movement, and he no longer heard that metallic shriek.

"Is the monster still there?" Linee whispered, rising to stand beside him, dagger shaking in her hand.

"I told you. There's no such thing as monsters. Now let's—"

A shriek slammed into his eardrums.

Light flashed.

Metal burst out from the gateway.

Cam shouted and leaped sideways. Linee shrieked and jumped the other way.

A creature of metal, rope, and spinning blades lunged onto the stairway. Orange eyes blazed. Cam raised his sword. A spinning disk slammed into the blade, chipping it. Circular saws thrust his way, and he ducked; one spun over his head. Rust showered. Cam leaped off the stairway, landing on the ziggurat's brick facade, and clung to the rough stone.

With clanks and screeches, the metallic contraption retreated back into the doorway like a snake into its burrow, leaving a shower of dust.

"Linee! Are you hurt?"

She crouched across the other side of the stairway, similarly clinging to the sloping facade. She was pale and shivering but seemed unhurt. Cam guessed that the ziggurat walls had once been smooth, sending people sliding down to the desert, but time had left pockmarks and cracks for purchase.

"A monster," Linee whispered, clinging on.

Cam shook his head. "A machine. Circular blades on ropes. A booby trap."

"But I saw eyes!" Linee said from across the staircase.

He nodded. "A doll has eyes. A trap can too."

He rifled through his pocket, found a bread roll, and tossed it onto the stairs.

The booby trap burst out again, saws spinning, eyes of glass reflecting the sun, old chains and ropes creaking. Cam stared, mumbling, memorizing. The contraption retreated back into the doorway.

Cam tightened his grip on his chipped sword. He reached into his collar, fished out his half-sun amulet—symbol of Idar—and kissed it for luck. He nodded, gulped, and began climbing back onto the staircase.

"Duck, then leap right, then back . . ." he muttered.

Linee gasped. "Camlin, stop—"

Before she could complete her sentence, the booby trap burst out from the doorway again.

Cam ducked beneath a spinning blade. He jumped to the right, closer to the archway, dodging another blade. He swung down his sword.

The blade sliced through a rope.

Cam leaped back.

The contraption screamed. A circular saw tore free and crashed down the stairs, showering sparks. A second blade broke loose and shot out, and Cam ducked; it flew over his head. Resisting the urge to leap back, Cam sprang forward, swung his sword again, and sliced through two more ropes.

Metal pieces tore free and scattered down the stairway. The booby trap collapsed. Blades clattered down. With a shower of rust, silence fell. The broken pieces rolled away.

Cam coughed and waved to scatter dust. A flying piece had scraped his side, and he winced to see blood. He struggled back onto the stairway. Linee joined him, coughing too. One of the trap's eyes—a sphere of murky glass—lay at their feet. Linee kicked it away.

"One monster slain," Cam said. "Do you see a clock hand among this mess?"

She placed her hands on her hips and glared at him. "I see a stupid, woolheaded shepherd's boy who almost got himself killed!" She slapped his chest. "How dare you attack spinning blades like that? You could have died."

He managed a shaky smile. "I'm still alive. And you sound like Bailey."

She stared, eyes flashing, but then her expression softened and she embraced him. "Just be more careful, you silly thing. Don't leave me alone in this desert." She kissed his cheek, then spat. "You taste of rust and sand."

In their right hands, they raised their blades. Their left hands clasped together. Stepping over the debris, they walked through the doorway and into the darkness.

CHAPTER FIFTEEN
THE WEAVEWORMS

They climbed the mountain, heading toward the worms—a scarred Qaelish woman in armor, a katana and shield in her hands; a diminutive assassin in black silk, daggers hanging from her belt; and a silent giant with a chest like a boulder and fists the size of heads. Above them, bulging over the rest of the island, loomed a city of iron spikes, strands of silk, and countless cocoons the size of men.

"There are monsters up there," Nitomi whispered, tiptoeing up the mountainside. The dojai assassin clutched a dagger in each hand; the blades were shaking. "Oh, Koyee, there are monsters there, I know it. Can we please go back? I want to go away. I don't want to face monsters. Maybe we can find a gear elsewhere, maybe in a gear store. Do you think they have gear stores? I saw a store once that only sold dollhouses. You wouldn't think an entire store would only sell dollhouses, but I saw it once in the south, and I wanted to buy one, I really did, but my mother said I'm too old, and then I wanted to buy a pet spider but—"

"Hush!" Koyee said. "Please."

Nitomi slapped her palm against her mouth, nearly stabbing herself with her dagger, and nodded. They kept climbing, silent but for the rustle of their clothes in the wind.

The village of the Montai folk was now a distant patch of light below. As they kept climbing the mountain, Koyee stared upward. Spikes of metal covered the mountaintop, curling and twisting; they reminded Koyee of the brambles in the dusk. Some coiled only several feet tall, and others pierced the sky, high as

towers, twisting and curling. Koyee wondered if these had been
the foundations of an ancient city, its walls fallen ages ago.
Countless strands of silk hung between the spikes like cobwebs,
and among them hung cocoons large enough to seal men. With
every gust of wind, the silky strands fluttered and the cocoons
swayed like bodies hanging from gallows.

Soon the companions were walking among the metal spikes
and hanging strands. Silk brushed against them, and Nitomi
squeaked and made to slice a strand with her dagger. Koyee
pushed the woman's blade down.

"Sheathe your dagger," she whispered. "Do not cut or
scratch anything here." She looked around her and smiled softly.
"This is a nursery."

When she raised her lantern, Koyee could see forms curled
up within the cocoons. Larvae hid inside, each as big as her. She
could see nothing more than their vague outlines through the silk.
When she brought her lantern close to one cocoon, the larva
inside squirmed as if blinded by the light. The companions kept
walking, navigating between the metal spikes that held the silk,
passing thousands of the hanging cocoons.

"If those are the babies," Nitomi whispered, "then . . . oh by
the flame, how large are the adults?"

Koyee hefted her shield and pointed ahead. "See for
yourself."

They crested a slope, parted curtains of silk, and beheld the
hive of the weaveworms.

Nitomi shuddered and covered her mouth, and even
towering Qato, a man who could remain silent for turns on end,
grunted. Koyee stared in wonder, torn between disgust and
marvel.

A ring of steel spikes rose ahead, as wide as an arena, and
upon each spike perched a weaveworm mother. Their bodies were
white and segmented, as large as whales, and their black eyes

spun, shrewd and bright. Clutching their perches, they undulated and pulsed, producing offspring in an endless stream. The babes—wet, gray, and wriggling—fell onto the ground and promptly crawled away, leaving room for their siblings to emerge. Koyee watched one newborn larva find a metal spike of its own, climb, and begin to weave a cocoon.

Within this birthing ring bubbled a pool of pale liquid. It smelled of sulfur and salt. Adult weaveworms—these ones winged and thinner than the mothers—flew above, carrying cocoons and dropping them into the boiling pool. As each cocoon splashed down, shrieks rose as the larva burned within. The winged adults hovered above, waiting as the cocoons cooked like dumplings. Once the larvae inside had died, the flying weaveworms fished out the boiled bundles and carried them away.

"They're cooking their babies!" Nitomi whispered, standing among the strands of silk.

"Hush!" Koyee said. "Look behind the pool."

Beyond clouds of steam, a great structure loomed over the pool of boiling cocoons. It rose as high as a palace, formed of salvaged scrap metal. Old shields, the hulls of boats, and suits of armor formed its base, held together with clumps of rope. Great spokes of metal turned on springs, moving strands of silk to and fro. Hammers rose and fell, wheels turned, and steam blasted as the machine operated. A belt moved along metal tracks, carrying boiled cocoons from the water into the machine. As each bundle entered the gauntlet, moving blades tore it apart. Hooks tugged on strands of cooked cocoons, spun them together, hammered and braided, and tugged the fabric onto spinning wheels. Up and up the structure the silk rose, track by track, wheel by wheel, until at its crest plates of red-hot steel—perhaps salvaged tabletops—clamped together, pressing the strands into sheets.

"It's a loom," Koyee whispered. "It's a great, mechanical loom the size of a palace."

Nitomi whimpered. "They're turning their babes into cloth."

At her side, the towering Qato lowered his head, and his voice was a mournful rumble. "Qato sad."

Clad in armor, Koyee touched their dojai outfits of black silk. "Where do you think silk comes from? The cocoons of weaveworm larvae . . . cooked by their own caretakers."

Nitomi shuddered.

Koyee stared back at the loom and narrowed her eyes. A gasp fled her lips and her innards tingled. Her eyes stung. She pointed.

"There," she whispered. "On the loom's crest. The gear."

At first she had not seen it. No larger than a wagon wheel, it nearly drowned among a thousand other moving pieces. But Koyee knew it was the right one; when she squinted, she could see the stars and moons engraved upon its teeth. She pulled out the page from her book and held it up. The illustrated gear and the gear in the loom matched.

She stuffed the page back into her pocket, passed through curtains of silk, and began walking toward the pool and the loom beyond.

"Koyee, where you going?" Nitomi demanded, whisking behind her and grabbing at her. "They'll eat you."

"Nonsense. They only eat . . ." She looked down at the poolside, saw human skeletons, and grimaced. "Never mind. It's too late anyway. They saw us."

Before her, along the ring of steel pillars, the weaveworm queens raised their heads. Their gleaming black eyes stared at her, and their abdomens kept contracting, birthing their spawn. Atop the pool, the flying weaveworms—the winged workers who boiled the cocoons—paused from their task, hovering and staring. As one, the animals—mothers and workers alike—opened their maws, revealing sharp teeth, and shrieked.

The sound rolled across the mountain. The metal pillars shook. The larvae, both the ones crawling away from their mothers and those already cocooned, whimpered and wriggled.

Nitomi squeaked. Qato grunted and drew his sword. Koyee raised her hands and called out, loud enough for all the weaveworms to hear.

"Weaveworms, hear me! I am Koyee Mai of Qaelin. I come in peace. I come offering friendship and trade."

The shrieks continued. The mountain itself seemed to shake. Only the great loom kept working away—clicking, turning, and weaving its silk, hundreds of feet tall and seeming as ancient as the mountain itself.

"You are a daughter of men!" rose the cry of a hundred worms; they spoke in one voice. "The children of man-flesh are forbidden to enter our realm. The bones of those who walked here lie around you. Your bones will join them."

Nitomi raised two daggers and snarled. "You'll have to fight us first, and I have dozens of daggers, and I trained in the Dojai School, and if you fight me, you'll die, weaveworms, so don't even think that you can win, because I—"

"Qato fight!" cried her towering friend and sliced the air with his sword.

"No!" Koyee shouted. "We will not fight."

The weaveworms flew closer, wings ruffling her hair. Strands of saliva quivered in their maws. Their stench assailed her, the smell of rotten fruit and old meat and wet earth. One eager weaveworm, a festering thing twice Koyee's size, lunged so close that it nearly hit her. Nitomi and Qato lashed their blades, but Koyee shoved them back, and the weapons missed the worm. The breath of the creature blasted her face, hot and fetid.

"Enough!" Koyee shouted. "Weaveworm—back! We are no humble villagers you can scare. We bear sharp blades and we're trained in war. Yet we come in peace. Close your mouths and open your ears. We come here to trade with you."

The weaveworm who hovered before her, wings beating, gave a horrible sound like gagging. It took Koyee a moment to realize it was laughing. A pattern of pale blue rings circled its body, and glowing bulbs of light tipped its wings. Its breath smelled like rotted flesh.

"You have nothing to trade with us," said the weaveworm. "We trade with the Montai folk, though we do not let them gaze upon us. We leave our silk upon their beaches, and we collect the scraps we find." It gestured at the loom behind it. "We have built a palace from the treasures washed ashore. The children of men are wasteful. They discard old metal, old pottery, old treasures they once loved. They litter and pollute and break. But we are weaveworms. We are weavers, loomers, fixers, collectors, builders, cleaners. We take the discarded bits of man-folk, and we shape them into beauty, into a tower of metal that pumps out glimmering silk like a spider pumps out gossamer. What have you that the sea cannot give us? What have you that we cannot find in the gutters of men? We care not for gold nor gems, for they are trifles to us, pretty things that have no use. A crude, ugly tool is worth more than a pretty, useless jewel. We care not for small, glittering things, but for rusted iron and scrap metal. Only for those would we sell our silk, and yet upon you, I see only a few old blades, barely worth more than a strand."

"I seek not silk!" Koyee called out, speaking both to the weaveworm fluttering before her and to its brethren which covered the mountain. "I seek metal too. I too am a builder—of less talent than weaveworms, but of no less passion. I seek a gear." She pointed at the towering loom. "I seek the gear from the crest of your loom."

The weaveworms stared at her for a moment in silence, and then they all emitted their sickening, bubbling laughter. Even the larvae seemed to gurgle in mockery, imitating their elders.

"You seek the Cabera Gear." They spoke as one, drool dripping, eyes shinning in amusement. "Others have come before you—travelers in days long gone. For thousands of years have children of men sought to steal our Cabera Gear, but it is precious to us. It is the centerpiece of our loom, the treasure of our tower. There is nothing you can trade for it. Now leave or fight us, but bore us no longer with your words."

Koyee reached into her pockets, pulled out coins, and held them out. "I have treasure. Here are coins from the empress of Ilar. They are worth more than—"

"We have spoken!" said the weaveworms. "The children of men never listen to words. For long years we have warned them. We have spoken of their folly, of their wastefulness, of the poison of their flotsam and jetsam. We have cleaned the seas to build our home, and still they pollute, still they do not hear. We care not for coins. We care for flesh."

They lunged toward her, mouths open wide, spraying saliva. Their wings beat. At Koyee's side, Nitomi screamed and tossed a dagger. The blade slammed into a weaveworm, and the creature bucked and squealed. Qato swung his blade, slicing into a wing. Teeth drove down toward Koyee, and she held out her shield, blocking the attack.

"Wait!" she cried. "Wait, weaveworms, and listen!"

They hissed around her, forming a ring of flesh and tooth, some bleeding, most laughing, and their tongues licked their teeth. "We have no use for words."

"I will not use words!" she said . . . and sheathed her sword. Instead she drew her flute—the old silver instrument she had played in The Green Geode as a yezyana. "As payment, I will offer you no coins . . . but music."

She brought the flute to her lips, and Koyee played her song.

The notes flowed, the old song called "Sailing Alone," the same song Little Maniko had taught her on the streets of Pahmey long ago. At first her song was soft, shaky, hesitant; she had not played in many turns and fear filled her. But as the notes rose, quivering like beads of light upon rain, the weaveworms ceased their onslaught and hovered, insects caught in moonbeams, listening. Her dojai companions paused too, tilted their heads, and lowered their blades.

Koyee closed her eyes, found her inner light, and her song grew in strength. With her eyes closed, she stood barefooted in Bluefeather Corner again, clad in only tattered fur, an orphan girl of sixteen years, so hungry and cold, so afraid, playing her song for coins. She stood upon the stage in The Green Geode again, a yezyana in a dress of black silk, a roof over her head and food in her belly but no less fear in her heart. She had played this song then, and she played it now, and it was not just the song Maniko had taught her, not just the song of a busker or a yezyana. Here it became the song of her life, the song of a girl grown by the dusk, a youth who sailed alone upon the Inaro, and a woman who fought and bled for her empire. It was the song of Shenlai, the last dragon of Qaelin whom she had guided into death. It was perhaps the song of all the night, of all souls lost, of all souls sailing alone upon a river, far from home. It was a song of darkness and of starlight.

When she opened her eyes, she saw that the hive had fallen still and silent.

"Oh, Koyee," Nitomi whispered, tears in her eyes. "It's beautiful."

The weaveworms regarded her. The mothers clung to their perches, no longer birthing their babes, and the workers had landed upon the rim of the bubbling pool. They stared at Koyee, awe in their eyes.

"I will play you many songs," Koyee said. "I will play you the songs of the night and of the day beyond. I will play you songs of loneliness and hope, of loss and joy. I will play you songs of moonlight on water, towers that rise glowing into the sky, of war and peace, of fear and hope, of distant cities of wonder and villages of solace. This will be my payment to you—the gift of song and the gift of my heart."

The weaveworms blinked and remained silent, as if too overcome with emotion to speak. Koyee smiled softly, and a deep sadness and pride welled within her, for she had sung to them the song of her soul, and she had moved them.

Finally their chief, the weaveworm with the blue rings upon its back, whispered in a hoarse, awed voice.

"It's beautiful."

Koyee bowed her head. "Thank you. I did not compose this music, but I have made it my own, and—"

The weaveworm shook its head and blasted out breath. "Not your music! Stupid thing. Never music! We care not for such rackets of coarse sound."

Koyee gasped and took a step back. She narrowed her eyes. "Coarse sound? But . . . I thought the music awed you, that—"

"Stupid daughter of men!" The weaveworm thrust its head near hers. Its eyes were the size of her fists, black and bulging and blinking. Steam rose from its mouth, and it licked its chops, dripping saliva. "The silver . . . the silver of your flute! The most precious, forbidden of metals . . . sweet silver . . ."

Koyee pulled the flute back, and the weaveworms hissed and mewled. "My flute is not for sale! I carried this flute through war, through poverty, through—"

"Sell it to us!" the weaveworms hissed, and though anger twisted their voices, she heard pleading there too, a longing like the cry of a starving man who'd forgotten the taste of food. "Forever the Montai mock us, forging their silverwork, and never do they sell us the precious metal like moonlight. Crude iron and cold copper and ugly tin they give us, scraps rusty and coarse, but we long for the silver, the sweetest of metals, the material of moonlight."

Koyee took a step farther away and hid her flute behind her back, much to the chagrin of the weaveworms who howled and beat their wings. "If I give you this flute, will you give me the gear?"

They squealed and squirmed. "She tempts us! She knows our craving. We will give you silk, daughter of men, as much silk as you desire, and we will give you our young, and we will give you precious wings, bolts of iron, and shards of steel, and we will give you our own song, our own stories, the very blood from our hearts. We will give you all this for a flute of silver."

She shook her head. "I don't want those. I want the Cabera Gear upon your loom."

They screamed. The pool bubbled with more fervor, and the larvae squirmed within their cocoons. "The loom is our life! The gear is its heart. Only with this heart can we weave our silk. We will give you anything, daughter of men, anything but that. Give us your silver! Give us the precious metal of moonlight."

She shook her head again. "No. I will not give you this flute."

"Then we will take it by force!" They bared their teeth and snarled.

Koyee shouted out, waving her shield before her. "Take this flute by force and you will have a shard of silver! But I can bring you more. I can bring you a silver heart for your loom. A great gear of silver I will bring you, the same size as your old Cabera Gear of plain iron. It will be a glimmering, precious thing, a pure metal of moonlight for your silk."

The weaveworms froze. They breathed raggedly. Their eyes dampened.

"A gear of silver . . . a silver heart . . ." Their chief tossed back its head and cried out to the starlight. "We . . . we have no words for such a blessing. We have no prayer for such holiness." Tears streamed from the worm's eyes. "Bring us a gear of silver, and we will not only give you this old gear of iron, but we will name you our goddess. Forever will Koyee Mai of Qaelin be remembered as a glorious deity of the weaveworms."

She couldn't help but smile. "I don't care about that. I just want to make a swap and be on my way. I will return with a silver gear, lord of weaveworms. I promise this to you."

As they walked downhill, leaving the hive of weaveworms and heading back toward the village, Koyee sighed, for those memories still pounded through her—memories of loss, hunger, fear—and though she was older and stronger now, a grown woman who had sailed through fire and rain, her song always broke a new part of her, revealing a wound of light that perhaps could never fully heal.

I lived in hunger, she thought. *I slept in alleyways, afraid, alone, hurt. I was an urchin, a busker, a soldier, and like I still carry the scars on my face and arm, I carry those scars inside me. Songs are the scars of the heart.*

Yet not all was dark and hopeless, and not all hurt, for in her memories she also saw a glowing lantern, a warmth in the cold. She saw Torin. She saw a man she had met in war, a man she loved, a man who guided her even here, so far from home. *You are a song inside me too, Torin, but you are not a song of sailing alone. In the music your memory plays inside me, we sail together.* Her smile tasted of tears.

"And did you see all the little ones in their cocoons?" Nitomi was prattling on as they walked. "At first I thought they're ugly, but they're kind of cute, in a slimy sort of way at least. Well, not cute like a wolf pup or a baby bird, maybe sort of like a wet baby fish. Do fish have babies? I've never seen a baby fish. They must have little ones, I'm sure, but aren't those just minnows? Do you think you can catch really big fish or even whales with weaveworms? Are there any fishing rods big enough? Qato, you used to go fishing." She tugged on the giant's arm. "What do you think? You'd need a massive hook, maybe one of those spikes they perch on, and . . ."

Koyee stopped listening, and her smile grew wider. In the cold of night and rain of memories, it was good to have friends.

"Hush, Nitomi. We're almost at the village. It's time to hire a silversmith."

CHAPTER SIXTEEN
IMPURE

Ferius walked through the ruins of Yintao toward his brother's grave.

The city was silent around him. He had invaded this place, perhaps the greatest city of the night, with shouting soldiers, booming drums, roaring beasts, and the screams of the dying. The hiss of dust, the thud of banners, and the caws of crows; it was the only song remaining.

Where once a million souls had lived, now only ghosts and shadows remained. Shattered blades, cloven shields, and burnt bones lay across the road's cobblestones. Homes, shops, and temples crumbled on the road sides, crushed by catapults, dark magic, and the flames of war. A burnt scrap of banner tore free from the roof of a fallen pagoda, scuttled along the street like a demon, and wrapped around Ferius's legs. It showed the moonstar upon its silk, sigil of the fallen empire. Ferius tore it free and watched it fly on. The banner fluttered over a cracked cannon, raced along blood-stained bricks, and finally draped across a skeleton.

An Elorian skeleton, Ferius thought, staring at it. The eye sockets were twice the usual size—eyes for seeing in the dark. The eyes he lacked. The eyes they had tormented him for.

Suddenly Ferius no longer stood in Yintao, the ruins of the capital. Once more he stood in Oshy, a humble village of the night, his home by the glow of dusk.

He was in a round clay hut, a mere child of ten years, his small, weak eyes blinking in the shadows, his dark hair oily, a creature in a land of fair, large-eyed Elorians with pale skin and hair like white silk.

"Meet your little brother," Mother said, smiling weakly in her bed and holding out the babe. "Meet little Okado."

Ferius stared at the small, pale creature. His mother had married an Elorian man only a year ago, a decade after Ferius's father—a Timandrian from across the dusk—had returned to the lands of light.

Ferius had inherited his father's small, dark eyes, but this babe had large blue eyes. Ferius had dark hair; this babe had milky white strands. A pure-blooded child.

A child to replace me, Ferius thought, trembling. *Mother replaced her husband only last winter . . . and already she replaces me too.*

"Say hello to him!" Mother said, holding out the babe. "Would you like to hold him? Say hello to your brother."

Ferius balled his fists at his sides. The walls of their hut seemed to close in around him. The babe whimpered and his eyes closed.

"My *half*-brother," Ferius said, speaking through clenched teeth. "A son you will not be ashamed of." His eyes stung with tears. "A pure child."

Mother's eyes softened. "I will always love you, Ferius. You are pure to me. You are—"

Ferius reached out and snatched the babe from her arms. "I am a freak!" His voice echoed in the hut, and his tears streamed. "That's what the other children call me. They say I'm a monster. They say you bedded a demon." Baby Okado woke and screamed in his grip. "Don't lie to me. You want to replace me!"

He turned, kicked the door open, and ran outside, still holding the babe.

"Ferius!" his mother cried behind him. The baby screamed. Okado ran.

He raced through the village square. A few lanterns rose upon poles, casting enough light for large Elorian eyes, but Ferius stumbled and nearly fell. He righted himself and kept racing, the baby screaming in his arms.

"She thinks you're better than me," Ferius said to it, grinding his teeth, digging his fingers into the creature. Its skin was red now, no longer pure white Elorian skin, and its large eyes narrowed into ugly slits. "She thinks you can replace me. I won't let you. I won't . . ."

Tears flowed over his voice. He ran on. He heard his mother crying behind him; she was chasing him. Villagers gasped around him, and one man—that fool Finian, the bead-maker who sometimes brought fish soup to their hut—tried to grab him. Ferius barreled past him, shoving the old man onto the cobblestones. He kept running until he reached the river.

He raced onto the boardwalk. The Inaro gushed before him, a flowing torrent, a mile wide and silver in the moonlight. To the west blazed the dusk, the orange light that forever burned upon their horizon, leading to Timandra, the realm of demons, the realm whence Ferius's father had emerged. To the east spread the black lands of endless night; the water would take the babe there.

Legs trembling, Ferius stepped forward and held his baby brother over the river.

"Ferius!" rose his mother's hoarse cry behind him.

"Stand back!" he shouted. "Stand back or I drop him."

Villagers were gathering on the boardwalk behind him, daring not approach, staring with those large eyes he lacked, those large eyes that made them feel superior. The babe screamed in his arms.

"I'll toss you into the water, Okado," he whispered. "You'll drown. Your body will float away. Nobody will ever say you're better than me, that you're pure and I'm broken."

The babe stopped crying. Its lips twisted as if trying to form words. It blinked as if trying to bring Ferius into focus, and its tiny, pale fingers reached out, and it seemed to Ferius that the babe smiled.

He's beautiful, Ferius thought, and his tears streamed down his cheeks. *He's everything I'm not.* He gritted his teeth and trembled and took short, shaky breaths.

"And so you must die."

The lights went out.

The three lanterns on the boardwalk died, and darkness cloaked Ferius, so thick he could no longer see the baby in his arms, the boardwalk beneath his feet, or the water ahead. Only the glow of dusk lit the night, a dim orange scar, a single faded line.

Ferius gasped. Sweat coated him and he stared at that western line, that great mouth of flame. The distant fire seemed to whisper to him, calling him home.

Shadows scuttled around him.

Hands grabbed him.

Ferius opened his arms, letting the baby drop.

Okado squealed, and a shadow darted away, and the sound of crying moved back toward the village. Lights flared—lanterns crackling to life. Ferius spun around, blinking, to see the villagers staring at him, holding tin lamps. All the village of Oshy had come to stare at him, a hundred souls, their eyes condemning, their mouths frowning, their faces cruel.

"You mock me!" Ferius screamed. "I will kill you all!" Saliva sprayed from his mouth. "And I will kill you, Okado. You will burn in my fire!"

They just stared at him, all of them, all those Elorians, all those perfect creatures. His mother stood among them, and one of the villagers—a young fisherman named Tien—placed her babe back in her arms. She stared at Ferius, weeping.

"I swear to you!" Ferius howled. "I swear I will kill your child!"

He clenched his fists, opened his eyes, and took a shuddering breath.

He was standing back in the ruins of Yintao, almost thirty years since that turn, no longer a frightened boy but a great leader of sunlight. And still that pain dug through him, an eternal shard cutting the flesh of his memory.

"I kept my promise," he said softly. "I killed you, my perfect half-brother." He licked his lips, walked around a shattered column, and beheld the grave.

The tombstone rose in a cobbled square, taller than a man, carved of white stone. A golden sunburst blazed upon it, and braziers burned around the grave. At first Ferius had wanted to toss Okado's corpse into the river, to hang it from chains until it rotted, or perhaps to send it to Koyee in her southern exile. But no. Okado would remain here, crushed under the stone of Ferius's victory, forever sleeping with the sun above him.

Ferius walked over the grave, rubbed his muddy boots upon it, and touched the tombstone. A thin smile twitched across his lips.

"You were a perfect son. You were a perfect warrior of the night. You were a husband, a leader, a hero." He spat. "And I spit upon your grave. I was a freak thing, half Elorian, half Timandrian, a monster to you. But now . . . now I am a god. Now all the savages of the night will burn in my fire . . . like you burned."

CHAPTER SEVENTEEN
LABYRINTHS

As soon as they stepped through the archway into the ziggurat, the desert sunlight vanished. Cam spun around, frowning. The archway still loomed wide open—only a foot away—and he could see the land outside: blue sky, bright sun, and golden dunes rolling toward the distant green haze of an oasis city. And yet no light fell upon him. He couldn't see his own hands when he raised them, and he could only hear Linee breathing beside him but not see her.

"Why doesn't the light enter?" she whispered, and he felt her hand grab his arm.

"I don't know. But we still have our lanterns from Eloria. They're in my pack."

"Our lanterns from where?" Linee sounded miserably confused. "Who's Loria?"

Cam groaned. "Eloria! You know . . . Nightside."

"It's called Eloria?"

With a groan, Cam lowered his pack off his shoulders, rummaged blindly, and found his oil lantern and tinderbox. He worked by sense of touch, seeing nothing. He could have stepped back outside the ziggurat to work in the daylight, but somehow, entering the ziggurat had felt like a great accomplishment, one he dared not undo. If this place was truly cursed and he stepped outside, who knew if he'd find his way in again?

Within a moment or two, he had filled his lantern with oil and lit the wick. Light flickered to life, falling upon a craggy hallway and a shivering Linee. He lit her lantern for her; it trembled in her hand.

"Do you think there are more monsters in here?" The light only illuminated several feet of the hallway. Beyond lay darkness. "I'm frightened."

With his finger, Cam drew a half-sun upon the dusty wall— the symbol of Idarism, same as the amulet he wore around his neck. Seeing the rune soothed him, and perhaps it would bless the building.

"That was a trap, not a monster, and there might be more, yes." He took a step forward. "So let's walk carefully and be ready to leap back from any springing knives."

They walked down the corridor. The bricks were craggy and sandy at first, but the farther they walked, the smoother they became; less sand and wind had pummeled them over the millennia. After walking for about a hundred yards, Cam frowned. From outside, the top of the ziggurat—a square of stone rising above the triangular base—was not much larger than his cottage back home. They should have reached the opposite wall by now, but the corridor kept stretching forward.

"This doesn't make sense. We should be . . . by Idar, we should be outside the ziggurat and hovering in the air."

Linee shrugged and stamped her feet. "Well, this feels like real stone to me. And look—stairs!"

After walking a few more steps, they indeed reached a stairway that plunged down into a chasm. When Cam stood upon its edge, he looked down and gasped. Dozens of stairways rose, fell, and crisscrossed in the shadows below. Firelight illuminated the dizzying scene, its source hidden. Cam could see no logic to the architecture. The stairways, all carved of the same craggy rock, stretched out in a bundle like a pile of discarded sticks. They plunged down for what seemed like miles into the pit.

"Is the clock hand down there?" Linee peered down the stairs.

Cam thought back to the painting in the tavern. "It's the arm of a mechanical man. If he's not up here, we'll search for him."

He stepped onto the first flight of stairs—the one connecting to the corridor—and began to descend. Linee walked at his side, holding her lantern. Other stairways rose and fell beside, above, and below them, emerging and disappearing from shadows. Aside from jumping across the chasm, Cam saw no way of reaching them. Linee and he kept descending their stairway. Soon they had descended hundreds of steps and still could see no end.

"We must be under the sand by now," Cam said. The thought chilled him. Who knew how far underground the stairway would take them?

His pack bounced across his back and his sword swung at his side. Finally—it must have been a thousand steps down—the staircase ended, connecting with another corridor. Cam shivered to think how far underground he must be, buried deep below the sand. Linee close behind, he walked down the corridor . . . and found himself facing a sunlit archway.

"The archway we entered through!" Linee said and pointed. "Look."

"Nonsense." Cam shook his head. "We've been climbing downstairs for hundreds of steps. How could we be back where we started?"

"It's the *same* archway." Linee mewled. "Look, I can even see bits of the smashed trap."

Cam grunted. He stomped farther down the corridor, heading toward the sunlit archway. He found his old footprints on the floor, droplets of spilled lantern oil, and the little half-sun he had drawn onto the dusty wall.

"Impossible," he whispered.

Linee stamped her feet and crossed her arms. "I told you it's the archway we entered through! How did we get back here?"

"Some . . . some illusion of the stairs." Unnerved, he turned back toward the darkness and marched along the corridor. "The stairs must have turned somehow, leading us back up. Let's try again."

When he stepped back onto the staircase—the one he had just climbed *down* for a thousand steps—he found it stretching *further* down into darkness. He blinked, confused, but began to descend.

Dozens of staircases again crisscrossed above, below, and to their sides. It felt like walking upon a single branch in a great tree. Cam barely knew what direction he was walking, not even up or down.

"Let's try those stairs instead," he said, pointing to a staircase which ran below theirs.

He steadied himself, took a deep breath, and dived off the stairs he'd been descending. He thumped down onto the new staircase, raising dust. He reached up and helped Linee switch staircases too.

They kept walking downstairs until, after about three hundred steps, they reached the ziggurat's ceiling. Cam spun around and realized that he had *climbed* the whole way; the staircases all spread beneath him, endless layers delving into the darkness.

Linee tilted her head. "How—? What—?"

"It's another trap." Cam grumbled. "It's more complex than the trap of knives. It's some damn maze."

He began racing downstairs. Linee ran at his side. They descended three steps at a time. But suddenly only Cam was descending, and Linee was racing *up* a staircase a dozen feet to his left. They froze and stared at each other across a chasm.

"How did you get there?" Cam said.

She tilted her head. "I was just going downstairs. How did *you* get *there?* Now come back here."

Cam shivered. "Wait. Just . . . keep climbing. The ceiling's above you. I'll meet you there."

She nodded and climbed her staircase. He turned around and climbed his.

"Camlin!" Her voice rose somewhere beneath him. "Camlin, where are you?"

"I'm here! Where are you?"

Fear filler her voice. "I think I'm lost. Camlin, can you hear me? You sound like you're below me."

Cam's knees were beginning to shake. "It sounds like *you're* below *me*." He stopped climbing and leaned over, seeking her on a lower staircase. Her head appeared from beneath the stairs he was climbing; she seemed to be clinging to the bottom of the staircase.

"Camlin!" she said. "What are you doing down there?"

"I'm up here!" He rubbed his eyes. "What are you doing *under* the stairs?"

She squeaked, her head vanished, and he heard her footfalls. Suddenly she came rushing up a staircase across the chasm, maybe a dozen yards away from him—only she was upside down, walking beneath the stairs. She paused and turned toward him, her feet clinging to the bottom of the staircase, her head hanging over the darkness.

"You're upside down," she said, pointing at him.

"You're the upside down one."

She hugged herself. "What's going on? I'm scared. How do we get back onto the same staircase?"

"Let's just both climb upstairs. Forget about going down into the ziggurat. Try to reach the ceiling again somehow." He tried to remain calm, but he heard the tremor in his voice. "All right?"

"I see stairs up there," she said. "I'm going to try to jump up."

She made to leap off her staircase.

"Linee, wait!" From where Cam was standing, it seemed that Linee would plunge down to her death in the chasm . . . only suddenly he no longer knew up from down, left from right. Suddenly he thought he was upside down, that Linee would jump up, fall up and up until she hit the ceiling.

"I'm jumping!" she said.

"Wait. Don't—"

Before he could complete his sentence, Linee closed her eyes, held her nose as if diving into water, and jumped off the staircase.

She fell, plunging downward into the chasm below. Her scream trailed for what seemed like miles until it faded into the darkness.

Cam fell to his knees, shaking. "Linee!" He leaned over the stairs, staring into the chasm, and his breath shook. "Oh Idar . . . Linee!"

For a long moment—silence.

Then—with a beauty that brought tears to his eyes—Linee cried out to him. "Camlin, I found the floor! I found the bottom. Jump down and join me!"

Cam grimaced and shouted down toward her. "You sound like you're a mile deep. I'd smash every bone in my body."

"Trust me!" rose her voice from the pit. "Just jump. The ancients carved this labyrinth for the brave. So be brave like me and *jump*."

Cam looked away. This was madness. Madness! Linee had found a way down, but she had jumped from another staircase. From where he stood, he would surely die. He climbed a few more steps, found himself walking *down*stairs, and turned around. He kept moving. There had to be another way, had to—

He froze.

Upon the stairs before him lay a skeleton.

Cam grimaced and covered his mouth.

Bits of cloth covered the skeleton—shreds of a white cloak and tunic. Leather boots still held its feet, and a half-sun amulet hung around its neck. Cam clutched his own matching amulet.

"It's me," he whispered.

No. No, that was impossible. Wincing, he stepped around the skeleton and kept climbing the stairs, only to find another skeleton, identically clad—or maybe the same skeleton.

"Others have walked here," he whispered. "They never jumped. They kept wandering the maze until they died of thirst or hunger. *I* died here." His amulet dug into his palm and his eyes burned. "The stairs bend time like they bend dimensions. It's my skeleton."

Linee's voice rose from below. "Butterfly bottoms, Camlin. Are you going to jump or not?"

Cam turned away from the skeleton. He closed his eyes. He walked to the side of the staircase until his toes rose above open air.

He whispered a prayer . . . and jumped.

He fell about three feet, landed hard, and opened his eyes.

He stood in a long, dark corridor, the staircases gone. Linee stood at his side, hopping with joy. She grinned and embraced him tightly. "Hullo, Camlin old boy." She planted a kiss on his cheek. "You found your courage."

He closed his eyes. *I found my bones. I found fear.* He opened his eyes and looked at Linee. *But I found my light too.*

Bouncing and still grinning, Linee tugged his arm. "There's another corridor. Let's go exploring and let's find that old king and his hand."

Holding their lanterns high, they walked into the depths of the ziggurat.

* * * * *

Past a bare corridor, Cam and Linee entered a chamber of gold, jewels, and more majesty than in all the courts of sunlight.

"Merciful Idar," Linee whispered, eyes growing almost as large as an Elorian's. She could barely breathe out the words. "It's . . . it's the most beautiful thing I've ever seen."

Cam blinked, not even knowing where to look first, how to make sense of such splendor. He wasn't sure if he faced an imperial hall, a treasure-trove, or a cross between them. Murals covered the walls, depicting scenes of merchants rowing reed boats, countless birds of every kind, trees and flowers, goddesses and serfs, soldiers and farmers, kings and queens, their forms all lined with silver and gold. A platinum sun covered the ceiling, glistening with jewels. Giltwood tables filled the chamber, topped with artifacts. Cam saw a jeweled ostrich-egg cup resting upon silver legs; a golden bust of a bearded king wearing a crown of emeralds, amethysts, and topazes; silver statues of cranes with ruby eyes; jugs painted with scenes of hunters returning with baskets of fowls; ivory statuettes of goddesses, cattle, and soldiers; and four sarcophagi shaped as a snake, a beetle, an ibis, and a shrew.

"It's like a palace." Linee walked between the artifacts, eyes bright, hands clasped against her cheek. "It's even lovelier than my palace back in Kingswall. Oh, Camlin, isn't it wonderful? Maybe we can stay here." Her eyes lit up and a grin split her face. "What do you think? Maybe after the war, we can move here and be King and Queen of the Ziggyroot."

"It's *ziggurat* and no." Camlin too began to walk around, staring at the countless jugs, statuettes, busts, and urns. "Help me look. Maybe the Cabera Hand is here somewhere. I—"

Shrieks rose, echoing in the chamber like steel against stone.

Cam winced and covered his ears.

Linee screamed.

From behind several towering vases emerged clanking creatures of gears, springs, and blades.

Cam scuttled back, slamming into a table, and drew his sword. The mechanical creatures scuttled toward him, moving like the hand-drawn toys he'd seen in the markets. There were four of them. One was a snake formed of a many bronze rings. A beetle the size of a small dog clattered on knitting needle legs. An ibis sported a blade for a beak. A shrew opened its mouth to reveal teeth of rusty nails. Glancing aside, Cam realized they were the same four animals the stone sarcophagi represented.

Linee gasped and pointed at the scurrying metallic shrew. "Finally! A zigzagging rat! I *told* you, Camlin! It's cute." She leaned down to pat it. "It— ow! It's biting me!"

She shook her leg madly, screaming. The shrew clung on, shrieking as it chewed. The other mechanical animals—the beetle, snake, and ibis—came clattering toward Cam.

With a grunt, he swung his sword, diverting the ibis's bladed beak. The snake wrapped around his leg, tightening painfully, and the beetle leaped onto his chest, scurried upward, and bit his shoulder. Cam screamed, ripped the metal insect off, and tossed it across the room. The snake clutched his knee like a vise. Cam fell. The ibis thrust its beak again, and Cam swung his blade, parrying a second time.

"Camlin, help!" Linee cried, trying to slap off the shrew. It was now racing around her torso like a squirrel around a tree. "The rat is zigzagging all over me!"

"I'm a bit busy, Linee!" he shouted back, parrying the ibis with one hand, tugging at the snake with the other. The beetle was already racing back toward him.

Finally he managed to tear the snake off. He tossed it across the chamber, where it wrapped around a statue, then slunk to the ground and came slithering back toward him. Blocking another ibis thrust, Cam leaped to his feet, only for the beetle to jump his way. He swung his sword, slicing the metallic insect in two. Its halves fell, spilling bolts and sprockets.

One of the sarcophagi—the one shaped like the beetle—shook. Dust flew through the cracks along its lid. Cam could spare it only a single glance; the other automatons were still attacking. When the snake rushed toward him again, Cam leaped back, tugged a granite bust off a table, and sent it crashing to the floor. The bust slammed onto the snake. The mechanical serpent looked up, body trapped under the stone, and gave Cam a look that seemed almost sad, almost shocked. Then its head collapsed, spilling oil. The snake-shaped sarcophagus shuddered and scattered dust from within.

Two automatons remained—the shrew and ibis. The mechanical bird was squawking metallically, thrusting its blade madly. Cam kept parrying, reached back with his hand, and grabbed the jeweled ostrich egg. He tossed it forward, shattering it against the ibis. The bird shook its head, confused, and Cam swung his sword down, severing its thin neck. Its head slammed against the floor. Its body—built of metal hoops, gears, and springs—remained standing a moment longer, then fell over and cracked. Once more, a sarcophagus shuddered and scattered dust.

"Camlin!" Linee cried.

She finally managed tearing the shrew off—it had left her armor scratched and tattered—and tossed it toward him. With a swing of his sword, he sliced the poor creature in two. The shrew-shape sarcophagus shook so madly its lid swung open. A mummified shrew—a true, dead animal of withered flesh—stood inside, then fell out and thumped against the floor. With a shudder, the remains collapsed into dust.

Linee dusted her hands against each other. "Well, we showed them."

"*We?*" Cam groaned and examined the scratches and welts on his leg.

Linee looked at her own leg and winced; several cuts bled there. She rummaged through her pack for bandages, and they spent a few moments tending to their wounds.

For the next couple hours, Cam and Linee rummaged through the room—opening stone chests, looking through wooden drawers, and shuffling items on tables, searching for the clock hand. They found amulets and necklaces, paintboxes and thimbles, statuettes and engravings, books and scrolls, but no clock hand.

A distant screech sounded, echoing far from below, the cry of a subterranean creature, almost human, almost mourning, hateful, hungry. Cam froze.

"You remember the painting," Linee said quietly, a ruby necklace in her hand. "The mechanical man. The clock hand was his arm." She looked toward a doorway opposite the one they had entered. It led into shadows. "It's down there somewhere . . . waiting for us."

Cam placed down the jug he was holding. He nodded. "Put down that necklace and we'll keep searching." When she pouted, he glared. "These jewels belong to the dead. We will not take them."

She gave the necklace a longing look, nodded sadly, and slung it around the neck of a golden statue. They left the chamber of treasures, stepped into the dark corridor, and walked into shadow as the scream rose again below.

Daniel Arenson

CHAPTER EIGHTEEN
THE CHILDREN OF NINE

To the song of birds and howls of hidden monkeys, Torin and Bailey climbed over ivy-covered boulders, parted vines and strands of lichen, and beheld the ruins of an ancient temple.

"Til Natay," Torin said, breath heavy. "We found it."

Bailey stood at his side, wiped sweat off her brow, and spat. "I told you I'd find the way."

During his time in Asharo, the port city in the night, Torin had once visited the beach with Koyee, sat under the stars, and dripped wet sand from his fingers into towers, walls, and homes of bumps and swirls. The temple before him, rising from mist and ferns, looked like a massive version of those wet sand structures.

A dozen upside-down cones of stone rose here, their bricks corroded, their mortar crumbling. Rising a hundred feet tall or taller, the towers now sprouted leaf, lichen, and moss like green fur, and birds and rodents gazed from holes upon their facades. Reliefs of robed philosophers adorned the walls; moss covered the stone bodies, and wind and rain had smoothed the bearded faces. Below these bell-shaped structures, the remains of walls snaked through the forest. Most were only several feet tall; some rose higher but ended with shattered edges. A few buildings still stood, their walls bearing engravings of pious women, their stone roofs punched full of holes; most lay fallen. One statue stood facing Torin—a sage in stone robes now green with moss, his hand raised, his eyes closed. Other statues lay fallen, half-hidden in the greenery, their eyes forever staring up at the sky, their hands raised in forgotten prayers.

162

Once this had been a great complex, a temple the size of a city, but the rainforest had taken over the ruins. Banyan trees grew from inside old houses, their trunks sprouting through holes in the roofs. Several banyans grew atop the remains of walls, their roots enveloping the old bricks like the tentacles of a wooden beast. One statue was all but hidden behind wood and leaf; the roots of a tree wrapped around its face, an ancient snake of stone constricting its victim. Everywhere Torin looked, he saw ferns and moss, birds and scuttling monkeys, and floating wisps of mist.

This was a place of haunting memory, of beauty and loss, of sadness and silent songs, but more than these old stones and old trees, it was the central tower—the tallest among them—that drew Torin's attention. It rose above the others, large as the grandest palace, cone-shaped and riddled with holes and cracks. Upon its crest, embedded into the rock, shone a brass number nine.

"There's our boy," Torin said.

"Bet I can climb up and fetch it before you." Bailey gave him a grin—the first one since their kiss under the waterfall—and began racing toward the temple.

Torin was so glad to see her smile he didn't even mind another challenge. As he ran behind her, ferns and vines slapping against him, he thought back to that turn. His wounds from the fight with Ishel were healing, but the pain in Bailey's eyes—pain he had caused—still dug through him like a metal shard. He had told Bailey that he loved her, and he had spoken truth. Even now, running with her, just the sight of her flouncing braids, bright eyes, and smile shot joy through him; he didn't think it was possible to be unhappy around her. Yet how could he forget about Koyee, a woman he also loved?

He winced as he ran. *How could I love two women at once? What if we fix the clock, if we defeat Ferius, if we win this war . . . and I have to choose?* He didn't know, and the guilt coursed through him. In old stories, the heroes always loved only one maiden; their hearts were true and noble. Since he'd kissed Bailey by the waterfall, he had felt less like a hero and more like a villain. He felt a little like Ferius, torn between day and night, pain always inside him.

Right now, focus on fetching that number nine, old boy, spoke a voice inside him. *All the world of Moth hinges upon it, and that world has no time for your fancies.*

"You're falling behind, Torin!" Bailey said over her shoulder, grinning toothily. "I'm going to beat you."

He nodded. He would refuse to think about any woman now—about Bailey *or* Koyee. He would love nobody, at least until the clock was fixed, the world turned again, and the flames of Sailith died. He tightened his lips and ran faster toward the ruins.

They leaped over a fallen log, jumped across a shallow stream, and ran through grass toward the crumbling outer wall—a mere four feet of stone, chipped and full of gaping holes.

With shrieks, a hundred figures leaped from the grass, landed on the wall, and aimed bows and arrows.

Torin and Bailey skidded to a halt.

"I knew we should have kept chasing Ishel . . ." Bailey whispered, frozen, hand hovering over the hilt of his sword.

Torin grimaced, staring at the archers ahead. He whispered from the corner of his mouth, "I'm not sure these are Ishel's friends."

The men upon the wall wore nothing but leaf skirts. Maroon paint covered them, overlain with coiling blue lines. Upon their bare chests, painted white, appeared the number nine. Bones jewelry hung around their necks and pierced their ears, brows, and lips. Their heads were bald, their feet bare, their bows strung with vine. Flint shards tipped their arrows.

Torin slowly raised his hands in a gesture of peace, but the warriors only hissed and drew their bowstrings farther back. They shouted out in their language, a chattering sound Torin couldn't understand. At his side, Bailey growled and her hand inched closer to her sword's hilt.

"Easy, Bailey . . ." he said. "Raise your hands slowly. We can still walk away from this."

He began to take slow paces backward. Grumbling, Bailey joined him.

They had taken three steps when one of the warriors—perhaps with anger, perhaps by accident—loosed an arrow. The projectile slammed down between Bailey and Torin's feet.

With a shout, Bailey drew her sword and began charging forward.

Torin grabbed her shoulders and pulled her back. "Bailey, no!"

The warriors ahead shouted.

Torin winced, waiting for arrows to slam into him.

A woman's voice cried out.

No more arrows flew.

Torin realized he had closed his eyes and was holding his breath. Holding Bailey against him, he peeked between narrowed eyelids. An elderly woman stepped onto the wall between the warriors. Her hair was long and gray, her eyes large and green. Her skin was painted crimson, and the number nine appeared upon her chest in white paint. She wore only leaves, and bead bracelets hung around her wrists. She held a staff crowned with a grinning skull and strings of bones. Wizened and barely taller than a child, she held no weapons, and her arms were thin as bones. And yet the archers all knelt around her, lowering their arrows.

The elderly woman stared at Torin and Bailey. Frowning, she spoke in a deep clear voice. "Who are you, travelers of northern lands, and what do you seek at the Temple of Nine?"

Torin blinked. "You speak Ardish?"

The woman nodded, her soldiers kneeling around her. "I am Xeekotep Who Speaks with Spirits, daughter of Hataf Who

Healed Many. I am a Child of Nine, and I speak many tongues, for many have come seeking the Nine."

Around her, her soldiers chanted together. "Nine. Nine."

The old woman held out her hands, and Torin gasped to see that she was missing one finger. When he looked around him, he realized that all the archers were missing the little finger on their left hand. Only stubs remained. He looked down at their bare feet. They were all missing a toe too, the stubs scarred over.

"We are the Children of Nine," said Xeekotep. "And I am our shaman. We are the guardians of the holy number. You must leave this place, for none but its worshipers may gaze upon the Nine."

The warriors chanted again. "Nine. Nine."

Bailey spoke from the corner of her mouth. "Idar's beard, they're loonies. They worship a number."

He frowned at her. "And we've traveled across night and day to find the same number, so who are the crazy ones?" He raised both hands, curling down one pinky. "Xeekotep Who Speaks with Spirits! We too worship the Number, for it appears in many of our old tales. I am Torin Who Tends to Gardens, son of Teramin Who Fought with Steel. With me is Bailey Who . . . Who . . ." He glanced at her, hesitating. "Who Is Often Covered in Mud."

"Torin!" She growled at his side.

He ignored her and kept speaking to the elderly shaman. "We have come to pray to the glory of Nine." He turned his head slightly and whispered to Bailey. "Bails, raise nine fingers."

Bailey dropped her sword and raised her hands, curling down her pinky. She called out for all the hear. "All hail the Holy Nine! Nine is wonderful. Eight stinks and ten's far too many. Nine's the bee's knees. I eat nine meals a day and got nine cats in my house. Praise the—"

"Okay, that's enough," Torin whispered.

Xeekotep gave the two hard looks, her mouth down-turned. At her sides, the archers raised their bows again. The shaman raised her staff, and its strings of bones rattled.

"Do you mock us?" the shaman said.

Torin gulped and winced. Bailey shook her head vehemently.

Xeekotep gave them another penetrating stare, then turned toward her archers. "Grab them. Tie them up. We will burn them in sacrifice to the Nine."

* * * * *

Only moments later, the Children of Nine marched among the ruins, carrying Torin and Bailey like trussed pigs.

"Why did you have to drop your sword?" Torin demanded. The ropes wound around him, pinning his arms to his side. Several Children of Nine held him over their heads, chanting in their language as they stepped over ferns, fallen bricks, and shattered statues.

Bailey glared at him, similarly tied. Her braids flounced as the Children of Nine marched below her, holding her up. "You told me to lift nine fingers, Winky! Damn you, this is all your fault. How can I lift nine fingers while holding a sword?"

Torin winced as the ropes dug into him. "Ever heard of a sheath, oh great warrior?"

As the Children of Nine carried him through the ruins, he looked around him. The crumbling houses and halls of the temple, built by an ancient tribe lost to time, now housed these new guardians. From every doorway, their eyes stared at him— mothers, children, elders. Soon Torin realized that outside every house stood nine souls. The warriors who followed the procession, bows in hand, marched in groups of nine. Nine arrows filled every quiver, nine squares of soil checkered every garden, and nine bracelets encircled every arm. One babe, lying in a basket, squealed in pain; Torin saw the bandaged stubs of a severed finger and toe.

"Burn them before Keyshora!" cried the wizened Xeekotep, walking ahead of the procession, her staff raised. "The stone god will judge them in the sight of the Nine."

The Children of Nine carried the prisoners over a fallen column, between the coiling roots of a banyan tree, and through an orphaned archway, its wall long fallen and its keystone green with ivy and moss. A shattered road stretched ahead, trees and grass pushing between its cobblestones, leading to the severed head of a statue. The statue's body lay fallen farther back, shrouded with vines and the coiling tree roots. The stony head stared, chipped and pockmarked but still frowning, a dozen feet tall from chin to scalp. Moss covered its cheeks, the number nine was painted upon its brow, and a green emerald—the size of a human head—gleamed within its right eye. Only shadows and cobwebs filled the left eye socket. The statue reminded Torin of his own eyes. When wrestling Bailey as a child, he had fallen, scratching his left eye on a rock. Since then, his left pupil had remained fully dilated, hiding the green iris, leaving him with mismatched eyes.

Fitting, he thought. *This was truly destined to be my final resting place.*

Before the statue rose his instrument of death: a pyre of branches, twigs, and dried leaves waiting to be ignited.

Xeekotep knelt before the pyre and stone head. She chanted in her tongue, then turned back toward Torin and Bailey.

"Behold Keyshora, god of punishment, guardian of the Nine. He is wise and mighty. He is a judge. Before his eye, you will be tried by fire."

Torin grimaced. "Tried by fire?"

Xeekotep nodded, waving her staff and letting its strings of bones clatter. "If your flesh burns before Keyshora, you are guilty. If the fire spares you, you are blessed and innocent."

Torin remembered seeing Ferius burn Koyee's father at the stake. The screams still haunted his dreams. "Is anyone ever found innocent?"

Xeekotep smiled thinly. "You might be the first."

At their side, Bailey squirmed in her ropes and screamed, nearly falling off the Children of Nine who held her up. "Untie me and fight me like men! I can slay you all. You are cowards! I spit upon your Nine." She spat onto the forest floor. "Xeekotep, face me in battle. Send all your men against me. I will take them all. Trial by battle! I—"

She screamed as the Children of Nine tossed her down onto the pyre. She landed on her back, branches and kindling snapping beneath her. When she tried to roll off, the Children of Nine tossed more ropes around her, securing her to the pyre. The statue's head gazed down, and it seemed to Torin that amusement filled its green eye.

With a crunch of branches, the Children of Nine tossed him onto the pyre next to Bailey. He slammed into her, his head banging against her shoulder.

"Ouch, Winky!" She wriggled and glared at him. "Stop hurting my shoulder with your head."

He blinked stars away from his eyes. "You're worried about your shoulder? We're about to be burned to a crisp. Show me your warrior moves!" He winced to see Xeekotep lighting a torch. "I bet I can escape faster than you, Bailey. I dare you to beat me. Go on!"

She growled. "You told me to stop with the challenges."

They wriggled madly, struggling to roll off the pyre or free their arms, but the ropes were too tight. The Children of Nine formed a circle around the pyre, chanting and raising their hands.

"Nine! Nine!" The stony head of Keyshora gazed down with its one emerald eye. Across the temple complex, rising from mist and a sea of trees, the teardrop tower loomed, the number nine reflecting the sun and gleaming like a beacon.

Xeekotep came walking toward the pyre, raising her torch.

"Trial by fire!" she announced, first in her own tongue, than in Ardish—simply, it seemed, to terrify her victims. "Keyshora will burn the victims in the sight of the Nine."

"Nine! Nine!"

Xeekotep began to lower her torch toward the pyre.

Torin turned his head to look at Bailey. She managed to wiggle down so her face was near his.

"Goodbye, Torin," she whispered, eyes damp. "I love you."

He thought of Koyee. He thought of his parents. He thought of home. He looked at Bailey, managed to reach out his tied hands, and clasped her fingers.

"Goodbye, Bailey. I love you too."

A hand grabbed his head.

Xeekotep pulled his face toward her painted, wizened countenance. "You will gaze upon the Nine as you burn. You—" She gasped. Her jaw dropped and her eyes widened. "You . . . your eye . . ." She leaned closer, scrutinizing him, then tossed back her head and howled. "His eyes! The stranger's eyes! One eye green, the other black and dead. A child of Keyshora!"

Torin breathed out in relief when the torch pulled back. "I'm . . . what?"

Bailey nodded vigorously. "Oh, yes, he is that. I worship him all the time. Hail Torin, child of Korshy, Lord of—"

"Keyshora," Torin corrected her.

She cleared her throat and shouted out again. "Torin, child of Keyshora! Worship him!"

To Torin's astonishment, the Children of Nine all bowed around the pyre.

Xeekotep handed her torch to one of her warriors, drew her knife, and worked at Torin's ropes. Soon he was climbing off the pyre and rubbing the welts the ropes had left. The Children of Nine bowed before him, chanting his name.

Xeekotep knelt. "Command us, child of Keyshora. You are a blessing unto our temple. Forgive us for our sins. We are yours to serve."

Bailey thrashed upon the pyre, still tied up. "Command them to free me, Winky! Command them or by the light, I'm going to beat you bloody."

Xeekotep leaped up, snarling, and raised her knife above Bailey. "You will not threaten the child of a god!"

"Me, threaten him?" Bailey fumed. "*You* nearly burned him to a crisp. Now I'm his foster sister and protector, so untie me now, before my wrath destroys this temple."

Torin raised his hands in a conciliatory gesture. "It's all right, Xeekotep. She's my loyal servant. Please untie her."

"Your *servant?*" Bailey's cheeks reddened. "I'll show you who's a serv—" When Xeekotep's knife drew close again, Bailey bit down on her words and nodded. "Oh all right, I serve the winky-eyed babyface. Now untie me, damn it."

Finally Bailey stood beside him, rubbing her wrists and glaring at him. The Children of Nine kept bowing, rising and falling like waves.

"What is your command, son of Kayshora?" asked Xeekotep, holding her staff before her.

Torin looked to his left. Beyond the kneeling tribesmen, the crumbling walls, and the swaying trees, he could see the teardrop temple rising from mist. It loomed like a mountain, a monument of ragged bricks, moss, weeds, and scuttling monkeys. Upon it, the metallic nine blazed in the sunlight, a beacon to be seen for miles around.

The number from the Cabera Clock, Torin thought. *It is holy, but perhaps not for the reason these folk know.*

He wondered if Koyee had found the gear, if Cam had found the hand. Often the notion of fixing a great, mountaintop clock that could make the world spin again, bringing night and day across both halves of Moth, seemed as outlandish as stone gods and holy numbers. But then again, two years ago, Torin would have thought hot air balloons, cannons, and dragons to be only fairy tales too.

He looked back at Xeekotep. "I've traveled from afar to see the holy Nine, the most blessed of numbers. I must take the Nine with me to the holy . . . nine mountains of . . . Cabera." He nodded, feeling a little guilty for twisting the truth, but deciding it was the best way to explain things. "There the Nine will rise to the halls of the gods, and a great blessing will descend upon the world."

The Children of Nine gasped. A few reached for their bows. Xeekotep rose to her feet.

"But child of Keyshora!" said the shaman. "Nine is the holiest of numbers, a master even unto your father. How can we forsake its guidance? No. This we cannot do. Even Keyshora's son, or the son of any lesser god, cannot claim the Nine, the father of all deities."

Bailey nudged him and muttered from the corner of her mouth. "Nice try, Winky."

Torin tapped his fingers against his thigh. If the people refused to surrender the number willingly, he'd have to steal it. The thought of thievery soured his belly, yet what else could he do? If he left the number here, the Sailith Order would continue to preach hatred, to burn and kill across the night. Only the number could bring daylight to Eloria and night to Timandra, invalidating Ferius's doctrine.

So we'll have to steal it.

Perhaps after this war ended, he could return with a duplicate number, a great nine forged from gold, a new god for the Children of Nine. Perhaps he could even return with a metallic ten, allowing these people to keep their fingers and toes.

He nodded and looked back at the elderly shaman. "You are correct, Xeekotep. I tested you with a false command, and you proved your loyalty to the Nine. Now you will hear my true bidding. My servant and I will climb the temple, touch the Nine, and worship it."

And steal it, he thought, cursing that guilt in his belly.

Xeekotep opened her mouth and seemed ready to reply when a thousand shouts tore across the temple grounds.

Birds fled and macaques shrieked and hid. The Children of Nine leaped up and nocked arrows. Xeekotep screamed.

Charging toward them, howling battle cries, came Ishel and a hundred Nayan warriors, tossing spears and leading leashed tigers. The Children of Nine roared, fired their arrows, and ran toward the intruders.

The temple grounds shook with blood, screams, and steel.

CHAPTER NINETEEN
THE RISING LIGHT

For the first time in years, Ferius rode into Oshy, his old home by the dusk. The pain clutched his chest and he could barely breathe. Perhaps sensing his distress, his horse nickered beneath him and sidestepped.

"It was here that I was born," he whispered. "It was here that they hurt me." He dug his fingernails into his palms and felt the blood drip. "It was here that Eloria created its nemesis."

He closed his eyes, and the memories pounded through him: the twisted boy, half of sunlight and half of darkness; the other children tossing him into the river and mocking him; the babe Okado, born to replace him; the endless pain, agony, fear, shame. He took a deep breath, trying to calm his pounding heart. He opened his eyes and gazed upon this old place of nightmares.

The huts were gone, razed to the ground, the villagers buried. He had slain them himself two years ago. Across the ruins bustled a hundred masons, climbing scaffolds, hammering and chiseling and laying down bricks. The shell of a temple rose here, a dozen feet tall already. When complete, it would form the greatest Sailith temple in the world, a monolith to dwarf even the grandest halls in both day and night.

"Here will be my seat of power," Ferius said, still tasting the old ash on the wind, still smelling the meaty aroma of burning bodies. "From here, the place where you hurt me, will I rule this broken world."

A flutter caught his eye. He looked up to see a moth flying overhead, its one wing black, the other white. Ferius reached out and caught it. The poor creature struggled in his grip, and Ferius stared at it between his fingers.

"A duskmoth," he said softly. Folk claimed that, with their mismatched wings, duskmoths looked like the world—one half light, the other dark. Ferius remembered the insects flying into the village in his childhood. The other children would call Ferius himself a duskmoth, a creature torn in two, a mere insect.

Pain flared in him and Ferius trembled. He wanted to crush this animal in his fist, to forget that memory, to make it bleed. Yet strangely, he found a new emotion flowing through him—not fear, not rage, not pain, but something . . . something both warm and cold, something he'd never felt before.

When he realized what it was, his head spun.

"Pity," he whispered.

He opened his fingers. The moth seemed to regard him for a moment, moving its feathery antennae. The creature seemed almost sad, as if it understood Ferius's pain. Then it took flight and fled, wobbling, back toward its home in the dusk.

Ferius watched until it disappeared in the distance, then wheeled his horse around. He turned away from his rising temple and toward the Inaro River.

Hundreds of ships filled the water, the combined fleets of northern Timandra. Once these had been the ships of separate kingdoms, the remnants of old Riyona, that sprawling empire that had fallen a thousand years ago into petty, battling nations ruled by fools. Today all these ships sailed under one banner again—*his* banner, the golden sunburst upon a red field, sigil of Sailith, of daylight, of his dominion. Carracks towered, their masts high as palaces, their many sails wide. Galleys filled the water like great centipedes, their many oars raised and ready. Galleons stood lined with cannons—the weapons of Eloria converted to sunlit might. Between them floated countless smaller vessels, from humble rowboats to simple reed dinghies carrying jungle warriors. The fleet stretched across the river west and east, lit with countless lanterns, so great it rolled into the horizon. Soldiers filled hulls and covered decks, awaiting the glory of final victory.

Ferius smiled thinly. In the southern lands of sunlight, a separate fleet mustered—the great forces of the desert, the swamps, and the savannah. They too prepared to sail. The two forces would meet in the last patch of Eloria still standing.

"All the forces of sunlight will meet in Asharo, capital of Ilar, and there . . . there the sun will finally burn the last children of the dark."

Ferius unhooked the silver horn that hung from his belt, raised it to his lips, and gave a long, wailing keen.

From every ship, a horn answered his cry. Hundreds of wails filled the night, a chorus like a song of bones, like screams of death, a symphony of purification.

The ships sailed.

Ferius stood upon the riverbank, watching them go by, carrack after galley, galleon after caravel, cogs and ballingers, and even captured Elorian junk ships which now hoisted the sunlit banners. Upon every deck they roared, the soldiers of sunlight, brandishing their swords and axes and hammers, worshiping him, singing for the death of the night.

And Ferius stood, watching them sail by, waiting until the last ship vanished downriver.

His horse tossed its head and nickered. Ferius stroked the beast's mane.

"No, my friend, we do not join them. Not yet. We will ride into the ruins of Asharo, but not yet. Ours is a different task."

He dug his spurs into the horse's flesh. The beast bucked, whinnied, and burst into a gallop. They raced across the darkness, heading toward the dusk. Ferius leaned forward in the saddle and rode into the light.

CHAPTER TWENTY
FOUR MIRRORS

The corridor narrowed into little more than a tunnel. They walked single file, the walls brushing against their shoulders. Cam was not a large man, and Linee was a slim little thing; he could not imagine larger folk like his old friends walking here.

Especially not Hem, Cam thought with a wince that turned into a sad smile. *He'd get stuck here like the big loaf of bread that he was.*

The tunnel went on and on, plunging downward. The air grew cold, as cold as the night. The ceiling dropped so low that Cam, short as he was, had to walk stooped over. Finally they reached a fork. He paused and Linee bumped against him from behind. Their oil lanterns flickered, casting orange light and dancing shadows.

"The tunnel curves left and right." He held his lantern toward each path, but he only saw more bricks leading into shadow. "Where do we go?"

Linee peered over his shoulder. "Right."

She sounded confident. Cam shrugged; one way was as good as the other. They walked down the right tunnel, plunging deeper into the ziggurat. He brushed his hand against the walls as they walked; they were etched with old Eseerian runes. When they reached another fork, he paused again.

"Left," Linee said and nodded.

He looked at her. "How do you know?"

"Trust me!" She pointed. "Left."

They kept walking and the tunnel narrowed further. Cam had to walk with his shoulders rolled inward, his head bowed. He worried that he'd get stuck here like a turnip in a glutton's throat. In his mind, he saw his skeleton again, those bones lingering here for years, finally fading into dust, forever lost in the depths of the ziggurat.

They kept walking, and at every fork Linee confidently chose a path. Finally, at a fork where Linee pointed left, Cam turned toward her and held her arms.

"Linee, how do you always know where to go? Are you just guessing?"

She smiled and brushed dust off his nose. "I *know*. Back in Kingswall, there was a maze of hedges in the gardens. At first I'd always get lost and cry, and Sir Ogworth would have to come rescue me. But I kept going back in there, because I heard there was a beautiful garden with butterflies and pretty flowers in the middle. One time I decided to draw a *map*. I took parchment and charcoal and drew as I explored the paths. I kept walking and drawing and walking and drawing and walking and dra—"

"Linee!"

". . . and finally, I mapped the entire labyrinth and found the garden in its center. I know that map by heart now, Camlin. I don't even need that old parchment. It's like the map's in my brain." She tapped her chest, then frowned. "Wait . . . where is the brain again? Somewhere in your belly, right?" She nodded and patted her stomach. "Anyway, the map's in there somewhere, and I'm taking us the right way."

Cam rubbed his eyes, aghast. "But this is a different labyrinth! Every labyrinth has different routes! How will your mental map from home help us?"

She rolled her eyes and blew out her breath. "You're not listening! Because it's the *same labyrinth*." She gestured around at the craggy stone walls. "I mean, back home the walls are nice green hedges, and you can see the sky above, and there are lots of butterflies and birds. But the paths are the same."

"That's impossible."

She placed her hands on her hips. "Have *you* ever been in a labyrinth?"

"No."

"And I have! I'm an expert. So follow me. Left!"

She began to march down the left tunnel. Reluctantly, Cam followed. Linee was perhaps crazy, but one tunnel was as good as another, he supposed.

They walked in darkness, Linee leading the way, for what seemed like hours. Cam began to wonder if this labyrinth was like the staircases higher up—a trick that would keep them moving in circles—when the tunnel finally led them into a towering round chamber.

Gingerly, he stepped inside and raised his lamp. A thousand other lights blasted out, nearly blinding him. He squinted and shielded his eyes with his palm. When Linee entered the chamber behind him, her own lantern raised, the light grew even brighter. It felt like stepping into the sun.

"I told you!" Linee said, squinting. "I knew the way."

Peeking between his fingers, Cam saw a round chamber the size of the pebbly village square back in Fairwool-by-Night. Four tall, ornate mirrors stood at each corner, each reflecting the others in an endless recursion, tossing back the lamplight countless times. Cam placed his lantern on the floor, beneath the reach of the mirrors, and lowered Linee's lantern too. The light subsided into a manageable glow.

Cam gasped.

"Oh Idar . . ."

This round chamber was not merely the size of Fairwool's village square; it was a mockery of it, a representation in metal and stone. One mirror's frame was shaped like Fairwool's Sailith temple where Ferius would preach, complete with a mock stairway and columns. Another mirror was shaped like The

Shadowed Firkin, the tavern back home; its top frame was molded into the shape of a tiled roof, and a bronze garden—one of Torin's gardens—lay at its feet. A third mirror's frame was shaped as the Watchtower, tall and dark, topped with battlements—the place where Cam and the rest of the Village Guard would watch the night. The final mirror was shaped like Cam's old house, a humble abode with a straw roof; several metal sunflowers rose around it.

In the center of the chamber rose a tree, a mockery of Old Maple back in the village. Its trunk was woven of coiling steel ropes. Its leaves were flat metal shards; they reminded Cam of the throwing stars Elorians wielded. A face appeared in the trunk, its eyes formed from bolts, its mouth full of nails for teeth. The metal leaves creaked, the tree's mouth twisted, and it spoke in a voice like grinding gears.

"Welcome home, Camlin Shepherd."

Cam winced. That voice tore at his ears like insects gnawing on flesh. He shuddered and drew his sword.

"This is not my home. This is an illusion—just like your trick of staircases." He sneered at the tree, trying to let hatred fill him; it helped subdue the fear that shook his fingers. "Who are you? And how do you know my name?"

The tree's grin widened with creaking metal and raining rust. Its trunk of metal ropes twisted, and three leaves fell to slam into the floor, cutting the stone.

"Do you not know me, Camlin Shepherd? I have always been with you."

Cam took a step closer and brandished his sword. "I slew your servants, the mechanical animals guarding the trove. I can cut you too. Who are you? I don't know you."

The metallic tree laughed. Bolts like acorns fell from its branches.

"I am only what you bring here with you, Camlin Shepherd. I am memory. I am fear. I am hope." The tree licked its lips with a tongue of coiling tin. "I am you. Your past, your present, your future. I am the labyrinth inside you—the labyrinth inside every man. I am Ziggurat. I am only what you are. I am only what fears and riddles already dwell inside you."

Linee stepped up beside Cam, holding her dagger out. She frowned. "What about me? What about *my* fears? Why don't I see any of that?"

The tree turned its metal eyes toward her. "You walked through a labyrinth of tunnels to find this place. You recognized it. You followed the same twists and turns as the maze back in your homeland. You walked up and down staircases. You knew when to jump down. Did you not recognize the staircases that run through the Palace of Arden, your old castle, the walls between them removed?" The tree's metal leaves shifted and glinted. "I am Ziggurat. I form myself from your fears. I am what you made me. I plucked the stairs and labyrinth from the mind of the young queen. And here, in this chamber of Camlin's mind, must the young shepherd choose his path."

Lights flickered and suddenly the mirrors no longer reflected the chamber. They now showed visions as from astral lands, their edges blurred, their distances too deep, their lines bending and smudged like dreams.

The tree spoke. "As your heart has four chambers, here you see four visions of your heart. Choose the truth, Camlin Shepherd. Gaze into the mirrors and choose the man you truly are. Step into the vision of truth, and you will find the clock hand you seek. Step into a vision of lie, and only fire and death will await you. Gaze into your heart. Gaze into four mirrors. Choose wisely. Choose the true Camlin Shepherd."

Cam turned from mirror to mirror, a vision in each. The true Camlin?

"Choose!" demanded the tree, creaking, metal leaves falling. "Choose and enter."

Cam sucked in his breath.

It's only a vision, he thought. *The whole ziggurat—everything from the archway to this room . . . only visions Linee and I created.*

He wanted to end this game. He wanted to attack the tree, to storm out of the chamber, to smash the walls. He felt invaded, violated, his most inner secrets tugged out like entrails from a fish, rearranged into traps to thwart him. Yet if he attacked, would he end up a skeleton like the one he'd seen? Had that been a warning—play our game or you'll fade into bones?

He grimaced. *So I'll play this game. I sailed across the night and traveled through snowy hinterlands. I fought in battles against hosts of sunlit warriors. I can defeat the riddles inside me.*

Clutching his sword, he turned toward the first mirror, the one shaped like his old home. Within the glass, he saw himself back in that home, sitting with his parents by the fireplace. Cam's eyes stung and his knees shook. The reflection inside the glass showed a younger him, not yet scarred by war, his cheeks softer and his eyes brighter. The boy sat in an armchair, speaking excitedly to his parents. His father, a kindly old shepherd with a white beard, smiled at his son. His mother, a petite woman with graying buns of hair, was sipping mint tea and knitting a scarf. Outside a window spread their pastures, green grass speckled with white sheep beneath a blue sky.

"Home," Cam whispered, tears in his eyes. "This is the mirror. This is the true me."

He took a step closer, ready to reach into that mirror, to step into the vision or whatever place it took him to. This mirror reflected his heart, his inner soul. He was no warrior, no adventurer, no soldier. He was that boy inside the glass, happy, at home.

When he took another step toward the mirror, Linee grabbed his arm. "Wait." Her voice was soft. "Look into the others."

It pained Cam to look away from this reflection, from the kind eyes of his parents, from the peace and beauty of his home. When he turned his head aside, it felt like a part of him ripped off. He rubbed tears from his eyes and turned toward the second mirror.

This mirror was shaped like The Shadowed Firkin, the tavern where Cam had spent so many hours with his friends, drinking and singing with Hem, Bailey, and Torin. When he stared into the glass, he seemed to see a future vision. A reflection of him was walking into the tavern, clad in Elorian scale armor, a sword in his hand. The villagers filled the common room—his friends, his family, all those he had grown up with, and they were cheering him. Beautiful Yara, the rye farmer's daughter, batted her eyelids and begged to hear tales of his adventure. Perry Potter, her long auburn hair cascading, leaned forward, kissed the reflected Cam's cheek, and called him a hero. Everywhere men bought him drinks, praised his name, and sang songs of his glory.

This is me returning from war, Cam realized. *We defeated Ferius. We won. And I'm a hero at home.*

He longed to step into this reflection too. All his life, he had been the shortest man in the village, a humble shepherd's boy with no coins in his pockets. The girls had never chased him, and the boys—aside from fellow misfits Torin and Hem—would only mock him. Yet here was the man Cam had always dreamed of being—adored, worshiped, no longer the cynical shepherd but a war hero. He took a step toward this reflection, aching to step inside.

A foot away from the mirror, he paused. The tree had warned him to choose the true reflection—not a dream, not a wish . . . but the true Camlin Shepherd. Was this him . . . or simply who he wanted to be?

Tearing his gaze away, Cam turned toward the third mirror.

This mirror was shaped as the village's Sailith temple, and Cam shuddered as soon as he turned toward it. He sucked in his breath and felt his eyes sting anew. His knees shook, and he reached out and clutched Linee's hand.

"Oh, Camlin," she said softly and hugged him.

He stared at the reflection in the mirror, barely able to breathe. He saw the ruins of Yintao, the great city of the night, smoldering after the battle with Ferius. Towers lay fallen, walls crumbled, and enemy troops marched over corpses. In the center, leaning against a shattered wall, lay the corpse of Hemstad Baker. Arrows pierced the large man's chest, and his eyes gazed at the stars. Cam remembered finding his best friend dead like this in the ruins; it had only been half a year ago. But in this reflection, Cam himself lay dead by his friend, his corpse trampled, arrows in his back.

"I should have died with him," Cam whispered, staring into the mirror at his own body. "I should have been there with you, Hem, but we were late for the battle. I wasn't with you when you died." His voice shook. "I'm sorry."

He took a step closer to the mirror, wanting to jump in, to be with his friend again. They had spent their lives together, and only through twist of fate, Hem had died and Cam lingered on.

"Camlin, please, stop," Linee said, holding him back. "That isn't you."

He turned toward her, eyes burning. "How do you know? How do you know that isn't the true me?" His knees shook. "I was meant to die there in the darkness. I would have died, but we were late, we—"

Linee growled—it was the first time Cam had heard her growl—and slapped him. Her hand connected with his cheek so hard he saw stars.

"Camlin Shepherd!" She dug her fingers into his shoulders. "Don't you dare say you should have died. Because I was there with you. We rode the same nightwolf. If you had died there . . ." Suddenly she was trembling. She pointed into the mirror.

Cam turned back toward the reflection and his chest deflated. He had not seen it at first, but now as he gazed at the destruction, he saw the corpse of a young, golden-haired woman, her body crushed and stabbed. It was Linee.

When he turned back toward the true Linee, she was crying. He embraced her and kissed her cheek. "It's all right. It's just a reflection, just a dream, just a possibility. It's not real."

She nodded and sniffed. "Look into the fourth mirror."

A lump in his throat, Cam turned toward the fourth mirror, this one tall and narrow and shaped liked the Watchtower. Inside he saw himself and Linee in a carriage, rolling into the village, dressed as King and Queen. He wore a golden crown and a cloak of samite, and Linee wore a blue gown and many jewels. Knights in armor rode alongside their carriage, jesters somersaulted and juggled and blew trumpets, and Dalmatians ran along the procession, yipping and wagging their tails. Upon the horizon, Cam could see the palace of Arden, a place he'd only ever seen in paintings.

"King Camlin and Queen Linee!" announced one of their jesters, his voice a faded echo inside the mirror.

Watching the reflection, Cam couldn't help but laugh. This was one mirror he thought it safe to avoid. Him—a king?

But Linee nodded and pointed. "This is the mirror to enter. This is the true you."

Cam watched himself as a king. Now the reflection showed him sitting upon a throne, Linee at his side, surrounded by guards.

"How can this be me?" He shook his head. "I'm not a king. I'm just a shepherd."

He turned away from the mirror and faced the metal tree. It stared back at him, its eyelids clattering, its boughs creaking. More metal leaves fell, slicing into the floor.

"Choose," said the tree, grin widening with menace, rust dripping from its mouth. "Choose the true Camlin Shepherd. Step into the true vision and live. Enter the lie and perish."

Cam looked from mirror to mirror. A boy back in his childhood home. A hero returned from war. A corpse. A king.

"It has to be the boy back home," he said, taking a step toward that mirror.

Linee grabbed his arm. "No! Camlin, listen to me." Her eyes flashed and her cheeks flushed. "Listen. That *was* you. That was you years ago. Are you still a carefree shepherd, a boy with rosy cheeks and an easy smile?" She shook her head vigorously. "That's only a memory, not a reflection. That's who you *were*, not who you *are*."

Cam breathed out shakily, feeling close to tears. More than any other reflection, this one tempted him, but Linee spoke truth. He was no longer that boy; it was a memory whispering.

"The war hero?" He looked into the second mirror. "A soldier returning home to glory? It must be. That's who I am now—a soldier."

Again Linee pulled him back. "No. Camlin, look at that reflection. Women are fawning over you. Men are buying you drinks. You're a hero there, craving glory, lapping it up. That's not you." She touched his cheek and gazed into his eyes. "I know you. You don't crave fame. You came here to fight Ferius, to save the night, to serve honor and truth. Not for glory. Not for a hero's welcome. That isn't who you are. I know it."

Cam lowered his head. Perhaps she was right. "But . . . that leaves only the corpse in the ruins. You said that wasn't me either."

"It's not." Linee held his cheeks in her palms. "Because you're alive. You're with me. That means the last reflection is true—you and me as king and queen, still together, married, living in a palace."

Cam laughed bitterly. "A fairy tale."

"The truth!" Linee stamped her feet. "Maybe the future will be different. Maybe we won't live in a palace. Maybe I'll never be queen again, and maybe you won't be king. But look more closely. It shows us together—at peace, strong, wise. Not craving glory. No longer silly youths. Not bodies in ruins. It shows . . . it shows who we are *inside*. I still feel like a queen inside." Tears streamed down her cheeks and she kissed him. "And you are a king. Maybe not out there." She pressed a hand to her heart. "But you are *my* king. I see who you are. That's the true you. With me. Step into the Watchtower mirror."

At their side, the twisting tree of metal creaked. Rust filled the air. Its voice rose into a shriek that made Cam cringe. "Choose! Choose now." Metal leaves shot out like throwing stars. One whistled over Cam's head, embedding itself into the wall behind him. Another slammed down by his foot, driving an inch into the stone floor. "Choose a mirror. Enter the true vision. Enter now or I will slay you in this chamber."

Cam turned again from mirror to mirror, holding Linee's hand. A boy. A hero. A corpse. A king.

More leaves shot out and Cam winced; one sliced his arm. Another whistled over Linee's shoulder, nearly cutting her ear. She gasped.

"Choose!" shouted the tree, a sound of crumpling steel.

Linee held Cam's hands and gazed into his eyes. "Trust me," she whispered. She pulled him toward the narrow mirror that showed him a king. "Trust me like you did when jumping off the staircase. Trust me like you did in the labyrinth. Trust me, Camlin." She kissed his lips. "Please."

He nodded, lips tightened, throat constricting. More shards flew. Cam and Linee took deep breaths, clasped their hands together . . . and stepped into the Watchtower mirror.

CHAPTER TWENTY-ONE
SHALESH

"I need a gear of silver," Koyee said to the elders of Montai. "Four feet in diameter with forty-eight teeth." She gestured at the cache upon the floor. "As my payment, I offer you all we own."

She stood in the Temple of Shalesh, the finest building in the coastal town. Marble columns, lined with silverwork, held the vaunted ceiling. Black and white tiles spread across the floor. A statue of the goddess Shalesh—a woman with six arms and no mouth, nose, or ears—stood behind an altar, her blue eyes staring down, burning with inner light. Koyee stood beneath that statue, and Nitomi and Qato stood at her sides, clad in their black dojai silks. Before her stood the Montai elders, their wrinkled skin dark as charcoal, their hair white as moonlight on snow, their eyes gleaming blue.

On the floor between them, Koyee had stacked her payment. Upon a blanket lay all her belongings: coins, hourglasses, jugs of wine, and fine Ilari armor of gleaming plates. Nitomi and Qato had donated their possessions too; Nitomi had even placed all her daggers save a single blade upon the pile. Most of all, Koyee's eyes stung to see her most precious memento— perhaps the most precious thing anyone ever owned.

My father's sword. Sheytusung.

The katana lay atop the pile, worth more than all that lay beneath it. Sheytusung had been forged in Pahmey by master smiths, its blade folded and hammered a dozen times. Koyee's father had carried this weapon to war in Ilar, and Koyee had wielded it throughout all her battles, from the streets of Pahmey to the ruins of Yintao.

But now we must part from that sword, Eelani, she thought, knowing her invisible friend could hear. She felt a hollowness inside her and a chill upon her shoulder; Eelani sat there and she grieved too. *We need a silver gear. We must part from this blade of legend, from this memory of Father, for the world to turn again.*

As she looked upon the blade, she knew that emptiness would always fill her.

The Montai elders looked at one another but did not speak. Koyee bit her lip, and at her side Nitomi bounced anxiously. Towering over the two, the giant Qato grunted, stared at his own sword upon the pile, but said nothing.

"Will you accept my payment?" Koyee said, her voice sounding too loud to her, echoing in the temple. "Will you forge me a gear of silver?"

Please, she added silently, staring at the elders. She could bring a silver gear to the weaveworms. She could swap it for the true Cabera Gear. She could see her beloved again—her dear Torin—upon the mountain of the clock. And she could fix that clock, could let the sun rise upon the night, could invalidate all of Ferius's preachings and end this war.

"Will you not speak?" she said, looking at the elders. "Why are you silent?"

The elders stared at one another again as if sharing silent words. All eyes turned back toward her, blue moons in midnight faces. Finally it was Siyun, the elder who had first greeted her in this town, who spoke.

"We do not crave your coins, armor, or blades."

Koyee tilted her head. "I have no other gifts to offer."

Siyun bowed his head. "You have your courage. You have strength. You have fought in the great battles of empires. We will forge you a silver gear, four feet wide and bearing forty-eight teeth. But we ask for payment of a different kind."

She narrowed her eyes. "What payment?"

The elders' eyes flicked upward, glancing to the statue of Shalesh, then back to her. Siyun reached out his hand. "Follow, children of night. And take your weapons."

Koyee glanced at her companions, but Nitomi and Qato seemed just as confused. The elders turned and walked toward the temple exit. When Koyee lifted Sheytusung, the comforting silk hilt and familiar weight brought tears to her eyes. This blade was a part of her, as much as her invisible friend Eelani, as much as her heart, as much as her memories of home. When Nitomi and Qato had reclaimed their own weapons, they left the temple and followed Siyun down a stone path.

They left the village, climbed to the hilltop henge, and stood between the stones and glowing runes. The worlds shone above, hanging in the night sky like lanterns, blue and green and red, siblings to Mythimna, this world Koyee fought for, a world men called Moth. Under the light of the skies, protected in the ring of stones, Siyun turned toward her, and sadness filled his eyes, and an ancient fear hovered upon his words.

"Here we can speak without the goddess hearing. Here Shalesh, whom we worship in temples and homes, cannot judge us. Only here in this henge can we share our secrets." Siyun looked down upon the village. "For too long has she forced us to love her. For too many years have we sacrificed our children to her cruelty. Every winter she demands a child. Every summer she returns that child—mute, deaf, simple-minded, six arms growing where only two had once moved. The faces of our children return to us blank—no mouths, noses, ears, nothing but two eyes. And oh, child of night . . . what pain we see in those eyes, what secrets they dare not—cannot—reveal." He stepped forward, pain and fear in his own eyes, and clasped Koyee's arms. "We will forge you this silver gear. But please, child of the night. Please. You must kill her. You must kill Shalesh."

Siyun turned away, trembling, and fell to his knees. He lowered his head and would say no more.

* * * * *

She curled deeper in the dark. She had been lingering for so long. She had been weaving her webs, lapping at the salty puddles, dreaming . . . dreaming in the dark . . . festering and fermenting and feeding upon the scraps of skin on bones. Too long. Too many moons had waxed and waned above, casting their light through the peering eye, the hole in the ceiling of her cave, all seeing, blinking, light and dark, a clock of the worlds.

The worlds can hide them, Shalesh thought, twitching, and her tailbone flicked, tapping against the wet rocks of her lair. The henge . . . the henge! The glowing runes. The worlds above, magnified, screaming in her skull, pounding against her, shrieking . . . begging . . . dying . . . Their screams deafened her. Their light blinded her. The old ones—the Montai folk—had stepped twice into the shrieking and light. Travelers scuttled among them.

Strange things of distant lands, yes . . . creatures . . .

They seek to hurt you. They will cut you. They will come to explore you, to shine light upon you, to see your shame.

Shalesh twitched, and her six hands lashed out, arms flailing, fingernails scratching at the stone. The pools of silver and violet water trembled below her, circles within circles, rings like the henge, like the dreams in her mind. Ancient. Ancient beyond knowing.

She remembered the sunlight. She remembered the cruel yellow fire blazing through the peering eye. It had died. It had left her here in darkness, rotting, reeking, rummaging for flesh.

Worship me.

Her spine uncoiled, cracking, and she reached out and grabbed one of the bones, one of those endless relics of those who had come to shine their light, to expose her nakedness. She crunched. She snapped. Her head bore no mouth; she had gotten rid of it. She had silenced her screams. She fed through the mouths of her hands, sucking like tree roots, lapping, gnawing, feasting upon the marrow and sweetness and old blood and scraps of skin.

Worship me.

"Mamma . . . mamma . . ."

The whimper rose in her chamber, echoing between the stalagmites, shuddering the pools of water. She looked up and saw them there—her children. The children she had claimed from the Montai, the children under the white disk. She had adopted them, nurtured them, morphed them, broken and reformed them, grew them like mushrooms into her own image. Once the children of men, they were now her spawn, blessed and infected with her old beauty like icicles on stone. Six arms grew from the cold, indigo torsos. She had erased their mouths, their nostrils, their ears, sealing all cavities, leaving only eyes, only two blue eyes on blank, hairless heads, eyes to admire her, to see out into the world for her, to worship her.

Worship me.

She held their hands. She fed them, disgorging her lumpy feast through veins and palms, passing the viscous goodness into their hands, their distending bellies, their minds. When they had grown strong enough, she would send them forth. She would return these deities made in her image. They would infest the village of men, things to praise, things to fear, a warning for all to worship her, for she could take their children, shape their children, send their children back as creatures with six arms, no mouths to scream, no ears to hear, only eyes of endless pain.

And they would worship her.

They would fear her, for she was Shalesh. She was ancient. She was the last among those who had seen the yellow light.

She pulled her hands free from theirs; they came loose with sucking sounds. She raised her head, a white oval, staring ahead through the cave. Things were drawing near. She could feel their vibrations in the rock. She could hear their thoughts like static in the air, crinkling, crackling, echoing. She had no ears, but their voices reverberated through her arms, her spine, her skull, racing up and down, crying inside her. The foreigners. She had sensed them in the village. Her discarded children, lying wrapped in cloaks in the village moonlight, had spoken in her mind of these travelers, and they were cruel, and they were dangerous, and they had come to hunt Shalesh, but she was an ancient huntress, and she had feasted upon many in her lair. They too would worship her. They too would become her. They too would sprout arms and lose their faces, things of the dark, things of water and rock and shame. They would be Shalesh sent forth into the world, small idols for the children of men to praise.

"Koyee!" cried the little one, a daughter of men barely larger than a child. "Koyee, can you see anything, I— ow!"

"Hush, Nitomi!" Another spoke now, the dangerous one, the daughter of men with the long white hair and ancient shard of steel, a blade drenched in much blood whose scent still filled the air, sickly sweet and sticky. "Keep your voices low. She's in here somewhere."

The little one stamped a foot, still distant but sending vibrations through miles of caves. "She's got no ears. You saw the statues. She can't hear. She— ow, all right! Let go and I'll be quiet."

A grunt shook the stalagmites; a giant walked there too, twice the little one's size, but still small and weak by the glorious, unfurling might of Shalesh. "Qato silent."

Shalesh stared into the dark, crouched, her six hands upon the ground, her spine raised, her legs ready to leap, long and pale, larger than three children of men, slick, white, waiting, all seeing, holy, sickly sweet, sticky meat. She was ancient. She was goddess. She was hungry and here in the dark of her cave, among the stalagmites and stalactites, among the pools of rotting fish and the white light peering through Hollow Eye, she would feed. She would nurture. She would make them her own. She would steal their voices.

She crept. Step by step. Over puddle and rock, over her children who cowered, reaching for her. Mamma. Mamma. She brushed past them, moving down a tunnel, through water, over boulders, slinking, always seeing, always hearing, waiting in the dark, her great blue eyes piercing the shadows. Her hunger rippled inside her, and the mouths upon her six hands opened in a gust of fervor, sucking at the cold water and mushrooms, waiting for the sweet meat. She would feast upon two, she decided—the giant and the little one. The huntress—the one with the steel shard, the one called Koyee—that one she would break. That one she would remake in her image.

She raced through the darkness. She leaped. She cocked her head and stared. Down tunnels, up walls, through burrows and echoing caverns, squeezing through wet places and swimming and racing along the ceiling, clinging like the bats she fed on, crunching them in her hands. She moved through the shadow, silent, a great white spider upon stone, until she saw their forms ahead, and she paused, held out her six palms, opened her six mouths, and shrieked.

The shrieks flowed from her arms, her body, her spine, the depth of her shame and despair, for she had been a child of men once, she had walked upon the world in eras past, a child, a female child of fear, and she had fallen here and lived and lingered and changed and screamed, and now all that scream of ancient, twisting malformation burst from her, shaking the cave. And they heard her. The three children of men heard and they covered their ears and they screamed too.

Palms open, her six mouths spoke . . . the old words, the words she had demanded for the endless years, the turn of seasons, the dance of the worlds that could still blind her.

"Worship me."

They stared at her. Two children of men in black, one small and one smaller, and they tossed their blades toward her, and they screamed as they cut at her, but Shalesh was ancient. Shalesh had lingered. Their steel shattered against her rubbery skin, and she sucked up the shards, absorbed them, turned them into armor, into a cold hardness inside her. She lashed her head, clubbing the larger one, the mindless one, the one called Qato. Her skull, long and hard and draped with her skin, slammed into him, shoved him against stone. Her leg lashed out, sprouting three clawed toes, a leg for climbing and slinking, for striking, and she slammed it into the one called Nitomi. The thing's daggers shot out, darts of pain, driving into her, but Shalesh only shrieked again, shoved the daughter of men down into the water, drove her foot upon her, and she saw into her, saw her shame, her secrets, her pain. A daughter of men failed. Banished. Outcast from the mountains and hurting inside.

Shalesh lifted the two in her hands, and her tongues emerged from her palms, licking, tasting, shuddering as the tongues' hooks brushed against the hot skin, feeling the blood flow beneath. Yet she would not dine yet. She would save them. She would savor them. She tossed them behind her, sweet meat for a long, languorous feast.

She cocked her head, blinked, and stared at the one remaining before her. The dangerous one. The bright one of inner light, a thing of the moon.

Her mouths spoke—a slow, sucking sound.

"Koyee . . ."

The daughter of men stood before her, sword raised in one hand, lantern in the other, and the light blazed, the light of the moon reflecting in the blade, and the ghosts of its slain cried out, countless voices of men. This blade had driven into the hearts of warriors, into dragon-flesh, into the light of the worlds, and Shalesh screamed as it burned her eyes.

"Sheytusung," her mouths spoke. "A blade of old steel from the worlds."

She remembered the stone and metal falling, crashing into the sea, driving a crater into the world, a ball of minerals and metal, full of the fire of the heavens. Its inner flames still burned in that blade. Now it drove toward her.

The shard dug into her thigh, raising smoke, crashing through her white skin, spilling black blood. Shalesh swatted it away, but it cut her hand, and she cried out again, and she reached for the daughter of men, for the huntress, and she grabbed her hair in her sticky hands.

She pulled the small head close. And Shalesh stared.

There was power in eyes. There was power in seeing. And Shalesh, grown in darkness, broken and transfigured in darkness, was a goddess of seeing. Her two eyes, large like the woman's head, stared with blue knowledge, and they *saw*. They saw a brother. They saw a river. They saw a shame . . . a shame of a mother who loved another, of a bastard boy fled to sunlight, of a rot returned to haunt, to cut, to burn. And from Shalesh's six hands a laughter rose, bubbling like blood in a wound, and they spoke into the girl.

"His name is Ferius and he is your secret. He is your shame. Have you told your kindred, your friends, the soft ones whom I will feast upon? Have you told the empress you serve? Have you told the Montai folk whom you swindle? Have you told the lesser gods who fear me?" Shalesh tightened her grip, pulling Koyee closer, even as the blade thrust into her side again and again. "I see your filth . . . your humiliation."

Her blade coated with black ichor, Koyee stared back.

Shalesh gasped and hissed and recoiled.

Koyee *saw*.

There was power in those lavender eyes, there was seeing, knowing.

There was old wisdom.

"And I see you, Shalesh," said the daughter of men, Koyee of the night. "I know who you are." There was no accusation in her voice, only sadness and pity. "You were like me once. You were a girl . . . only a girl who got lost in the dark. Who drank the deep waters. Who changed." Tears streamed down Koyee's cheeks. "You fell ill, and the illness took your mouth, and your nose, and your ears . . . it took your voice, your hearing, your memories. I'm so sorry, Shalesh. I'm so sorry."

The scream of Shalesh tore through the caverns, shaking the walls. Dust fell and rocks rolled and cracks filled stone.

"Look away!" Shalesh pulled back and covered her blank face, hiding her shame, hiding her eyes. "You know me. Do not look upon me. Do not shine your light upon the shame . . . my humiliation."

Koyee stepped forward, and Shalesh scuttled back, but always the young woman advanced, her blade alight, her lantern piercing the shadows.

"You told the Montai you were a goddess." Koyee's voice shook. "You made them fear you, worship you. You changed their children, infecting them with your disease. They grew four new arms and lost their faces." Koyee shook her head, eyes pained. "Why? You lied. You said you remade them in your image, the image of a goddess to praise, but . . . it's only a disease. You didn't remake them; you contaminated them. How can I cure you?"

Shalesh swung her head, slamming her skull into Koyee. She knocked the daughter of men down.

"You will not cure me! There is no cure. You will see, daughter of men. You will scream with no mouth. You will morph into my shape. You—"

The sword blazed.

The light blasted out, falling upon Shalesh again, and she cowered, for in the light her shame was exposed, her deformity, these strange arms, this vanished mouth, and inside her she felt it, she felt it move, she felt *her*. The child she had been screamed inside her, weeping, trembling, so afraid, so afraid . . . so ashamed . . . and her name was Sen. And she begged.

The creature she had become retreated, slinking like a spider into its secret holes, abdomen swinging, hands like claws clattering.

"Please . . ." the creature begged. "Please don't look upon me. Please don't speak of my shame to the Montai. For I was one of them. For I was born in that village under the moonlight, and I still remember the worlds. And their eyes still hurt me. They will not worship me. They will look upon me in disgust, and I will be naked before them. Please, daughter of men. I am Sen. I am afraid."

Koyee took a step closer, her blade reflecting her lamplight, her eyes peering, seeing, eyes like moons. "If I keep your secret, you must leave this island."

Shalesh took a step back, cowering, quivering, and she hid her head behind her legs, and she shrieked. "I have lurked in this cave for thousands of winters. I have risen from this island, and I have—"

"Then all will know your shame." Koyee raised her chin. "I will return to the Montai. And I will travel the night. And I will speak of a child named Sen, a child diseased, deformed, who betrayed her mother, who drank forbidden water, who—"

"You would kill us!" The voices rose from her six hands, but they were no longer the voices of Shalesh, shrieks like shattering glass, but the whimpers of a child, high and trembling. "Please, Koyee. Please. I'm in here. I'm inside her. Please don't tell them what I've become. I've been a bad girl. Please. I'm ashamed."

Pity filled Koyee's eyes . . . pity that stabbed like ten thousand swords. "Then run. Flee this island. Swim across the sea and find another place to dwell, some barren rock where no children of men can see you. Feast upon fish and may only the darkness keep you company."

"Who will worship me?" The child's voice quivered, emerging from five hands; the sixth spoke as Shalesh.

"I will," Koyee said. "I will worship that child that you were, a child of moonlight, of joy, a child whole. I will praise your name, Sen. Always." Koyee reached out gingerly and placed a hand upon Shalesh's shoulder—perhaps the shoulder of Sen, a forgotten child not encased in hard white skin. "I will always see you as you were."

At Shalesh's sides, figures stirred. The two others—the two children of men clad in black—rose to their feet, and their lanterns burned too, and their eyes too gazed upon her, and they knew. They knew her true name.

"Sen," whispered the daughter Nitomi.

"Qato sees," said her tall, pale companion.

They stared at her. Six eyes like her six hands. She stood before them, exposed.

And so I will flee, she thought. *And so I will fade. And so I will become Sen again.*

Palms upon the floor, mouths tasting the water, she scuttled through the cave, escaping their eyes, their knowledge, cloaking herself again in shadows. A deformed child with too many arms, unable to scream, she raced through the tunnels and water and darkness, and she emerged—diseased and bloated—into the world. The moonlight burned her, and she wept, for once she had danced beneath this moon and her laughter had rolled across the hills.

She slunk and scuttled toward the shore. She entered the water. She swam into darkness, and none in the island of Montai or in any other realm of night beheld her curse again.

* * * * *

Koyee sat in the boat, watching the island of Montai fade into a distant glow.

"Do you think she'll be all right, Eelani?" she whispered. "Do you think she'll find peace?"

She spoke too softly for her companions to hear. Nitomi was busy chattering behind her to Qato, rattling off tales of six-armed goddesses, floating worlds above henges, and weaveworms the size of men—as if the towering, pale assassin had not lived the same adventure. But Koyee, sitting at the stern, knew that her invisible friend could hear. Eelani was always there for her.

"She was like me once, Eelani." Koyee's whisper floated on the wind. "The goddess Shalesh was once but a girl . . . lost in the dark, far from home. I wonder if she, like I did, cowered in shadows, begged for food, survived year after year . . . growing cold, dark, twisted." She thought back to the streets of Pahmey—the spice, the thieves, the rats and trash and endless fear. "I wonder sometimes if you're real, Eelani, or just my imaginary friend. I know not all believe you truly exist. But maybe . . . maybe our dreams are real. Maybe our imaginations manifest, mist rising into ghosts. Hers was a disease, a dark dream that made her a tortured goddess." She thought she felt a little warmth on her shoulder, a small figure nuzzling her cheek, comforting her, and Koyee smiled. "I'm glad you're with me, Eelani."

Koyee thought of the children found in Shalesh's cave—children infected with the disease, deformed into the goddess's image. Koyee had returned them home to their village, yet still she grieved for them. *There is no cure for their illness,* she thought and lowered her head. *But perhaps their souls can now heal.*

She reached down and caressed the great, iron gear that lay at her feet. It was old beyond reckoning—forged before the keeping of books or the memories of songs. It had turned inside the clock of the world. It had woven silk that clothed the night. And now it lay here, black iron without a dent, scratch, or speck of rust, smooth and pure as if freshly forged. She had taken a silver gear, made by the masters of Montai, to the weaveworms. She had swapped the precious metal, the greatest joy of the worms, for this artifact. She had climbed mountains, crawled through caves, and fought a goddess for this gear. Perhaps all her hardships, since sailing alone upon the Inaro to Pahmey two years ago, had been to find this ring of metal.

"Have you found the number nine, Torin?" she whispered to the waves as the island faded over the horizon. "Have you found the hand, Cam?"

Nitomi's voice rose louder behind her, and the boat rocked as the diminutive assassin bounced around. "And I struck her with my dagger, but her skin was like armor! And then . . . and then she hit me, and I flew through the air, and I crashed into the water, and I think I blacked out a little, but then I was up again, but Koyee was taming her somehow! And then . . . and then . . . " She had to pause for breath. "And then we went back to the weaveworms, and gave them the gear, and—"

Qato groaned as his companion ran in rings around him. "Qato *knows.*"

Nitomi seemed not to hear him. "Oh, and the weaveworms boiled their babies! Isn't that disgusting? And . . . and . . . and I saw giant worlds in the henge, and—"

"Qato tired," said the giant. He covered his ears, lay down, and tried to sleep as Nitomi tugged at him, struggling to rouse him as she regaled him with more tales.

Koyee looked at her two new friends, and she smiled.

Yes, Eelani, I think she will find peace. I pray that we all will.

Their boat sailed through the endless night . . . a night that might soon fade under the rising sun.

CHAPTER TWENTY-TWO
ENTOMBED

Light and sound.

Color and whispers.

Wind blew and tinkly laughter echoed, and all around floated shards of reflection like lost stars.

He had no body. He had no thought. With only a wisp of being, a consciousness broken and reforming like beads of water, he reached out and grabbed her.

They tumbled through shadows and moonlight inside the mirror, flowed down tunnels of darkness, and thumped onto cold stone.

For a long moment, Cam merely sat, groaned, and blinked.

"I want to go again," Linee said at his side. She tugged his arm. "Please can we jump through the mirror again?"

Ignoring her, Cam struggled to his feet. The world was blurred. His lamp lay fallen at his feet, flickering. He lifted it, shining a light ahead. He stood in a towering tomb, the floors tiled, the walls covered with runes and paintings of men bowing to a great, towering king upon a throne. Scraps of metal, bolts, blades, and springs lay across the floor, spreading into shadows.

Many feet above, Cam saw a round hole in the wall; it was no larger than his fist. A ray of light shone through the hole, dancing with dust, and fell upon a sarcophagus in the chamber's center. The stone coffin was shaped as the king painted on the walls. It stood upright, stern and staring, seven feet tall. Engraved upon the lid was the king's bearded likeness. His stone hands clutched a sword, and stone snakes coiled around his feet.

"It's him," whispered Linee. "The tomb of King Kaeorin the Conqueror, Son of Asharpel, Blessed King of Ancient Eseer. My old books had paintings of him. Do you think . . ." She gulped. "Do you think his body is in there?"

Cam drew his sword. "I don't know, but I'm not looking for the corpse. Do you remember the mechanical animals we fought?"

Linee nodded. "I do."

"The automatons were protectors of the dead, shaped like the mummies they guarded. The painting in the tavern showed a king of metal; he wore the Cabera Hand as an arm." He took a slow step forward, sword held before him. "We don't need the body. We need to find its mechanical guardian."

Linee gulped and raised her own lantern, but the light only spread out several feet. Aside from the sun ray falling upon the sarcophagus ahead, shadows cloaked the chamber. "Where is the guardian?"

Cam took a deep breath. "He's here with us."

Linee gasped and stared from side to side. "Where? I see nothing."

Cam winced and sucked in a slow breath. "He's here. He's everywhere. He's in the shadows watching us. Do you see him, Linee?"

Her voice shook. "No!" She spun around, but only a wall now rose behind them, the mirror gone. "I'm scared. What do you see? Where's the automaton?"

Cam nodded slowly. He took a step closer to the sarcophagus. "We don't seek to hurt you!" he called out, his voice echoing. "We seek only the clock hand that belongs to all Mythimna. Surrender the hand, Guardian of Kaeorin, and we will leave in peace."

A laughter sounded across the tomb, deep as thunder, high-pitched as steam, echoing, crashing against the walls, aching against Cam's ribs. The room shook, and the metal debris across the floor—bolts, nuts, springs, and rings of metal—bounced and clattered.

Linee mewled and swung her lamp from side to side. "Where is he, Camlin? I can't see him."

"He's everywhere." Camlin nodded a took a step closer. "He's in a thousand pieces. Look for the clock hand. Grab it before—"

But it was too late.

The scraps of metal moved toward one another, bunching and clattering together. Springs leaped onto bolts. Screws drove into rings of steel. A skeleton of metal rose, coalescing, taking the shape of a man. Two bronze circles opened, forming eyes, blazing with red light. Hoops like the rings of barrels formed ribs, and chains formed veins and tendons. An iron bear trap snapped, a rusty mouth. From the ray of light it descended, three feet long, a shard of polished brass—the Cabera Hand, alight like the sun. The ancient relic connected with the creature and rose in condemnation, a limb of metal, pointing at Cam.

The automaton spoke, its voice like grinding gears and breaking bones. "You have done well, Camlin Shepherd of Arden, and you have come far. You have traveled through fire and darkness to enter your tomb."

Cam shook his head. "This is the tomb of Kaeorin."

"And of all who enter here." The automaton took a step forward, shedding rust. "For many years I lay shattered, screaming silently, waiting for one to wake me. You have ended my long desolation. Now you too will lie in pieces, but yours will rot and fester, and your bones will fade into dust."

Cam snarled and sliced the air with his sword. The blade whistled. "Your pets lie in shattered pieces, Guard of Kaeorin. This blade shattered them. Come and taste it."

The automaton raised his second arm, this one formed of chains, and flexed fingers formed of daggers. The mechanical king shrieked, the sound shaking the chamber, and sprang forward.

Cam swung his sword.

The automaton flew through the air. Cam's blade drove through it, crashing through ropes and tin, cleaving the machine in two with a rain of rust and bolts.

The automaton's halves crashed to the floor, flailing.

Cam breathed in relief and Linee gasped.

"You killed it, Camlin," she said. "Oh Idar, you killed it."

The king's halves twitched. Its legs kicked. Its mouth worked silently, and its eyes spun. Its rust covered the floor like blood. It seemed almost a pathetic creature, too hurt to scream, dying in the shadows. Wincing in disgust, Cam reached down toward the Cabera Hand, hoping to tug it free.

Before he could grab the hand, the broken half jerked across the floor. Cam started. The king's bottom half scuttled and connected with the upper half, snapping into place. With more rust and creaks, the automaton stood again, shrieked, and leaped toward him.

The Cabera Hand thrust forward like a blade. Cam sidestepped and parried. The king's second hand lashed, and its fingers—formed of daggers—slammed into Cam's side, denting his armor and nicking his flesh.

He cried out, kicked, and drove the king back. He slammed his sword down, scattering nuts and bolts. The automaton laughed, lunged toward him, and sank its teeth into Cam's shoulder.

Cam screamed as the bear trap punched through armor and into his flesh. Linee screamed too; she was slamming her dagger against the mechanical king, but the blade only clattered between its moving parts, doing the machine no harm. Cam grabbed the automaton's metal jaw and twisted, forcing it off his shoulder. The daggers sliced again, cutting Cam's thigh.

"Linee, attack the king!" he shouted. He swung his sword, severing the automaton's ropy arm. It crashed to the floor, then leaped back up, reconnecting with the torso.

"I am!" she cried back, driving her dagger into the machine's back.

"The real king!" The Cabera Hand thrust. Cam diverted the blow, but the brass digit still sliced along his side, scattering scales from his armor. "The dead one in the sarcophagus!"

"But . . ." She stood still, confused. "But he's already dead."

"I know! Stab him! He—"

A scream cut off his words. The automaton barreled into him, daggers tearing his armor, scaling him like a fish. Cam fell onto his back, and the automaton leaned down, teeth digging, tugging off armor, scratching Cam's neck.

"Linee, the sarcophagus!" he shouted, holding the automaton's head back.

He glimpsed her tugging the coffin's stone lid. She cried out, tears in her eyes. "I'm trying! It's stuck."

"Pull harder!"

He drove his sword upward, slamming the crossguard into the automaton's face. Metal dented. Iron teeth fell out and scattered, then leaped back into the mouth and bit again. Blood sprayed Cam's hand, and his sword fell.

"Linee!"

The teeth drove into his shoulder again. Cam rolled, shoving the machine down. He grabbed its head and slammed it against the floor, again and again, denting the metal. It reformed every time. He scuttled back, kicked hard, and snapped the automaton's ribs, only for them to mold back into place.

The Cabera Hand thrust.

Cam jumped sideways, and the hand scraped across his waist, cutting through armor and cloth and skin. He screamed and grabbed the hand. It dug into his palms, but he clung on, twisting, trying to wrench it free.

"Camlin, it's too heavy, I can't open it!"

The automaton leaned forward, grinning and laughing, and licked its chops with an oily metal tongue. It spoke in a voice like shattering glass. "And so . . . here you die, Camlin Shepherd. Here I will break you. You tried to break off my arm . . . so I will start by ripping off yours."

As Cam clung to the brass hand, the automaton closed its iron jaws around Cam's arm.

He screamed. Those jaws tightened like a vise. The teeth cut his flesh. The automaton began to tug back, pulling Cam's arm, and he screamed. He kicked. Tears budded into his eyes. He felt like a prisoner on the rack.

"Linee!" he shouted, voice torn in agony.

Through a haze, he saw her standing by the sarcophagus. Its lid was still closed. She looked at him, hair golden in the sunbeam, eyes bright green, and she was beautiful. She was so beautiful she soothed his pain, and he could barely feel the creature ripping him, tearing him apart. It seemed to Cam that in the light and mist, she stood back in her gardens of Kingswall, a queen in a gown, smiling at him, wreathed in flowers and angelic light. He would die here, he knew, but he would die gazing upon her, and that was all right. It no longer hurt.

But she tore her gaze away.

She stepped into shadow.

She vanished behind the sarcophagus, and the pain returned, and the creature was tugging again, biting, feeding, and his blood spilled. It laughed as it ate him.

Linee shouted.

The sarcophagus tilted.

Dust rained through light.

The sunray split into ten beams, scattering across the chamber.

The coffin, shaped like King Kaeorin, tilted further. The stone king upon its lid stared at Cam, eyes dark and knowing. Like a bird of prey, it swooped. It fell. It crashed against the floor and cracked, shattered, broke like a jug, broke like Cam's body was breaking.

Inside, among the shards of stone, it lay—the true body of King Kaeorin, wrapped in a shroud, clad in jewels. Its face and hands were still bare, the skin blackened, the eye sockets staring.

The automaton shrieked, clutching Cam in its jaws.

Linee knelt above the wreathed corpse, looked up at Cam, and drove her dagger down.

The blade crashed through the dead king's jewels, drove through the shroud, and sank into mummified flesh.

The automaton screamed.

Cam kicked the machine off and scampered backward, his blood seeping.

Smoke rose from the corpse. Linee shouted and released the dagger; it glowed red and welts rose on her hand. She raced toward Cam and knelt beside him.

The corpse twisted, coiling inward, churning like black water. Bare feet thrust out from the shroud, nails black, and the legs bent. The corpse's mouth opened in a silent scream. The spine snapped. It seemed as if a giant, invisible fist was crumpling the corpse into a ball.

At its side, the automaton—this mockery of the body—emitted the scream the corpse could not. Its ribs snapped. Its legs broke off and shattered. It fell, weeping, begging. Its skull dented, imploding.

"Thieves . . ." it whimpered. "Grave robbers . . . I curse you. I curse you! You killed us . . . you doomed us . . ."

Linee clung to Cam. They knelt together, watching. The corpse gave a last jerk, then collapsed into dust. Its jewels spilled across the floor. The automaton gave a last cry, then broke apart, its pieces spilling like the jewels—springs and sprockets and gears rolling everywhere, clattering against the floor.

Linee gasped and pointed. "Camlin, what's that?"

He stared and shivered. From the metallic remains rose pale smoke, forming the shape of a man. A king floated before them, a misty apparition, little more than dust in the sunbeam. The ghost rose into that beam as if trapped, steam floating in a tube. It rose higher—sucked up—flowing up the sunbeam until it passed through the hole in the ceiling . . . and vanished into the sunlight beyond.

"It was the king's soul," Cam said. "It was in the automaton all these years, trapped in a mechanical body, guarding its old flesh and bones." He blinked rust and tears out of his eyes. "I can think of nothing sadder. We freed him, Linee. We freed him from a torturous half-life."

Linee stared at the sunbeam for a moment longer, then spun toward Cam and gasped. "You're hurt. You're bleeding all over."

He struggled to his feet, wobbled, and swallowed. Linee helped him stand, her arm around him. He stumbled forward, kicked dust and bolts aside, and saw the Cabera Hand lying at his feet.

"All this way," he whispered. "Through the night and dusk. Along the river and through the markets of Kahtef. Past riddles and shadows and blood. And here it is. The clock hand. Hope." He turned toward Linee and smiled wanly. "Let's lift it together."

She nodded. They leaned down and their hands closed around it. The brass was cold and smooth. They straightened, holding the relic before them.

With his free hand, Cam held his head. "I . . . I think I'm dizzy. The chamber is spinning."

He swayed and Linee caught him. "I feel it too!"

The bolts rolled across the floor. The dust bounced. Cracks raced across the walls, and a chunk of the ceiling fell, slamming against the floor only feet ahead of them.

"It's an earthquake!" Linee said.

Cam shook his head. "It's the end of long pain."

A chunk of wall fell, revealing a tunnel. Far ahead, Cam saw the light of day. He began stumbling forward, skirting cracks and chunks of stone. Linee ran at his side, holding the Cabera Hand to her chest. Dust rained around them, walls cracked, and tiles thrust up from the floor like teeth. The rumbling of stones rose as loudly as thunder.

They raced down the tunnel, rocks pelting them, and emerged into a hall lined with columns. A gateway rose ahead, and through it Cam saw the desert, the sunlight nearly blinding him. Columns cracked. One shattered and fell.

They ran toward the gateway between raining stones.

When Cam reached the gateway and began to pass through, Linee clutched his arm, holding him fast.

"Camlin, look!"

He spun around. They stood within the gateway, staring back into the hall.

"It's her," Linee whispered, holding him, her eyes damp. "It's Queen Ferisi. The queen he built this ziggurat for."

Cam stared, scarcely believing his eyes. The ancient queen stood between two columns, clad in white, golden jewels around her arms and neck. Her face was a silver mask. Her left hand rose, a gesture of peace . . . of farewell.

"Goodbye, Queen Ferisi," Linee whispered, raising her hand too. "Rest now. You're free."

More rocks fell from the ceiling. The columns around Ferisi cracked. Dust rained.

Cam and Linee turned and fled from the mausoleum. They raced down the outer stairs, ran across the sand, and finally spun back toward the ziggurat. Dust burst out from its gateway. Its columns cracked and fell. The entrance collapsed, and debris fell down the building's facades with a rain of dust and pebbles. The upper tower, the square atop the triangle, collapsed into itself . . . and lay still.

When the dust settled, the ziggurat stood before them, self-mummified, its secrets forever entombed, its doorways gone—a dead relic for the sands of time.

Cam fell into the sand and winced. Finally he allowed himself to feel pain.

Linee rummaged through her pack, pulling out their medical supplies—spirits, ointments, and bandages. "I'm going to bandage you up good. When I'm done, you're going to look like a mummified king yourself."

He winced. "Don't remind me of him. Please."

She opened her mouth to object, then closed it. She nodded. She worked silently, tending to his wounds. Beside them in the sand, the Cabera Hand pointed skyward, gleaming in the sun.

CHAPTER TWENTY-THREE
FALLING

The horde of howling Nayans raced forward, brandishing spears and shields, their tigers leaping. Hundreds of the warriors ran among the trees, trampling grass and ferns. Tiger pelts hung across their shoulders, and fang necklaces jangled upon their chests. Their red braids swung, clanking with beads, and bloodlust filled their eyes.

Standing upon a fallen log, facing the charging mob, Torin and Bailey drew sword and arrow.

"Hello again, my friends!" cried Ishel. The wild woman led the charge, riding upon her tiger, the great beast Durga. She laughed, her mane of fiery hair billowing. "Are you ready to taste my blades again?"

Bailey closed one eye, aimed, and fired an arrow. It slammed into Ishel but snapped against her breastplate. The Nayans kept charging, only heartbeats away.

Bailey spat and shouted, "Couldn't face us alone so you brought an army?" She drew her longsword, leaped off the mossy log, and ran toward the horde. "I cut your arm last time, Ishel. Now I cut your neck."

Torin winced, memories of war returning to him—from the first skirmish in Fairwool-by-Night to the clash of empires in Yintao. His knees shook and sweat soaked him, but he gritted his teeth, jumped off the log, and ran with Bailey.

Around them, the Children of Nine roared and ran too, firing arrows and tossing javelins.

"Nine!" they cried. "Nine, Nine!"

With steel, stone, and screams, the battle crashed around Torin.

Tigers pounced and lashed claws, and Torin swung his katana, knocking them back. Nayan warriors bellowed, spraying saliva, their beards clattering with bones, and their spears lashed his way. He parried madly. Bailey fought at his side, her braids swinging with her sword. All around them, hundreds clashed together, killing and dying.

Ishel and her warriors were Northern Nayans, dwellers of the Sern's riverbank. They were tall and broad, and they knew the secrets of metalworking and writing. The Children of Nine were the southern dwellers of the deep rainforest, a smaller, humbler folk, and they knew only of stone and wood. And yet this southern tribe, guardians of the number, fought with just as much ferocity. Their stone-tipped arrows tore into the enemy. Their spears lashed. Their slings slammed stones into the invaders' heads. They spilled blood and they chanted for the Nine.

"Torin, watch out!" Bailey said, sounding more annoyed then afraid. She tugged him down an instant before a javelin flew over his head. With a glare, she yanked him up. "Now stop gawping and fight with me."

They stood back to back, swinging their swords like in that first battle against the Sailith monks in Fairwool-by-Night. But their defiance was short-lived. With a roar, a tiger leaped onto them, knocking them down. Claws scratched Torin's armor, denting scales. The beast's jaws wrapped around Bailey's arm, and she screamed. The rider upon the tiger laughed, hair blowing like a flame.

"Ishel." Torin grunted and pushed himself to his feet. Her spear drove toward him and he parried.

Bailey managed to stand beside him. Durga still gripped her arm, the tiger's teeth clattering against the vambrace. She thrust her longsword against Ishel, but the woman swung down her scimitar. The blades clanged.

"Our fight continues!" Ishel licked her lips. "Let our armies battle it out. We fight here alone."

Around them, the two Nayan tribes clashed and died, spears and arrows driving into flesh. Bailey kicked, slamming her boot against Durga's head, finally freeing herself. The steel of her vambrace was dented but her arm seemed unharmed. She and Torin circled the tiger, swords raised.

"What did Ferius promise you?" Bailey said. She spat at Ishel and checked the woman's lashing scimitar. "A castle in the night? A dream of power? A chest of coins?"

Atop her tiger, Ishel snickered and thrust her scimitar at Torin. He diverted the attack away from his chest, but the blade scraped along his arm, slicing through armor to nick his skin.

"He promised me blood." Ishel raised her sword to her lips and licked Torin's blood off the blade. "When I slew that friend of yours, the fat fool of a baker, I got a taste for the blood of traitors."

Torin felt as if an invisible fist punched his chest. "Be silent! You—"

Ishel laughed and drove her blade toward him again; their swords clanged. "Does the truth hurt, child? What was the fat one's name? Hemstad Baker? Yes, they were my arrows that drove into his flesh." She pouted. "Was he a dear friend of yours? Don't worry. Soon you'll be joining him in the afterlife."

Torin's eyes burned. "You will not speak of Hem that way. You lie." He sprang toward her, swinging his katana, but she knocked the blade aside.

Bailey too was screaming. Her eyes were red. "I will have revenge!" Tears streamed down her cheeks. "I am a child of Fairwool-by-Night. He was my friend. Now you die."

With a wordless battle cry, Bailey leaped into the air and landed on the tiger.

As the two women battled atop the beast, Torin stood, frozen for a moment, a strange clarity coming over him. Through the battle raged all around and blood splashed the ferns, all fear, pain, and sadness left him. He felt as if he floated above the fray, as if this bloodshed were but a tick of an ancient clock, another battle among thousands.

He died for us, Torin thought. *Hem gave his life for us to win this war—not to kill for him, not to die for him, but to stop this madness. To stop bloodshed.*

He nodded, stepped forward, and grabbed Bailey's shoulder. He pulled her off the tiger.

"Bailey, run!" he shouted. He grabbed her hand and began pulling her away.

She gasped and tried to shove him off. Durga snapped his teeth, narrowing missing them.

"Winky, what are you—"

"Run with me!" he shouted, switching to Qaelish, the language of the night, which the Nayans would not understand. "To the number. While everyone is fighting—to the Nine!"

"Nine, Nine!" the tribesmen shouted around them, racing toward Ishel. The tiger reared and Ishel screamed, for a moment separated from Bailey and Torin.

"Winky, let go!" Bailey tried to free herself from his grip, and her eyes blazed. "She killed Hem. Oh Idar, she killed him. Let go!"

He shook his head and kept tugging her through the battle. They moved between racing Children of Nine. "The best way to fight her is to grab the number. That is our task. That is our prize. That's what can win this war."

Bailey snarled. "My blade will win this war."

He wouldn't release her. He pulled her several steps back. Bailey was perhaps faster, braver, and stronger than him, but now Torin blazed with determination. For the first time in his life, he led the way, and he dragged her along.

"Your blade, Bailey? And if it cuts Ishel, what then? Hundreds fight around her. Grab the number with me." He looked into her eyes. "Please. Trust me. Follow me once like I always follow you. Just once trust me and follow."

She trembled, wiped her eyes, and nodded silently.

Ishel shouted behind them. "Cowards! Come face me!"

A dozen Children of Nine were attacking the woman, thrusting spears. An arrow slammed into her tiger, and Ishel screamed and fell from the saddle. The tribesmen mobbed her, driving down spears. A dozen Northern Nayans, Ishel's warriors, leaped into the fray. Torin did not stay to watch. He ran, holding Bailey's hand, racing over fallen logs, around trees, and across boulders. The towers, walls, and shattered statues of the temple rose around them, archers upon their roofs. Vines dangled and the roots of trees rose around them, taller than men.

The ringing steel, screams, and roars of the battle rose behind them. They raced under a crumbling, orphaned archway, weeds growing between its stones, its keystone still bearing a relief of a woman's serene face. They ran over another stone face—this one as large as a boat, fallen and overgrown with moss and grass—and across a dilapidated bridge that spanned a rivulet. Fallen statues of lions lay chipped, vines and ivy clutching them like green snakes. The teardrop-shaped temples rose around them, statues of ancient priests guarding their doorways. Holes filled the walls, and banyan trees grew from them, their roots creeping along the bricks.

Ahead, past a grove of kapok trees, Torin saw it. The largest temple rose from mist, tall as a palace, a great bell of stone. Upon its top beamed the Cabera Number.

"Climb with me, Bailey!" he shouted, racing toward the temple. "I dare you to climb. Let's see if you can beat me now."

"Oh, you cocky boy!" she shouted back. Her arms pumped as she ran, moving ahead of him.

They hurdled over a fallen wall and reached the temple. Several young Children of Nine, mere boys, saw them and scattered. As they ran across a cobbled courtyard, Torin and Bailey shrugged off their armor, weapons, and packs. Bailey reached the dome first, leaped onto the wall, and began to scuttle up, placing her hands and feet into the cracks between the old bricks. Torin reached the wall a few breaths later, pulled his grapple from his pack, and began to climb too.

"No grapple!" Bailey shouted, climbing several feet above him. "That's cheating."

"Bailey, enough!"

They had climbed fifty feet or more—Torin slamming his grapple between the bricks—when he looked over his shoulder. He saw the battle across the ruins below. He winced. Most of the Children of Nine lay dead; Ishel and her warriors, with their tigers and superior weapons, were tearing through the humbler tribe. Torin felt a pang of guilt. Those tribesmen were giving their lives to protect the Nine, and here he was, climbing up to steal it. He froze for a moment, unable to continue.

"Winky, hurry!" Bailey said, climbing above. "I'm beating you."

Torin nodded, swallowed, and kept climbing. He could return here someday with a new nine for the tribe, but if he could not grab this number, Ferius's armies would tear across all of Moth. Torin tightened his lips and climbed with more vigor, shoving his grapple into nooks and crannies. When he looked up, he saw the Cabera Number bolted into the stone, bright as a beacon. He climbed faster, almost catching up with Bailey.

A dozen feet below the number, it became harder to climb; countless years of wind had smoothed the bricks down like sandpaper on wood. Torin tried to slam the grapple into the stone, but even the iron claws could not find purchase. He grunted and slipped two feet. His heart nearly stopped, but he managed to grab hold of a crevice and halt his fall.

"I can almost reach it," Bailey said, a few feet above him. She reached out, straining, and her fingertips grazed the number. "I'm . . . almost . . ."

Whistles filled the air.

Arrows slammed into the walls around them.

Torin cried out as one arrow scratched his shoulder, drew blood, then snapped against the wall.

He looked over his shoulder to see several Children of Nine, the shaman Xeekotep among them, standing below. They nocked new arrows into their bows.

"It's the only way to defeat the enemy!" Torin shouted down. "Xeekotep, listen to me! I need this number to stop Ishel's army, to—"

More arrows flew.

One slammed into the wall only inches away from his head. Another sliced along Bailey's calf, tearing her leggings and ripping off skin. She yowled and stared down to the courtyard where lay her armor, pack, and weapons.

Torin gritted his teeth and kept climbing. More arrows clattered around him. He grabbed a bulging brick, pulled himself up, and reached the top of the temple. The number nine was bolted to the stone bricks, the size of a sword. Bailey reached the number an instant later and clung onto it.

"If you shoot me, you'll hurt the number!" Torin cried down to them. "Lay down your bows."

The Children of Nine stared for a moment, silent, hesitating.

Then more arrows flew.

Torin winced and swung aside, clinging to the number with one hand. Several arrows slammed into the wall around him. Two hit the number, snapping against the brass. One arrow drove into Torin's shoulder, and he screamed in pain.

"Torin, unbolt the number!" Bailey said . . . and let go.

"Bailey!"

She slid down the sloping wall, thumping against each bulging brick. Arrows clattered around her. She screamed as she slid. When her feet hit the ground, she ran. Not pausing, she scooped up her shirt of scales, slung it over her head, and drew her sword. She raced toward the Children of Nine, howling in rage.

Torin wanted to slide after her, but he forced himself to turn back toward the number. He slammed his grapple against the wall, chipping the stone, struggling to tear the bolts out. He glanced over his shoulder only once, saw Bailey battling the Children of Nine, then looked back at his work.

With a grunt, he pulled one bolt free.

Howls rose below. He glanced down to see Ishel and her warriors race into the courtyard under the temple.

He turned back to the number. He tugged, freeing another bolt.

More arrows flew, and one scraped along his side. With a scream, Torin grabbed the number with both hands. He tugged wildly, feet pressed against the wall.

With a crack, the last bolt tore from the old stones.

The number came free in his hands.

Torin fell.

For a moment he tumbled through open air, the number clasped to his chest, an arrow in his shoulder.

His knees slammed against the sloping wall.

He slid, thudding against every brick. The arrow came free from his shoulder and snapped. His blood spurted.

With a grunt and blinding light, he slammed against the ground.

For a few heartbeats, he could see nothing, hear nothing, feel only pain.

Then he felt hands grabbing his shoulders and tugging him up.

"Run, you winky-eyed babyface!" somebody shouted in his ear. "Clutch that number and run!"

He ran, the world hazy around him, his ears ringing. He was vaguely aware of somebody running at his side, an old friend perhaps, a tall young woman with two yellow braids.

"Bailey?" he asked, confused as he ran with her between ferns.

"No, it's Ferius's grandmother. Of course it's Bailey!" She grabbed his wrist and tugged him. "Faster!"

They ran, ferns slapping against them, grasshoppers and frogs fleeing before them. Arrows whistled, sinking into the earth around them. They hurdled over the fallen statue of an ancient monk, raced down a slope, and crashed between rushes and mangroves. A stream flowed ahead, and reed boats swayed nearby, tethered to pegs.

Clutching his wound, Torin stumbled down the riverbank and into a boat. Bailey leaped in with him and slashed the tether. The stream caught the boat, pulling them eastward. They bounced over rocks, swung over a sunken log, and splashed down. Arrows hit the water around them, and one drove into their hull.

Bailey snarled, drew an arrow of her own, and fired. A Nayan along the riverbanks fell. She shot again, hit another man, and sent him splashing into the water.

Their boat picked up speed. Rocks filled the stream, tossing them up and down. Water splashed and Torin grunted with every bounce, his wound aching. Through the rushes on the banks, he saw many Nayans pursuing. Some were Children of Nine, calling out for their stolen idol, and others were Ishel's warriors. Torin clutched the brass number to his chest.

Laughter rose behind them in the stream, and Torin turned to see a boat pursuing them. Ishel sat within. She met Torin's gaze, smiled, and raised her spear. The weapon came flying toward Bailey and him.

Torin winced. Their boat hit a half-submerged log and flew into the air. The spear slammed into the hull, piercing the reeds and emerging between him and Bailey. They crashed down into the water with a blinding splash and kept flowing downriver, moving as fast as galloping horses.

"I see your blood, Torin of Arden!" Ishel shouted from her boat. "I will drink it!"

Bailey grunted and fired her bow, but Ishel swung her scimitar, diverting the arrow. With a curse, Bailey reached into her quiver and found it empty. Grumbling, she leaned across the boat, tugging at Nayan arrows which pierced its hull.

"Uhm . . . Bailey?" Torin said.

She grumbled, struggling to wrench arrows free. "Not now, Torin!" She ducked with a curse as more arrows flew from the riverbanks, narrowly missing her head.

Torin gulped. "Bailey, I think you better sit down."

She growled, tugged an arrow free from the boat, and laughed. "Not now, Winky!" She nocked her arrow and closed one eye.

"I really think you should—"

"Torin, what?" She spun toward him, face red . . . and paled. She sat down and clung on.

Torin grimaced as they shot toward the waterfall ahead.

"Can I use my grapple now?" he asked.

"Yes, damn you!" Bailey shouted. "Use your damn grapple!"

He swung the grapple on its rope. Mist rose ahead. The boat jostled madly. A boulder slammed into the hull, snapping reeds. Ishel screamed behind them.

"Bailey, hold onto me!" Torin shouted.

He held the number with one hand, the rope with the other. Bailey wrapped her limbs around him and clung. Fallen logs filled the water, slamming into the boat. Several boulders jutted upon the waterfall's edge, stone teeth rising around spilling drool.

For a heartbeat, they tilted over the brink, strangely still, strangely peaceful. Torin could see the water cascade a hundred feet, slamming into a rocky pool below.

Then their boat went over the edge.

Torin tossed the grapple. The iron claws swung around a boulder.

They fell.

The boat came free below them, plunging down.

The rope snapped taut. Torin's palms blazed but he held on. Bailey clung to him. They swung on the rope, swaying through mist and water.

Screaming, her boat shattering against the rocks, Ishel came tumbling over the waterfall. As she fell, her eyes met Torin's. She reached out. She tried to grab him. He kicked, slamming his boots into her belly. She grunted . . . and she was gone, crashing down into the mist.

"Winky, you crazy bastard!" Bailey clung so tightly to his neck she nearly tore his head off.

Torin grunted and kicked. They swung, the water crashing against their backs. His boots hit a jutting boulder, and he pushed them several feet back.

Battle cries rose above and arrows rained. Torin looked up to see the Children of Nine upon the cliff, firing from between the rushes. Torin kicked the boulder again, and they swung, emerging from the waterfall.

They grabbed a vine that dangled down the cliff. They climbed down, shielded from arrows by an outcrop of stone. When Torin reached the forest floor, he wanted to collapse into the ferns, nurse his wounds, and sleep, but the Children of Nine still howled above. The tribesmen began climbing down vines in pursuit.

"I'll race you to safety!" Bailey said, flashing him a weary grin, and burst into a run.

Clutching the number to his chest, Torin ran with her. They plunged into brush, disappearing into a sea of green.

CHAPTER TWENTY-FOUR
THE SHORES OF NIGHT

With steel, flame, and gunpowder, the fleet of sunlight arrived in the last bastion of night.

They covered the sea, a thousand ships or more, a city of masts, sails, and warriors chanting for the blood of Eloria. Once there had been eight kingdoms of sunlight; here they fought as one force, a swarm to drown the night. Their torches burned, raising smoke that hid the clouds. Their swords and armor gleamed. Their cannons—once unknown to the sunlit demons and stolen from the cities they had crushed—turned toward the walls of Asharo like hundreds of baleful eyes.

Before them—a smaller force, clustered together—sailed the fleet of Eloria, the combined ships of fallen empires and one last, free island. Through the dark waters they rowed, heading toward the crackling armada of the sun. Atop their decks stood the soldiers of darkness, clad in steel, their eyes large and gleaming, their skin orange in their lanterns' light. All stood silent. No cheers rose from them, not even from the halest warrior. They stood still, staring ahead across the water, seeing their death approach, for here was their final stand. Here was a last fight under the darkness—the free children of Eloria, raising steel for one more battle . . . one last charge before the light rose.

Riding upon Pirilin, the white dragon of the north, Jin soared above his fleet and cried out for all to hear.

"Eloria!" His voice was young and high, but it carried on the wind, and he knew all could hear. "Eloria, fight with courage, fight with honor, fight for darkness. We are the night!"

From the a hundred decks rose the cries of soldiers. Sailors, archers, swordsmen, and gunners all raised their voices. The cry stormed across the water. "We are the night!"

Beneath Jin, Pirilin the dragon coiled across the air, wingless and limbless. She was like him, the crippled boy born of siblings, his limbs missing, and yet Pirilin was mighty, and flying in her harness, Jin felt mighty too. A thousand enemy ships sailed toward him, and they sought to slay him, to slay all the children of night, but he would be strong. He would be brave.

I will be a leader.

"I fight with you, Eloria!" he cried down to his soldiers. "Pirilin fights too. Cast back the sunlight!"

Pirilin roared beneath him, and a second roar answered hers. To Jin's right, black scales flashed. Strapped into the saddle, he turned his head and saw Tianlong fly with him, the black dragon of the south, his beard red, his horns long. Upon the beast rode Empress Hikari, clad in lacquered plates, a bow in her hand. Her visor was pulled down, shaped as a snarling face, and her hair streamed from under the helmet, a white banner.

"We fight together, Jin!" she cried out to him across the wind.

Less than a mile now separated the fleets. The Timandrian vessels covered the sea. His friend Torin had told Jin about the forests of Timandra, the trunks of strange living creatures called 'trees' rising together. This must have been how a forest looked, a thousand masts rising. The sunlit sailors jeered at the smaller Elorian fleet. Their drums beat. Their horns blared. Their soldiers shouted out, calling for the death of darkness. Upon their decks, their archers nocked arrows, and their gunners lit fuses.

"Eloria, light your cannons!" Jin cried from his dragon. "Light burning arrows and light the darkness."

Across his ships below—a fleet so small by the wrath of the day—archers dipped arrows into braziers, lighting the tips.

Gunners lit cannons' fuses. The night ships sailed forth, their oars moving to the beat of drums, their battened sails opened wide for extra speed. Their iron figureheads—shaped as dragons—spewed smoke to conceal their locations.

With countless battle cries, the fleets of both day and night fired their weapons.

Arrows sailed through the night like ten thousand comets, their tips ablaze. With blasts that nearly deafened Jin, cannons spewed fire and iron. Across the two fleets, flames blasted, wood and clay shattered, and sails burned. Men screamed and fell.

"Hang tight, little one!" Pirilin said beneath him. The white dragon twisted her head, looked at Jin, and grinned toothily. "Ready yourself for some battle."

With a roar, Pirilin turned back forward and dived.

Wind shrieked around them, whipping Jin's hair. They flew across the masts of their own ships, dived across the water, and charged toward the enemy.

Timandrian carracks rose ahead, larger and bulkier than the Elorian ships, their sails wide. Archers fired from their decks, and Pirilin roared again, dodged the projectiles, and dived.

"For Eloria!" Jin cried as the dragon lashed her tail, clubbing a ship's mast.

The mast crashed down, spilling a sailor. More arrows flew and Pirilin soared. Arrows clattered against her scales, snapping and doing her no harm. Jin shouted wordlessly, feeling more afraid, excited, and alive than ever before. At his side, he saw Tianlong plow into a second ship, ramming its hull. Planks of wood cracked, water gushed into the ship, and the black dragon soared through a stream of arrows.

Beneath them, through clouds of smoke and flying metal, the two fleets crashed together.

Figureheads—shaped as dragons on the Elorian fleet, shaped as animals of land and sky on the Timandrian fleet—

rammed into hulls. Sailors screamed and fell. Planks thudded down and warriors ran from deck to deck, swinging swords. Cannons blasted and flames raced across sails. Masts cracked and smoke billowed over the battle.

Jin shouted as Pirilin rose and dipped, lashing her tail. An arrow scraped across his cheek and blood dripped, but he felt no pain.

The battle seemed to last for hours, maybe for entire turns. Flames lit the water and red smoke covered the sky. The arrows flew, the cannons blazed, and blood filled the water. When Jin looked behind him, he saw the city of Asharo perched upon the coast. The walls rose above the sand, and the black pagodas rose behind them, thick with archers.

Behind those walls, the people of the night hide—mothers and children, elders and babes. We cannot let those walls fall.

"The ships are breaking through!" Jin cried out.

A dozen Timandrian vessels had crashed through the Elorian fleet. Charred but still topped with soldiers, the carracks made their way toward the city. In the east, Jin saw a dozen more Timandrian ships smash through a squadron of Elorian junks, navigate around the sinking vessels, and sail toward the coast.

"Pirilin, they're going to reach the city!"

The dragon growled beneath him, spun in the sky, and flew in pursuit of the Timandrian ships. Fifty now sailed away from the raging battle, heading toward the coast. With a roar, Pirilin swooped, lashed her tail, and cracked the hull of a caravel. The ship listed and water roared in. Arrows flew and Jin screamed as one whistled by his ear. The dragon soared, then plunged down and swung her tail again, cracking a second ship. Men fell into the water. The walls of Asharo loomed ahead, crackling with torches, awaiting the assault.

Jin whipped his head from side to side, seeking Elorian support, but the other ships still sailed deeper in the sea, engulfed in smoke and flame. Tianlong the dragon roared in the distance, too far to aid them. Everywhere else he looked, Jin saw the enemy ships sailing toward the walls.

Pirilin dipped to attack another vessel when cannons blazed.

All Jin saw was smoke, blood, flame.

The dragon screamed and wind shrieked.

They crashed into the water with a force that rattled Jin's teeth, pounded his body like hammers, and knocked his head so far back he thought his neck might snap.

Iciness engulfed him. Jin shouted and bubbles rose. They sank. They bobbed up, broke above the surface, and Jin gulped air.

"Pirilin!" he shouted.

She groaned beneath him and her blood filled the water. The enemy ships surrounded them, arrows flew, and Pirilin sank again. Jin cried out underwater.

"Pirilin! Fly!"

He could see the light of lanterns above the water, gleaming like stars in a murky sky. Pirilin's blood rose around him, coiling and dancing. She swam underwater then breached again, and Jin took a deep breath and coughed out water. The other ships sailed farther away now.

"Jin . . ." said Pirilin, turning her head in the water. Her eyes were glazed and blood trickled down her forehead. "Watch over them, Jin . . . watch over the night."

Her eyes closed.

She sank.

They plunged back into the depths, sinking between bubbles and dancing blood.

"Pirilin!" Jin cried, strapped into his saddle, but she would not wake.

The lights above grew distant.

Jin thrashed, struggling to free himself from the saddle. With no limbs, how could he unbuckle his harness? His lungs ached for air. The water seemed to crush him, pushing against him with the force of a constricting boa. He screamed into the sea, thrashing, banging himself against the straps, knowing that he'd die, that he would forever remain under the water with Pirilin, that—

One strap snapped free.

Jin struggled with renewed vigor. A second buckle opened, and like a fish squirting out of a fisherman's hands, Jin blasted upward.

He wriggled his torso. He swam like a fish, pushing himself upward, head aching, lungs blazing, only heartbeats away from breathing in water. He wouldn't make it. He was too deep, too slow. He had to breathe, his lungs were collapsing, he—

Pain exploded. He opened his mouth for a deep breath.

He burst over the surface.

Air flowed into his lungs and stars floated across his eyes.

He lay on his back, floated, and looked around him. The battle still raged in the northern waters. Hundreds of ships were firing cannons and arrows, and countless soldiers vaulted from deck to deck. In the south, many Timandrian ships were still sailing toward the walls of Asharo, and more kept joining them. Burning flotsam bobbed around Jin. The body of a sailor floated by him, then sank.

"Pirilin!" Jin shouted, seeking her. Surely she had managed to swim above the surface too. Surely she couldn't have died; she was a great, ancient dragon, wisest among them. "Pirilin, please!"

A roar sounded above and scales flashed in the sky, and hope leaped in Jin, but it was Tialong, his scales black and his beard red. The dragon dived toward him, smoke pluming between his teeth. Gentle as a mother wolf lifting her cub, Tianlong held onto Jin's tunic with his teeth and lifted him.

"We have to find Pirilin!" Jin said to Empress Hikari who sat in the black dragon's saddle. "She's hurt."

Tianlong soared higher, turned his neck around, and placed Jin into the saddle too. Hikari wrapped her arms around him, held him close, and kissed his head.

"We must go to the city now, Jin," she said. "The fight will continue."

When he looked below him, Jin saw that the naval battle was over. The Elorian fleet lay sunken; only the tips of their masts rose from the water. Burning flotsam and floating bodies covered the water. The enemy fleet—hundreds of its ships still sailed— was moving toward the city. Across the warships, men were lowering rowboats into the water. Troops chanted inside the landing craft, heading toward the beaches.

"Where's Pirilin?" Jin asked in a small voice, seeking her in the night, but he knew the answer.

You're with him now, he thought, eyes stinging. *You're with Shenlai. He will look after you. He was the greatest being I ever knew.*

"Tianlong, to the city!" the empress cried.

The black dragon roared and flew faster, heading toward the black walls. Below them upon the shore, the first Timandrian troops—thousands of them—leaped from their rowboats and ran toward the walls . . . toward the last, flickering life in Eloria.

CHAPTER TWENTY-FIVE
THE PATH OF TIME

On the spring equinox, Bailey and Torin walked toward Cabera Mountain, the broken heart of the world.

"By Idar," Bailey whispered. She stopped in her tracks and widened her eyes.

The mountain loomed above them, taller than any mountain she had ever seen. Grass and pines covered the foothills, giving way to rocky slopes and a cloudy peak. It rose from the dusk, its western slope gilded with sunlight, its eastern slope shrouded in indigo shadows. Hills rolled around the mountain, swaying with grass, rushes, and wild flowers on the sunlit side, barren and smooth on the night side. High upon the mountainside, crowned with wisps of cloud, shone a single round jewel, still too far to see clearly but bright as a star.

Bailey pointed toward the lofty beacon. "The clock."

Smiling, she turned to look at Torin. He stood at her side, and seeing him—just looking at him in open daylight, no more night or rainforest around them—lifted her spirits just as much as that mountain.

He's changed, she thought. Two years ago, when they had left Fairwool-by-Night, he had been a callow boy, soft of cheeks and timid as a pup. He had gained strength in the night, donning armor and lifting a sword and finding his inner conviction. Now he stood beside her like a ragged doll. His clothes were tattered, his cloak thick with burrs, his boots almost falling apart around his feet. His hair had lengthened and hung across his ears, and a beard—grown in the jungle—shaded his face.

He looks like a grungy alley cat, she thought, *but he's just my little kitten.*

She grabbed his hand, squeezed it, and kissed his cheek. "We're finally here."

But he would not smile or squeeze her hand in return. He stared ahead and worry veiled his eyes. When he spoke, his voice was raspy with weariness. "Do you think the others made it? Cam and Linee and . . . Koyee?"

Bailey narrowed her eyes and loosened her grip on his hand. She had heard that pause, that longing in the last name. Sometimes Bailey wondered if he cared about Koyee more than the fate of the world itself.

"It's the spring equinox," she said. "It's when we agreed to meet here. They'll make it." She nodded. "Cam is quick and clever, and Koyee is . . . Koyee is . . . well, Koyee had two dojai assassins to help her, and I'm sure they're well trained." She tugged Torin's arm. "Now come on, Winky! To the mountain! Stop gaping like a babyfaced country bumpkin and let's go."

Tugging him along, she walked through fields of wild grass that rose to her knees. Grasshoppers and bumblebees bustled around her, and chickadees and blackbirds flew overhead between scattered ash and birch trees.

This almost seems like home, Bailey thought, and suddenly her eyes were watering. Fairwool-by-Night too loomed by the shadow, forever caught between day and night. In Fairwool-by-Night, they would run like this through the fields, Bailey tugging him along. The memories filled her like dreams: him and her in their innocent youth, chasing fireflies, racing to the distant carob tree and back, seeking fairy burrows among the trees, and stealing honeycombs and then fleeing the bees into the river.

"Soon it'll be over," she whispered, tears in her eyes, as they ran toward the mountain. "Soon the world will be healed. Soon we can go back to joy." She looked at Torin as they raced through the grass. "Hot apple pies on the windowsill. Our fluffy feather beds and Grandpapa's stories by the fireplace. Cold ale and hot apple pie in The Shadowed Firkin. Soon we can go *home*, Torin."

He nodded but no joy filled him. "Not yet. Not until the clock is fixed. Not until we know Cam and Koyee made it here too." Pain filled his eyes. "How do we know it'll work? How—"

"You worry too much!" She growled at him, reached to her belt, and patted the brass number nine she carried there like a sword. "It'll work. I believe."

After an hour of walking, they reached the foothills and began to climb the grassy slopes. A faded path seemed to coil up the mountain, overrun with weeds and rocks, leading up toward the distant, gleaming disk.

"Race you," Bailey said.

Torin groaned. "Not everything needs to be a ra—"

She did not let him finish his sentence. With a grin, she burst into a run, kicking dust onto him. She heard him moan behind her but follow.

Sweat dripped down her back, and after traveling the rainforest for two months, she was weary and thin, but she wouldn't stop running. The clock was so near—just there above!—and this war could end. And so she kept racing, even as she panted and her legs ached.

And yet . . . as she ran up the mountain path, fear filled her along with her hope. For many turns, she'd been alone with Torin—just her and him in the rainforest. Her heart leaped to remember their kiss under the waterfall, their bodies pressed together under blankets, and just the presence of him—all hers. Would that end now? When they reunited with the others, would he forget about her, would he run to Koyee and her time with him would be over?

"You are mine, Torin Greenmoat," she whispered as she ran up the mountainside. "You were always mine. We've always been together and we always will. Never forget that."

She looked over her shoulder to see if he'd heard, but he was running a dozen feet behind her.

"Bailey, slow down!" he said.

She shook her head and ran faster. They left the valleys and hills far below. The path zigzagged up the slope, soon becoming so thin and steep Bailey had to climb on hands and knees.

Soon it'll be over, she thought, tears in her eyes. *Soon we'll go back to our old, thatch-roof cottage, and Torin will tend to his gardens, and things will be good again . . . away from this war and away from Koyee.*

The path rose steeply, and she saw it above—the great dial of the ancient clock. From afar it had shone like a star, but here she saw a great sun, a disk so large she could have stood in its center, stretched out her limbs, and not reached its circumference. It was thousands of years old, but time had not touched it; she saw no rust, no pocks, no cracks. The dial's hand was missing, as was the number nine. Beneath this glimmering brass disk, a doorway was set into the mountainside.

Standing outside the doors, watching them approach, she stood.

Koyee.

Bailey froze, stared at the young woman, and her dreams of a home with Torin crashed down around her.

* * * * *

For the past turn, Bailey had kept talking of returning home, but Torin found less hope inside him.

As he climbed the mountain behind her, heading toward the clock, worry gnawed on him. What if the others hadn't found the missing clock pieces . . . or what if they hadn't survived? So close to the clock—this place that could heal the world—more pain than ever clawed through Torin.

Even if we do return home, we lost a friend. We lost Hem. Returning to Fairwool-by-Night without his friend, that gentle giant of a baker, would feel like a pale victory. How would songs in the tavern, fishing off the docks, and harvest festivals ever be the same?

As he mourned Hem, the fear of losing more friends tore through Torin.

Will you meet us here, Cam? he thought, dropping to hands and knees to climb the steep slope. He longed to see the small, sharp-featured shepherd with his quick smile and quicker wit.

And I miss you too, Linee, he thought, remembering the young queen's bright eyes, easy laughter, and kind heart.

And most of all I miss you, Koyee, he thought, a lump growing in his throat.

He paused from climbing for a moment, closed his eyes, and thought of all the hours he'd spent in Koyee's chamber, laughing with her, reading books together, and speaking of their distant village homes. He remembered kissing her lips, making love to her, stroking her pale cheek and snowy hair. And he remembered her courage—the quiet, dignified strength in her eyes, the steel of her heart shining through. He had first seen her two years ago, a hurt young girl, a precious doll to protect, and he had watched her grow into a warrior who led armies.

The sound of Bailey climbing ahead died.

Torin opened his eyes, looked up, and saw Bailey staring ahead . . . at Koyee.

The young Elorian wore the armor of Ilar, the black plates dented and scratched, and several fallen birch leaves filled her white hair. Her sword hung from her left hip. Against her opposite hip leaned a large iron gear.

She smiled softly, a warm sadness in her eyes.

"Hello, Bailey," she said, then looked at Torin. Her voice dropped to a whisper as if she were struggling not to cry. "*Sen sen,* Torin."

For a moment, Torin stood frozen, only able to stare.

Several feet ahead, standing upon the path, Bailey spun around toward him. Pain filled her eyes; damp and hurt and wide, they seemed almost as large as Elorian eyes.

Torin wanted to run forward, to embrace Koyee, even to weep, but he could only stand upon the mountain, staring at them both, the two women of his life.

Bailey lowered her head and stepped off the path. "Go to her, you babyface," she whispered and managed a trembling smile, and he thought he saw a tear in her eye.

He looked back at Koyee and she smiled too, the shy smile he remembered, her old scar tugging up one corner of her mouth, twisting her lips into that crooked shape that melted his heart. And finally he could move. He stepped up toward her, and the sunlight fell upon her, gleaming like fireflies. She was a pillar of white light, the beacon he'd fought for all these years.

He reached out, meaning to hold her hand in his, and her fingers grazed his arm, and then—he wasn't even sure who initiated it—they were embracing desperately, arms wrapped around each other, and her face burrowed against his neck, her tears warm.

"Torin," she whispered. "Torin . . . I missed you."

He touched her hair, and she lifted her head and smiled, a huge smile that showed her teeth, and a tear sparkled on the tip of her nose.

I missed you too, he wanted to say.

I love you, he almost whispered.

Marry me, his mouth ached to utter.

"And hello to you too, Eelani," he found himself saying, looking at the empty space above Koyee's shoulder.

Koyee snorted, then laughed, then squeezed him tighter. "You silly thing."

An uncomfortable clearing of the throat sounded behind them.

"Well, isn't this a lovely reunion," Bailey said, "but we have only two pieces here. The number nine and the gear." She whipped her head from side to side, braids swinging. "We still need the hand. Where are those woolheads Cam and Linee?"

Still holding Koyee in his arms, Torin turned his head to scan the mountain. The clock dial stood above him, embedded into the rock. The doorway in the mountainside stood closed. The hills and valleys sprawled out below into misty horizons—lush and green on one side, lifeless and dark on the other.

"Where are you?" Torin whispered, the wind in his air.

Footfalls sounded to his side.

He spun around and his eyes widened. Two figures were trudging up toward him. They must had taken a different path, hidden behind boulders and pines. A short man walked there, a woman beside him. Both were clad in heavy cloaks, hoods hiding their faces.

Torin grinned, the weight instantly lifting off his shoulders.

"Cam, old boy!" he cried to the climbing figures. "Linee! You made it. Come on, hurry up, will you?"

They two kept climbing, still hidden in their cloaks and hoods, and Torin frowned. Koyee took a step back, reaching for her sword, and Bailey tilted her head.

With a roar, a tiger leaped from behind a boulder, a great striped beast of fangs, fevered eyes, and claws like daggers. Before Torin could even react, the two figures raised their heads, pulled back their hoods, and smiled thinly.

Torin drew his sword, feeling the blood drain from his face. His words barely left his stiff lips.

"Ferius and Ishel."

CHAPTER TWENTY-SIX
AN OLD SONG

The enemy slammed against the city walls like a wave of lava.

They spread across the coast, holding torches and blades, their armor blazing red in the firelight. Their banners, sporting the sigil of Sailith, rose like a thousand suns. Upon the beaches, catapults fired flaming barrels, ballistae shot bolts of iron the size of men, and trebuchets slung boulders spiky with metal shards. And still the troops kept surging. Every moment another boat reached the sand, and more Timandrians emerged, roaring for victory, and ran toward the walls. Battering rams swung on chains, trumpets blared, and arrows filled the sky.

Jin sat upon a tower's battlements, gazing down onto the battle, and whispered feverishly, his voice all but lost under the din.

"Please, Koyee. Please." He shivered as boulders slammed into the walls, shaking the city and showering dust. "Please, Koyee, fix the clock. We have no more time."

The tower rose from a hill, looking down upon the battle. Dozens of similar towers, black and craggy and crowned with crenelations, rose around him, and archers stood atop them, firing arrows across the city walls and onto the beaches. Yet for every Timandrian slain, ten more emerged from the landing craft. Behind the enemy, far upon the horizon, a few last Elorian ships burned and sank.

"Fight for Eloria!" Jin shouted from the tower, perched between two merlons. "For the night!"

He did not know if his words inspired anyone. He did not know if anyone heard. Yet he could not fight, and so he shouted to his soldiers, trying to be a leader, trying to be brave, but feeling like a frightened boy.

Please, Koyee. We need you.

Thousands of Elorian soldiers stood upon the city walls below, firing down arrows, spilling burning oil, and blasting cannons. A man lit a hwacha—a metal plate full of fire arrows—and a hundred shards of death shot down toward the beaches, slaying many, yet still the enemy surged. Empress Hikari flew above the beaches, her dragon dipping down to crush men between his jaws. Hot air balloons flew above the battle, archers in their baskets, and their arrows rained. As Jin watched, a Timandrian archer fired upward, hit a hot air balloon, and the vessel burst into flames and crashed down onto the beach, burying soldiers beneath its burning cloth.

"Slay the enemy!" Hikari cried upon her dragon and dived. Tianlong's jaws and Hikari's arrows took out several men, and then they soared again. "Eloria—for the darkness!"

Yet Jin knew those were hollow words; they felt no more inspiring than his. What could words now do? Words of poison had brought the enemy to these walls, yet words of courage could not undo the bloodshed. Below upon the sand, a hundred soldiers—clad in bright steel, sunbursts upon their breastplates—swung a battering ram that hung from chains, its head shaped like a black bird with blazing red eyes full of embers. With every swing, the gates shook, and even the arrows of the defenders above could not stop the attack.

"And so it ends here," Jin said softly. "Here upon the shores of a southern, dark island, the last children of light will burn."

A snort rose beside him, and a gruff voice answered. "There will be time for goodbyes, Emperor Jin, but not yet. This is still our time to fight. And I'm not burning without taking a few of those bastards with me."

Jin turned his head to see the oddest soldier he'd ever laid eyes on. The little man stood no taller than a child, yet a white beard flowed from his chin to the ground. Rather than a breastplate, a frying pan was strapped across his chest, yet his head was large and topped with a true helmet. In one hand he held a flute; in the other, a knife that seemed as large as a sword in his grasp.

The dwarf gave a little bow. "I am Little Maniko, a humble busker, now a soldier in your service, my emperor." He gave Jin a sly smile. "Neither one of us looks particularly warlike, but I think we're both handling ourselves fine so far."

Jin couldn't help but laugh weakly. "I'd trade bodies with you."

Maniko shrugged. "My body's getting too old, but perhaps old age needs no longer concern us." He gestured toward the city walls. Arrows still flew there, and siege towers were now joining the fray. "This seems like a good tower for our last stand. Poor souls down on the walls won't enjoy the fun as long, but this tower will give us enough time for some final prayers."

Jin lowered his head. "It also gives us time for aid. A friend of mine, she's . . . she's on a quest for . . . I can't say, but if she succeeds, there is hope." His eyes dampened. "I must believe there is hope."

Maniko's face grew solemn. "There is always hope, even in the darkest shadow. I learned that on the streets of Pahmey."

Jin's eyes widened. "You fought in Pahmey?"

Maniko laughed mirthlessly. "For over forty years on the streets . . . and about two turns in battle. The Timandrians slammed at our gates with that very ram." He stared down at the great, black bird of iron slamming against the city doors. "They charged in, stepping over corpses, and we could not stop them.

Not even the Girl in the Black Dress, the great heroine of the war. But I lived. And she lived. There is always hope."

"The Girl in the Black Dress?" Jin asked.

Maniko nodded. "The bravest woman I'd ever known. I knew her before the war. I taught her to play a flute like this one." He raised his instrument. "We were buskers on the dirty streets, partners in grime." He barked a laugh, but then his eyes watered. "When the enemy marched in, she stood before them alone, sword raised. She's only a foot taller than I am and definitely thinner, but she's braver than any soldier I'd known." He wiped his eyes. "She slew many of the enemy. They say she wounded the demon Ferius himself. I don't know what happened to her, but every turn since that battle, I've missed her. I wish Koyee could be with us here—for one last battle, one last chance to raise her sword . . . and perhaps to play one last song together."

Jin's eyes widened. "Did you say . . . Koyee?" He blinked. "A young woman with purple eyes, three scars on her face? From a village named Oshy?"

Maniko almost dropped both flute and knife. The little busker-turned-warrior gasped. "You know her?"

Jin looked back toward the beaches. Countless Timandrians covered the sand. A catapult's boulder slammed into a guard tower, sending it crashing down in a rain of bricks, roof tiles, and blood. The city gates cracked and the enemy cheered. Elorian soldiers stood in the courtyard behind those breaking doors, swords drawn, waiting.

"She is my friend. She is strong. And she has strong companions with her." Jin could barely speak, and his breath shook in his lungs. "We must believe. We must give them time. We will be strong, Maniko . . . strong for our people and for Koyee."

Maniko seemed ready to say more when a crash shook the city.

Jin winced as the gates below—a few hundred yards away beyond barracks and homes—crashed open with a shower of metal shards. Roaring for the sun, the Timandrian knights charged into the city on armored horses, thrusting lances. In the courtyard, the warriors of Eloria cried out for the night and charged to meet them, riding panthers and swinging katanas. The two forces crashed together with a shower of blood and broken metal. Behind the gates, countless more enemy soldiers stood in the sand, firing arrows, climbing ladders onto the walls, and replacing every man who fell.

"We don't have much time left," Maniko said, standing beside Jin on the tower. The soldiers around them were busy firing arrows, but Maniko was too small for a bow. "What say you to some music before the end?"

Jin grimaced, the sight of the dead below driving into him like throwing stars. Every heartbeat, another soldier of Eloria died. Deeper in the city, the women and children hid, cowering behind doors and in cellars, waiting for the blades and fire.

"Will music stop the enemy?" he asked.

Maniko shook his head and raised his flute. "No, but if we die, let us die with a song. I will play an old tune, one I taught our dear mutual friend a long time ago in simpler times."

Screams, cannon fire, clashing swords, and tumbling bricks rose in a cacophony below. Upon the tower, Maniko played the old bone flute. Jin did not know what the song was about, but it sounded like a song of sadness and hope, or water and sky, of a lone soul seeking light in the darkness. It was the most beautiful thing he'd ever heard, more beautiful than whispering rivers or crackling fireplaces, and it made tears well up in his eyes and warmth fill his chest. It was perhaps an old song, but it was also *her* song, Koyee's song, and it brought him hope even as the enemy flowed toward them.

Boulders crashed into the walls below, holes gaped open, and more Timandrians rushed in. Like a red river through a crumbling dam, the forces of sunlight flowed into the city.

Daniel Arenson

CHAPTER TWENTY-SEVEN
BAILEY'S RUN

Bailey drew her sword and howled to the sky. All her hope—for a fixed world, for a fixed life, for a home with Torin—crashed around her. Legs shaking and fire burning through her, she leaped forward, nearly falling, and lunged toward the enemy.

"Ferius!" she shouted, eyes burning. "You've come here to die."

He stood upon the mountainside, about the length of a ship's deck away from her, and smiled thinly. He wore crimson armor beneath his cloak, and a helmet circled his head, sporting a sunburst motif in gold. At his side, Ishel smirked, clad in her old tiger pelts, while her live tiger snarled.

"Bailey Berin!" Ferius called toward her. "Torin Greenmoat! Koyee Mai! I've come here to die? No . . . no, my old friends. I've come here to end this little game of ours." He smiled at his companion. "Ishel, you take the two Timandrians. The little Elorian girl is mine."

The jungle warrior smiled, nocked an arrow, and aimed. "With pleasure."

Bailey screamed and charged toward them.

Ishel's arrow flew, and Bailey ducked and swiped her blade; the arrow slammed against the sword and flew aside. Bailey kept running, sword held before her, pebbles cascading under her boots. Behind her, she heard Torin run too and shout wordlessly.

Yes, the game ends here, Bailey thought, teeth bared. *In the dusk, here between day and night, this ends.*

246

She tried to reach the monk, but the tiger pounced toward her, slammed into her chest, and knocked her down.

Bailey screamed as Durga clawed at her. His paws sparked against her armor, ripping off scales, and she screamed as one claw found her flesh. The tiger's fangs drove down, trying to reach her neck, but she twisted and they hit her armor, denting the steel. She screamed, swung her sword, and drove the crossguard into Durga's head.

The beast roared, strings of saliva between his teeth. Bailey tried to shove him off, but the animal pinned her down, several times her weight, nearly crushing her, and stars floated before her eyes.

"Ferius!" she screamed.

Durga leaned in to bite again.

Fangs punched through armor and tore into her shoulder, and her blood spurted, and her head slammed against the rocks.

For a moment she floated through light and darkness, and she remembered sailing with Torin two years ago upon the Sern River, back in the sunlight and warmth of their youth, and she wondered if she was dying, if the afterworld was a lazy boat ride along a sunlit river.

"Bailey!" he cried, her Torin, the boy she loved.

Her eyes snapped open.

The tiger still roared above her, her blood on his fangs.

No, she thought. *No, I cannot die here, not like this. Torin needs me.*

She roared and reached into her boot.

Durga drove his fangs down again, prepared to tear out her neck.

She drew her dagger and drove it upward.

The blade sliced the tiger's cheek, tearing through fur, skin, and flesh.

She expected Durga to roar again, to bite in rage, but the tiger only mewled. He looked at her, eyes wide and hurt, his expression almost betrayed, as if he hadn't just tried to kill her. She raised her dagger again, prepared to slay him, but paused. The animal's eyes, looking down upon her, seemed so large, almost Elorian-sized.

Durga lowered his head, licked at her blood, then stepped off her. The weight lifted off her chest, she breathed in deeply, and when she turned her head, she saw the tiger fleeing down the mountainside.

I'm alive, she thought. *Idar, I'm alive.*

Sword in one hand, dagger in the other, she rose to shaky feet.

Ahead of her, standing upon the pebbly mountain path, Torin and Ishel were dueling with swords. Blood already covered Torin's arm. Farther back, under the clock dial, Koyee darted through the doorway and into the mountain.

"Come face me, Ferius!" Koyee called out from the shadows. "Battle me in the dark, if you wish to see me dead."

Brandishing a flanged mace, the monk stepped into the mountain too, disappearing from view.

Bailey stood torn, bloody weapons in hand, not sure which duel to join. Another glance at Torin and his bloody arm, and she chose him. She ran, blades held before her.

"Stand back, Babyface!" she said, trying to ignore the blood flowing down her chest. "Let me handle her."

Bailey stumbled and her knees hit the path. They still fought ahead of her. She had thought them so close, but they were still far, and Bailey blinked furiously, slapping the blood off her. Damn blood! Damn wounds! She pushed herself to her feet, growling, and fell again, banging her knees hard. It took a third attempt to stand and keep running.

Because I'll always keep running, she thought, tears in her eyes. *I've been running all my life—across the fields with Torin, and away from my home, and into darkness, and into war.* Her tears flowed like her blood. *I've been running since the day our parents died, since Torin came into my home, a fellow plague orphan, and I won't stop running ever. Not until the world is fixed. Not until I'm fixed.*

She reached the duel, tears on her cheeks and blood on her chest, and shoved Torin aside. She sprang toward Ishel, blades swinging.

The Nayan warrior grinned. "Hello, Bailey! I've been waiting for moons to fight you again, you Ardish worm. Come to die."

Bailey screamed and drove forward. She slammed Ishel's spear aside with her sword and thrust her dagger, but the blade only crashed against the woman's breastplate, doing her no harm.

"You killed Hem," Bailey said through clenched teeth. "You killed my friend. Never make that mistake." She roared and swung her sword down. "I am Bailey Berin, a child of sunlight, a warrior of darkness, and I will have my revenge."

At her side, Torin swung his sword too. Ishel fought with both scimitar and spear, parrying both attacks at once.

I will kill you, Ishel, Bailey thought as she thrust and parried. *And I will kill Ferius. And I will save the night. And I will save our village. And—*

She realized her blood was seeping down her legs now. Damn wound! She hadn't thought the tiger had hurt her this badly, but she ignored the pain, and she lunged forward in another attack . . . but crashed down again.

She found herself on her knees.

Ishel's spear thrust, driving into Bailey's shoulder, and she screamed.

Bailey dropped her weapons, gripped the spear with both hands, and pulled it free from her body with a wet, sucking sound and gush of blood.

"Bailey!" Torin screamed, still swinging his blade, trying to find a way past Ishel's defenses.

Bailey rose to her feet, still holding one end of the spear's shaft; Ishel held the other end. Blood dripping, Bailey didn't even bother lifting her weapons.

She leaped forward, barreling into Ishel and knocking her down onto the mountainside.

"I'm not as good a swordswoman as you," Bailey said, shoving Ishel's head against the rocks. "But I'm a farm girl and a damn good wrestler."

Ishel screamed below her, still gripping her sword, trying to swing the blade into Bailey's back. Bailey leaned in like a tiger herself, driving her teeth into Ishel's shoulder, and she tasted blood, and the two women rolled.

They tumbled down the mountainside, pebbles jabbing them, the sky and earth spinning around them, the night and day sides rolling, and it almost seemed to Bailey that the world turned again. Rocks dug into her. Pain drove through her, and her leg twisted, and her elbow slammed against stone and blazed. Still she tried to claw, to bite, to tear out Ishel's neck.

With a thud and cracking wood and blazing pain, they slammed into a pine and lay still.

Bailey blinked. The clock was now high above her like a sun. Torin was running downhill but she barely saw him, and Bailey smiled because she no longer hurt. The fall had somehow healed her . . . or hurt her too badly for pain.

Vaguely, she was aware of Ishel rising to her feet. The woman still had her bow, and while some of her arrows had snapped, most were still whole. Standing above Bailey, she nocked an arrow. She pressed her boot against Bailey's chest, pinning her down, and aimed her bow up the mountainside.

"Torin!" Bailey screamed. "Torin, watch out!"

The arrow whistled. Bailey looked up to see the projectile slam into Torin's thigh, and he cried out and fell to his knees.

"Torin . . ." Bailey whispered, trying to struggle, to rise to her feet, but she could not. Her blood leaked around her, so much blood, and she could barely breathe, barely see.

A face thrust down before her—Ishel's face, cruel and mocking. The woman caressed her cheek, kissed her forehead, and whispered, "I will kill him first, Bailey. I will kill him first as you lie here dying. When I kill you, I want you to be staring at his severed head."

With that, Ishel drove down her fist. Pain exploded against Bailey's face with white light, and she couldn't breathe or see, and she floated upon the sea.

When she blinked, all she saw was mist. Was this the fog of the afterworld? She thought that a figure was moving ahead—Ishel walking uphill toward Torin, laughing, already nocking another arrow.

Bailey tried to rise.

Her eyes rolled back, and she gazed upon clouds, and her head rested among flowers, and it was beautiful. It was so beautiful. Moths flew above her, their wings black and white, and she smelled the hearths of home and felt the warmth of her old bed.

No.

She pushed against the earth.

You will stand up now, Bailey Berin, spoke a voice inside her. *Do you hear me? You will stand up now, and you will not die here. Not this turn. Now like this. Not now. You will still run.*

She shoved herself up.

She stood in blood, weaponless, and balled her hands into fists.

"I will still run."

Wobbling, almost blind with pain, she began to trudge up the mountain. To battle. To Torin. To be the woman she'd been born to be, to fight the fight of her life. For him and for this whole world of Moth.

He was on his knees, her Torin, an arrow in his thigh. He still held his sword, but he did not move. He only looked up, pale, staring. A dozen yards away from him, Ishel stood upon a boulder, smirking, a new arrow nocked in her bow . . . aiming at Torin.

"The last one was hard to aim," Ishel said. "This time I won't hit your leg. This arrow is going into your heart, little boy."

Torin turned his head and looked at Bailey.

Their eyes met and Bailey cried.

There he was—her foster brother, her brother at arms, the man she loved. There he was, so close to her but heartbeats from death.

"We will always run together," she whispered.

Smirking, Ishel pulled back her bowstring.

And Bailey ran.

She had been running for years—through fields, meadows, forests, and battles—but this was the run of her life. Here was the run she'd been born for—across the mountain of time, not just the time frozen in the clock above, but all the time spanning her life. Her boots raced through the rye field south of the Watchtower back home. They raced through meadows of flowers, tugging Torin behind her. They were small feet, shuffling, upon woolen rugs when she was just learning how to run. And he was always there, always a light in her life, even now at the end.

She ran and she leaped and she lunged toward him, to be with him again.

The arrow flew.

Bailey soared through the air between Torin and the projectile.

Pain drove into her chest with a shower of light.

She fell.

Torin leaped to his feet, and she thought he was running toward her, but he jumped over her and screamed, and his blade lashed, and though the world was smudged, she saw his sword drive forward, crash into Ishel, and sink into her chest down to the hilt.

Ishel never even screamed. Her mouth opened silently. She gasped. She seemed almost in shock, as if she had never believed she was threatened. The rainforest warrior tilted her head quizzically, opened her mouth as if to speak, but no words emerged, only blood.

Torin pulled his sword out of her flesh.

Ishel stood for just a moment longer, then crashed down and rose no more.

The sword clanged to the ground, and Torin left the body and rushed toward Bailey.

He knelt above her. He placed one hand against her cheek, the other under her head, and his eyes watered.

"Hi, Winky," she whispered, lying on the ground. The arrow thrust out of her chest.

"Bailey," he whispered back.

She nodded, smiling. "There are arrows in us." She gave a weak laugh that became a cough. "But . . . you'll be all right. I promised Grandpapa. I promised I'd look after you. And you'll be all right . . . I know it." Her voice was so soft, barely a whisper. "But . . . I won't, I think."

His breath shook. He placed a hand around the arrow in her chest, meaning to pull it out, but she stopped him. She shook her head.

"You'll be fine, Bailey," he said forcefully, but his face was pale and his eyes were damp. "I'm not going to let you die here. Do you hear me? You're coming home with me. Back to Fairwool-by-Night."

She laughed softly and tasted her tears. "No, Torin. I'm going on another run now. I'm going on the longest run yet, and you don't have to race me this time." She reached up and caressed his cheek. "This is one run I won't drag you on. I'm going here alone . . . to a new field under strange skies."

He shook his head, his hand cradling her cheek, his other hand stroking her hair. His voice was hoarse, torn with pain. "I won't let you."

"You never could stop me. You never could tell me what to do, you know that. Nobody could. Kiss me one last time."

His tears fell, and he kissed her lips, and he held her so close.

"I love you, Torin," she whispered into his ear. "And I want you to do something for me."

"What?" he whispered, seeming unable to say more.

"I want you to be with Koyee . . . to love her, to build a life with her, to never let her go. I want her to be yours . . . and you hers." She smiled, held in his arms. "I didn't give my life for you to mope alone forever, damn it. So marry the girl."

"Bailey!" He gripped her hand. "Bailey, no. You can't leave now. Do you hear me? Bailey, do you hear? I'm not letting you go." He blinked and shook his head and his voice dropped to a hoarse whisper. "I don't want you to go."

Her fingers trembled, but she managed to reach up and pinch his cheek . . . one last time.

"Hold me," she mouthed silently.

He held her in his arms. The sunlight fell upon them, and flowers rustled around her, and she could see a grove of maples below. She had always loved maples.

She closed her eyes and thought of home, and she imagined lying in the grass of Fairwool-by-Night upon the hill, Torin at her side, a place of safety and warmth, of crickets and flowers and endless sunlight. It was like falling asleep in his arms. She smiled softly. She was running again, heading into haze and light and another adventure, exploring the hidden meadows and secret forests of the undiscovered country.

A

Daniel Arenson

CHAPTER TWENTY-EIGHT
THE ORRERY SUN

She ran down the tunnel into the mountain, shouting over her shoulder.

"You want me, Ferius! Face me in darkness." The stone walls were narrow around her, roughly hewn, and even her Elorian eyes could barely see here. "Fight me in shadow."

As she ran, her heart twisted in worry for Torin and Bailey, but here in this mountain, she had to face him. The demon of sunlight. The man who had murdered her father, her brother, and countless of her people.

Ferius. My half-brother.

She heard him grunting behind her, chasing in the darkness, and when she looked over her shoulder, she saw his stocky form. A red light gleamed upon his sunburst helmet and waxy face, turning him into a creature of flame. His eyes burned like embers, cruel and hungry for her flesh. Koyee spun her head back forward and saw the firelight ahead. It bathed her with heat, but she couldn't see its source.

A few more steps brought her into a round chamber the size of a temple. Koyee gasped; she had never seen a place so strange. The walls were carved of the same rough stone, but the floor was an intricate astrolabe of metal tracks, turning gears, and clicking sprockets, the pieces flat and smooth enough to walk on. Great rings of metal rose from the floor to fill the chamber, as if some giant had tossed down armlets large enough to loop around homes. Upon these rings, metallic spheres spun in a lazy dance, and small maps appeared upon them. Koyee remembered

256

standing within the henge of Montai, gazing up at great, round worlds in the sky. These were the same worlds, she realized, but forged of brass, iron, and silver. It was an orrery—a map of the skies.

In the center, among all the rings, blazed a brazier as tall as her. It was perfectly round, formed of an iron grill that encircled embers and flame. It looked like a mechanical sun. The metallic worlds all orbited around it, some supporting little moons on rods. One sphere looked like Mythimna; upon its surface appeared a map shaped like a moth. As the sphere moved around the sun, traveling along its round track, only one side faced the mechanical sun. The flames lit only one of the wing-shaped continents, leaving the other in shadow. The other worlds all spun around their axes, but Mythimna—this world they called Moth— remained frozen.

"So much for darkness," Koyee whispered.

She spun around and saw Ferius enter the chamber. The monk stepped toward her, mace in hand. His sunburst helmet blazed in the firelight like a secondary sun. The scar Torin had given him at Bluefeather Corner shone on his cheek, and Koyee felt her own scars sting.

We are more alike than ever, she thought. Born of one mother, they had the same triangular face, broad forehead, pale skin . . . and now both bore similar scars.

"You've come so close, Koyee," he said. "You've come to the very heart of time. It's fitting, I think, that here—right by your hope for victory—you will fall."

Koyee shook her head, and her eyes stung. "Why? Why, Ferius? You're my brother. You don't have to do this. You—"

"Your *half*-brother." His face twisted and pain filled his eyes. "Your people like that word. Half. When I was a child in Oshy, I heard it a lot. Half-boy. Half-creature. Half-brother to Okado. I killed him myself, did you know? He burned in my fire."

Her eyes stung. "So much hatred, Ferius. So much anger." She could barely speak, and tears burned in her eyes. "We would have welcomed you back into our family. We would have loved you. Why did you take this path?" Her sword wavered in her hand. "Why did you turn to bloodshed, to hatred, when we could have offered you love?"

He shook. For a moment Koyee thought he'd weep, but instead he roared, a cry of agony that tore through the chamber, shaking the worlds on their tracks. The floor and walls shook; the mountain trembled.

"Love?" he screamed, voice hoarse. "What love was there for me as a child—when your people tormented me, when our own mother bore a new son to replace me? You drove me to this!" He advanced toward her, eyes red and watery, teeth bared. "You will pay for your sins, filthy Elorian. I made all the others pay. And you will suffer more than any. I will not kill you here. I will treat you as others treated me. You will become a freak, a twisted thing, outcast, scorned. When you're the last Elorian alive, I will place you in a cage, and I will parade you around the world, city to city. Mothers will shriek at your appearance. I will make you hideous. I will turn you into a creature like your emperor. I will rip off your limbs, but I will not let you die. Children will cry to see your deformity. Men will toss filth your way." His shoulders shook and his tears spilled. "You will suffer like I suffered."

He lunged toward her, mace swinging.

Koyee sidestepped, and his mace slammed against one of the orrery's tracks. Sparks flew and the worlds shook. Koyee swung her sword, aiming for his neck, but he lurched back and the blade scratched along his armor.

Their dance began.

Perhaps they'd been dancing for two years now, since that day he had killed her father. Perhaps she'd been performing this dance all her life—since she'd been born in a humble village, the daughter of a fisherman's wife with a secret old lover and a torn, lost child. Here Koyee fought within a great orrery, the secret machine of Moth, and here the secrets of her own family clashed with steel.

His mace slammed against her armor, and Koyee screamed and fell to her knees, swung her sword, and slammed it against the greaves protecting his legs. She leaped back and the mace swung again, and its flanged head crashed against the floor, cracking the metal. She jumped to her feet. Their weapons swung. The dance continued. They leaped between the round, metal tracks. The worlds spun around them, creaking back and forth like wagons in a mine, and the mechanical sun blazed at their side, a furnace bathing them with light and heat.

Koyee remembered her first battles, her first sense of fear. She had been a child running across the moonlit plains, a spear in hand, hunting for meat. She had battled nightwolves then, and they had scarred her face and hardened her heart. Leaping within the orrery, she remembered leaping across the roofs of Pahmey, firing her arrows down at soldiers, and battling Ferius in Bluefeather Corner. Again she fought in Sinyong's gauntlet on the southern coast, in the ruins of Yintao, and in deep caves on a dark island. All those battles merged as her sword swung, as the demon of sunlight stood before her, the slayer of her people, the light of the sun and the terror of the night—her half-brother.

"I'm sorry, Mother," she whispered as she fought, hair damp with sweat. "I have to kill him . . . I have to kill your son."

Her sword swung again, but he deflected this blow too. His mace's head drove forward like one of the metal worlds. It crashed into her shoulder and knocked her down.

"Brother . . ." she whispered.

The mace plunged down like a comet.

She rolled aside, crushing her hurt shoulder, and the mace slammed into the floor beside her, chipping metal and scattering sprockets.

Screaming, she tried to rise. One of the worlds—an iron sphere craggy with canyons and mountains—came swinging down its track. Koyee ducked and the sphere—larger than her head—whooshed over her. The mace came swinging behind it, and she rolled away again, jumped to her feet, and swung her sword.

Sheytusung slammed into Ferius's armor, doing the steel no harm. He fell back two steps and slammed into a bronze door. It swung open, revealing a chamber full of gears, springs, and the inner side of the clock's dial. The clockwork was still and dead. Snarling, Ferius drove forward again, and the door creaked shut, hiding the frozen heart of the mountain.

Another world trundled toward them, creaking on its tracks, and Koyee pulled aside. Ferius ducked, narrowly dodging the ball of bronze. With the world past them, their weapons thrust again. Mace and sword crashed together, tilted sideways, and banged against one of the circular tracks. Koyee wobbled, and when the mace swung again, she stepped so close to the mechanical sun the heat seared her cloak and hair.

She ducked under the mace, skirted Ferius, and swung her sword again. She aimed for his neck. The mace rose, deflecting the blow, and Sheytusung sliced off the tip of his ear.

Ferius hissed, bringing his hand to the wound, and Koyee thrust her blade again.

With a growl, Ferius lashed his mace, slamming it against Koyee's fingers.

She screamed, feeling a finger snap. A world came racing down a track. It slammed into her blade, tearing the katana from her wounded grip. Sparks blazed as the world kept moving, dragging her sword along the track.

Koyee stood, weaponless, her hand throbbing, as Ferius grinned and stepped toward her.

She tried to take a step back, but her back grazed the mechanical sun, and she winced in the heat. She stepped sideways, but a world swung by, forcing her back. Ferius licked his chops and his tongue darted; he looked like a snake ready to strike. He raised his mace above her.

"And thus, here in the mountain, I bring light and purity to the world." Ferius's eyes blazed with internal fire. "Here in the very light of the sun I will crush you, a creature of darkness."

"Brother, I—"

His mace drove toward her.

The weapon crashed into her chest like a horse's kick. She screamed. One flange drove through her armor, cracking the steel, cutting into her flesh. She fell backward, and her back hit the sun's grill, and the flames roared and she cried out in pain.

The mace rose again.

Koyee barreled forward, catching the blow on her shoulder. Barely able to see, she shoved against Ferius. He was bulky and strong, and she was slim and short, but she shoved him with all the pain, rage, and fear in her. She smelled her hair burn, and her wounds screamed, but she kept pushing, knocking him against an orrery track.

One of the worlds came loose, rolled across the floor, and slammed against his foot. They fell together.

He crashed atop her, crushing her, and she screamed. His mace thumped against the floor, and his hands wrapped around her throat. She tried to gasp, unable to breathe. She tried to kick him, but her knees only banged against his armor. He laughed above her, his saliva dripping onto her, his face red in the firelight. His fingers felt like they could snap her neck, and she couldn't even wheeze.

"Don't worry, little child," he said. "I won't let you die. You'll just go to sleep."

She scratched at his hands, tearing his skin, and he roared like an animal. He leaned in and bit her ear, and pain blasted through her. She wanted to scream but couldn't even breathe. He pulled his head back and spat out a chunk of her earlobe. The red glob flew into the mechanical fire.

"Just the first bit I remove from you," he said.

Koyee's eyes rolled back.

Her body loosened and she lay limp.

Darkness began to spread across her eyes.

I'm sorry, Torin, she thought. *I'm sorry, Eelani. I'm sorry, Eloria. I could not defeat him.*

Beads of light flowed above her, and she was only a heartbeat or two away from unconsciousness. When she awoke, she would be tied, tortured, beaten and deformed, forced to watch the night blaze as she lingered in a mockery of life.

I'm sorry . . . I'm sorry, Torin, I love you.

Trundling metal sounded behind her like a wobbly wheel.

Koyee forced her eyes open.

No. I will not give up yet. I am Koyee of Eloria. I am the night.

With her last burst of strength, she floundered, kicked, and shoved him upward.

The darkness cleared from her eyes.

Still kneeling over her, his fingers around her neck, Ferius grunted as she shoved him. His head rose a foot higher.

A metal sphere the size of a cauldron—the world shaped as Mythimna, its continents like moth wings—slammed into his head.

Blood spurted across Ferius's face. With a squeal, he fell back, his hands leaving her throat.

Koyee sucked in air, a breath that tasted of blood and ash— the sweetest breath she had ever taken. Bleeding and broken, she rose to her feet. Ferius knelt beneath her, his nose crushed, his mouth bleeding. He stared up at her, sneering, and reached for his fallen mace. His voice bubbled through blood and mucus, and a tooth fell to the floor.

"You are Elorian filth!" His voice rose to a shriek. "I will tear off your face, and I will bring light to the world, and—"

Koyee placed a foot against him. Tears filled her eyes, pain flowed through her, and she screamed. For the loss of her family. For the death of her people. For two years of heartbreak and pain. The worlds danced around them—the dance of night and day—and she pushed her foot forward, shoving with all her might.

He fell backward and pressed against the mechanical sun's grill. Sparks flew across him.

"Return to the sunlight," she said. She shoved him again.

The grill snapped. He crashed through the metal and into the blazing flames.

Koyee stood before him, and though her body was bleeding and broken, she stared steadily into the fire.

The sun crackled like a pyre, belching out sparks, smoke, and heat. Inside the blaze, Ferius shrieked—a sound like steam, like cracking metal, like the death of an empire. His black form writhed within the fire, a demon inside the sun, and he laughed.

"You cannot burn me!" rose a demonic voice from the holocaust. "I am Sailith. I am woven of sunfire itself. You only give me strength."

Koyee grimaced and took a step back.

Hands held before him, a living torch, Ferius—now more demon than man—stepped out from the sun.

The flames raced across him, but his flesh did not burn. He advanced toward her, laughing within the inferno. Koyee took a step back, ducking under a metal ring, and he kept moving toward her, flaming arms raised.

"It's over, Ferius!" she shouted, voice echoing in the chamber.

He laughed within the blaze. "Do you know how your brother died, worm? I approached him like this, wreathed in a cloak of fire. I burned him. Now I burn you. I am a god of flame."

He reached toward her, and she kept walking backward. Her back hit the wall, and she stared at him, weaponless, wincing in the heat and light.

"A god of flame?" she shouted over the roaring blaze. "You rub yourself with the milk of *taromi* mushrooms. Spicers in the Green Geode rubbed it on their fingertips to hold their hot pipes. I smelled it on your cloak and armor. I saw the glaze on your skin. You have no magic, only simple tricks!"

He reached a flaming hand toward her, laughing. "You will still burn."

She shook her head. "No, Ferius. But you will. Do you feel the heat?"

He froze, his hand inches away from her. He gasped as welts blazed to life across his face. He gave a strangled yelp.

"What—" he began, his cloak blackening, his skin peeling.

"*Taromi* only protects from regular fire!" Koyee shouted, the heat blasting her, the inferno shrieking. "You stepped into sunfire itself, into heat and energy fallen from the true sun above. Your tricks cannot protect you nor can your faith."

He fell to his knees. He screamed. His face melted. His eyes bubbled. His fingers curled backward, blackened, and he tried to grab her, but she jumped back. His cries seemed inhuman, the cries of falling walls, crumbling towers, and nations burned in war.

"Sister!" he wailed. "Sister, please! Mercy! Pity!"

She stared down at the burning wretch. "Ask the sun for mercy." Suddenly she was shaking, her eyes burning, and she screamed with fury. "Burn like you burned my family."

She pressed her boot against him, shoving him across the floor, and knocked him back into the mechanical sun. He crashed down, and the flames blazed so high they touched the ceiling. Ferius screamed, burning away, crumpling . . . and fell silent.

Before her eyes, he curled up and collapsed into ash and memory.

The flames lowered.

Koyee fell to her knees, hurt and trembling, burnt and bloody. She lowered her head and her tears fell.

"It's over," she whispered. "It's over."

Shouts rose behind her. She turned her head and saw a figure running into the chamber—a pillar of white light in the smoke, her guiding star, her Torin. She smiled and her eyes closed.

CHAPTER TWENTY-NINE
STONES AND FLOWERS

Cam groaned as Linee hopped up the mountain path ahead of
him, her hair flouncing as she sang.

"Linee, please." He panted as he climbed, his legs aching
and sweat dampening his tunic. "Please no more singing. You've
been singing the same song for months. Please. I'm begging you."

She kept on skipping, ignoring him. She wore a white tunic
and a tasseled shawl, clothes from Eseer, and ribbons filled her
hair. She sang out loudly as if performing for a crowd of
thousands.

"And the kittens and the puppies and the turtles and the
guppies, and they all went hopping awayyyy. And the bumbles and
the bees and the doggies and their fleas, and they all went—"

"Linee!" Cam covered his ears. "By Idar!"

They had been traveling up the dusk for ages. The last of
Linee's jewels had bought them a couple donkeys, which they had
left to graze in the valley below. After suffering Linee's songs all
the way from the desert, Cam was sure the poor beasts would be
making a dash for freedom now. He and Linee had climbed most
of the mountain already, heading toward the clock above. The
missing Cabera Hand hung from Cam's belt like a sword.

"Are you there waiting for us, Torin and Bailey?" he said
softly, but with Linee's racket, only the wind heard.

Cam sighed and looked down to the hills and valleys below.
Half the land lay in sunlight, green and rustling and full of flowers.
The other half lay in shadow, bare blue hills rolling toward an
indigo horizon. Could they really make this old world turn again,

letting light and darkness forever dance? Had his friends found the other missing pieces?

Cam thought that more than he wished to save the world, he wanted to see his friends again: Torin, wise and somber, the noblest person he knew, but not too noble to share an ale and laugh with; Koyee, shy and quiet yet a great warrior of darkness; and Bailey . . . headstrong, temperamental Bailey, the leader of their gang, whose flashing eyes masked the greatest kindness he'd known in a person. Would he find them here upon the mountain?

As he stared below at the valleys, a strange silence fell across the land, and he realized that—without him noticing— Linee had stopped singing.

Cam turned to look back up the mountain and found the exiled queen standing still, her arms hanging at her sides.

"Linee?" Cam's heart burst into a gallop, and he raced up toward her. She was pale and her eyes were wide. "Linee, are you all right?"

She pointed up the mountainside. Cam looked and felt the blood leave his face. The entire mountain could have collapsed beneath him, and he would have felt no less fear.

Behind a pine above, Torin was kneeling over a bloodied, frozen Bailey. Koyee stood farther back, her head lowered, her hands clasped together as if she were praying silently; blood and burn marks stained her armor.

"Bailey . . ." Cam wanted to run forward, but his legs would not move, and his breath shuddered. "Oh Idar . . . Bailey?"

Torin raised his head and looked down toward him. The gardener's eyes were dark and haunted like the halls of drowned nations.

* * * * *

They buried Bailey upon the mountain on a small, grassy plateau overlooking valleys of flowers and mist.

Torin stood above the open grave, staring down at her. He had cleaned her of blood and removed the leaves from her hair. Lying below, she seemed peaceful. She almost looked asleep, and he kept waiting for her to wake up, to leap out, to pinch his cheek and muss his hair and call him Winky. She lay in the armor of Eloria, the steel scales polished and bright. A ring of dandelions crowned her head; Torin had woven it himself, the only gift a humble gardener knew how to give. Her shield and sword lay upon her chest, anemones upon them.

Torin looked at his friends who stood beside him. Cam and Linee, clad in the white tunics of the desert. Koyee, her armor dented and her eyes solemn.

But my dearest friend—the closest, oldest friend I ever had—will never stand with us again.

He looked back at Bailey and his eyes stung. "You always liked climbing, and you always liked heights," he said in a choked voice. "This is a good place for you to rest, Bailey. It's high up the way you like it."

Linee led them in prayer to Idar and then sang softly, the songs to carry Bailey's soul to the world beyond. Koyee knew little of Idarism, but she played an old tune of the night upon her flute, and she whispered prayers in the tongue of her people. When the grave was covered, the soil soft and crumbly upon it, they each placed down a single stone and flower, gifts of the earth. A boulder rose as a tombstone, engraved with her name, kissed with sunlight.

Torin stood above the grave, head lowered.

"Goodbye, Bailey," he whispered. "Goodbye, daughter of sunlight, warrior of moonlight, child of Moth."

Arms enveloped him—Koyee holding him close. Cam and Linee joined the embrace, and the four stood together, tears in their eyes, silent.

I won't stop, Bailey, Torin swore silently. *I will finish what we started, and we will fix this world. For day and night . . . and for your memory. Goodbye, my foster sister, my best friend, my love. Goodbye, Bailey.*

CHAPTER THIRTY
THE GUARDIAN OF TIME

Koyee and Torin walked into the mountain, past the orrery, and through a small bronze door. They found themselves entering a room of gears, springs, and pulleys, the machinery rising high above their heads. Upon one wall, they saw the inner dial of the clock, ten feet wide. The gears were silent and still; the clock was frozen.

Koyee tilted her head back, gaping at the towering machine. So many pieces comprised the clockwork that she didn't know where to begin. Despite her wounds—her finger blazed where the mace had struck it, and a bandage covered her ear—awe and joy spread through her.

"This won't be easy to fix," Torin said. He stood beside her and chewed his lip. "My head hurts to look at it. Sort of like looking at those Qaelish runes you force me to learn."

He tried to sound lighthearted, but she saw the pain that still filled him—the pain of his wounds and of his loss. Bandages wrapped around his thigh, and he walked with a limp, but worse was the hurt in his eyes, a hurt Koyee knew might forever fill him. She wanted to embrace him, to comfort him, but now the fate of the night depended on them. Now they had to fix this clock . . . or all those deaths had been in vain. Cam and Linee were outside upon the mountainside, trying to climb onto the dial and reattach the number and hand. Here inside the mountain, Torin and Koyee held the gear between them. They would have to make that clock hand move again.

"Well, we just have to find a missing spoke." Koyee walked deeper into the chamber. "Or . . . rod. Or . . . sprocket? Whatever a gear fits onto. What does a gear fit onto, Torin?"

He sighed. "We should have read some books about clocks."

"Well, we're already here, and I'm not traveling all the way back to Asharo Library." Koyee ran her hands along the metal parts around her, walking among them. She felt like an ant trapped inside the winding innards of a metal conch.

She was walking near the inner dial when creaks sounded at her side. A voice rose, old and soft like a beloved, well-worn garment of silk.

"I believe I can fix this clock for you, daughter of men." A shadow stirred behind the machinery. "After so long, I will place this gear into its proper place."

Koyee and Torin spun toward the source of the voice. The strangest creature Koyee had ever seen emerged from behind springs and gears, stepping toward her. She recognized the creature drawn in the old book.

A little smaller than a nightwolf, the animal sported thick golden fur. He walked upon six legs, and two arms stretched out under his neck. His snout was long, his eyes large and amber; they seemed sad eyes to Koyee, damp and full of memory. She did not know why, for she saw no white hairs or wrinkles upon this creature, but Koyee thought him very old, more ancient than the wisest elders she had seen in the night.

"Hello," she said hesitantly, still holding the gear. "I'm Koyee. With me is Torin."

The creature nodded, and it almost seemed to Koyee that he smiled. "I am First of Four, a Clockwork Cleric. Welcome to Cabera Clock. Welcome to the heart of the world."

Torin leaned toward Koyee and whispered from the corner of his mouth, "It's talking! A giant spider-bear creature . . . is talking. Are you seeing this too or am I dreaming?" He rubbed his eyes. "This high mountain air."

First of Four gestured toward a gear that thrust out like a bench. Koyee and Torin sat, and the old cleric spoke for a long time.

He spoke of many years long ago, an era when mankind had been young, when Mythimna had spun around its axis and night followed day. He spoke of war, of hatred, of three ancient empires soaking the world in blood. He told them of breaking the clock, hiding a piece in each old empire, so that the children of men would lay down arms, join together, and heal the world.

First of Four gazed upon them with his sad amber eyes. "Is the world healed, children of men? Have you brought all the missing pieces . . . and have you brought peace?"

Koyee sighed and lowered her head. Peace? The world was drenched in more blood than ever. How could they fix the clock now, the hope of the clerics unfulfilled?

She glanced at Torin and saw the same pain in his face. She looked back at First of Four.

"There is no peace in this world," she said. "Hatred and war rage across Moth. Daylight and night clash. But we fight for peace." Never removing her eyes from the Clockwork Cleric, she clasped Torin's hand. "I am a daughter of the night, and Torin is a son of the day. Our people hate, fear, and fight . . . but we stand together. We fight too but not for blood or victory. We fight to join our people, to fix the clock, to show the world that all men and women are one."

As she spoke, tears filled First of Four's eyes. They dampened the golden fur on his cheeks and dripped onto the floor. He lowered his head.

"Then it was in vain," said the cleric. "I sought to bring peace, yet I brought more pain and war. I sought to let the children of men stand together, and yet across the border I made, they stood apart."

"We stand together!" Koyee said firmly, rising from the gear she sat on. "Our union will be a beacon for others. We can show this world that Timandrians and Elorians are one people. But we cannot do it alone. We need the world to turn again. When sun rises in the night and darkness falls upon day, they will see." She held out the reclaimed gear. "Fix the clock, wise cleric, and we will bring peace to this weeping world."

The old cleric raised his head, blinked those gleaming eyes, and took the gear from her hands.

* * * * *

They sat in the valley, the grass soft beneath them, four friends . . . four hurt, weary souls. Wildflowers rustled in the western light. Shadows spread in the east and a distant star shone. Linee had bought several honeycakes from a farm along the road, and Torin had picked wild apples from a tree. They shared the meal now, listening to the birds and watching the sky.

"Do you think there are fluffy unicorns above the clouds?" Linee asked. She sighed and smiled. "I think there are."

At her side, Cam rolled his eyes. "The only fluff is between your ears." And yet there was a softness to his words, and there was love in his eyes when he looked at her.

Linee chewed her meal slowly, seeming lost in thought. She stared at Koyee, blinked shyly, and said, "Koyee, there's something I always wanted to know. It's an important question . . . to me at least, and . . . I never had the courage to ask. Maybe with all our secrets revealed now—about the clock, about Ferius's mother, and everything else—it's time to answer one more question."

Koyee nodded. "What is it?"

Linee bit her lip. "Do Elorians have eyelids?"

"Oh wormy sheep hooves!" Cam cried, raising his hands to the heavens in indignation.

"What?" Linee kicked the grass. "Their eyes are really big and I want to know!"

But Koyee only laughed. "Yes, Linee, Elorians have eyelids." She blinked. "Do you see?"

Linee nodded and grinned.

They sat for a long time, watching as the sun set. The twilight cast red and orange mottles across the sky like watercolor stains. Beams of light burst through the clouds, columns in a celestial temple, and the sun seemed to sway and melt as it touched the horizon. Soon it was only a semicircle the shape of Idar's sigil . . . then only a glowing crest upon a distant hill . . . and then it was gone.

"The first sunset in ten thousand years," Koyee whispered, and a smile stretched across her face. "Are we supposed to go to bed now?"

Linee yawned, stretching out her limbs. "Yes! I'm so tired I can sleep for the next ten thousand years." She lay down in the grass and tugged Cam down beside her. "You'll warm me up at night, Camlin, and don't steal our blanket this time."

Koyee watched them curl up together on the grass and pull a blanket over them. She smiled softly, then looked at Torin. He wrapped an arm around her, and she leaned against him and kissed his cheek. Both were wounded and bandaged. Both had lost so much. Pain still filled them; perhaps it always would. But now, for a short while, they were at peace. They watched the sky, silent, holding each other for warmth and comfort. The moon glowed and a shooting star shot overhead.

"Fluffy baby unicorns . . . no . . ." Linee mumbled at their side, shifting in her sleep. "You can't eat *all* the cupcakes."

A yawn stretched across Koyee, and she lay down and Torin lay beside her. She cuddled against him, kissed his lips, and slept with his arms around her.

If dreams filled her sleep, she did not remember them, for which she was thankful.

She awoke with soft light upon her, opened her eyes, and gasped. The sun was rising in the east, spreading pink, feathery fingers across the sky. Birds chirped. Flowers bloomed. The others woke around her, and they sat and watched the light.

"Are you all right?" Torin asked softly, holding Koyee's hand.

She nodded and pulled a blanket over her head. "The light stings a bit, but I'm fine." She smiled. "I'm more than fine. I'm happy. We did it, Torin. We fixed it."

"And yet our quest does not end." He rose to his feet. "Sailith still spreads across the land. War might still be raging in the east. We must return to Ilar."

Koyee nodded and stood up too. "The sun rises here. It has rises in Eloria too." She shivered to think that blood might still be flowing. "One journey has ended. Another begins."

CHAPTER THIRTY-ONE
SUNLIGHT

The enemy was streaming through the streets of Asharo, breaking down doors and smashing walls, when dawn broke across the night.

The battle—the last stand of Eloria—had been raging for turns now. Jin still sat upon the tower top, the devastation rolling around him. The city walls lay smashed upon the sand, fallen to the catapults, cannons, and black magic of the sunlit demons. Through the streets and squares they swarmed—the soldiers of Timandra, clad in bright steel, waving the banners of the sun. The monks of Sailith, that twisted faith, led their soldiers into homes, shops, and barracks. They smashed, looted, and slaughtered both the city defenders and civilians. Blood and shattered glass covered the streets, gleaming under the light of torches and lanterns.

Some soldiers of Eloria still stood—the remnants of the night's old empires, now fighting as one army—but they were falling fast, overwhelmed by a sunlit swarm that seemed to never end. The soldiers flowed deeper and deeper into the city, capturing street by street, ever driving up toward Ilar's palace— the heart of this island, the last fortress of darkness.

"By the bard's stars," Little Maniko whispered, standing beside Jin on the tower. The bearded busker stared eastward and lowered his flute. "Light. The light of the sun."

Jin looked to the east and his eyes watered. Pink, orange, and yellow smudges rose across the sky, and soon beams of light broke through the clouds, flaring out like heavenly blades. The sun itself—it had to be the fabled sun, a great disk of fire too bright to stare at directly—rose across the distant, lifeless hills.

"It's true," Jin said, tears falling. "The legends are true—the world turns. Koyee did it." He laughed as he cried, even as blood and death sprawled below him. "Koyee fixed the world."

Below in the city streets, the battle died. Soldiers stared to the east, gasped, and shielded their eyes with their palms. For a few long moments, silence fell upon Asharo. Jin could hear only dust in the wind, a distant cry from a wounded child, and the clinking of armor. He could have heard a pebble dropped across the city, he thought. The people of Moth stared into the light, too awed for battle. In the golden dawn, Jin could barely distinguish between the Timandrians and Elorians. For one moment, awash with shadows and light, they looked like one people.

Finally it was a monk of Sailith who broke the silence. The burly, bearded man cried from atop his horse, "The sun rises in the night! Sailith is blessed. Our faith lights the darkness!"

Jin's heart wrenched in horror. Across the streets, the enemy soldiers waved their swords and cheered the sun. They chanted together, voices shaking the city.

"The sun rises! For the light!"

With renewed vigor, the enemy attacked, surging along the streets.

"Fight them!" Jin cried atop the tower. "Children of Eloria—fight the enemy! Look away from sunlight and fight!"

Yet his soldiers were losing heart. They winced in the sunlight, covered their eyes, and cried in fear. Panthers hissed and fled into shadows. Warriors fell to their knees, praying to stars that no longer shone. Jin shook. Koyee had fixed Moth, but had she only given vigor to Timandra?

"Tianlong!" Jin shouted. "Tianlong, I need you!"

As the Timandrians shouted and slew his people below, Tianlong, the last dragon in Eloria, roared above and flew toward him. The beast's black scales clanked. His red beard fluttered like a banner, its tip crackling with fire. His fangs and claws gleamed in the rising sun. Upon his back sat Empress Hikari, blood staining her spear. The dragon circled around the tower top where Jin perched.

"The city cannot survive much longer!" Hikari shouted from the saddle. "Jin, into the saddle—we must flee."

He shook his head. "No. I cannot abandon our city. Tianlong! Fly to Cabera Mountain. It rises where dusk once glimmered. You must find Koyee and Torin. You must bring them here."

Tianlong panted, tongue lolling, blood on his teeth. "I will not leave you, little emperor."

"You must! The world must see Koyee and Torin, a daughter of night and a son of daylight. They must speak to the children of Moth. Fly, brave dragon. Fly and do not rest until they're here. We don't have much time."

Upon the saddle, Hikari fired her last arrow; it sailed across several streets to slam into an enemy. She nodded, leaped off the dragon, and landed on the tower beside Jin.

"Fly, my friend!" Hikari said to Tianlong and slapped his scales. "Bring them back."

With a roar, Tianlong soared. Beams of light blazed around him. He coiled across the sky, soon becoming a distant strand, then a speck, then finally vanished over the horizon.

The battle raged on.

More streets fell.

The enemy reached the base of the tower, and Hikari hissed and hugged Jin close. A battering ram swung below, slamming into the door. Soon the Timandrians would climb the coiling stairway within. When they reached the tower top, when they reached Jin . . .

"We will die with blood on our blades," said Hikari.

Little Maniko nodded, tossed his beard across his shoulder, and grinned. "My blade is ready." He raised his knife.

Jin stared at the swarm of Timandrians that covered the city—a sea of steel and fire—and shook his head.

"Night falls," he whispered.

The sun sank below the western horizon, darkness cloaked the city, and the stars emerged. The Elorian warriors below—the last survivors—cried with new vigor. The Timandrians cried in fear.

"The sunlight abandons us!" one soldier shouted.

The Elorians charged against their foes, their blades sinking into flesh.

The sun was rising again when Tianlong returned, shimmering in the light, bearing two riders.

* * * * *

Torin looked down upon the city. Countless soldiers covered the beaches, the streets, and the hills beyond, all the might of Timandra and Eloria clashing together.

"We're too late," he said. "The city has fallen. Day has conquered night."

Sitting in the saddle before him, Koyee shook her head. "No. There is no more day and night. And there is hope."

Tianlong had carried them here, flying faster then an arrow. Meanwhile, Cam and Linee were making their way north, back home . . . back to Fairwool-by-Night. Torin had ached to go there too, but here was his most important task. Here below him throbbed the diseased wound of the world.

They flew above the city of Asharo, moving between pocked towers, crumbling walls, and burning pagodas. Arrows flew around them and cannons still blasted below. Half the city lay in ruin, soldiers racing across hills of bricks and bodies. Smoke rose in plumes, and ruined ships lay upon the beach like the skeletons of whales.

Torin rose in the saddle—the way he had stood with Bailey. He would be brave like her this day.

"People of Timandra!" he shouted to the armies below. "Soldiers of sunlight, hear me!"

They looked up, swords bloody.

Koyee stood in the saddle behind him, clinging to Torin. "Children of Eloria!" Her voice was higher than his but no less powerful. "I am Koyee, the Girl in the Black Dress, a daughter of darkness. Hear me!"

Torin held up a charred helmet shaped as a sunburst. "The world turns again. We all share day and night. Ferius the False is dead!"

The helmet—a last remnant from the inferno in the orrery—caught the sunlight. Torin tossed it down. It tumbled into the army of Timandra. The soldiers stared up at him. No more arrows flew. No more swords swung.

Torin shouted out, flying over the city, moving over street by street. "The Sailith Order told you that day is righteous, that night is evil, that the sunlight must crush the shadows. Yet Moth turns again! No more are we torn between day and night. There is no more Dayside and Nightside; we are one." His voice was hoarse and the wind whipped him, scented of fire. "I was born in sunlight. I was sent into darkness. I fight with a woman of Eloria, a woman I love."

They stared up at him, and he saw fear in their eyes. In some eyes he saw tears. Most of these Timandrian soldiers were youths, Torin realized, younger than him. He had left home two years ago, eighteen and frightened, a boy entering a war too big for him. Many of the soldiers below were no older, simple boys from farms and workshops, fed lies and hatred. When he looked down at them, he saw himself two years ago, a young man drafted into an army, given a sword and shield, and sent to kill.

"I too fought for sunlight!" he shouted. "I too shed the blood of the night. No more. I reject the lies of Sailith. You see these lies as the sun rises in Eloria; darkness now cloaks Timandra. What has this war brought you, my brothers? How many of your friends have died in shadow? How many of you bear wounds—on your bodies, in your souls? Don't die and kill far from home. Your homes, your families—they need you. They await you in the west. Turn against the lies! Turn against the monks of Sailith who poisoned your minds. I am one of you. Come home with me."

For long moments, it seemed nobody in the city moved, only stared up at him. The sunlight lit armor and swords, and in the glow, it seemed like the forces of Timandra and Eloria were one, a great sheet of metal draped across the city like scale armor over a wounded warrior.

It was a young soldier in Ardish armor—a boy barely old enough to shave, blood on his arms—who spoke first.

"My brother died at the walls of Yintao's palace!" Standing upon a hill of rubble, he tossed down his sword. "He died alone in darkness. Ferius told him to give his life for the sun, but now darkness covers our home." The young man tore off his breastplate and tossed it down. "Let the monks fight their war. I'm going home."

Another soldier—this one a young woman in Mageria's dark robes, her face smeared with ash—tossed down her sword and shield. "I once worshiped Idar! I joined Sailith for the glory of sunlight, but our ship sank upon these very shores. My father burned and my friends drowned. Praise Idar! I return home."

More voices rose. More soldiers tossed down weapons and turned to leave. Men and women spat and cursed Sailith, clutching wounds, crying of dead friends and family, of farms lying fallow, of children and wives waiting at home. As the sun rose higher, they walked toward the city gates, calling for their comrades to follow.

"The monks won't let them leave without a fight," Koyee said, settling back down in the saddle.

Torin sat too, and beneath them the dragon glided upon the wind, circling the city. "Watch."

Below, a Sailith monk moved to block the gates. The man sneered and swung his mace, holding back the crowd of deserters. He shouted and cursed the soldiers, calling them sinners and cowards, urging them back to war.

A few of the deserters hesitated. One—a Verilish woman clad in fur and iron—kept riding her bear forward. The monk swung his mace. The bear growled and clawed; the monk fell and the Verilish warrior rode on. The other soldiers of Timandra shouted in approval. When more monks rushed toward them, swinging their maces, the soldiers fought back. A young man with red hair thrust a spear, impaling one monk. Another soldier cut down a monk with his axe. Soon the forces of Timandra were no longer fighting the Elorians but their own cruel leaders.

"Idar!" one man cried from a tower top. "Praise Idar! Cast out the false faith."

Torin wrapped his arms around Koyee in the saddle. "For every Sailith monk, there are a hundred soldiers: boys and girls, mothers and fathers, peasants and artisans, all far from home. They sun rises . . . and they are waking up."

As smoke rose and as dust still flew, the soldiers of Timandra marched out of the city like poison seeping from a wound.

Koyee turned in the saddle to sit backwards. Facing Torin, she embraced him and laid her head against his chest. "Is it over now?" she whispered.

He kissed her forehead as the dragon flew, as the wind whistled, and as the city smoldered below. "For many years, we will have to rebuild. For many years, these wounds will hurt. The scars might always remain. But the war is ending. The world is healed. Now mankind can heal too."

She held him close and cried against him. He stroked her hair and thought of all those he had lost. He thought of Hem, of Okado and Suntai, of Shenlai, of Bailey . . . and of the thousands who had died around him.

For your memory, we will rebuild, Torin vowed. *For your memory, we bring new life to a shattered world.*

CHAPTER THIRTY-TWO
CHILD OF DUSK

As the flames of war faded, two famous weddings gave Arden—
that old kingdom in a place once called Timandra—a little light,
song, and comfort.

The first, in the capital city of Kingswall, was a lavish affair.
Jugglers, jesters, puppeteers, and bards ambled through the palace
gardens, performing for a crowd of thousands. Knights stood
with ribbons on their armor, wine flowed, and jewels sparkled.
Across the entire city, flowers bloomed in vases, minstrels sang,
and the smells of baking cakes and pies filled the air; even the
poorest folk were invited to feast.

Queen Linee of House Solira—restored to her throne—
beamed in a green gown, a crown upon her head. She spent half
her time entertaining her guests and half watching the puppet
shows with the children. Her new husband, Camlin Shepherd,
stood in a doublet, cloak, and leggings, looking as uncomfortable
as a sheep caught in a wolf's lair. Whenever he tried to flee the
gardens, Linee rushed toward him and dragged him back.

"Well, I'm a king now," Cam said to Torin. "Blimey."

The two had sneaked behind a hedge of honeysuckle for a
respite from the festivities. It was the same place where, two years
ago, King Ceranor had recruited Torin into the war.

"King *consort*," Torin reminded his friend. "Linee is the true
monarch. You're just, well . . . sort of like one of her puppies."

"Good! I'd prefer to be a dog than a monarch." He sighed.
"I miss home. I wish I could return to Fairwool-by-Night. But . . .
dang it, it's just not the same back home now, is it?" Cam lowered

his head. "I wish he could have been here today. That lumpy loaf. And I wish she were here . . . even if she'd tug my ear, twist my arm, and call me a woolhead."

Torin's throat tightened. He watched a bumblebee travel from flower to flower. He missed his friends too, so much that he didn't trust his voice to remain steady if he spoke. It had been almost a year since Bailey had died; longer since Hem. And still the pain felt fresh, especially on days like today.

Perhaps the world is healed, he thought. *But not for me. And not for Cam. Maybe not for anyone in this world. Not after so many had fallen, not after so much hurt.* The wound in Moth was healed; the scars remained.

Arden's second famous wedding was a far humbler affair.

They gathered in Fairwool-by-Night, standing in the shade of Old Maple, that tree Bailey would climb so often. Cam and Linee were there, and so was Mayor Kerof Berin, seated in a wicker chair, his eyes watery. Many Fairwoolians felt too ashamed to stand here today; old followers of Sailith, they now hid in their homes. But some had come as guests: a few farmers, a potter, a brewer's boy, good souls and old friends.

Torin stood in the shade of the tree, looking around him, and a deep sadness dwelled inside him, for this was not his old home.

In many ways, the village of Fairwool-by-Night was better than he'd ever known it. The plague no longer raged here. The Sailith temple was gone; the old stone building, its columns tall and wide, had become a library full of books Linee had donated from the capital. Strangest of all was the eastern side of the village; no more darkness lay there, no more of that borderline they had called the dusk. The forest now stretched toward distant green hills. The grass was spreading into the old lands of Eloria, and sunlight now lit them.

A lump in his throat, Torin turned to look at the marble statue that rose outside the library. It depicted a tall, proud woman in armor, her chin raised, her two braids falling across her chest.

I miss you, Bailey, he thought. *You always got me into trouble, but you always looked after me too. I hope you're happy for me.*

Her last words echoed in his mind: *I want you to be with Koyee . . . to love her, to build a life with her, to never let her go.*

A pale figure, draped in white, stepped from behind the maple tree. Torin turned toward her and warmth and ice swirled through him.

Koyee approached him slowly, clad in a cloak and hood of white silk, the marriage garment of her people. Beneath the cloak, she wore a simple ivory dress with a blue sash, and she held a silver lantern, a candle within. When she reached Torin, she pulled back her hood and stared at him solemnly, her eyes large and lavender, and in them he saw her love, her pain, and the memories they would always share: of war, of blood, of fear in the dark, and of the love they had found in these places.

She handed him the lantern, and she spoke in Qaelish, her voice soft. "You are my light in the darkness. You are the mate of my soul. We will walk the shadowed paths together. Our lights will shine as one." She smiled shyly and spoke her next words in Ardish, his tongue. "You are the sun and I'm the moon. Together we are whole."

A loud sniffle sounded beside them, and they turned to see Linee weeping and blowing her nose into a handkerchief.

"Sorry," the queen said, tears on her cheeks. "I'll . . . I'll wed you right after I cry my eyes out." She glared at Cam, who stood at his side. "Why can't you ever be so romantic?"

Cam only groaned.

That night—it still seemed strange to Torin to think of nights in Fairwool-by-Night—he took Koyee into his home, the old cottage he had shared with Bailey and still shared with Mayor Kerof. They sat for a long time by the fireplace, squeezed side by side in an armchair, as Kerof sat across from them, and they told old stories of those they had lost, family and friends.

"I lost a granddaughter," the elderly mayor said to Koyee, tears in his eyes. The old man's hands shook when he held hers. "But I found you."

When the fire burned low, Torin took Koyee into his old bedroom. A wooden bed stood by the window, topped with quilts. A table laden with books, scrolls, and toy soldiers stood beside a chest. Paintings of landscapes hung upon the walls.

"I wish I could build us a home of our own," Torin said, suddenly feeling awkward. "But . . . I can't just leave Kerof here alone, and . . . well, I don't have any money. And—"

"Hush." She placed a finger against his lips . . . then kissed him.

They kissed for a long time, then lay upon that old bed, huddled under those warm quilts, and made love as the stars and moon shone outside.

* * * * *

The next evening, light and song filled The Shadowed Firkin, the old tavern in Fairwool-by-Night. Fires roared in the three hearths, and the smells of apple pies, waxy candles, and oiled wood filled the room. The villagers drank, ate, and sang. Two shepherds stood upon a table, waving tankards of ale, while in a cozy corner, several women whispered and laughed. A group of farmers sat at the scarred oak bar, arguing about who grew the larger squashes.

The four companions sat at their own table—the same place Torin and his friends would always sit, the old table for four. Today two of their original gang were gone; Koyee and Linee now filled the empty seats.

Torin looked at the second new statue in town—a statue of Hemstad Baker, which stood by the fireplace. The beefy, bronze baker held a loaf of bread and a rolling pin. Some had wanted the statue to show Hem in armor, bearing sword and shield, but Torin had refused those designs. Hem would want this, want to just be a baker in a tavern.

You're still with us here, Torin thought and raised his mug of ale.

Cam, Linee, and Koyee raised their own drinks. They slammed the mugs together, then drank.

When their thirst was quenched, they stared at one another in silence for a long time.

It was Torin who spoke first, voice low. "Things are not well in Arden, perhaps not across all of Timandra." He reached under the table and clasped Koyee's hand. "Our farms and gardens wilt in the night. When dawn rises, our plants are weak, frail, struggling to bloom again. They've spent too many years in endless daylight. And so have we." He looked around the tavern. "Half the people here are covered in bruises. They still stumble in the dark. Children cry whenever night falls, even some adults."

Cam nodded. "It's the same in the capital. When night falls, chaos reigns. Burglars stream across the streets, and our guards cannot stop them. The Sailith temples are gone from Kingswall, but many still miss the endless day."

Koyee looked into the crackling fireplace. Her voice was so soft the others had to lean in to hear. "And in Eloria, my home, it is worse. Skin reddens in the sun. Eyes are blind. I myself must wear this cloak and hood everywhere." She caressed the garment. "Our mushroom farms wilt and die in the sunlight, and our fish flee into the depths where we cannot catch them. People cry that the stars have abandoned us. Some say the day is a curse of Sailith, and they hide in cellars until darkness falls again." Her eyes dampened. "I thought we fixed the world, but maybe the world was never broken, only the hearts of men."

Her hand squeezed Torin's tightly under the table. She looked at him with those large eyes; eyes he had first seen so long ago in the darkness; eyes that had peered, frightened, from around a boulder as he wheeled her father's bones toward her; eyes he had followed into shadow and fire; eyes that still drove into his soul, the twin beacons of his heart.

The dry leaves of fall covered the land as Torin and Koyee returned to the mountain.

Clad in warm woolen cloaks, they walked up that old, pebbly path. Red and yellow leaves covered the trees, rustling in a great, fiery carpet upon the hills and valleys below. Mist floated over grass, and geese swam in pools of gleaming water. This mountain had once risen from the dusk, splitting the land in two, but now both sides of the world bloomed with life. Sunlight lit the mountainside, and the clock dial ticked above, its hand moving again.

When they reached the grassy plateau, Torin and Koyee approached the grave that lay between wildflowers. Dry nettles lay like a blanket upon Bailey's grave, and ivy grew around the boulder that served as her tombstone. Torin knelt, dug a shallow hole, and planted the sapling there.

"It's a maple, Bails," he said, patting the soil down around the plant. "It's from Old Maple, the same tree from home we used to climb. It'll grow tall and strong, and it'll shade you, and people will see it for miles around." He bought his fingers to his lips, then touched the tombstone. "And I'm not climbing this one!"

He stepped back toward his wife, took her hand, and kept climbing the mountain.

When they finally returned to the valleys below, Koyee smiled softly, and they did not speak. They walked over fallen leaves and under the shade of ash and birch trees, geese honking above. Sunlight shone in the west, golden upon the land. In the east, stars glowed upon the deep blue horizon.

As they walked through the wilderness, Torin placed an arm around Koyee, pulled her close, and kissed her cheek.

She smiled, eyes downcast, and held the new amulet that hung around her neck—a small brass gear.

Spring's warmth flowed across the land, gardens bloomed in Fairwool-by-Night, fresh leaves budded upon Old Maple, and in the fields the farmers sang as they plowed and planted new seeds. Laughter sounded again in homes, and children filled the new library, reading books of ancient lore.

East of the dusk, spring rose too. No plants bloomed in the darkness, but the ice melted in the river, and across ancient cities workers bustled, rebuilding walls and towers and homes, singing again to the stars. In the ruins of Oshy, new life rose. The Sailith temple was smashed, and its bricks formed new huts for the survivors of the war. Once more, boats swayed in the Inaro River under the moon, lanterns shone upon the boardwalk, and fishermen—refugees from the devastation in the east—trawled nets through the water, collecting crayfish and bass. In old cities and young villages alike, the prayers of Eloria rose into the starry sky.

In this new spring, flowers blooming in gardens and birds singing in Old Maple, a child was born in Fairwool-by-Night.

She was a special child, though she would not know it for several years. Her skin was pale as moonlight, her hair dark as night. Her eyes, twice the size of any other child's in the village, gleamed a deep purple, wide and curious.

Not long after the birth, the child's mother stepped out of her home, stood in a garden of honeysuckle and sunflowers and lilac, and let the babe see the world for the first time. She then turned, cradling her daughter to her chest, and walked down a pebbly path, across a rye field, and into that place they called the dusk. The child's father joined them, dirt beneath his fingernails and soil staining his knees. They walked until they stood upon a hill between two worlds. The light of Timandra shone to one side, casting orange mottles across the trees. The shadows of Eloria rolled to the other side, leading to indigo skies strewn with stars.

Koyee kissed her daughter's forehead. The babe seemed to smile and reached out tiny fingers to tug at Koyee's hair.

"What will we name her?" Torin asked.

Koyee smiled softly. "Billy . . . to remember a good friend." She kissed her daughter's fingertips. "Billy Greenmoat."

Torin's eyes softened. "If Bailey is watching, she is honored, but . . . Billy Greenmoat? You do realize the other children would call her billy goat."

Koyee laughed and tickled the babe. "My little billy goat. Let Billy be her middle name then. For her first name . . . Madori."

Torin raised an eyebrow. "That was your name in The Green Geode. Your yezyana name."

"It was also the name of Xen Qae's wife. It's a blessed name in the night. And that name is a part of me—like she is." Koyee caressed the girl's cheek. "Madori Billy Greenmoat."

Torin smiled but soon his smile faded, and he tightened his cloak around him. "A child half of sunlight, half of night. Koyee, what if—" He choked on his words and swallowed. "Is she good? Is she kind?"

Koyee looked up at her husband, and sudden anger filled her. Was he comparing her sweet Madori to . . . to him? To the demon Ferius? How dare he? She wanted to scold him, but she saw that true fear filled his eyes. Koyee lowered her head and rocked her daughter until the babe slept.

"She will be good, kind, and wise," she said. "We will raise her to heal this world, to show the world that night and day are one—the way they are one in her. Perhaps some will think us cruel, bringing a torn baby into this world, but I don't see her as torn. I see her as the only whole child in Moth."

Sleeping now, Madori mumbled and kicked, perhaps dreaming.

May your dreams always be good, my child, Koyee thought, looking upon her. *May we build you a life better than ours . . . a world safer than the one we fought in. Your parents love you, little Madori, and we will always protect you.*

Madori calmed, still asleep, and Torin leaned down and kissed her forehead. Koyee was meaning to turn back home when movement caught her eye and she froze.

A duskmoth came flying down toward them, one wing black and the other white. It landed on Madori's head, and the babe stirred and seemed to smile but did not wake. The moth tilted its head, twitched its antennae, then took flight and vanished into shadows and light.

A new story will begin in . . .

DAUGHTER OF MOTH

The Moth Saga, Book Four

NOVELS BY DANIEL ARENSON

Standalones
Firefly Island (2007)
The Gods of Dream (2010)
Flaming Dove (2010)

Misfit Heroes
Eye of the Wizard (2011)
Wand of the Witch (2012)

Song of Dragons
Blood of Requiem (2011)
Tears of Requiem (2011)
Light of Requiem (2011)

Dragonlore
A Dawn of Dragonfire (2012)
A Day of Dragon Blood (2012)
A Night of Dragon Wings (2013)

The Dragon War
A Legacy of Light (2013)
A Birthright of Blood (2013)
A Memory of Fire (2013)

The Moth Saga
Moth (2013)
Empires of Moth (2013)
Secrets of Moth (2014)
Daughter of Moth (2014)

KEEP IN TOUCH

www.DanielArenson.com
Daniel@DanielArenson.com
Facebook.com/DanielArenson
Twitter.com/DanielArenson

www.ingramcontent.com/pod-product-compliance
Lightning Source LLC
Chambersburg PA
CBHW071448170626
46811CB00007B/2509